# THE FABRIC OF CHAOS

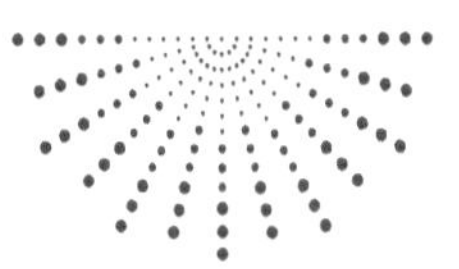

CURSE OF THE CYREN QUEEN BOOK III

# THE FABRIC OF CHAOS

## HELEN SCHEUERER

*For Anne Sengstock*

LOWER REALMS
Saddoriel
Talon's Reach
Lamaka's Basin
Lochloria
Csilla
Isle of Dusan
Endon River
Akoris
N
W E
S
The Five Daughters
20 20
BEEE

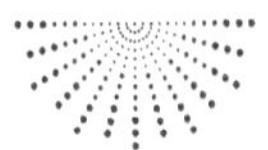

Time was a wretched, sleeping beast in the dark cells of Saddoriel's Prison. It refused to move at anything other than a glacial pace: months bled into years of solitude, each more silent than the last.

Another half-decade had passed since Cerys the Elder Slayer had last seen her daughter and she clung ferociously to the memory of that wide-eyed nestling, recalling the way her chubby fingers had gripped the bone bars of the cell with no fear. From those few seconds alone, Cerys could tell that Rohesia was her husband's child. Cerys lingered in that thought as she looked to the dead water warlock who kept her company, to the man who shared her daughter's nose, and in his more tender moments, her inquisitive gaze.

But the preserved figure before her didn't truly reflect the warlock who'd fought and schemed at her side. In death, his darker nature had been immortalised. His smile, which had once warmed Cerys' heart and pressed against her skin, was now frozen in a half-snarl, his kind eyes blazing with frozen fury.

'Eadric,' Cerys breathed, reaching for him between the bars of bone. But as always, he was a hair's breadth beyond her fingertips, a cruel and deliberate choice by her gaolers. Gods, she missed him. Nothing would ever quell that deep pit of longing for him.

She supposed she should be grateful that they'd had the luxury of growing together over the decades and eventually the centuries, too. But shadows had always loomed over them as they dreamed of better realms. Their visions of the future had been so grand, so ambitious, that even with all their infinite wisdom, they hadn't understood how small they truly were in the world that was unravelling around them.

Their plans had gone awry. And they both had become monsters before the end.

Picturing their daughter again, Cerys sighed long and heavy. 'I wish you could see her,' she told him, her voice raw from disuse. But she believed in no afterlife, she harboured no dreams of her lost love sitting alongside the gods in the skies, looking down on the living, waiting for her. Eadric would never see his own child, for dead was simply dead.

Certainly not for the first time, the unfairness of life struck Cerys anew like a blunt force to her chest. How had Eadric walked the realms for so long and yet been snatched from the earth just before setting eyes on his own flesh and blood? How was it that she remained here in shackles, while others less deserving roamed freely? How was it fair that her innocent infant had been forced into a gold circlet of shame?

Rage barrelled through Cerys, in a way that she'd forgotten was possible, filling her entirely, coursing through her limbs. She threw herself against the bars of bone with a strangled scream, and then at the walls of her cell, dragging her unsheathed talons across the stone, through her countless carvings of that godsforsaken symbol —

'Is this a bad time?' A crisp, melodic voice spoke.

Cerys whirled around wildly, spit hanging from her mouth, her talons bleeding. 'Deelie.'

The figure before her bristled, her rustling wings casting shadows into the dim cell.

Cerys almost smiled. She knew how much Delja the Triumphant hated being reminded of her younger, less regal self; it was a small but satisfying barb Cerys could wield against her.

'What's the matter, Cerys?' Queen Delja asked, her brows knitting together in concern as she pressed her fingers to her chin.

Cerys took a deep breath and gathered herself. 'Bored,' she drawled.

'I imagine so, after all this time.' It was a verbal swing back from Delja. She loved to mention *time*, knowing how it passed down in the dark depths.

'Is there something I can do for you, Deelie?' Cerys asked pointedly, stalking towards the bars of her cell again. She knew she would regret not prolonging the conversation, not using it for the opportunity that it was: a way to pass the seconds, the minutes. But in that moment, she despised Delja, dressed in flowing finery, the crown of coral with the birthstones of Saddoriel gleaming proudly atop her head.

'I thought you might like news of your daughter,' Delja said sadly, making to leave. 'But if you'd prefer not —'

'No!' Cerys practically shouted, lunging at the bars, snatching at the bait dangled before her. 'I do,' she gasped. 'I *do* want news.' Her desperation dripped between them like blood, but she didn't care. Any news of Rohesia was news she would kill for.

Delja nodded. 'As you wish … She is doing well. She is being well cared for.' Delja spoke as though the conversation was occurring across a dinner table, not in the dank corners of Saddoriel's Prison.

'You put a circlet around her head,' Cerys ground out, the thin line of gold flashing clearly in her mind.

'What did you expect?' Delja bit back. 'You think I want to uphold such a cruel tradition? It is the Law of the Lair. My hands were tied.'

Cerys took another deep breath and waited.

Delja continued. 'She does not go without. I saw to it that she was provided with the tools and guidance to learn to draw. Her mentor says she has an eye for architecture, even at such a young age. I used to have a great appreciation for art, in case you don't remember.'

'I remember.'

'I hear she is enjoying her lessons. She's a bright little thing.'

'She's *my* daughter,' Cerys snapped unnecessarily, not liking the oddly possessive tone in Delja's voice, nor that she had taken an interest in shaping Rohesia's talents to match her own.

Something flickered behind the queen's eyes then and her nostrils flared, a viper about to strike. 'Her mentor did mention one thing.'

'What?'

'That there was an open lessons day for the nestlings, for their parents to attend —'

What little food Cerys had eaten curdled in her gut, just as Delja had intended with her measured words.

'Rohesia was very upset that she had to attend these lessons alone. Apparently, she was the only orphan there. The other nestlings asked her where her parents were. Some teased her. It was a hard day for her.'

Cerys eyed the winged cyren. Long ago, it had been Delja who had been the outsider in the lessons room, and Cerys had been the one to see her better than the rest. Was Delja remembering that, too? Cerys swallowed the rock of granite that had formed in her throat. 'I'm sorry to hear it,' she managed.

'As was I,' Delja replied, surveying the walls of the cell. If the queen had been reminiscing, she showed no sign of it. 'I shall see you again, Cerys,' she said.

Cerys simply nodded, watching on as Delja swept her skirts up in her hands and left. She had no doubt she would see the Queen of Cyrens again. Deelie never could leave her alone.

·  ·  ·

Later, when Cerys had sunk back into her solitude and churned over Delja's words countless times, she went to the far corner of her cell. There, she removed a loose brick from the wall and prodded with her talon until she dislodged a worn, creased piece of parchment. In the waning torchlight, she carefully unfolded it, noting how delicate it was, nearly falling apart after all this time.

Cerys stared at the sketch she smoothed out. Centuries and terrible conditions had marred it significantly, smudging the charcoal lines and wearing away the parchment. But it was the same drawing an eight-year-old had given her several lifetimes ago.

*'Whoa, this is amazing,'* she had said back then. The two nestlings hadn't ever discussed the drawing, it had been pinned to the wall above Cerys' bed for years.

Staring back at her was her own likeness as a nestling, and Delja's too. Only the artist had drawn them with great wings outstretched behind them. The illustration of a dreamer, or so Cerys had thought. As much as she wanted to trace the lines, she didn't, for fear of damaging the already fragile sketch. Instead, her eyes drifted to the lower right corner, where the creator had scrawled her name in thick, loopy writing.

*Deelie,* it read.

Cerys ran her talons through her hair, remembering herself and Delja as they had been when they first met: innocent and eager, ready to explore the realms together. How things had changed … Cerys returned the drawing to its hiding place and curled up on her damp cot, drawing the thin blanket up to her chin.

As they always did, Cerys' thoughts went to her daughter, who somewhere in this godsforsaken lair of bones, was alone, longing for family. It cracked Cerys' heart. How she yearned to be with her child, to hold her hand and wipe away her tears. Rage didn't find her again, only an all-consuming sadness that weighed down her entire body. Despair dug its talons into Cerys often, but this … the pain of knowing Rohesia was missing her … it was too great —

Something moved in the cell.

Cerys leaped up, scrambling backwards, squinting through the darkness, her heart hammering wildly.

*There!* The thing floated slowly towards her.

*It can't be …* She took a tentative step forward. *Can it?* She inhaled sharply as her eyes adjusted and recognised the floating mass: a water bird, water warlock magic.

She drew closer to it, knowing its master instantly.

'You fool,' she muttered. To use magic like this was such a risk in Saddoriel, treasonous. But all the same, she gazed at the water creature, which hovered before her and dropped a small scroll into her outstretched palm.

Cerys unrolled it, her eyes desperately scanning the words.

*I know she came to see you. I know what she likely said. But I want you to know, R is well. She is happy. See for yourself.*

Frowning now, Cerys looked back up at the strange bird beating its wings. She gasped. Inside its transparent breast, it held a vision. Cerys peered longingly into the watery image.

'Rohesia ...'

The nestling was ten years old now, sitting happily with two other cyren youngsters, one about the same age, the other perhaps a decade or so older. They had their heads huddled together over something and Rohesia ... Rohesia was *laughing*. But there was more than that, Cerys realised, drinking in the image as though it would quench a lifelong thirst.

Even through this strange warlock magic, Cerys could feel her daughter's presence. No, not just her presence – her *power*. It thrummed as strongly as though Cerys was standing right beside her.

Tears blinded Cerys momentarily, but she blinked them away, not willing to part with the picture of her nestling just yet. The pulses of power rolled in waves from Rohesia, unbeknownst to the nestling herself, or her friends.

Cerys let her tears spill then. It didn't matter if she was there or not. Rohesia had everything she would ever need. For there was no denying who she was. She was the daughter of Cerys the Elder Slayer, whose voice had changed the very tides of history.

And Rohesia's song would bring the world to its knees once more.

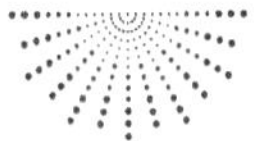

# CHAPTER ONE

The town of Thornhill glimmered on the horizon and Roh was in disguise. Deodan's enchantments and cosmetics hid the scales at her temples and the dark nails that could unsheathe as deadly talons. But there was no disguising the deathsong that now hummed within her, a force of unrelenting magic, a presence that pulsed constantly as she and her companions rode towards the village.

Thornhill beckoned to them with blinking torchlights and graceful plumes of smoke that curled into the darkening sky. Squinting, Roh could make out the line of a surrounding wall, and beyond it, rows of steep sloping roofs. They were deep in the human lands now, and deathsong or not, Roh didn't fancy their chances against an entire town, a town they'd learned was likely equipped with talismans to protect them against cyren magic. She would have avoided the village altogether, were it not for their scarce supplies, and so they were to enter the village as humans themselves, young men and women simply seeking a hot meal and a place to rest their horses.

'This stuff itches,' Harlyn muttered to Roh's left, touching her fingers to her own temples, where Deodan's tricks hid her true nature.

'Once we've found rooms you can wash it off for the night,' Roh told her. 'It's not that bad.'

'I still think this is a terrible idea,' Odi, the only human among them, muttered, shaking his head at the sight of them.

'We won't make it to Csilla without replenishing our supplies. Do you have a *better* plan?' Harlyn retorted, adjusting her grip on her reins with her good hand.

'I've told you, send me in alone,' Odi said, twisting in his saddle to Roh, hands raised in exasperation. 'Or with Deodan at least —'

The water warlock shook his head. 'We can't carry all we need between the two of us. And two men buying supplies for six is suspicious in these parts. Roh is right, they need to come too. Worry not, friend. The cosmetics and enchantments —' he waved a vial of water at the human, 'will keep the cyrens safe.'

Odi sighed and ran his long, half-gloved fingers through his hair. 'Don't say I didn't warn you.'

'Finn, how much longer?' Roh asked the Jaktaren, who sat straight-backed atop his horse at the front of the group.

He turned to face her, his dark brows raised. 'At this pace?'

She stopped herself from rolling her eyes and didn't reply. He knew what she meant.

'Not long, provided none of these beasts collapse on us anytime soon.'

Roh surveyed the horses – their coats gleamed with sweat and hot, frustrated breaths expelled from their noses. The Jaktaren was right, the horses had been ridden hard across the lands, not to mention they had been on edge ever since —

As if in answer to Roh's thoughts, the creature in her breast pocket stirred with an unhappy cry.

'What are you complaining about now?' Roh muttered, peeking into her pocket. Tiny, razor-sharp fangs clamped around her exposed finger, causing fat drops of blood to well at the puncture marks. 'Ouch!' Roh jerked her hand away and glared down at the molten-gold eyes that blinked back at her from the folds of fabric.

'What's wrong?' Yrsa asked, moving her horse nearer.

'The usual,' Roh replied, flashing her bloody finger at her friend, not taking her eyes off the sea drakeling that emerged from her pocket. With a scurry of his short legs and a flick of his barbed tail, his long body settled on her shoulder. The creature was only the size of a small lizard, but his eyes were bright with intelligence and his movements fast and unpredictable, never failing to make the horses nervous. Perched on Roh's shoulder, he stretched his small, membranous wings luxuriously, basking in the sun's final, weakened rays.

Yrsa laughed. 'He's a moody little thing, isn't he?'

Roh was inclined to agree, although the drakeling's temperament was what had allowed Yrsa to identify his gender. The Jaktaren had told Roh that according to lore, male drakes were usually aggressive at a young age, but 'mellowed out' in maturity, wherein the females became the true danger. For a moment, she thought of her drakeling's mother, who had followed them across the seas on the way to Akoris and then some. There had been no sign of the beast since then, but they were much further inland than before. If the egg Roh had stolen had hatched, did that mean the others had too? Perhaps it was only a matter of time until the mother drake took to the skies to hunt for her lost youngling.

The little creature gave a satisfied squawk and flapped his wings.

'Still no name,' Roh murmured, turning her attention back to him as she sucked the blood from her finger. It had been two weeks since Roh's deathsong had exploded from her and the drakeling had hatched from its stone-cold egg. It had taken those entire two weeks for the shock to thaw from Roh's core. Sometimes she still couldn't believe that she'd sung at all, and that the strange creature had been attached to her ever since.

'Nothing suits him,' Yrsa was saying.

The drakeling growled in her direction and another laugh escaped Yrsa.

'Don't insult him,' Roh warned. 'Next he'll be chomping down on my earlobe.'

'Well, don't expect me to intervene,' Odi said, suspiciously eyeing the creature. Of all Roh's companions, Odi was still skittish around the drakeling, usually going out of his way to put several feet of distance between them. As though sensing Odi's dislike, the creature gnashed its teeth in the human's direction, albeit half-heartedly. Roh tried to keep a smile from tugging at her mouth, recalling how she too had held similar disdain for the human once upon a time.

'Are you nearly done?' Finn's sharp voice interrupted Roh's thoughts. She glanced back to where Deodan and the Jaktaren had stopped their horses, and Deodan was leaning in his saddle, gently applying more cosmetics to Finn's temples. Roh couldn't help the grin that split across her face. It was the most uncomfortable she'd ever seen the highborn. She made sure to avoid meeting Harlyn's gaze, knowing that if she looked at her childhood friend, there would be no stopping the laughter bursting from her.

But apparently, she wasn't hiding her glee well at all.

'Glad you find this so amusing,' Finn ground out.

'Get over yourself,' Harlyn retorted.

Finn squirmed in his saddle, clearly weighing his options: prolonging the closeness between the warlock and him, or walloping Harlyn.

'Done,' Deodan announced.

Finn moved his horse on immediately, scowling.

Roh quickly surveyed her fellow cyrens, inspecting Deodan's handiwork. At a glance, she could no longer make out the scales at their temples, their talons were hidden and Deodan had used water magic to hide the telltale lilac of Harlyn, Yrsa and Finn's eyes as well as the zigzag patterns in the Jaktaren's hair.

Unlike the others, Roh didn't need the additional magic. Despite having found her deathsong, her eyes had disappointingly remained the same moss green they'd always been.

As they rode on, Roh felt her horse sway beneath her. The poor beast was utterly exhausted. In contrast, Roh felt wide awake. The air had cooled as they had journeyed further north and inland, and the fresh breeze kissing her skin brought goosebumps rushing across her arms. However, Roh knew it wasn't only the wind causing her skin to prickle, it was what stalked beneath it, too. Magic and poison, interlaced so intricately that she didn't know where one ended and the other began. It made her restless. As though sensing her thoughts again, the drakeling nuzzled her neck, his scales surprisingly soft. Roh truly didn't know what to make of the creature. One moment he was aggressive and fussy, the next it was as though he sought comfort and empathy from her. She reached up and stroked the top of his small head with her finger. His body, taut with tension, eased, and after a few more strokes, he huffed a small sigh and retreated to her breast pocket once more.

When Roh next looked at her companions, irises of human hues stared back at her. There was something utterly unnerving about Yrsa, Finn and Harlyn with blue eyes.

In the fading light, they crossed the last of the plains, following the braided bed of Endon River north-east to the village. As her horse lurched forward, Roh fantasised about sleeping on a proper mattress. Her back and shoulders ached from her heavy pack and sleeping on the hard ground every night. Though Roh knew they had more difficult nights ahead of them, especially if they took the mountain-pass route to Csilla, she'd be forever grateful for a full night's sleep in a soft, warm bed. However, the thought of the mountain pass sent an eerie shiver down her spine, stirring the poison that had laced her system since undertaking the Rite of Strothos in Akoris. Ever since her submersion in that dreaded pool, she hadn't felt herself, had sensed the foreign substance shifting within her and toying with her cyren magic, like a serpent toyed with its prey. The pass offered a cure, or so said the torn library-book page Finn had stolen before they'd left that godsforsaken territory.

Unsure of the full effect of the drug she'd consumed, Roh still hadn't made up her mind about whether or not to brave the mountain pass. She had already asked so much of the others and the thought of putting them in further unnecessary danger didn't sit well with her. Though they all knew she hadn't been quite herself, only Finn knew of the cure, but he'd said nothing more about it to her, making it clear that this was her quest, her choice.

Gripping her reins, Roh's fingers itched for her sketchpad and stick of charcoal; they had always offered her a sense of comfort during troubled times. But it was no use, for the pad's pages were full, not a single space left for her to draw so much as her name.

Roh felt the drakeling stir in her pocket, seeking the heat of her chest. The little creature slept a lot, but whether in dream or reality, he didn't leave Roh's side.

'Roh?' Harlyn's voice called from behind her.

Roh twisted in her saddle. In the waning sunlight, she saw that Harlyn's face was tight with worry, and something else … fear.

'What is it?' she asked, her voice suddenly strained.

'Did you hear that?' Harlyn asked cautiously.

'Hear what?'

Harlyn looked around wildly, though Roh could hear nothing but for the sound of the horses' hooves hitting the earth.

'I swear I can …' Harlyn started, her eyes wide and her attention far away.

'Swear what? Harlyn,' Roh said sharply. 'What do you hear?'

Around them, the others slowed, their brows knitted in concern. The attention seemed to snap Harlyn out of her daze. She scanned the faces before her, her gaze at last landing on Roh. She seemed to gather herself.

'Nothing,' she said, shaking her head. 'I heard nothing.'

It wasn't long before they reached the closed gates of the village and Roh realised for the first time that their disguises put them all on even footing. No longer were they Jaktaren, bone cleaners, a water warlock and a human. For one night, they would be the same, all human, no hierarchy and no prejudices, at least not on the surface.

'Who goes there?' boomed a voice from a small watchtower that loomed over them.

Roh jerked her chin in Odi's direction.

A muscle twitched in his jaw, but the human looked up. 'Common travellers, my good man,' he called. 'We are in desperate need of rooms and supplies. Our horses are weary. As are we.'

'From where have you ridden?' The man's tone was suspicious.

Roh shifted uneasily in her saddle, resting her hand on the sling at her belt. Yrsa had made it for her and she'd worn it ever since. Roh had promised herself she'd never be caught unprepared again, so she also wore her father's quartz dagger sheathed at her thigh.

'I hail from the Isle of Dusan,' Odi shouted back. 'But my companions and I have been on the road from Clearmoor,' he cited a western human town.

'You have come a long way, then.'

'Indeed. We have gold to spend at your inns and markets, sir. We have dreamed of soft beds and hot meals in our bellies for days.'

There was a pause as the village guard seemed to deliberate on their tale. There was a sudden, loud groan.

The gate swung inwards.

'Then soft beds and hot meals is what you shall have,' the guard told them. 'Welcome to Thornhill.'

'Thank you,' Odi called, waving to the gatekeeper and urging his horse forward.

Roh exhaled a shallow sigh of relief, although she knew this wouldn't be their only test.

'Follow the main road to the town square,' the gatekeeper called after them. 'On the corner there, The Thorn is the best inn in the village.'

Roh and the others followed Odi and Deodan. She wasn't sure they needed the *best* inn of the village, but she didn't protest, figuring they had enough Akorian gold for one night of luxury.

As they rode down the dirt street to the village centre, Roh could feel eyes on them from the rows of townhouses on either side. It didn't matter that she had been stared at her whole life, she never got used to the sensation of being watched, of being the source of curiosity at best, and outright loathing at worst. But this was mere interest, she realised. To the untrained eye, they were only fellow humans, after all. The group didn't stop until they reached a narrow, grey building on the corner of the intersection.

A faded timber sign read: *The Thorn.*

Roh could hear laughter and chatter within.

'I'll duck inside and ask for the nearest stables,' Odi said, dismounting from his horse in a single easy swing.

Roh simply nodded, hardly registering him leaving as she took in the town square. She had never been in a human settlement like this before; the dome tents of the Gilded Plains had nothing on this established colony. She supposed the basic structure of it was not too dissimilar to the entrance of Saddoriel: open space with a platform of sorts in the middle where crowds could gather around and look inwards. But the brick townhouses were strange. The buildings in Akoris had been made of sandstone, crafted to slot into the russet tones of the hillside, whereas these ... The architecture here was *ugly*. There was no other word for it. Even in the glow of the street lamps, the structures were grey and unappealing. Despite that, the town itself wasn't far from the beautiful Endon River and the mountain passes. Why had they not taken inspiration from nature for their designs?

Roh's thoughts were interrupted as Odi emerged from the inn, a young boy in tow. 'This is Samuel,' Odi told them. 'He'll take the horses for us.'

Roh looked dubiously at the youngster, but Odi had already started removing their featherlight packs and belongings from the saddlebags. She dismounted and followed his lead, careful not to disturb the sleeping drakeling in her pocket. The last thing they needed was for him to make an appearance before they'd even stepped foot in the inn. Shouldering her near-empty pack, Roh followed Odi and Deodan up the steps and into the rowdy establishment, her hand still on her sling and glad for the dagger at her thigh. It was always best to be prepared.

Music hit Roh's ears. And not just any music. Music from a *piano*; the instrument she and Odi had built from scratch in the second trial of the Queen's Tournament. She'd recognise that sound anywhere: the tinkering of the keys and the sweeping melodic notes. It wasn't anything like the songs Odi played, though. Roh craned her neck, but couldn't see the musician sitting at the piano at the far end of the bar. Whoever it was didn't have close to half of her friend's talent. But still … it was *music*, and she hadn't heard music in so long. With Odi and Deodan talking with the woman at the front desk, Roh closed her eyes and allowed herself just a moment to appreciate the sound streaming towards her, wrapping around her.

'Roh.' A sharp elbow hit her side. 'Snap out of it,' Harlyn hissed.

Roh's eyes flew open. For a second, she'd forgotten where she was, that she was hiding her nature from the world.

Luckily, it seemed no one had paid her any heed. The inn was full with enough drunken revellers and small commotions that for the most part, Roh and the others had gone unnoticed.

'You can stay here to settle up with a deposit, while your friends are shown to their rooms,' the hostess was saying as she handed over two keys.

'Not a problem,' Deodan said smoothly, passing the keys along to Yrsa and Finn.

'First floor, three doors down on your left, loves,' the woman told them, before turning back to Deodan and batting her eyelashes.

Deodan leaned in close, flashing a mischievous grin. Roh had to stop herself from scoffing. The flirtatious nature was typical of the water warlock when he wanted something, and more often than not, it worked.

'He'll be fine here,' Roh muttered to Yrsa as they started up the stairs.

'No doubt.' Yrsa laughed under her breath.

With Finn, Harlyn and Odi close behind, Roh led them up the carpeted stairs and down the hall, finding the doors to their rooms easily enough.

'Can we put the males in one room, females in another?' Yrsa asked Roh quietly.

'Of course,' she replied, sympathising with the Jaktaren's yearning for privacy. It had been a long fortnight on the road with three males in tow.

'Harlyn, Yrsa and I will take this one,' Roh announced, as though she herself had come up with the idea. She jutted her chin towards Finn and Odi, then the second door. 'You two and Deodan can take the other. We'll leave our packs inside, then head back downstairs for food.'

'Fine,' Finn muttered, already unlocking his door and disappearing inside.

Yrsa unlocked the door to their room and held it open for Roh.

'Thanks,' Roh said as she entered their chambers. It was nice, big and airy, with its own small fireplace crackling in the corner. Two four-poster beds stood next to each other with a privacy screen on the far side, a pile of fresh towels waiting for them on a stool.

'It's taking everything I have not to jump on this right now,' Harlyn announced, springing one of the mattresses beneath her palm.

'I imagine the sheets would be a different colour if you did,' Roh warned.

'Exactly why I'm refraining. That, and the fact that I'm *starving*.'

Roh's stomach gurgled in response. They had run out

of food a day and a half ago, and they had nothing in their bellies but water and a disgusting river weed Deodan had insisted was safe to eat. The rich aromas of roast meat and mulled wine wafting up from the tavern below made Roh's stomach ache hungrily and she swore to herself that they'd fill their empty packs to bursting before they set out again.

Yrsa was already waiting at the door. 'Well, come on, then.'

Roh hesitated. 'What about …' She pointed to her breast pocket. 'I don't want him to jump out at the smell of food. You know what he's like.'

Yrsa chewed her lower lip. 'You might be right there. Perhaps it's best to leave him here? We won't be long.'

Roh found herself nodding. As gently as she could, she scooped the sleeping drakeling from her pocket, marvelling at his light weight, and placed him carefully on one of the pillows. Although the little creature stirred, he did not wake up.

Roh looked across to Yrsa, who had been her base for all drake knowledge.

'What?' the highborn asked.

'Do you think I should be worried that he hasn't flown yet?' Roh asked quietly, rubbing the tension at the back of her neck as she tiptoed towards the door. It was hard to keep up with her numerous worries.

Yrsa shook her head. 'No, he's only little. His wings just aren't strong enough to support his body weight yet. See how tiny they are?'

'But he weighs nothing.'

'It's all relative.'

Roh swallowed. 'What if, without his mother, he never learns to fly? What if I've robbed him of that skill? That freedom?'

'I don't think it works like that,' Yrsa said. 'Flight will be an instinct for him, when the time comes. But as I keep telling you, my knowledge is of *serpents*, not these legendary creatures. Everything I tell you is a guess.'

'An educated guess,' Roh corrected. 'Better than anything I'd come up with.'

'So, stop worrying, then. He'll find his way.'

Roh let her gaze linger on the Jaktaren. Yrsa had thrown herself into the role of helping and supporting everyone, particularly Roh with the drakeling. Roh knew it was because she desperately missed her partner, Piri. Sometimes, her sorrow was so poignant Roh could almost hear her thinking about the warrior back home. But there was nothing to be done. Roh had sucked Yrsa into this quest and only its end, one way or another, would take her back to her other half.

Roh reached the door without making a sound. 'Let's go,' she said quietly.

They left the room, wincing as the door clicked closed behind them and the key crunched in the lock. Finn and Odi were waiting, the Jaktaren's arms crossed impatiently over his chest, but only when Roh was sure there were no sounds of disturbance from within the room and had checked their disguises, did they head for the stairs, the smell of roasting meat luring them.

As she walked, Roh admired the elaborately framed

paintings that lined the walls. Numerous oil-on-canvas works that she'd failed to notice before. But as her foot hit the final step, she froze at the sight ahead. Her stomach plummeted.

Deodan was surrounded by menacing villagers.

With five glinting blades held to his throat.

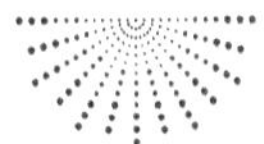

# CHAPTER TWO

Roh's hand shot to the bone grip of her dagger, but the sight of Deodan's arms raised in surrender made her hesitate. The villagers pressed their blades firmly against his throat, threatening to break the delicate skin there.

*We've been discovered,* she panicked, her gaze flitting from one poised sword to the next, the taste of danger thick in the air. Their ruse had lasted mere moments. How could they have thought that cosmetics and water spells would mask what they were? They were *Saddoriens,* for Thera's sake. A tight knot formed in Roh's gut as she calculated their odds. She had no doubt that the Jaktaren and warrior warlock could handle the five before them, but what of the rest of the inn? There was no knowing who else was armed and how many might jump at the chance to intervene. This was *bad.*

'The coin you carry is marked by Akorians,' one of the

men said, his eyes narrowing. 'What dealings have you had with those savage creatures? Are you in league with them?'

'None,' Roh answered quickly. 'No dealings at all! And gods, no! Of course we're not in league with them. What do you mean the coin is marked?'

Without removing his blade from Deodan's throat, the man nodded to another, who showed Roh the base of a gold disc, where a teal marking stood out. 'That is a cyren brand,' he told her.

Roh studied it, cursing the Akorians and then cursing herself for not noticing such a detail. Thinking fast, she made her eyes go wide and her lower lip tremble – she'd seen Tess, the human girl, look small and frightened in this way.

'Gods,' she gasped, horrified. 'We must have been scammed on the road. That man we bought the wine from … He … he knew we wouldn't know what such gold looked like.'

While the men didn't lower their weapons, a breath of relief seemed to flow from them all.

'Well …' The man studied Roh's pitiful expression, clearly deeming her harmless. 'The boss needs some other form of payment. He's tempted to throw you out just for bringing this into his place of business. It's bad luck.'

Roh forced herself to remain calm and quell the urge to point out the irony of the man's ridiculous superstitions. 'Well, there's no need for violence,' she said, her voice steadier than she felt. The truth was, the more the man talked, the more she wanted to batter him with her sling.

'We thought you were in league with the Akorians. Besides, your companion here has no more gold to offer, so you can understand why we're holding him,' the man replied testily.

'I'm sure we can come to some sort of arrangement.' Already, her mind was panning through the options. It was so typical of Adriel to mark his damn gold, the greedy, possessive letch. And if the villagers weren't accepting riches from Akoris, there was no way they would accept the bronze keys she had in her sock upstairs, not that they'd be nearly enough.

They needed to pay. What was the alternative? To be thrown out into the streets with empty bellies and no supplies for their journey? Or to be discovered? Which left only one option. It wasn't much, but it was all she had.

The broken halves of her circlet, pure gold —

'You there!' a voice boomed.

Roh jumped, ripped from her whirlpool of thoughts by a newcomer, who was now pointing his sword at *Odi*, the one *actual* human among them. Roh slipped her dagger from its sheath and made to step in front of her friend, all pretence of being a trembling girl gone. But the newcomer was already lowering his weapon, his mouth agape.

'I know you,' he said, trying to sidestep Roh and get to Odi. 'You're him.' His words were a murmur of awe. 'You're the Prince of Melodies!'

Roh almost choked. It took every fibre of her willpower to stop her talons from unsheathing and tearing through the riding gloves she still wore.

'I saw you play once,' the man continued, his eyes wide. 'Me brother and I, we climbed the fence, hid in the bushes to watch. You ... you were ...' He searched nervously for the right word. 'It *is* you, isn't it?'

Roh bit her lip, tasting blood as she watched the cogs of Odi's mind turn. He seemed to assess the situation: the blades still poised at Deodan's throat, their disguises on the verge of being uncovered. His amber gaze flicked to Roh before he squared his shoulders and raised a brow.

'I am indeed,' he said, his voice strong and clear. 'What's it to you?'

The man blinked, awestruck by the musician in his presence. 'You were only young when I saw you perform. Years ago now. But even then, you were ... incredible.'

'Why thank you,' Odi replied smoothly with a bow. 'Odalis Arrowood, pleased to make your acquaintance. Now, could you unhand my friend there?'

The man hesitated. 'I'm told he can't pay the bill, Master Arrowood. You see, I'm the owner here, and we can't be letting him go without —'

'As the lady said,' Odi waved to Roh with a flourish. 'I'm sure we can come to an arrangement. Especially now you know who stands in your midst. At the very least, be civil and lower your weapons.'

It was Roh's turn to blink. She'd never heard Odi speak like that. Like ... a highborn, someone who commanded a room. Nor had she *ever* been referred to as a *lady*.

The man nodded to the others and they dropped their swords to their sides, though they didn't step away from Deodan, who looked equally impressed with Odi.

Odi cleared his throat. 'If you'll just allow my travelling companions and me a moment in private to discuss —'

The man was already shaking his head. 'I can't be letting you outta sight until the deposit has been settled. I'm sure you understand, Master Arrowood?'

The muscle twitching in Odi's jaw said otherwise. 'Then what is it that you want?'

'Well, I *did* want gold.'

'And now?' Odi's words were terse.

'Now I've seen you … I reckon we'll have ourselves a performance.'

Roh made to step towards the innkeeper, as did Harlyn behind her. No one was forcing Odi to play. Not again.

'That *could* be arranged,' Odi allowed, gripping Roh's arm and pulling her back. 'But a performance by the Prince of Melodies is worth more than a deposit on a room or two. The crowd alone that will flock through these doors upon hearing my name will generate a week's worth of revenue for a place like this.' Odi glanced around the inn, his top lip curled in distaste.

The innkeeper seemed to consider this carefully. 'What do you want?'

Roh baulked. How had Odi turned this dangerous

situation into an advantage? He'd been spending too much time with Saddorien cyrens, by the looks of things.

'The bill for our rooms and meals covered for the night. And forty gold pieces.'

'Forty?' The man laughed. 'You must be mad.'

'You're right. Let's make it fifty. You'll make that at least four times over when I play. Don't think I don't know my own worth.'

'Thirty,' the innkeeper bartered.

'Forty-five. Plus, wine and ale for the evening, too.'

Roh glanced at the others, who were just as shocked as she was. They'd never seen Odi behave this confidently.

The innkeeper thrust out his hand. 'Deal.'

'Deal,' Odi agreed, grasping it in a firm shake.

'Then let's find you a booth, Prince of Melodies.' He spoke loudly, emphasising Odi's title. Immediately heads turned. Clearly, there would be no waiting to announce Odalis Arrowood's presence. The publicity started now.

The men surrounding Deodan fell away at once, and at last Roh sheathed her dagger, exhaling a long-held breath of relief.

The innkeeper's determination to make Odi's presence known to the whole establishment tripled; he evicted a group of tradesmen from a booth to make room for 'the Prince of Melodies', he ordered the best wine for 'the Prince of Melodies' and waved over several serving staff to tend to 'the Prince of Melodies'.

'What is happening?' Harlyn hissed in Roh's ear, watching everything unfold before them with a scowl as they slid into their seats.

'He's on the ledger,' Finn ground out. 'Does that not tell you enough? The Jaktaren don't go after ordinary folk.'

Odi looked up and grinned at Finn from across the table. 'So, you're saying I'm special?'

Finn clenched his jaw. 'No.'

'I think that's *exactly* what you're saying,' Roh added, reaching for the basket of fresh bread that had been placed between them.

'For Dresmis' sake,' Finn muttered, shaking his head and taking a generous swig from his tankard.

'Isn't anyone else worried that this might send a message?' Deodan asked quietly.

'What do you mean?' Harlyn mumbled between mouthfuls.

'Didn't Roh take Odi from the lair? When the council wanted him? And now he's going to be performing in the human lands for all to see? He's practically a beacon. And Roh ... Well, you might as well have spat in the elders' faces.'

*There's an elder or two who would deserve it*, but Roh didn't voice the thought. Instead, she sighed. 'What other option was there?' she countered. 'Were it not for Odi, we'd be being chased out of this town as we speak, or worse. And he's managed to get us gold for the supplies we need.'

'We could have handled them,' Finn grumbled.

Roh ignored him and turned to her human friend. 'I'm sorry it means that you're forced to play again.'

'What's one more performance under duress?' the

human replied darkly.

Roh's stomach roiled uncomfortably. How many more times could she allow this to happen? Would Odi ever truly trust her to get him home safe to the Isle of Dusan, with his love of music still intact? His amber eyes shifted around the inn, wary of the numerous patrons who were trying to catch a glimpse of the renowned musician.

Roh reached for him. 'I'm sorry. I wish that things were —'

But a warning look from Deodan silenced her. 'Best to keep your apologies and wishes to yourself around here.'

Roh followed Deodan's wary glance around the room before clumsily buttering her bread, still wearing her gloves. 'Noted.'

A burst of hot breath on her neck made her jump and within seconds panic bubbled up inside her once more.

'What's *he* doing out here?' Harlyn hissed, almost half out of her seat, looking around wildly, her expression as distressed as Roh felt.

But Roh still didn't dare move, for fear of drawing more attention to herself, and to the feisty creature who had appeared on her shoulder, eyeing the food greedily.

'Is that a *Battalonian gecko*?' someone gasped.

*Too late.*

Roh couldn't move, couldn't flee to the privacy of her room. She was boxed in immediately by half-a-dozen humans crowded around the booth, all staring at the little beast who'd leaped onto the table. He seemed to bask in their attention, showing off the spikes running down the length of his spine and tail, scurrying around on his four short legs, his claws scratching against the table surface.

'Whoa,' another voice murmured. 'Never thought I'd see one of *those* in Thornhill.'

Roh found herself nodding. If their attention had to be anywhere near her, it was better off on the drakeling, whose tiny wings were cleverly tucked away so they weren't noticeable. Better to play the part of a proud owner of an exotic animal, than a Saddorien cyren in the heart of a human territory.

'Yes,' she replied, forcing a note of satisfaction into her voice. 'He's a Battalonian gecko. We know a breeder down south.' The words sounded awkward, but no one seemed to notice, transfixed as they were on him. With his narrow skull and lean, long body that made his movements smooth and effortless, Roh might have called him elegant, were he not such a menace.

Impressed murmurs followed and the strange little creature puffed out his chest and sized up the small crowd that had gathered around.

'He's so sweet looking.'

Roh snorted. 'Sweet?'

The drakeling let out a low noise that Roh knew to be his version of a growl and she shifted in her seat, readying herself in case the little beast lunged at anyone. Gods, they didn't need *that*.

'What's his name?' someone called.

'His-his name?' Roh stammered.

'Aye, his name,' said another. 'Surely a wee beasty like that has a name?'

'Of course he does,' Finn interjected, clearing his throat.

Roh only just managed to thwart the instant urge to clap her hand over Finn's stupid mouth.

'His name is Vallius. Valli for short.'

Roh shot Finn an incredulous look. He knew better than to test a name out on the creature, let alone in front of an eager human audience. She sucked in a breath, waiting for the drakeling to attack in protest. Every name they'd trialled so far had ended in bloody fingers and moody hisses. A few nights ago, Harlyn had tested out the name 'Tagoor' on him. The drakeling had clawed her good arm, hard enough to draw blood, before retreating to Roh's pocket in a huff. He hadn't resurfaced until the next morning. Now, Roh braced herself for a similar tantrum.

But it didn't come.

Instead, the creature tilted his head, as if considering the name.

Forgetting the humans, Roh stared in disbelief. '*Really?*' she whispered. 'Valli?'

The drakeling's molten gaze met hers. He paused a moment, before burying his face in her bowl, slurping greedily. The small crowd laughed with delight.

'Valli it is, I suppose.' Roh frowned once more.

'Ladies and gentlemen,' Odi announced, standing suddenly. 'My companions and I will be here tomorrow evening, if you'd care to join us then?'

A polite but clear dismissal, and with a few

disgruntled comments the villagers dispersed at last, leaving the group to their meals.

Roh stared at Odi. Who was this socially savvy gentleman? She tried to share a sceptical look with Harlyn, but her friend was too baffled by Valli, who was half submerged in Roh's soup.

'He's a bottomless pit,' she remarked.

'Gods,' Roh muttered, pulling him out and dabbing him dry with her sleeve.

Odi huffed his disgust and inched further away in his seat.

'Well, that was some introduction to the townsfolk,' Deodan said. The warlock was a little pale and had barely touched his food. He glanced up at Roh. 'I'm sorry. I had no idea the gold would be a problem.'

Finn eyed him suspiciously. 'How did they even know it was Akorian?'

'Didn't you see? Each piece had a little teal engraving,' Roh explained. 'Another way for Adriel to mark what's his, no doubt.'

'This doesn't look good for you, Warlock,' Finn warned.

'Finn,' Yrsa interjected. 'Leave him be. He wasn't to know. None of us were.'

'You'd *think* after all these years and dealings with Adriel, he'd have some experience in the matter,' Finn pressed.

Deodan's eyes went to Roh's again. 'I swear to you, I didn't know.'

With the Mercy's Topaz currently hidden in their

rooms upstairs, Roh didn't have the reassuring thrum of power against her skin to tell her that the warlock was being sincere. But there was something in his gaze, in his body language, that told her he was. For better or worse, Roh had started to trust him again.

She waved him away. 'Forget it.'

Finn downed the rest of his mead, but said no more.

'It's been a long few days,' Roh heard herself say. 'Let's eat our fill and make the most of those beds —'

Harlyn snorted.

'That's *not* what I meant,' Roh warned.

But that didn't stop Harlyn suggestively wiggling her eyebrows at her.

Roh leaned back in her seat. 'Oh? And who would you take from this motley lot?'

Harlyn burst out laughing. 'No idea, it's slim pickings …'

The tension around the table eased and a few smiles broke out among the group, although Roh could have sworn Finn's eyes flicked in her direction.

When at last the companions had eaten their fill, they didn't linger in the dining area of the inn. Roh scooped a very bloated Valli from the table and led the group back up to their rooms. As she did, Odi walked beside her, massaging his hands.

'Are you alright?' she asked quietly.

The human gave her a sad smile. 'Honestly? I don't know.'

'Is there anything I can do?'

He paused outside the door to the males' room.

'Asking helps,' he told her. 'But no. It was my choice to step in.'

'You don't want to talk? We could get another drink …?' Since Odi had told her how he felt about everything in Akoris, Roh was doing her best to keep an eye on him, to make sure he was alright. She had the sinking feeling she'd been failing him miserably.

Odi shook his head. 'The innkeeper will give us half the gold in the morning, so we can get our supplies then.'

'Once again, I'm indebted to you and your music,' Roh murmured.

A cloud passed over Odi's face, as though he was recalling the last time he played for her. The image came to her: Odi's long fingers in half-gloves, dancing across the bone keys of the piano they had built together. His stepbrothers, too, forced to play their fiddles from within a bone cage, until exhaustion overcame them.

Odi cleared his throat. 'Rest well, Roh.'

Before she could say anything else, Odi ducked into his chambers after Finn, and Deodan shut the door behind them.

Despite having longed for a warm, soft bed for weeks, Roh was suddenly restless. While Harlyn and Yrsa took turns to wash behind the privacy screen, she sat on the rug before the dying fire, stroking Valli's full, round belly as he basked sleepily in the heat. It was in these quiet moments that Roh was very much aware of the new magic that now coursed through her veins, the embodiment of the deathsong she had sung two weeks ago. She hadn't spoken of it since, not even to Harlyn. But it was always there, stalking beneath her skin.

*I suppose I'm still in shock that I sang it at all*, she thought. Every day, she thanked the gods that Odi had been wearing his protective talisman. She had sung on instinct, without a thought for the vulnerability of those around her. Her gratitude aside, she hadn't allowed herself to think more deeply about the consequences her song could have had, or what she would have done if Odi had fallen prey to it. And yet she also couldn't help but revel in it, this newfound magic that danced within.

She wanted to tell Ames, she wanted to tell Orson … wherever she was now. Roh even wanted to tell *Cerys*, though why she didn't know. Her mother was still an enigma to her. In Roh's almost eighteen years, her mother had been lucid for precisely one moment, and all it had done was confuse Roh even more. And there was much to be confused about. Her free hand wandered to the bone hilt of the dagger at her thigh. She had always wanted something belonging to her mother, but it seemed it was her father's token she was to have.

*One of two*, she remembered her mentor's hurried words back in Akoris.

'*Please don't tell me it's another object I have to find,*' she had pleaded.

His reply had been as cryptic as always: '*It will find you.*'

Roh was lost in her thoughts when Harlyn's sharp voice interrupted.

'Someone's outside.'

Roh's eyes went to the door, where she could see a shadow beneath. Leaving Valli in front of the fire, she loaded her sling in seconds and wrenched the door open.

'Thought you might need extra hot water for bathing.' Finn was there, offering a large, steaming pail. 'We didn't have enough, so figured you could use some more, too,' he added.

Slightly dazed and flushing, Roh stuffed her loaded sling into her pocket and took the pail from him, her hand grazing his. 'Thank you,' she replied, not hiding the surprise in her tone.

'I was going anyway,' Finn told her warily. Then left her staring after him.

'Who was it?' Yrsa called from behind her.

Roh closed the door with a click. 'Finn. He brought us more water.'

'Good, you'll need it. I've just about used the last of ours,' Yrsa said, unfazed.

'Right.' Still puzzled, Roh ducked behind the privacy screen and began to peel off her travel-worn clothes. As she scrubbed the dust from her skin, she sank back into her thoughts of quartz daggers and deathsongs, Ames' words echoing in her mind once more:

*There is no limit to what you can do or what you can endure, Rohesia,*' he'd said. '*Birthed by a cyren, fathered by a warlock, named for a human girl ... Maybe you are the one to bring us together, after all.*'

Later, when Roh was clean and settled beneath the thick quilts, despite the soft warmth of the bed, she still did not sleep.

# CHAPTER THREE

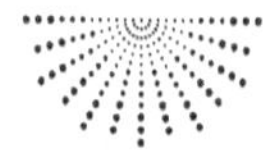

The following morning, true to his word, the innkeeper handed Odi a purse of gold at first meal, and armed with an array of directions, the companions headed out into the early sun. With their cosmetics and enchantments reapplied, they split into three groups, ready to buy much-needed supplies for the rest of their journey to Csilla. Roh left Valli sleeping in their room and was relieved to find Harlyn at her side as they searched for a stall at the local markets that sold fur pelts for colder climates.

'I wonder if these are like the trade sector back in Saddoriel,' Harlyn mused as they wandered through the rows of tables and tents, where craftsmen flogged their wares.

Roh stayed close to her friend, incredibly aware of her magic pulsing close to the surface. Neither of them had ever been in a place like this, and as she had been since she'd left Talon's Reach, Roh was caught in a constant wave of discovery of the new worlds around her. However, the hurried, jostling bodies reminded her of the swarms of fanatics in Akoris and she had to tell herself between deep, steady breaths that she was no longer trapped there, no longer at the mercy of the Arch General, Adriel.

'Are you feeling alright?' Harlyn asked her quietly.

Roh grimaced. 'It just reminds me …'

Harlyn nodded with understanding. 'Me too,' she said. 'But we're safe, we got out of there.'

'We did,' Roh agreed.

Thankfully, there was no incessant drumming, nor did Thornhill smell like the sickly-sweet hallucinogenic herbs of the cyren territory. A vision of burning fields and dark columns of smoke billowing into the sky came to Roh. She and the healer, Incana, had seen to the destruction of those herbs, severing the leash of control Adriel had held over the Akorians. Roh only hoped the remaining effects had worn away, and the cyrens had come to their senses about who their leader was and what he had done to them. But despite the wrecking of those fields, sometimes Roh thought she could still smell the faintest hint of those dangerous herbs. She shook the thought from her head. Out here, the aroma of freshly baked bread filled the air, as did the sound of lively chatter and bartering.

'There!' Harlyn pointed to a stall at the end of the row. 'That's the place the innkeeper mentioned.'

'Good eye,' Roh offered, heading straight for the small tent.

Outside, dozens and dozens of furs hung on hooks. Some had been dyed in bright colours, while others looked more natural.

Roh pointed to a bright-lavender cloak. 'We should get that one for Finn,' she said with a grin.

Harlyn snorted. 'That'd go down well.'

'May I offer some assistance, ladies?' said a gravelly voice from within. An elderly woman appeared, wearing an unnecessarily large fur across her shoulders and smoking a pipe similar to the one Deodan carried.

Roh and Harlyn exchanged glances.

'Yes,' Roh said. 'We're in need of six cloaks, preferably lined with wool. For a cold journey.'

'A cold journey, eh?'

'That's right.'

'Let's see what we have for you, then … I think I have a few from Havennesse.'

'The winter continent?' Harlyn gaped.

'The very one. Wait there.'

The old woman shuffled past the partition, disappearing out the back of the stall. Roh peered around at the array of cloaks.

'I've never seen so many different pelts,' she told Harlyn.

'I import them,' the woman called out. 'I've got the biggest range south of Valia.'

Roh gave Harlyn a meaningful look. If the shopkeeper was as worldly as she implied, then perhaps it was worth asking a few questions. A little information to complement their supplies wouldn't go astray.

'How do you import?' Roh asked boldly.

The woman returned to the front of the stall, a pile of furs bundled in her arms. 'How?' she repeated. 'Built up relationships all over the realms, girl. That's how business works, eh?'

'So, you have connections everywhere?' Roh ventured as the woman flung a cloak at her.

'You some sort of spy?' The woman's brow crinkled.

'No,' Roh said smoothly. 'And I'm not in the pelt game, don't worry.'

'Never do. It's why my face stays so young.' The woman reached out, straightening the cloak across Roh's shoulders. 'Fits like a glove, eh?'

Warmth instantly blanketed Roh. It was easily the most luxurious thing she'd ever worn, including the highborn fashions she'd donned for the Queen's Tournament back in Saddoriel.

'Where are you heading off to, then?' the woman asked, pushing Harlyn towards the other cloaks she'd brought.

Roh felt Harlyn's look of warning on her, but she forged ahead. 'Around the eastern mountain pass.'

'Around? My dear girl, go through it. It will cut *days* off your travels. No humans need fear it.'

Roh swallowed. Given their current disguises, there was no way she could ask what creatures *should* fear it without raising suspicion, so she continued as if the woman hadn't spoken. 'We intend to head north of Csilla.'

The woman's brows shot up. 'That's no scenic trip, lass.'

'No,' Roh agreed.

'Your business is your business.' The shopkeeper shrugged. 'But I'd be wary of those parts. Strange, dangerous folk up there.'

Roh tried to press for more details, but the woman merely shook her head and proceeded to charge them an exorbitant sum for the cloaks.

Later, their arms laden with palma-fur cloaks and the shopkeeper's vague warning fresh in their minds, Roh and Harlyn sat in the shade beneath a large oak tree on the edge of the village square eating sweet pastries. Roh didn't know how Odi tolerated wearing his gloves every day; it was cumbersome.

'How do you think the others are getting on?' Roh asked between mouthfuls, realising that this was the first time they'd gone separate ways in weeks. It felt odd without their usual entourage.

'Between two Jaktaren, a warlock and a human, I think they've got it covered,' Harlyn mumbled.

They sat quietly, watching the humans bustle by on their daily business, free and content. Roh marvelled at it all, drinking it in: the sunshine, the laughter … Suddenly, the bone shavings and waning torchlight of the workshop back in Saddoriel were incredibly far away.

Harlyn dusted the flour from her gloves onto her

pants and considered Roh. 'I've been meaning to ask you …' she started awkwardly.

Worry filled Roh instantly. 'What is it?'

'I was wondering … I …'

'Spit it out, Har.'

'Jesmond,' she blurted. 'She didn't say goodbye to me in Akoris.'

Roh raised a brow. 'That's not a question.'

'I know, I —'

A smile tugged at Roh's mouth, enjoying her friend's discomfort just a little.

'Did she say anything to you?' Harlyn pressed.

Roh took her time deliberately chewing the remaining mouthful of her pastry.

'Oh, for Dresmis' sake, Roh!'

Grinning, Roh nodded. 'She said to say goodbye. Why?'

'No reason.'

'Really?'

'Really. Let's leave it at that.'

'If you say so.'

'I do.'

Roh shrugged. 'Fine by me.'

After a pause, Harlyn spoke again. This time, her tone was serious. 'Can I ask you something else?'

Roh met her gaze. 'Always.'

'Do you remember your dreams?'

The decadent pastry curdled in Roh's stomach. 'What?'

'I … I don't mean to pry,' Harlyn said gently. 'But it's

been the same, every night since we've left Akoris. You don't remember me waking you? Ever?'

Roh's skin prickled, and slowly, she shook her head. No memories came to her, of dreams or of Harlyn at her bedside. 'What happens?' she asked. 'Do the others know?'

'I've done my best to keep it private,' Harlyn told her. 'But it's hard when for the last two weeks we've slept only a foot away from one another. It always starts with you muttering something in your sleep. Sometimes, it's the words to that lullaby —'

At its mention, the words sprang upon Roh's tongue:

*Little nestling, little nestling,*
*Follow my voice, to the land of sleep.*
*Hush hush, little cyren, so strong yet so small,*
*For down in deep Saddoriel, we let no tears fall.*

'Sometimes, it's a name – Eadric. Or Marlow. Or Adriel. Sometimes, you speak of wings and masks. But the worst has been ... Well, a few times you've screamed, but ... It's a muted scream.'

Roh's face flushed. To think that the others had heard her muttering and shrieking in her sleep like some terrified nestling.

'It's alright, Roh,' Harlyn said, moving closer, wincing as she jarred her bad arm. 'There's nothing to be ashamed of.'

'But there is!' Roh pushed Harlyn away, albeit gently. 'I'm supposed to be their leader, their future queen,' she argued. 'They shouldn't see me like that, weak and pathetic.'

Harlyn's voice became stern as she spoke. 'You may be our future queen, Roh. But you're also one of us: a Saddorien cyren. And we all saw what you went through. Both in the lair and in Akoris. It's enough to give anyone nightmares.'

'But …'

'But what?'

'I don't *remember* them, Har. I don't even remember going to sleep. It feels like I never sleep. And now I find out that not only have I been sleeping, but crying out and waking everyone? It feels like it's happened to someone else.'

Harlyn gave her arm a gentle squeeze. 'I'm sorry.'

'You don't think I deserve it?'

'No,' Harlyn said firmly. 'I don't.'

Roh nodded to herself, trying to shake the souring thoughts from her mind. 'Right.' She got to her feet. 'We'd best head back and hope the others got everything else we need.'

Offering Harlyn her hand, she helped her up and the two cyrens grabbed their new cloaks.

'Well, I doubt they've got anything as exotic as these. Can you believe they're from *Havennesse*?' Harlyn replied, clearly trying to lighten the mood as they set off towards the inn.

'Can you even point to that on a map?' Roh quipped.

'Not a chance.' Harlyn grinned.

.   .   .

To both Roh and Harlyn's surprise, the inn was already busy when they stopped by to drop off their newly purchased cloaks. The booths were quickly filling up with eager patrons, hours before nightfall, which marked Odi's impending performance. Unburdened of their wares, with a sleepy Valli in her pocket, Roh soon saw why as she turned down the next street, Harlyn shaking her head in disbelief at her side. The innkeeper had plastered any blank space with a parchment detailing Odi's likeness and the words scrawled beneath:

*One-time performance in Thornhill.*

*The Prince of Melodies at The Thorn.*

*From sundown.*

'They're everywhere,' Roh breathed, plucking one from a nearby post. 'Deodan's right. It's a damn beacon.' The sketch of Odi was rudimentary at best, though it had managed to capture his mop of dark hair well enough.

'Looks nothing like him,' Harlyn snorted, taking the poster from Roh and frowning at it.

'Come on,' Roh said, nudging her friend. They headed to the stables to tend to another matter on their list.

Harlyn pocketed the crumpled piece of parchment and winced at the movement.

'Are you alright?' Roh asked, hovering at her side.

Harlyn massaged her forearm, still grimacing. 'It's been playing up lately,' she admitted, fishing her sling from her pocket.

Roh helped her get it over her head and position it across her shoulder. Gently, she threaded Harlyn's arm through the gap and rested it against the fabric.

'I haven't been doing those exercises often enough,' Harlyn mumbled.

'Why not?'

'It's hard … They hurt and there's no guarantee that my arm will ever be the same again. Some days, it just feels pointless.'

Roh nodded. She wasn't about to reprimand her friend for something that she herself couldn't understand. 'Maybe Odi can help?' The human did have a knack for these things, likely because he suffered from chronic pain himself.

'He's been trying to. I've … I've not been overly receptive,' Harlyn said with a sheepish smile.

'We can do the exercises together when we get back to the inn, if you like?'

Harlyn sighed. 'Alright.'

They started down the street once more as Roh silently chanted the directions to herself. She had a lifetime's experience of navigating the passageways and tunnel networks of Talon's Reach, but these simple human streets confused her to no end.

At last, she located the stables. She checked that the small purse she carried contained enough gold coins before striding up to the entrance, where she had spotted the young boy from the night before.

'Samuel, was it?' she asked, the name coming back to her.

Startled, the boy jumped.

'I didn't mean to scare you,' Roh said.

'You didn't *scare* me,' Samuel said defiantly, eyeing her

suspiciously. 'How can I help?'

'We need a new bit for one of the horses,' Roh told him. Harlyn's had broken early on in their journey from Akoris and she'd had to swap mounts with Deodan, who was a much more experienced rider.

'And some of our tack needs repairing,' Harlyn added.

Samuel nodded, leading them into the stables. The sweet scent of fresh hay and manure filled Roh's nose and she gazed at the neat rows of stalls lined up on either side.

'Your horses have been fed and rubbed down. My brother said he'd take them out to graze in the paddocks later,' Samuel was saying. 'Your friend gave us an extra gold coin for wiping down the tack, too, so we've done that. I can have the mending done by the end of today and a new bit … probably by next week.'

'Next week? That's too long.' Roh peered into one of the stalls, spotting her horse with its head lowered to a golden bale of hay, chewing happily. She handed the boy a gold coin.

'Two days,' Samuel countered, his eyes bright at the sight of Roh's purse.

Harlyn turned to face him, her face stern. She was not known for suffering greedy fools gladly.

But Samuel's attention snagged on Harlyn's sling. 'What happened to your arm?' he blurted.

Harlyn met his gaze, a challenge glinting in her eye. 'A teerah panther attacked me,' she told him bluntly.

Samuel barked a laugh. 'Those don't exist.'

'Oh?' Harlyn's eyes narrowed. 'Wanna bet on that?'

Wincing again, she was already removing her sling. 'Tell me what sort of beast makes a scar like this …'

With his curiosity piqued, the boy didn't hesitate as he moved closer to Harlyn, his mouth agape as he examined the thick, pink scar that dragged down her forearm.

'Nearly killed me,' Harlyn added, with a wink at Roh.

Roh didn't think there was anything to wink about. The beast *had* nearly killed her. But it seemed Harlyn had read the youngster perfectly.

'Whoa,' he breathed. 'That's …'

'Ugly,' Harlyn finished for him with a shrug.

'No,' he countered. 'It's amazing.'

Harlyn huffed a laugh. 'I suppose it is. Now, how soon can you really get this bit, boy? If you're helpful, I might just tell you the story of how this happened …'

The inn was heaving upon their second return and Roh and Harlyn had to push their way inside, flashing their room key to prove they were staying there. Yet again, Roh cringed at the press of bodies around her. Would she ever be able to stand crowds? It didn't bode well for her future as queen.

'You're safe,' Harlyn said in her ear, gripping her hand.

Roh shot her a grateful look as they squeezed into the main bar, the noise of the revellers so loud that Roh couldn't think straight.

'Over there!' Harlyn shouted above the raucous laughter and chatter.

Roh followed Harlyn's pointed finger to a booth in the

far corner, where Deodan sat smoking his pipe. She could see the tops of Yrsa and Finn's heads as well, though they had their backs to her.

'Where's Odi?' Roh asked by way of greeting when they'd reached them.

'Upstairs,' Deodan replied, relighting whatever herbs he'd stuffed in the bowl of his pipe. 'Folks wouldn't leave him be, so he's going to stay in our room until the performance.'

Roh nodded, sliding into the booth beside the warlock, while Harlyn pulled up a stool to sit at the end of the table.

'Did you have any luck?' she asked the trio.

Yrsa nodded. 'We got all the supplies and then some.'

'What do you mean?'

Deodan cleared his throat and chewed the end of his pipe. 'We heard a few tales along the way … It seems our Csillan friends in the northern gorges keep to themselves,' he said, glancing around warily. 'For the most part, their clan is small and scattered. But their leader …'

'What about their leader?'

'All we heard was that they're … Well, they're known as The Carver in these parts.'

'*The Carver?*' Roh sagged in her seat. 'And how does one gain a name like that?'

'How do you think?' Deodan said tersely. 'Everything we heard about the Csillan Arch General leads to bloody speculation and a widespread fear. The tales we heard make Adriel look like a fluffy bunny.'

Roh let her head fall into her hands. 'Gods,' she murmured, the weight of the tasks ahead bearing down on her anew. She wrung her hands beneath the table and toyed with the frayed holes in her gloves.

Deodan nudged her gently. 'It's not so bad,' he said.

'Isn't it? I have to prise the stone away from someone known as "The Carver", *not to mention* deal with the fact that I can still be challenged at any time?'

Deodan squeezed her shoulder. 'These are the burdens of a future queen —'

Across the table, Finn opened his mouth, but Roh beat him to it.

'I know, I know,' she snapped. 'I'm not your queen.'

That seemed to satisfy the Jaktaren.

Suddenly, Yrsa's hand was up, waving someone towards them.

'What are you doing?' Roh hissed.

'Getting you a drink,' she said with a laugh. 'You look like you could use one.'

'You might be right.'

They sat watching the inn fill to capacity as they waited for the Prince of Melodies to take the stage. Roh sipped on sweet cider, wary of all she had been told. She tried to distract herself, surveying the humans around them. Men and women ate and drank merrily, the air brimming with anticipation about the upcoming festivities. They moved with such ease, apparently all familiar with one another, all on good terms. When Roh had first left Talon's Reach, she had been surprised to learn how many human settlements were scattered across the lands, having always been taught that cyrens ruled over all. But that was clearly not the case. For here, it was the cyrens who were the outlanders.

Valli poked his head out of her pocket and huffed, obviously irritated by all the noise and revelry.

'You *can* stay in the room, you know,' Roh told him. But the drakeling blinked up at her as though that was the stupidest thing she could have said.

Roh smiled to herself. Though she'd never admit it, she liked that the drakeling rarely left her side. He seemed to be attached to her and it made her feel … well, special, that the little beast had chosen her above the rest.

'I think it's nearly time,' Harlyn said, twisting in her stool and craning her neck towards where the noise had doubled.

Thunderous applause broke out all around them and the crowds parted in one respectful wave to make way for …

The man who walked across the bar wasn't the Odi Roh knew.

Straight-backed, his toffee hair swept off his face and his long fingers bare, Odalis Arrowood, Prince of Melodies strode towards the elevated piano and took a seat.

Quiet washed over the room. Even the drunkest of revellers fell silent in the presence of the master musician.

No ceremony or introduction was needed.

Odi simply lifted his elegant hands to the keys, and began.

## CHAPTER FOUR

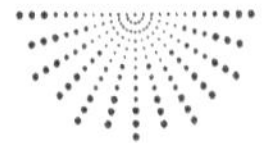

Music cascaded into the room with the force of a mighty waterfall. Grateful she was already seated, Roh swayed at the waist as the notes poured from the piano at Odi's touch and danced around the inn. Each stroke of the key, each perfectly timed push of the pedal enriched the melody crafted by the master musician before their very eyes. The crowd was utterly transfixed on him, Roh included. The song was one she had never heard before, delicate and soft at first, then building into a powerful current, capable of sweeping everyone away. Even Valli had left the comfort of her pocket to watch from the table.

The rhythm wrapped around Roh, calling to the magic that stirred restlessly within her. She could feel her deathsong dancing, her power mesmerised by the rich, resonant sounds and Odi's mastery of its dynamics. The melody he played seemed to have its own spirit, its own energy that affected everyone it touched. In dips and waves, it told its own truth.

Abruptly, the song finished. Applause burst out across the inn. Odi bowed his head in thanks, before lowering his fingers back to the keys.

A new song filled the room. A sound incredibly different to those Roh had heard previously. It was joyous, a burst from the soul, a celebration of life. The humans around them seemed to understand this better than anyone. For no longer did they stand still, rooted to the spot in awe. Chairs scraped back, tables were pushed to the side and all at once, people were *dancing*. The humans moved with complete and utter abandon, their heads thrown back in delight, big, toothed smiles splitting their faces. There was no order, no formality. It was a beautiful chaos.

Roh watched on in wonder. *Have I ever danced like that?* Before the thought was even complete, she knew the answer. A lifetime in the bone workshop had not provided such opportunities. Her drink forgotten, Roh continued to sway to Odi's music and gaze upon the twirling humans around them. Beneath the table, her boot tapped against the floor. She felt the music deep in her chest, flooding her senses and filling whatever fissures had cracked inside her during this quest. For a moment, she closed her eyes, letting it take complete hold of her, and when she opened them again, she found herself drawn to her feet. Harlyn, Finn and Yrsa were standing now as well, all of them taking slow, longing steps towards where Odi played. Roh went with them.

Before she knew it, her body was moving, swaying in time to the rhythm, as though the melody was in her very veins, an extension of her. Harlyn's fingers threaded through hers, and together the friends whirled about the tavern, the humans parting for them, as equally enraptured by the piece pouring from Odi's fingertips. Finn and Yrsa danced together, too, their eyes bright with pure joy.

*Joy, that's what this is*, Roh mused as Harlyn spun her again, a laugh spilling from her lips.

Odi continued to play, his upper body swaying as his long fingers flitted across the length of the keys, his eyes closed to the rest of the world, as though he was pretending it was only him and his music.

'Easy, Roh,' someone murmured in her ear.

Roh faltered, blinking at Finn, stunned, as though an enchantment had been broken.

'I can feel your power building.' His eyes were full of warning, but that wasn't the only thing Roh noticed.

Instead of blue, Finn's eyes were cyren-lilac and his talons were unsheathed.

A scream cut through the magic of Odi's melody.

'Cyrens!' one of the humans yelled. 'There are cyrens in our midst!'

The music ceased and Roh froze, her gaze scanning from Harlyn and Finn to Yrsa. The warlock magic was gone – there was no more hiding who they were: Saddoriens, the deadliest of cyrenkind.

All at once, a wave of panic barrelled through the

tavern, the crowds surging around Roh and her companions, shoving and screaming.

'Deodan,' she shouted across the room, elbowing a human off her.

The warlock forced his way towards her, cursing. 'It's the music,' he said between his teeth when he reached her, pressing a thrashing Valli into her chest.

Roh took him, heart pounding as the drakeling dived for her pocket.

Deodan pushed a human away from them. 'Your cyren magic is growing stronger in its presence. It's overpowering my enchantments.'

Glass shattered somewhere.

Finn dealt a powerful punch to a human's nose, sending the poor man crumpling to the floor.

Yrsa gave Deodan a sharp look. 'Do something.'

'Are you mad? It's too late! We have to get out of here!'

'They're among us!' the innkeeper shouted, aggressively pointing at Roh and the others from the bar. 'There! Get them!'

Roh heard the distinct sound of a sword being unsheathed from its scabbard.

A hand shot out from nowhere and grabbed her. Roh didn't think. Her lessons from Akoris snapped into place and she brought her arm down on her attacker, dislodging their grip from her and slicing at them with her talons.

The whole tavern seemed to inhale as her true nature became clear and then … chaos exploded.

Fists and chairs went flying. The crowd surged across

the room, towards the stairs. Tankards and plates clattered to the ground. Everyone was shouting.

'Go!' she urged the others, who were also defending themselves.

'Take the servant's stairs,' Deodan hissed in her ear, hauling her away from the fray. 'There's something in your rooms you *cannot* lose.'

*The crown. The Mercy's Topaz.*

'I'll get to the others. Meet at the stables,' Deodan shoved her in the opposite direction.

'The paddocks,' Roh rasped. 'The horses are out —'

'Got it.'

'And if not there?' she pressed, eyes wide as she watched the humans turn on each other with their fists and hidden weapons.

'The foot of the eastern mountains, by nightfall after next,' Deodan gave her another shove. 'Now *go!*'

Forcing thoughts of Odi and the others from her mind, Roh sprinted for the hidden stairs. Taking them two at a time, she reached the first floor quickly, where several fights had overspilled from the ground level. Sheathing her talons, Roh prayed she looked like a terrified young woman fleeing to her rooms as she ducked between the various brawlers.

Her room door was ajar.

Someone had been here already.

By some miracle, though, Roh's pack was untouched, half shoved under the bed. She grabbed it, hauling it up on her shoulders and swiping her new cloak from the settee —

The door was kicked in.

'You're one of them,' a man said, brandishing a sword.

'No, I —'

'I've found one —' the man's booming voice was cut off.

Roh's deathsong poured from her, fierce and unstoppable. Originating in her heart, it gathered all the power within her, surging through her body and bubbling up out of her, finding its mark in the sword-wielding human in her doorway. The weapon clattered to the ground, and the man fell to his knees.

Her magic still thrumming in her blood, Roh darted past him, hoping she hadn't gone too far and left a heap of bones in their rooms. But she didn't linger to check. She snatched the sling from her belt and sprinted down the corridor, praying that she would run into the others along the way.

But there were only humans fighting.

Roh placed a stone from her pouch in the cradle of her sling, hoping that she wouldn't have to use it at close range. Even so, the weapon comforted her as she wove between the swinging fists of inebriated men, hurried down the main stairs and burst from the inn. The fighting had spilled to the streets, too, and there was no sign of her friends. Roh didn't know if that was good or bad. There was nothing for it now but to make a run for the paddocks beyond the stables.

Panicked, Roh retraced her steps from earlier that day through the darkened streets. She cupped her hand to her breast pocket as she ran, making sure Valli didn't go flying from her shirt. He growled in protest, but she didn't care as her boots pounded the dirt road beneath her. Drawing closer to the stables, she slowed her pace to a brisk walk to avoid attracting unwanted attention. With her loaded sling clutched in her hand and her back to the wall, she edged around the side of the stables.

*The paddocks can't be too far beyond the main building,* she told herself. Squinting in the darkness, it was a strange moment to realise that this was the first time she'd been truly alone since the beginning of the Queen's Tournament. Besides when she had snatched the egg from the drake's nest, this was the first time she had acted on her own instinct, solely for herself. Her heart thumped wildly as she spotted a flicker of movement up ahead and voices sounded close behind her.

Roh cursed under her breath. She was trapped. Gripping her sling, she decided she had a better chance against the lone figure up ahead, rather than what sounded like a group of men trailing her. Aware that the pack and fur across her shoulders hindered her slightly, she dropped into a crouch and stalked towards the figure, legs burning, trying to recall every detail of attack strategies the Jaktaren had taught her back in the monastery.

*Aim for the soft parts. Don't let them take you to the ground* ... Roh poised her sling for impact and leaped forward —

She gasped.

A strong arm connected with hers, blocking her attack with alarming precision and pinning her to the wall behind. Fear spiked as she struggled against the man, his body covering hers —

Water hit her attacker right in the face, a powerful stream shot from a muddy puddle nearby.

'What in the realm …?'

Roh *knew* that voice. Usually, it was laced with disdain for her.

'Finn?' she blinked at the lilac eyes boring into hers.

His grip loosened. 'What are you doing?' he hissed, angrily wiping his face with his sleeve.

'It wasn't me.' Roh looked down at the puddle and pointed. Valli stood at its edge, his molten-gold eyes full of fury, his chest puffed out, emitting a low growl.

'That little —' Finn stopped himself, his face still dripping. He frowned. 'What good was that supposed to do?'

Roh tried to inch back, but there was no room, and Finn's strong body was still pressed up against hers. 'It shocked you enough, didn't it? Besides, I imagine that sort of power will have a different meaning when he's bigger,' she said quietly. She smiled at the drakeling. He'd leaped from her pocket and come to her defence.

Finn was shaking his head and he took a step back. 'Well, he's not —'

Roh lunged towards him and clapped her hand over his mouth. 'Shhhh.'

Terror latched its claws into her heart as torchlight flickered in the direction she had come from. It had indeed been a group of men trailing her, and now, they had caught up.

A thick lump formed in Roh's throat, as though she wanted to scream but couldn't.

*Sing* – she had to sing her deathsong. Who knew if it was powerful enough to take on a whole group, but it was all she had, the only thing she could do. But as she dug deep to find that melody, she felt the shield in place around the men. *Talismans.* She could sense their magic from here, more powerful than any of those she had come into contact with before, even the one Odi wore.

She and Finn were done for.

Unless …

As the approaching heavy footsteps grew louder, Roh launched into action, grabbing a fistful of Finn's shirt and shoving him off her, twisting them around so it was *she* who had *him* pinned against the wall. She mussed up his hair, pulling it forward around his face, smearing dirt from where the muddy water had hit him across his skin, hiding where his scales shone through the cosmetics.

Roh leaned in, wrapping her hands around the back of his neck and drawing his face to hers, so close she could feel his warm breath on her lips.

'You there!' a deep voice boomed.

Roh pulled away from the Jaktaren, feigning surprise and pressing her hand to her mouth. She didn't have to fake the blush that heated her cheeks as one of the men raised the torch to see them more clearly.

'What do we have here?' the leader of the group said.

Catching on, Finn's hands went to his belt and he turned his back to the men, as though embarrassed.

'I …' Roh stammered.

Someone gave a rough laugh. 'Just one of the stable boys rutting in the dirt.'

Roh flushed redder still.

'Leave them be,' the gruff voice said. 'Poor lad works for Mickael, he needs a good time every now and then.'

'I'll say,' another man said in agreement. 'Just be sure to walk that lass home, there's brawling in the streets.'

'Yes, sir,' Finn mumbled, giving a flustered wave.

More laughter followed, but the men's footsteps retreated and the torchlight faded into the distance.

Roh bent at the waist, bracing her hands on her knees, unsure if she was going to be sick or not. She dared to glance over at Finn.

He was pushing his hair from his eyes, a bewildered expression on his face. 'That was ...' he trailed off.

'You're welcome,' Roh told him, straightening as Valli crawled up her side and positioned himself on her shoulder. 'Come on,' she said. 'We have to get to the paddocks.'

Finn didn't speak as Roh led them down the length of the stables and through the corral at the back. They climbed the fences in silence and stumbled in the dark across the grassy field. The quiet danced along Roh's skin, where she could feel the phantom press of Finn's body against hers.

'I told Deodan to meet here,' she whispered.

'I know. Why do you think I'm here?' Finn replied.

Roh ignored this. 'Do you see the horses?'

'Yes, I've developed sudden abilities that allow me to see in the pitch black,' Finn said with slicing sarcasm.

Roh could have cuffed him over the head, but instead she turned to the drakeling. 'How about you?' she asked softly.

The creature leaped from her shoulder and scurried away. Roh could only hope it was to find help. She started to pace.

*Where are the others? There was no sign of them. Surely, they should be here by now?*

'You're going to wear a hole in the ground,' Finn muttered from nearby.

Roh gritted her teeth. For someone who had travelled and fought extensively all over the realms, Finn wasn't exactly what she'd call *helpful* in stressful situations.

'They'll be here,' he said, more gently this time.

'How do you know?'

'Yrsa wouldn't let anything happen to them.'

*Ah, of course*, Roh thought. *Finn and his undying loyalty for his fellow Jaktaren.* The thoughts came to her angrily, though she didn't know why. Perhaps she was just nervous; standing out in the paddocks like this made her feel vulnerable and exposed. *And now where is Valli?* She squinted through the darkness, but not even her keen cyren eyes could spot a flicker of movement out in the field. Why was it that they were able to see in the dark depths of the currents, but not out here?

'Roh ...' Finn whispered.

'What?' she snapped.

He crept to her side, knees bent in a fighting stance. 'Someone's out here,' he said slowly, palming a dagger.

'Where's your crossbow?' she asked, readying her sling.

'Wasn't time —'

A glowing lantern appeared before them.

Roh shielded her eyes from the sudden brightness. 'Who's there?' she demanded. But as her eyes adjusted to the light, she saw exactly who it was.

'Samuel?'

The boy from the stables was holding an axe, though the weapon was trembling in his grasp.

'I *knew* it was you they were looking for,' he said, his voice unsteady.

'We're not going to hurt you,' Roh told him, taking a step towards the frightened boy.

'I'm making no promises,' Finn muttered.

'Why don't you go back to the stables, where it's warm?' Roh made her voice gentle, as she'd heard Orson do with the workshop nestlings when they were upset.

But the boy shook his head. 'My pa and his brothers are on their way. I told him I'd get you. I told him you'd come out here.'

'No …' Roh breathed.

Beside her, Finn took a step towards the boy. The Jaktaren would kill him in a heartbeat, axe or no axe.

Roh grabbed his arm, just as something tugged on the hem of her pants.

*Valli.* He was pulling her in the opposite direction.

'Finn,' she said. 'We have to leave.'

'I'm not going anywhere without Yrsa.'

But in the near distance, torchlight flared to life. Roh counted over a dozen.

'You're done for.' Samuel brandished his axe.

Roh tightened her grip on Finn's arm and wrenched him towards where Valli was pulling her. The thought of leaving the others behind made her airways constrict. But there was no other choice.

'If Yrsa is as good as you say, she will meet us later.'

'Jaktaren don't leave each other behind —'

'Nor do bone cleaners,' Roh spat. 'But what good will we be to anyone if we're captured? And I'm not killing a child.' She pulled his arm again, at last spotting her horse. Valli had herded the poor creature towards them.

The mob of men were closing in, following the beacon of Samuel's lantern right to them.

'Finn!' Roh yelled.

Something seemed to snap in the Jaktaren and he sheathed his dagger. Together, they fled towards the horse, Finn grabbing Roh's pack from her and shouldering it himself.

The shouts of the angry humans drew closer and closer.

Roh launched herself up onto the horse's bare back, grateful that at least the reins were still tethered around its face. A moment later, Finn was up behind her, his arms gripping around her waist.

'Valli?' Roh cried, blindly scanning the grounds.

'He's here,' Finn said. 'Go!'

Trusting him, Roh didn't hesitate. She squeezed the

horse's sides with her heels and the beast sprang into action, lurching into a canter across the grassy field.

'I don't know where I'm going,' she hissed, focused on staying upright, terrified without the support of a saddle and stirrups beneath her.

The torchlight and yells were nearly upon them.

Finn gripped her tighter still, one of his hands finding her grasp on the reins. 'Just ride,' he said.

And together, wind whipping their faces, they hurtled into the darkness.

# CHAPTER FIVE

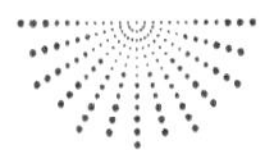

They left Thornhill far behind, with clouds of dust in their wake. Soon, the town was nothing but a speck of dim light against the inky night. They had crossed various fields and at last found the dirt road. Finn directed them using the positioning of the stars and it wasn't long before they found themselves following the Endon River north at a brisk walk once more.

Roh couldn't believe she'd chosen to leave the others behind. She couldn't believe she was on the road with Finn Haertel at her back and a horde of furious humans potentially still on their tail. It was a mess. The entire plan had gone awry, and now who knew where they'd all end up. Roh had experienced firsthand how these decisions impacted her friends and their lives —

'We did the right thing.' Finn's voice in her ear made her jump. He was so incredibly close, she sat between his thighs, each powerful step of the horse jostling them together. But for all her discomfort, it was the press of his chest against her back that stopped her from shivering in the crisp night air.

'I thought you said we couldn't leave them —'

'Yrsa would have killed me if we'd waited there for them,' he added, his breath tickling her neck.

Roh didn't respond, her thoughts were too intense and the fear was still raw in her heart. Only time would tell if she'd made the right call.

They rode in silence for the next few hours as infinite stars blinked and the yellow moon beamed down on them, illuminating the grass and rocks in their path. Beside them, the sound of the rushing river filled the pocket of quiet, its steady rhythm offering a small sense of comfort.

It was in the dark and windy hours of the morning that Roh brought them to a stop, spying a small cluster of rocks just off the main path by the river. The river foamed white and the grass tugged in the gale.

'We should rest. Take shelter for a bit,' she said, trying to figure out how to dismount with Finn so close behind her.

To her surprise, he didn't object. He slid easily from the horse and offered her a hand as the wind whipped through her cropped hair. As soon as her boots hit the ground, Valli jumped from Finn's shoulder to hers with an unhappy sound.

'Here,' Finn said, handing her the pack. 'I imagine you'll want to keep this close.'

Roh took the heavy bag from him, shifting awkwardly

from foot to foot. She and the Jaktaren weren't often alone and she felt hyper aware of his presence, his movements and his gaze on her.

'You didn't manage to get yours?' she asked; he held nothing else.

Finn shook his head. 'There wasn't time. I wish I'd at least grabbed my crossbow, but the rooms were overrun.'

Roh noted that he *did* look different without the weapon peeking from behind his back, and she felt a pang of pity for him. She knew what it was like to leave the things you loved behind. With a mumble of thanks, she headed towards the mountain of rocks, where a mouth of a small cave beckoned.

She turned to Finn. 'After you,' she said.

'Told you in Akoris,' he said, 'I don't like enclosed spaces, remember? I'll stay out here.'

Roh frowned. 'It's cold.'

'I'll be fine,' he said stubbornly.

Well, Roh wasn't going to let her teeth chatter until they chipped for the sake of a stubborn highborn. She ducked into the cave and set her pack down on the ground, feeling instantly protected from the chill. For a moment she wondered if it would be safe to start a small fire, but dismissed the thought almost as soon as it had entered her head. She was too tired and too sore to bother with that sort of effort, not to mention that it would be a beacon for those still hunting them. From where she sat, she could see Finn's outline in the moonlight, pacing by the river to keep warm.

*Pigheaded fool.* She clicked her tongue in frustration as she got to her feet once more and stalked over to him.

His eyes widened at the sight of her. 'What —'

Roh thrust her fur cloak at him. 'Here,' she said. 'Wear this.'

'No, you —'

But she was already walking away and dismissed him with a wave. 'It's plenty warm in the cave.'

He didn't follow her and Roh was glad. She didn't have the energy to argue with him.

Back in the shelter of the cave, she curled around her pack and lay her head on her arm. Just a brief rest and they'd be back on the horse heading for the foot of the mountains. The others would meet them there. They had to.

Roh jolted awake with a ragged gasp, a cold sweat between her breasts and panicked wheezes caught in her throat. Terror lanced through her and wrapped around her, like the suffocating python had back in Akoris.

*Where am I? What's happened? What —*

'It's alright,' a voice said. 'You're alright.'

The gentle hands on her were too big to be Harlyn's.

*Finn,* she remembered. His face came into view. He was crouched beside her, holding her hand, his brows furrowed with concern.

'What … what happened?' she managed, still panting, her fur cloak falling away from her shoulders as she sat up. *How did that get here?*

'You were dreaming,' Finn told her.

But Roh's mind was blank. She sifted through it, finding nothing; no memory of the horrors that had plagued her. She looked at Finn, suddenly realising where he was.

'You're here,' she said dumbly. 'In the cave.'

'Well, I couldn't let your screams alert every human within a hundred leagues of here to our location, could I?'

Heat rushed to Roh's cheeks. 'Was I that bad?'

Finn shrugged.

Roh ground her teeth.

'Harlyn usually helps you,' he added. 'I'm no good at this.' Finn shuffled back from her with a grimace of pain.

Roh frowned, following his tentative movements. 'Are you injured? When did that happen?' She couldn't recall him limping in the paddocks and they hadn't come to any blows after that. Perhaps he'd been injured before but the shock had kept the pain at bay?

Finn waved her away. 'No, no. It's nothing.'

'Doesn't look like nothing,' Roh pushed, reaching for him.

He was dragging his left foot, and trying to shield it from her view.

'What happened?' she demanded, angry now as she followed him from the cave. Why was it that it was alright for her to be vulnerable in front of him, but not vice versa? Plus, if he was injured, she needed to know. It affected their —

The soft orange glow of dawn greeted her, and around them, the wind had stilled. How long had she been asleep? Long enough for Finn to hurt himself, apparently.

Finn faced her, defeat in his eyes. 'It's not new,' he relented.

'Then it's an old wound?' Roh asked, more gently this time. She knew that every bit of Finn's being would be fighting against telling her the truth.

'It's not a wound.'

Ceasing her questions, Roh leaned against one of the rocks and sighed. *Fine, it's Finn's tale, he'll tell it in the way he sees fit.* There were some things that couldn't be forced out of a cyren.

'We could be there by noon tomorrow, depending on our pace.' Finn limped to where the horse had been tied and was grazing happily. Taking Roh's pack, he threaded his arms through the straps before he laced his fingers together and offered her a leg up without another word.

As the sun rose above the horizon, they started their journey once again. Ice-blue water streamed through the braided riverbeds, sweeping away any debris from the previous night's winds. Around them, verdant grass fronds rippled in the gentle morning breeze. Although no one chased them now, Roh couldn't shake the tension from her body. It didn't matter how calm it was out there in the vast plains, there was simply no knowing what awaited them, be it here or in the mountains beyond. The wild lands and their inhabitants were nothing if not unpredictable.

Finn shifted behind her, carefully adjusting his position, instantly snatching her attention back to every inch where their bodies touched. His torso rocked against her back, hot and rigid as the saddleless horse trudged along the riverbank, and his arms wrapped firmly around her waist, filled with quiet strength.

Roh was careful to take an even breath, determined that he sense no change in her, or her awareness of *them*. There was no doubt in her mind that this close, he would detect even the most minor of differences. She let her thoughts distract her for once. It wasn't that she was uncomfortable … It was that she couldn't quite believe where the last few months had brought them.

'*Watch where you're going,* isruhe …' Those had been Finn's first words to her, at the tournament gala in the Queen's Conservatory. If only she could have seen where they'd end up. Not quite friends. She couldn't go that far, could she? But certainly not the enemies they had been, either. At least she hoped not.

'I can practically hear you thinking,' Finn muttered in her ear.

'What's it to you?' Roh retorted.

'If your mind is whirring on and on like that, you may as well provide us with some entertainment on this long and treacherous road.'

'Did I hear you correctly?' Roh mocked. '*Finn Haertel* is asking a lowly *bone cleaner* to *share her thoughts* with him? As though they matter?'

'Don't flatter yourself. I'm bored.'

'Well, why don't you regale us with tales of your Jaktaren heroics? I'm sure they're far more superior to anything I can offer.'

'True. But …'

'But what?' Roh challenged, twisting to give him an incredulous look.

Finn hissed, jerking back as much as the breadth of the horse's back would allow. 'Easy there,' he told her, repositioning himself.

Roh couldn't help it. She laughed. Loudly.

'You think endangering the future of the Haertel line is *funny*?' Finn asked in mock disbelief.

Roh snorted, tears forming in the corner of her eyes. 'A little. I can't say the realms need more of you.'

Finn huffed a laugh of his own. 'You might be right there.'

But suddenly, the thought of the Haertel line unnerved Roh, more specifically those who had come before the one whose thighs she sat between. Their families shared a bloody history, or so Finn had said, back in Saddoriel.

*'That murdering piece of filth rotting away down in her cell … The Haertels owe her a death debt.'*

Those had been his exact words, Roh would never forget them. A cyren death debt was not something to be trifled with. It was a promise that could span generations, and millennia.

'I can still hear you thinking.' Finn's voice tickled her ear.

'I …'

'Spit it out.'

'The death debt,' Roh blurted, despite the fact that

reigniting the hatred between them was the last thing she wanted.

'What about it?' Finn asked quietly.

There was no going back now. 'What do you know of it?' she said.

Finn inhaled deeply, his body pressing closer as he did, generating a heat between them.

For a moment, Roh wondered if he'd deny her, if he'd revert back to the near-growling Jaktaren she'd loathed in Talon's Reach. But Finn exhaled evenly and adjusted his grip on the reins.

'My great-grandmother was part of the elder council when your … when *Cerys* went mad,' he said slowly. 'She was one of the first to be slaughtered in the Council Room. She bled from her ears and eyes upon hearing the slayer's song.'

Roh was glad she couldn't see Finn's face. She didn't twist in the saddle, nor did she reach for his hand as she might for another friend. There was grief there, a grief she couldn't possibly understand.

'I know it was six hundred years ago – or thereabouts. I *know* I didn't *know* her —'

'You don't have to explain yourself to me,' Roh interjected.

But Finn ignored this. 'I've heard stories of her, of my great-grandmother. Through distant relations, through family history archives. She was … like me.'

'How do you mean?'

Finn paused, guiding their horse down a rocky slip in

the terrain. 'She just was,' he replied. 'My life would have been different with a cyren like her in it,' he told her.

Roh knew there was more there. She wanted to ask if this was the reason he had been raised by the Wards rather than his own flesh and blood, but she knew now was not the time to press him.

'Had she lived, my grandparents may have been different. My father might have been different …' His voice took on a faraway quality, as though he'd forgotten where he was and to whom he spoke. 'The death debt was declared the following day by my great-grandfather. He hadn't been there at the time. It's been passed down the Haertel line ever since. The hatred of the Elder Slayer has been carved into us all, literally.'

At this, Roh *did* twist in the saddle. 'What?'

Finn rolled up his sleeve, revealing his tanned bicep where a thick scar marred the skin, a messy letter *C* …

'A death debt is promised through blood,' he said.

Roh stopped herself from running her fingers over the scar that vowed her mother's death would come to pass. 'Your family did that to you?'

'So I am told. I don't remember.'

'Why not?' Roh wasn't sure she wanted to know the answer.

'Whenever a new family member is born, the debt passes to them. I was only a nestling when it happened.'

'Gods,' Roh murmured, chilled to the bone. She turned back to the path ahead, her stomach queasy.

'What were you expecting?' Finn asked quietly.

'I don't know,' Roh admitted. 'If the debt has existed

this long, why has it not been carried out? Why has no Haertel killed my – Cerys?'

'I'm told the prison is impenetrable.'

Roh faltered. There was nothing in Finn's voice telling her he suspected otherwise. But she knew it for the lie it was, the lie that had been passed down to him along with the blood promise and a fight that wasn't his.

Quiet fell between them once more, the rhythm of the horse's steps the only sound. This time, though, Roh could have sworn she could hear *Finn* thinking. She chewed her lower lip, running through the various ways she could restart the conversation. Each seemed stupider than the last. She wished they could return to their jokes, but the time for those was over.

Around noon, Valli emerged from her pocket and proceeded to irritate their horse, scurrying up its neck and trying to burrow into its mane. The horse jerked forward, shaking its head and trying to rid itself of the menace.

'Valli!' Roh chastised, trying to snatch the little beast from the poor horse's forelock.

But the drakeling ignored her completely. Full of mischief, he darted wherever he pleased, seeming to enjoy the discomfort he caused. The horse became so unsettled he nearly threw Roh and Finn from his back.

'That's it,' Finn growled, reaching around Roh to draw the reins up short. Once stopped, he slid from the horse's back and limped away to the river. 'You have to do something about that thing,' he called back to Roh. 'The horse is scared out of his wits.

And riding without a saddle doesn't make things easy.'

Sighing, Roh dismounted inelegantly. 'Pest,' she muttered in Valli's direction. If she didn't know any better, she would have bet all the bronze keys in her spare socks that the drakeling had grinned at her in response.

The horse whinnied as Valli raced down his hind leg and darted into the grass.

'So, he just wanted to stop,' Roh said to herself, shaking her head, incredulous. She wondered just how much the drakeling understood them. He certainly seemed to have motives of his own at times.

Roh took the opportunity without Finn and Valli breathing down her neck to see to her needs, grateful for the privacy and the fact that for once, she didn't have to announce her intentions. Afterwards, she brought the horse to the water's edge to drink, and nearly fell in.

Downstream, Finn crouched at the riverbank, splashing water on his face and over his bare torso. Muscles rippled across his back, betraying the power behind even the slightest of movements. He pushed the chestnut hair from his brow, running his fingers over the zigzag pattern shaved into the side of his head.

Roh couldn't look away, even though her mind was screaming at her to bolt before he caught her watching.

The Jaktaren's hands paused back in the water, before he reached for something, brows furrowed.

Roh squinted, trying to make out whatever he had plucked from the foliage of the riverbank.

Oblivious to her careful approach, Finn studied a leaf

of sorts. Roh's stomach lurched, realising that it looked sickeningly familiar to her.

'What's that?' she demanded, his broad, bare chest forgotten. But as the words left her mouth, she fully recognised the dark-green vine and the star-shaped leaves and she lunged, batting it from Finn's hands. 'Don't touch that,' she practically yelled.

But in doing so, the foliage skimmed across her own skin, and she jerked back, as if burned. Shock barrelled through every nerve ending in her body, as though the plant recognised itself in her and had awakened its essence from slumber.

'It's alright —' Finn started, reaching for the fallen vine.

'Don't!' Roh shouted, suddenly unsteady on her feet. She lurched forward and only Finn's swift grip on her arm stopped her from falling face-first into the river.

'I only thought to bring it with us as a sample, in case we can't find the antidote,' Finn told her, still holding onto her arm. 'The antidote to a lot of poisons can be created from the poison itself.'

Roh exhaled shakily. 'Did you feel anything when you touched it?' She studied her hand where the plant had brushed against her skin. A line of raised, red bumps trailed up her forearm.

'No …' Finn followed her gaze to the marks. 'Are you alright?'

Roh shivered. The rash on her arm burned, but she didn't know how to explain to Finn that it wasn't a mere surface reaction, that something stirred within her, taunting her cyren magic, trying to coax it to come out. The powers within Roh were at war with one another, making her knees buckle.

'I'm fine,' she answered at last, though she knew she hadn't fooled the Jaktaren.

With a lingering look of concern, Finn simply dropped her arm and nodded. 'If I wrap the leaf in something, do you mind if I bring it? If the cure isn't in the mountain pass like the book said, it might do us good to have it to show a healer?'

'Are there healers on the way to Csilla?' Roh asked flatly.

Finn tore a strip off his discarded shirt and plucked a fresh vine from the nearby foliage. 'No idea.'

Roh gritted her teeth. 'Do what you want, then. Just don't touch it with your bare hands.'

Unsure if she could trust herself to stay upright, she left Finn by the riverbank and retrieved their horse.

There was no more conversation as they rode on into the afternoon. Despite Finn at her back and the sun beaming down upon the plains, Roh felt cold. There was a strange hollowness within her that she couldn't shake and a chill that bit deep into her bones. She thought of the Strothos vine tucked away in Finn's pack. Had coming into contact with it caused her to relapse into that weakened state she'd experienced in Akoris? Every time her mind began to drift, she could feel the vines from the rite tighten around her throat, and her eyes bulge out of her skull.

*It's over. It's over now*, she told herself, trying to focus on the small details around her to ground herself: the steady staccato of the horse's hooves, the song of the river beside them, the silken scales of the drakeling nestled in the crook of her neck. But her skin crawled all the same.

Roh knew if they spoke, even if it was just trading insults, the time would pass more quickly, but she didn't have the energy. She was completely sapped of strength. All she could do was hold onto the reins and long for night to fall, which meant the hours passed at a grinding pace.

By the time the sun lowered to the horizon, Roh could hardly see straight. She didn't care where they set up camp, she didn't care that Finn had to help her down off the horse, and she didn't care that Valli scurried off again into the underbrush. All she cared about was lying down. Exhaustion had her in a death grip and she was ready to surrender. The rash had spread across her arm.

Silently, Finn set them up against a large rock by the riverbed. Roh let him lead her right to it, her knees giving out as he pushed her gently to the ground. The Jaktaren was limping significantly more, but he didn't stop moving, didn't stop ensuring everything was in order. He pressed a canteen into Roh's hands, but she sat numbly, unmoving, so he brought it to her lips, letting the water trickle into her mouth.

'Have you seen?' he asked, breaking the silence at last.

Roh couldn't find her voice. She didn't know what he was talking about. She could see nothing except for imagining the silver of the poison racing through her veins.

'Look.' Finn pointed.

Roh lifted her head, following his finger northwards. There, on the horizon, misty grey mountains loomed.

'We're not far, Roh,' he whispered. 'We're not far.'

# CHAPTER SIX

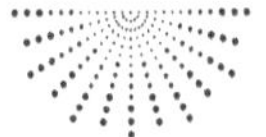

Roh was on fire, she was sure of it. The chills that had racked her body had been overrun by flames. Everything burned. She could feel the beads of sweat trickling between her shoulderblades, and suddenly she was in a dimly lit chamber, a dark puddle pooling at her bare feet on the tiled floor. Council Elders she didn't recognise from her own time gathered around a stone table, fear etched on their faces, looking up in surprise. The scene before Roh was somehow muffled, but she understood when their hands shot up in surrender and they began begging for their lives. Roh couldn't see whom they addressed, but the crawling of her skin told her that deep down, she knew who advanced upon them. Their pleas fell silent and their eyes widened in horror. The puddle at Roh's feet was red.

A relentless, violent chaos swept through the room, filling it with blood and talons and song and death. A powerful magic surging forcefully and then the council elders were screaming.

A silent cry left Roh's own lips and she knew where she was. She was back in the hollow in Akoris, watching horror after horror unfold, the drug clouding her senses and showing her what she did not wish to see. This was it, the moment Cerys had become the Elder Slayer —

'Wake up,' said a familiar voice. 'Wake up, Roh.'

But she wasn't dreaming. She was in Akoris. She had to be. There was no mistaking the sickly-sweet scented herbs that wafted around her. There was no mistaking the hollow or the dark, creeping vines that —

The voice broke into her thoughts again. 'You're having a nightmare.'

*Finn.*

Finn Haertel of the Jaktaren guild held her by the shoulders with firm but gentle hands.

Roh blinked slowly at him, trying to ascertain how long she'd been out and where she was. Her back hurt where a jagged piece of rock poked her. How had she slept here? Out in the open like this? She could feel the chill drifting from the rushing river nearby.

Finn pressed the back of his hand to her brow, the movement incredibly tender. 'You've got a fever.'

'Water?' Roh croaked, her throat raw, as though she'd been screaming. Had she been?

Finn brought the canteen to her lips and let her drink. The crisp, icy water soothed her parched tongue and dribbled down her chin.

'Sorry,' she muttered, pushing the canteen away, weakly.

'Forget it,' Finn said.

Roh hauled herself up into a sitting position, her entire body aching. 'What time is it?' she asked, palming the grit from her eyes.

'Just before dawn.'

'I've been asleep that long?'

'You needed it,' Finn allowed. 'I think that vine did something to you.'

Roh found herself nodding, rolling up her sleeve to the rash that had spread north of her elbow. 'It brought whatever poison remained in me to the surface again. I … I can't keep going like this,' she admitted in a whisper. She sought Finn's gaze, expecting impatience, frustration even, but when her eyes locked with his, she saw something else. His gaze was clouded with pain of his own.

'What's going on, Haertel?' she asked quietly, her fever forgotten. 'You're not yourself.'

He opened his mouth as if to argue, but instead, he loosed a heavy sigh. 'I suppose you'll find out soon enough, anyway,' he said, crouching with a wince and pushing up the leg of his pants.

Roh frowned as he carefully removed his boot and sock. She stared, barely breathing. For where Finn's foot and lower leg would have been, a strange silvery substance glimmered. It held the same shape as the limb, but … it didn't seem solid.

'I-I don't understand,' Roh stammered at last, unable to take her eyes off it.

Finn let her stare. He ran a talon down the substance, causing it to ripple, as though it was liquid. 'I was born without a leg from the knee down,' Finn told her, examining the shimmering replacement himself, his expression hardening. 'It's not an injury. It's a limb difference. I've always been like this.'

Roh found herself moving closer to him. The Jaktaren eyed her warily, as though bracing himself for her pity. But she had none of that for him.

'Then why is it hurting now? I've never seen you in pain like this.'

Finn tilted his head slightly, apparently surprised at her response. He gestured towards the lower half of his leg. 'This assistance is created by a tonic I've been taking every day since I was little. It generates a brace of sorts for my leg and foot, constantly adjusting to the terrain and the strength I have. My stores of the tonic were in my pack … which I no longer have.'

'Oh.'

Finn nodded. 'I've missed a dose already. Today will make it two. By tomorrow, any support it gives me will be gone. I will be as I was born: without a limb south of my left knee. The great-grandmother I mentioned? She had the same condition.'

'I see. Can we do anything for the pain?' Roh watched as Finn self-consciously pulled his sock back on and rolled the leg of his pants back down.

'It's a combination of withdrawal from the tonic and

these damn pins and needles I get where my foot would be,' he said.

'Can we get more? Who made it?' Roh asked, trying and failing to imagine the panic Finn must be feeling.

'A world-renowned healer from Battalon. Ethelda from the fire continent is famous, the best of the best. But even she couldn't grow a limb out of thin air,' he replied, sitting on a nearby rock and looking to the golden horizon. 'Taro and Bloodwyn scoured the realms searching for someone to *fix* me …' His tone turned bitter as he spoke his parents' given names.

'How have you kept this a secret?' Roh gaped at him. He was one of the best Jaktaren in history, so the rumours told, fierce and unflinching.

Finn pinched the bridge of his nose. 'They were ashamed to have a son, an heir, like me. They told no one. Anyone who witnessed my birth was paid off, or … disappeared. For the first decade of my life, they kept me hidden away.'

A sour taste filled Roh's mouth.

'My cage was a tiny room in their apartments in the Upper Sector. I wasn't allowed out.'

*'I don't like enclosed spaces, remember?'* he had told Roh.

'Yrsa's aunt, Winslow, she discovered what they were doing, and on the queen's orders took me from their care. That's why I grew up with Yrsa.'

'Gods,' Roh murmured, her stomach squirming uneasily.

'The tonic Ethelda created helps a lot. But I trained harder and harder with each passing day. Every day I adapted to work around my limitations. Yrsa helped me, she kept my secret. But it didn't matter how fast I could run, or how well I could fight. It never mattered. Taro and Bloodwyn wouldn't acknowledge me as their own.'

'I'm sorry,' Roh said quietly.

Finn looked up sharply. 'What do you have to be sorry for?'

Roh shrugged. 'I know what it's like to not be acknowledged.'

Finn stared at her for a moment before nodding and pushing off the rock. 'We should get moving again.'

'You're sure there's nothing we can do for the pain?'

'I've gone through this once before, when a shipment from Battalon was delayed. There's nothing to be done but to weather the storm, and in this case, learn to live with it. There's no magic tonic hidden behind these rocks.'

Roh nodded, quelling the urge to ask Finn more. She knew how unlike him it was to tell her at all, which prompted her to speak again. 'Finn?'

'What?'

'Thank you for telling me.'

'Wasn't like I had much of a choice.'

'I guess not,' Roh said, grabbing her pack from the cave, noting her weakening grip. Gods, they made a pair now. 'How far do you think it is to the foot of the mountains?' she asked.

A renewed sense of urgency had awakened within her alongside Strothos' poison. They needed to get to Csilla, not only for the Willow's Sapphire, but for Finn. Plus, the gods only knew what state they'd find the others in. Roh silenced the little voice in her mind that added darkly, *if we find them at all.*

'If we leave now, we can be there before noon,' Finn replied.

Roh had a vague recollection of seeing the mountains in the distance at some point the previous day, but the memory was murky.

She spotted Valli standing proudly on the horse's rump. 'Then let's move,' she said.

'Can you ride?' Finn asked.

Roh nodded. 'Can you?'

'I'll manage.' Finn favoured his good side heavily as he reached out and offered his hand.

Without thinking, Roh took it.

'Do you think the others will be there?' she asked, when they were both back atop their horse.

Riding onwards, she could feel Finn's shrug behind her. 'I don't know. We can only hope. Have you got a plan if they're not?'

Roh swallowed the hard lump in her throat. Truth be told, she hadn't let herself consider that possibility, hadn't allowed herself to imagine an alternative.

'They'll be there,' she said quietly.

The closer they got to the mountains, the more majestic they became. Even if Roh had had her sketchbook and charcoal with her, there was no way she had the skill to capture their likeness. Rugged slopes, craggy peaks, golden light and layers of shadow from the looming clouds as the dawn sun broke through. No manner of technique would capture the sheer *depth* of them. Nor the scope. It wasn't until Roh focused on how miniscule the trees were, that she realised the vastness of the mountains, and even then, that sense of scale was lost moments after because there was just so much to look at, so much to take in.

'You've not seen mountains before, then?' Finn asked in her ear, clearly having heard her intake of breath.

She shook her head.

'You should see the ones in Lochloria,' he said, apparently equally in awe. 'They're much bigger than these and even in the warmer seasons are covered in snow.'

Roh recalled him telling her that he'd been. 'What's your favourite place? From all your travels?' she heard herself ask, entranced by the deep rhythm of his voice.

Finn paused for a moment. 'The Isle of Dusan,' he said quietly. 'Where Odi's from. The chalk-white cliffs by the sea, the salt air, the luscious greenery ... It's a place unlike any other. I can see why he wants to return.'

'Empathy for a human, Haertel? You must truly be unwell,' Roh retorted.

'I believe I'm the one holding you up in the saddle,' he bit back.

'Hardly,' she said, though his words brought her attention to his arms around her waist, firm and strong.

'Whatever you need to tell yourself,' he scoffed, urging their horse on. But there was a gentle note to Finn's words and he seemed to sense that Roh welcomed the distraction from the burning rash across her arm and the aching that had suddenly gripped her joints.

Roh listened as Finn told her about the incredible landmarks he'd seen throughout his travels, no doubt trying to divert her attention from the writhing poison within her. He spoke with ease, in a way that was new between them. He had left the 'bone cleaner' and '*isruhe*' barbs far behind them. Instead, his voice was deep and calming, with notes of melody hidden within, leading Roh through each tale with care.

They arrived at the foot of the mountains an hour before midday. None of their companions were there.

'We're early,' Roh said, more to herself than to Finn as he helped her dismount. 'Deodan and I agreed, by nightfall. Wait here,' she told him. 'I'll wander around for a bit, they might be —'

'We stick together,' Finn interjected.

Roh's brows shot up in surprise. 'Oh?'

'Yrsa would kill me if I lost you.'

Roh sighed, swiping a thick stick from the ground. 'Then you'll need this.' She held it out to him. 'Use it to support your left side.'

'I know what to do,' he snapped, snatching the branch from her.

But the sharpness of his words didn't faze Roh.

Together, they walked around the partial base of the mountain, hoping to run into their friends at some point.

But there was no sign of them and the pair returned to where they'd tied the horse and shared a hardened bread roll in the shadow of the mountain. Roh gave half of her ration to Valli, who chewed at it reluctantly, clearly missing the finer meals he'd experienced at the inn.

Roh took a swig of water from her canteen and sighed. 'We should have gone around that damn village,' she muttered.

'And survived *on what* when we got here?' Finn countered. 'We didn't have a choice.'

Roh ran her fingers through her tangled hair and looked out onto the plains they had crossed. 'What if —'

'They'll be here,' the Jaktaren said firmly. 'All we can do is wait.'

And wait they did, long into the afternoon, long after night had swallowed the sun once more.


Torchlight flickered on the faint line of the dark horizon and Roh nudged Finn awake.

'Can you see how many?' she hissed, getting to her feet and squinting into the dark before her.

'Two horses,' Finn murmured. 'But I can't make out the riders they bear.'

Valli emerged from Roh's pocket and sat upon her shoulder, his bright eyes latching onto the movement up ahead. Whoever they were, the drakeling held a keen interest for them.

Roh nearly cried with relief as Deodan and Odi came

into view, supplies strapped to their backs and saddlebags. But the relief didn't last long.

Finn was already upon them. 'Where's Yrsa?' he demanded.

'Good to see you, too, Jaktaren,' Deodan quipped, dismounting.

'*Where is she?*' Finn took a step towards the warrior warlock, leaning heavily on his makeshift staff.

Deodan's gaze slid down to where Finn's pant leg dangled above the ground and then back to the stick he clutched, but he made no mention of it. 'We don't know,' he replied evenly. 'We saw her and Harlyn in the paddocks, but we split up – the villagers were upon us and that seemed to be the best option. She knows to meet us here, though. I thought she'd beat us to it.'

Finn's face fell.

Without thinking, Roh went to him and placed a comforting hand on his arm. 'If anyone can navigate the plains and find us, it's Yrsa.' She turned back to Deodan and Odi, who had dismounted as well and now stood beside the warlock. 'Harlyn was with her when you split?'

Odi nodded solemnly. 'I didn't want to leave her, Roh, but … It seemed like the best idea at the time.' His tone was laced with guilt.

'It's not your fault,' she told him. 'You made the right decision. They'll catch up.'

*They have to*, Roh added silently.

'So, what is the plan from here, once the others arrive?' Deodan asked, leading his horse to where Roh's stood grazing nearby. 'We're going around the mountain, yes?'

'Through,' Finn said boldly.

Deodan didn't hide his surprise. 'Why —'

'We haven't decided yet,' Roh interjected. 'I want this to be a choice we make together.' She had long since learned that the best decisions were not made with one mind, but many.

'There's no choice,' Finn retorted. 'Roh is unwell, she has been since the Rite of Strothos in Akoris.'

The panicked gazes of both Deodan and Odi fell upon her and it took all of Roh's willpower not to snap at Finn. This wasn't his tale to tell. But now … Now it was already out there.

'The poison from the rite still lingers in my body,' she admitted. 'Finn found a book in Akoris that suggested there would be a cure for it in the mountain pass, which is why we're considering that route.'

Deodan frowned. 'You couldn't have shared this information with the rest of us?' he ground out.

'I'm sharing it now,' Roh replied.

But the warrior warlock only seemed to grow angrier, the crease between his brows deepening, a muscle twitching in his jaw. 'We deserved to know,' he said. 'Do you have *any idea* what this mountain pass is?'

The woman from the stall in Thornhill flashed in Roh's mind. *'No humans need fear it …'*

'I …' Roh stammered.

'You foolish, ignorant cyren.'

'Warlock …' Finn's voice was laced with warning.

But Roh would handle the warrior herself. 'I haven't made any choice yet,' she told him sternly. 'I don't want to force anyone into danger.'

'A little late for that,' Odi scoffed quietly.

'Roh's been getting worse,' Finn said. 'The nightmares were one thing, as you know, but yesterday —'

'*Haertel!*' Roh hissed in warning, heat flushing her cheeks. The others didn't need to know about her weakened state. They didn't —

'She touched the same plant by the river,' Finn ploughed on, ignoring her protests. 'It seems to have awakened whatever poison was still in her system lying dormant.'

'Why in the realms were you touching that?' Deodan rounded on Roh.

She thrust a finger at Finn. 'I was trying to stop *him* from touching it!'

'I was fine!' Finn growled. 'It had no effect on me.'

'How was I supposed to know that?' Roh bit back, fury catching ablaze within her, making her dizzy. 'I was trying to help you —'

'I don't need your help —'

'Enough!' Odi raised his voice. 'We find the cure. It's as simple as that,' he said matter-of-factly.

Deodan laughed darkly. 'Simple? You really do know nothing. Even you.' He turned to Finn, his anger boiling to the surface. 'Even a worldly Jaktaren knows nothing of the mountain pass?'

Finn folded his arms across his chest. 'I've heard the rumours. That it's haunted by spirits,' he snorted.

'Nothing but superstitions. Stories told to deter children from exploring. Old wives' tales. Humans and your kin love that sort of nonsense.'

Goosebumps rushed across Roh's skin, further irritating the rash that now covered her whole arm. She checked her sleeve was pulled down to her talons. 'What's he talking about?' she asked Deodan.

'About the cyrens' ability to believe nothing but their own lies,' the warlock spat, his eyes darting to scan the trees. 'The pass is a deathtrap for your kind. The last surviving warlocks of Lochloria made it so as they fled south during the Scouring. An attempt to stop their hunters.'

'*How* is it a deathtrap?' Roh pressed, preferring the truth to the possibilities whirring in her mind.

Deodan dug his pipe from his pocket and stuffed the bowl with a pinch of herbs from a pouch at his belt. 'It's enchanted.'

'I gathered as much. How?' Roh demanded, her patience wearing thin.

'It's designed to mirror the effects of Saddoriel, the lure of the lair, only … Only it targets your kind. It will call to you, toy with your senses, your mind and take you into its darkest depths, never to be found again.'

'Oh.'

'Yes. *Oh.*'

'So, we go around, then,' Roh replied. 'We avoid it altogether.'

Finn closed the gap between them with a single, lurching step and grabbed her arm, yanking up her sleeve. Roh hissed in pain as her raw, red skin pulsed, stinging under his grip. She wrenched her arm back.

'What are you doing?' she snapped.

Odi sighed, looking from her arm to Finn. 'He's showing us that we don't have a choice.'

Finn nodded and turned to Deodan. 'You see now?'

'I do …' The warlock sounded resigned.

'Can you not whip up some sort of immunity enchantment?' Finn asked Deodan. 'Like the tokens the humans use against our lair and our deathsongs?'

But Deodan was already shaking his head. 'No. From what I know of the pass, the enchantments are adverse to any smaller spells like that. My ancestors wanted no mercy for cyrens, not when they had been hunted down and slaughtered like animals.'

Roh chewed her bottom lip. 'I see.'

'I doubt very much that you do.' Deodan's voice was harsh, cold. 'I cannot undo the magic that slumbers in these mountains. Nor would I if I could.'

Roh stared at him. She knew she would never truly understand the trauma that had passed to him from the generations before, nor would she ever understand the layers of complexity to their friendship because of it.

'I would never ask that of you,' she told him, stopping herself from touching his arm.

'Nevertheless,' Finn said firmly. 'We need that antidote.'

Roh ignored Finn's angry glare. 'If Deodan says we can't go through, then we can't.'

'I didn't say we can't,' Deodan murmured. 'I said you were foolish and ignorant.'

Valli growled. Roh took a steadying breath, her hairline growing damp with perspiration. 'Well, now that you've reinforced that point, what *do* you say?'

Deodan lit his pipe and began pacing. 'Odi and I will be unaffected by the enchantment.'

'Why me?' Odi asked. 'Why am I safe?'

'Water warlocks never had any qualms with your kind. We are similar, after all. We always abhorred the way cyrens treated you —'

'And yet you let them use your enchantments to lure my people to their deaths —'

'Enough,' Finn warned. 'Roh's nearly toppling over. Can it be done or not?'

'I believe it can,' Deodan answered. 'With mine and Odi's guidance.' He gave Finn a pointed look. 'So, I'd watch yourself or you might find that you wander down the wrong dark passage —'

'We wait for Harlyn and Yrsa,' Roh interjected, 'then we make a decision together.'

'Yrsa would vote for the cure,' Finn declared. 'To take the pass.'

'And I imagine Harlyn would feel the same,' Odi agreed, gritting his teeth.

Roh clicked her tongue in frustration. Where were the girls when she needed them?

'What about you?' Deodan was saying, with a pointed look at the staff Finn held.

'What about me?' Finn challenged, his lilac stare full of defiance.

'I clearly don't know the whole story, nor do I require it.'

Finn sneered. 'How noble of you.'

'But it would be amiss of me if I didn't ask: are you sure you can manage the mountain?'

Roh practically felt the rage pulse from Finn as he took a measured step towards Deodan.

His tone brimmed with the promise of violence. 'Don't concern yourself with what I can and cannot do, Warlock. My abilities are my own business.'

Deodan opened his mouth to protest, but Roh cut him off.

'If Finn says he can handle it, he can handle it,' she heard herself saying. Despite his own pain, it had been *Finn Haertel* who had looked after her over the past two days. *Finn Haertel* who'd woken her from her nightmares and made sure she drank enough water when the poison took her in its grip. She would not do him the dishonour of doubting his strength and endurance now.

'Actually,' Odi said. 'I have something for you, Haertel.'

Finn frowned. 'What?'

They watched, bewildered, as Odi went around the other side of his horse and unbuckled something there.

'What are you doing?' Roh called out.

But when Odi returned, it was obvious. For in his hands was Finn's beloved crossbow.

'Here,' he said, holding it out to the Jaktaren. 'Figured you'd want this.'

For the first time since she'd met him, Finn Haertel was speechless as Odi pressed the weapon into his hands.

'You're welcome,' Odi muttered before turning back to Roh. 'When do we leave? Should we wait for the others? Until daybreak?'

Roh was still watching Finn drink in the sight of his crossbow, as though it was a long-lost friend he thought he'd never see again.

'Can we afford to wait?' Deodan asked.

Roh tore her gaze away from Finn, hating that she knew the answer. Ever since she'd touched that godsforsaken plant, she had been up against an hourglass that was losing sand grain by grain. Though she stood with her back straight and spoke with a steady, confident tone, she could feel herself slipping.

'No, we can't.'

Finn swore, then slinging his crossbow over his shoulder, he unsheathed his dagger. 'Then we head for the pass. And hope the others catch up by the time we reach it.'

All Roh could do was stare as he limped towards a large, flat-faced rock, and in the dim torchlight, started to carve something there. Only when he stepped back, did Roh realise what it was. A pattern, the same pattern that both Finn and Yrsa had shaved into the sides of their hair.

'She'll know we were here,' Finn explained. 'She'll know to keep going and catch up.'

A wave of nausea barrelled through Roh and she gripped a nearby branch to steady herself. Valli whined against her neck, as though sensing her discomfort. Roh swallowed the build-up of saliva.

'Are you all sure you want to do this? And now? In the dark?'

'We have torches. We'll have to let the horses loose, anyway, whether it's tonight or tomorrow morning,' Odi said. 'Every moment we stand here idle, is another moment you may succumb to the poison, right?'

Roh nodded stiffly, silently hating herself. None of them complained though. Instead, they set about distributing their supplies evenly between the four of them. Valli dived into Roh's pocket as she shouldered her pack once more, nearly staggering beneath its weight. She didn't doubt Finn would make it up the pass, but whether *she* would, was a different matter entirely. Roh did her best not to let it show. The last thing she needed was an argument.

'Do we have everything?' she asked no one in particular.

'Everything we can carry,' Deodan replied, adjusting the straps of his own pack and taking the torch from Odi. 'Shall I lead?'

'I've got the map,' Finn countered. 'And Roh has the topaz. We'll take the front.'

'Fine.' Deodan waved him away. 'Though, Roh, you should probably wear the crown if you want that topaz to be of any use in guiding you.'

Odi dug it out of her pack for her, to save her from having to take it off. When he handed her the crown, disapproval was clear on his face. She didn't blame him. It was made of bones, after all. But something within her settled as she placed it atop her head; she could feel the reassuring thrum of the Mercy's Topaz.

'Let's go, then,' she said. Roh asked no more details of Deodan. He would tell them his plan when he was ready. And perhaps for now, it was best not to know what awaited them.

*Focus on one obstacle at a time,* she told herself, eyeing the rocky incline ahead.

They each held a torch as Finn led them around the base of the mountain, all the while leaving Jaktaren symbols for Yrsa to follow. He paused for just a moment as they came to the beginning of the path, clutching his staff. Roh watched the crossbow rise across the breadth of his shoulders as he took a deep breath.

Then, they started their ascent.

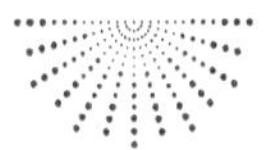

# CHAPTER SEVEN

Roh's back burned right down the middle from the weight of her pack and the steep incline. Despite the chilled night air, her shirt quickly grew damp with sweat. She wasn't the only one struggling – the laboured breathing around her was proof enough – and it wasn't long before she realised that climbing to the pass in the dark of night was a mistake. She couldn't see more than two feet in front of her, the torches each of her companions carried barely illuminating the uneven terrain and jagged rocks. Snapped branches scratched at her exposed skin and the earth beneath her boots slid under each step. But they were there because of her, as always, so she would not give up, and she certainly wouldn't be the first to complain.

The four of them pushed on, ignoring the pain and the bite of the harsh wind that had started only moments ago.

'What was harder?' Roh called back to Odi. 'Climbing the Five Daughters, or this?'

There was a pause. 'I almost died climbing the falls,' he replied, his words echoing up to her.

How could Roh have forgotten? Harlyn had been the one to save him, grabbing onto his cloak as the rest of him had detached from the rockface, his limbs flailing. Roh remembered the terror thick in her throat, unable to scream.

'You climbed the Five Daughters?' Deodan asked, a note of awe in his voice. 'That path caved in years ago.'

'We did,' Roh told him.

'Then this should be child's play to you.'

'I wouldn't go that far,' Finn said between gritted teeth, using his staff to steady himself.

Roh watched in admiration as he tackled each step forward with determination and precision, all the while consulting the map and leading them. Finn was true to his Jaktaren nature, she'd give him that.

Another hour passed and another. Roh lost herself in the monotonous rhythm of the hike, suppressing the desire to ask how long they still had to go. Asking never made the journey shorter. She tried to ignore the chattering of her teeth and the black spots that came and went, making her vision swim. The poison within stirred her magic, her deathsong burrowing further inside her, as though hiding from the drug's effects. She could tell the burning rash had spread to her shoulder and neck because the straps of her pack were rubbing her skin raw. Roh clenched her jaw against the pain and pushed on.

Conversation between the companions came in short bursts. An attempt to distract themselves from their exhaustion that was thwarted by their need for air and concentration on where they were stepping.

Finn stumbled in front of her, swearing as he lost his footing entirely and fell to the ground.

Roh gasped and reached for him. 'Are you alright?'

Finn muttered a string of curses as he patted the ground, trying to find his staff. 'I'm fine,' he snapped, though he was unable to hide his wince as he tried to get back up, ignoring her outstretched hand.

'Don't be a fool,' she bit back softly so the others couldn't hear. 'Sometimes being strong means knowing when to accept help.'

'Everything alright?' Odi called from behind them.

Finn paused for a moment, the hard lines of his face softening as he considered Roh's words. With a reluctant sigh, he met the challenge in her gaze and his hand grasped hers. She pulled him up, staggering herself.

'We're nearly there,' was all Finn said.

But Roh didn't move. 'Can you smell that?' she asked, breathing in the crisp night air.

Around her, the others did the same.

'Smoke,' she muttered. 'We're not the only ones aiming for the pass.'

'Should we wait?' Odi asked. 'The last thing we need is to run into a bunch of people and have a brawl on the mountain side.'

The idea didn't appeal to Roh, either, but nor did

waiting in the dark in the hope that whoever was ahead of them would move on.

'I'll go,' she told him. 'You wait here.'

'No,' Finn said firmly. 'We go together. All of us.'

Deodan moved to the front of the group and stood beside Finn. 'I hate to agree with the Jaktaren, but he's right. All or none.'

Roh threw her hands up in frustration. 'Have it your way, then.' The movement seemed to disturb Valli, who poked his head out of her pocket with an aggressive gleam in his gold eyes. Huffing, the little drakeling leaped from Roh's chest onto the ground and scurried ahead.

'What's he doing?' Odi asked with a moan. 'He'll give us away.'

'He will not.'

'Will so.'

'What are you, a child?' Roh retorted. She recalled how Valli had found a horse for them back when they had fled Thornhill. 'He's scouting,' she said with a quiet realisation.

It didn't stop her from jumping when they heard the crunch of branches snapping beneath boots up ahead. Her hand went to her sling hanging from her belt. She had it loaded and poised to bludgeon in seconds; Yrsa had taught her well. With their torches blazing in the dark, they were a beacon to any attacker. It was too late to extinguish the flames. They had been found.

Deodan gripped his cutlass, while Odi palmed a pair of daggers and Finn loaded his crossbow, knowing it was far too close quarters for sword combat as the footsteps drew closer.

With her heart lodged in her throat, Roh gripped her sling tighter, prepared to shatter —

'It's about time you showed up,' a familiar voice sounded.

Squinting into the dark, Roh lifted her torch to illuminate whoever approached them. Her steps were measured, confident, and when she stepped into the light, Roh recognised the sling held casually in her hand, and the golden drakeling sitting upon her shoulder —

'Yrsa!' There was uncontained joy in Finn's voice.

Roh exhaled a shaky sigh of relief. 'Gods,' she muttered, pocketing her sling. 'How did you get here before all of us? How did you know to come here? Is Harlyn with you?'

'She is. But first things first,' Yrsa said, glancing at Finn's support staff and Roh's dripping brow. 'Come and rest by the fire. You all look horrendous.'

Roh snorted. 'Thanks.'

Moments later, with Yrsa in the lead, they came upon a small, flat clearing – the dark mouth of the mountain pass, where a small fire blazed. And there was Harlyn.

Roh lunged for her friend, a powerful wave of relief washing over her. Until she saw that Harlyn was cradling her injured arm to her chest, her face lined with pain. Roh skidded to a stop and knelt in the dirt before her.

'What happened?' she asked, her strained voice threatening to break. 'Did the villagers catch you? Were you attacked?' She realised that Harlyn held a wet poultice to her arm, something that Yrsa had made, no doubt.

But to Roh's surprise, Harlyn laughed. 'Nothing as exciting as that, I'm afraid.'

'What, then?'

In the light of the fire, Roh could see the pink tinge of embarrassment on her friend's cheeks.

'I fell asleep on my horse,' she admitted. 'Slid right out of the saddle like a prized idiot.'

Roh couldn't help it, she clapped a hand over her mouth to stifle a laugh.

'Glad you find my pain so amusing, Rohesia.' But Harlyn's tone was light.

'Only a little,' Roh countered, reaching across and grasping her friend's hand. 'It's good to see you, Har.'

Harlyn smiled. 'And you.' She gave the others a wave as they set down their packs and huddled around the fire. 'Though, how you survived Haertel this whole time, I don't know.'

Roh took up a place beside Harlyn. 'It wasn't all bad,' she muttered.

She felt Harlyn's side glance on her and she waited for the sarcastic jab that was due any moment. But instead, her friend touched her shoulder lightly.

'Roh?' Harlyn asked, twisting to face her fully.

'Hmm?'

'You're shaking.'

'What?'

'Your whole body, it's shaking.'

Sure enough, when Roh studied her hands, they

trembled, and as soon as she noticed that, she felt it through her whole body.

'Are you cold?' Harlyn asked, motioning for Yrsa to join them.

'That's not it …' But as Roh began to explain the poison's effects, a cold shiver raked down her spine and a barrage of whispers flooded her mind. She gasped, her head whipping around, her gaze latching on the mouth of the mountain pass. Dozens of voices sounded from within, though she couldn't discern one from another.

'We hear them, too,' Harlyn told her, following her line of sight, a grim understanding on her face.

'You haven't entered, have you?' Deodan's voice sounded.

'No,' Harlyn said. 'Yrsa said to wait for you. And to be honest, what I hear isn't exactly welcoming.'

Deodan nodded. 'I imagine not.' He turned to Yrsa. 'You know? About the pass?'

'A guess,' Yrsa said. 'My aunt, she has many books on the Scouring. I know the importance of this place for warlocks. For the refugees of Lochloria.'

'How'd you know we'd come this way?'

Yrsa rubbed the back of her neck. 'I … I'm not entirely sure.'

'What do you suspect?' Deodan insisted.

Yrsa gave Roh a strange glance. 'It was like I could feel you – your song, your energy – pulling me in the right direction.'

'I felt it, too,' Harlyn offered. 'It was definitely you.'

Roh frowned. 'Perhaps it was the topaz? Maybe it can guide the bearer's company, too?'

'Perhaps,' Yrsa said, clearly unconvinced.

'You truly think it was my magic?' Roh asked, ignoring the crawling sensation across her skin.

'Definitely,' Harlyn said confidently. 'It *felt* like you. Like you were right in front of me.'

Roh rubbed her aching eyes. *Strange,* she thought. There had to be some sort of explanation, but with the voices from the pass sending her body into a fresh set of tremors, she didn't want to delve too deeply.

Roh let Deodan, Odi and Finn relay their situation to Harlyn and Yrsa. Finn and Odi had been right about their stance on the matter, and the company decided to rest for an hour to regain what little wits and strength they could before pressing onwards. With exhaustion once again latching onto her bones, Roh lay down by the fire, Valli curling up at her side, basking in the warmth. She felt as though her body did not belong to her. She could feel her cyren magic warring with the awakened poison of Strothos' vine. Her mind churned through every dire possibility that might befall them once they entered the mountain pass, all the while, the voices didn't cease, only seeming to grow louder with each passing minute.

Unable to sleep, she watched the others go about their business in a daze. Though they were missing a bag or two, Deodan seemed to think they had enough supplies to get them to Csilla. She saw Yrsa approach Finn, who had propped his bad leg up on a log.

'Thought you might need this,' Yrsa said to him, dropping a pack at his side.

'You took mine instead of yours?' he asked, hope gleaming in his eyes.

Yrsa shrugged. 'Figured you'd need yours more.'

Finn was already rifling through one of the side pockets. From where Roh lay, she could hear the clinking of glass vials.

'Thank the gods,' Finn murmured as he held one up to the light. 'And you, friend.'

'You did well to get here without it,' Yrsa said. 'But don't double up on doses, you hear?'

'I know, I know …' Finn uncorked the vial and tipped its contents into his mouth. When he had swallowed it, he stretched out his leg and looked up at Yrsa, his eyes full of gratitude. 'Thank you.'

'What's that about?' Harlyn whispered, laying a palma-fur cloak over Roh's torso.

Roh thought of all that Finn had told her on the road. 'You'll have to ask Finn,' she said weakly.

Harlyn held her gaze for a moment, before she shrugged. 'Fair enough.'


'Roh,' Harlyn whispered. 'It's time.'

Roh awoke bleary-eyed to her friend gently shaking her shoulder, the pain from the rash searing her skin. Shocked that she'd managed to sleep at all, she sat up, trying to rub the grit from her eyes. Deodan and the others were waiting for her at the dark mouth of the tunnel. Odi and Yrsa were lighting torches for everyone, while Deodan and Finn held thick lengths of rope in their hands.

'I can't say this is my favourite of all the wild plans we've come up with so far,' Harlyn grumbled as she helped Roh get to her feet.

'Why does that not surprise me?' Roh muttered, reaching for her crown of bones.

Harlyn eyed it questioningly.

'Figured we could use all the guidance we can get,' Roh said, arranging it on her head. She stood, shouldering her pack with a wince. It was too dark to check, but she didn't need light to know that the rash had spread even further across her torso. Valli tugged at the hem of Roh's pants with an unhappy growl. The drakeling flared his gold wings, as though he meant to launch himself into the air, but nothing happened. Valli growled again and Roh scooped him up in her hand.

'You'll get there,' she told him, praying that Yrsa was right and that the skill would come to him as an instinct.

'Roh?' Harlyn nudged her, jutting her chin to where the others waited restlessly.

'We'll tie ourselves together,' Deodan told her. 'Odi at the rear, me in the lead. We should be able to guide you through the pass, pull you back in line when you stray.'

'We're trained to deal with enchantments,' Finn muttered, scowling at Deodan as he looped the rope around the Jaktaren's waist and knotted it tightly.

'No,' Deodan said quietly. 'You're not.'

'You have no idea what I'm trained for, Warlock, or what I'm —'

'If it's anything like Saddoriel,' Odi interjected coldly, 'you'll be powerless. Knowing the lure is there makes no difference. It'll take you all the same, and you'll lose yourself.'

Roh shuddered, remembering the trance-like state in which she'd found the human by the Pool of Weeping, as though he might drown himself in it. Her eyes met Deodan's. 'You're outnumbered by us,' she said, with a pointed glance at the cyrens in their group. 'What if we're too strong? What if you can't contain us, can't keep us in line?'

'There's no other choice,' the warlock replied.

'You could escort us through one by one?' Harlyn offered.

But Deodan shook his head. 'It would take too long, all the while leaving you vulnerable here. I think my presence has kept the enchantments contained to the pass itself, but … I can't guarantee that would remain so without me.' Deodan reached Roh and threaded the rope around her waist, tying her to Harlyn.

Odi cleared his throat, clearly unnerved by the sight of the cyrens being bound together. 'Deodan and I will look for the antidote, the rest of you won't be in the right frame of mind.'

'Then you'll need this,' Roh said, patting down her pockets and retrieving the page from the Akorian library book. 'It's got an illustration on the back.'

Odi nodded, taking the paper wordlessly and sliding it

into his pocket. Roh's fate was in his hands now, it seemed.

Yrsa handed Roh and Harlyn a torch each. In the glowing light, Roh saw how wide Harlyn's eyes were, how her mouth was slightly parted as she stared into the narrow entrance.

Roh gently squeezed her free hand. 'We'll get through this,' she told her, sounding more confident than she felt.

Harlyn's voice came out as a croak. 'You don't hear her, do you?'

'Hear who?'

Harlyn chewed her lower lip. 'Orson.'

Roh's blood chilled. 'No … I … It's just a trick of the enchantment.'

'This isn't the first time I've heard her,' Harlyn said.

'Harlyn …' Roh didn't know what to say.

'I know,' her friend replied, tearing her eyes back to Deodan, who was now double-checking everyone was secured in place.

'Outside Thornhill,' Roh recalled aloud. 'You heard her then?'

Harlyn nodded. 'Yes. And a few times after, when we were riding here. What's wrong with me, Roh?' she asked, her eyes pleading, her face drained of colour.

'I don't know, Har,' Roh said. 'Can you hear her now?'

Harlyn waited a moment. 'No …'

Roh struggled to find the right words.

'Don't bother,' Harlyn waved her off, a poor attempt at nonchalance. 'There's nothing to be done, at least not now.'

'Is everyone ready?' Deodan asked.

Roh squeezed Harlyn's hand again and looked from her friend to Yrsa on her other side. 'As we'll ever be,' she answered.

'Good.' Deodan tied himself to Finn at the front of their line and drew his sword from its scabbard.

'Are you expecting company?' Yrsa asked.

Deodan scanned them warily. 'Only the company I've got now.' He nodded to Odi, who hesitantly unsheathed his own blade, glancing apologetically at the cyrens.

Roh took a deep breath, shuddering again at the voices growing louder. 'Let's get this over with,' she said.

'As the Queen of Bones commands,' Deodan replied. Without hesitating, he strode forward, into the mouth of the pass, pulling the cyrens and Odi along with him.

# CHAPTER EIGHT

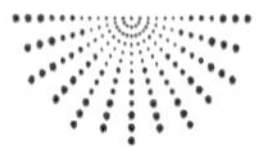

As soon as they crossed the threshold, the buzzing whispers ceased. A wide, dark tunnel greeted them, its glimmering black stone walls lined with a thick chain on either side. Sconces trailed all the way down, out of sight. Deodan touched his torch to one and the entire path came to life with light, that one touch setting off a sequence of reactions all the way to the other side of the mountain.

'I feel no different,' Harlyn announced, looking expectantly around the cavernous passage.

'The enchantment is clever, subtle,' Deodan called back to her. 'It is not a sudden onslaught, but a quiet questioning of the mind.'

Roh swallowed the dry lump in her throat. Her mind had been toyed with enough these past few weeks.

From what Deodan had told them, the pass was a relatively flat tunnel that cut through the heart of the mountain and opened up on the other side facing Csilla. But there were offshoots from the main path, just like the passageways of Talon's Reach, and *that* was where the dangers would lie.

As they trekked deeper into the mountain, Roh felt the hollowness within her yawn wider still and her skin itched furiously. Her limbs felt more and more like liquid, while her mind began to wander to the darkest corners of her imagination.

*Is this it? Is this the enchantment kicking in?* she wondered. *Gods, it's hard to tell when my thoughts naturally descend into chaos ...* She touched her hand to the topaz sitting in her crown and it warmed beneath her fingertips. No, there was no enchantment at play, not yet. The scramble in her head was all her.

Harlyn's hand shot out, gripping Roh's arm painfully. 'She's here,' Harlyn whispered. 'Orson's here.'

Roh tried to loosen Harlyn's grip, her talons peeking from her fingertips. 'She's not,' she said, trying to soothe Harlyn. 'It's the warlock spell.'

Harlyn's throat bobbed as she looked around wildly. 'She's here,' she insisted.

The length of rope encircling Roh's waist tugged her forward and she stumbled after her friend, torn between comforting Harlyn and delaying them further, subjecting them to the enchantment for longer. Was it the warlock trickery when Harlyn had heard Orson long before entering the mountain pass? Around them, the walls shimmered. What was this quest of hers doing to them all?

Harlyn babbled behind her, calling out to their friend as though she was only a few yards away.

'It's alright, Har,' she heard Odi's voice behind them. 'I've got you.'

'But, Odi, she's right over there somewhere, she wants us to find her,' Harlyn protested, straining against the rope, tugging Roh in the opposite direction.

'Listen to me, Harlyn,' Odi said, his words calm and soothing. 'You have my word, she's not there. The lure doesn't affect me. I can see clearly. She's not there, I promise.'

Harlyn's pulling at the rope ceased. 'You wouldn't lie to me.'

'No, I wouldn't,' Odi told her.

Harlyn exhaled a sigh of relief. 'Alright.'

Odi gave her a gentle push forward, nodding to Roh to keep moving.

Roh's skin crawled; it was just as Deodan had warned. Not an onslaught of the senses, but a subtle questioning of the fabric of one's reality.

Up ahead, she noticed Yrsa and Finn walking close together, despite Finn's still prominent limp. Their heads nearly touched as they whispered to one another.

*But that's not possible*, Roh realised. Yrsa was tied to her. Finn was tied to Deodan up ahead. And yet she saw them, walking alone, as though they were the last two people in all the realms.

*What are they talking about?* Roh wondered with a twinge of envy. The Jaktaren were at complete ease with one another, a casual intimacy that only came with being raised together. The same sort of relationship she'd once had with Harlyn and Orson. One day, she hoped to have that again with Harlyn, but Orson … Roh had to accept that she would never see her friend again. Perhaps Harlyn was going through the same grief. Perhaps the voice she was hearing was part of that process.

Roh's head spun as her mind flitted from thought to thought, each one sapping more energy from her already drained body. She could feel herself trembling, so hard her body ached. Her knees weakened with each step, but she was alert, waiting for something, or someone to call out to her from the shadows, to lure her into an unknown fold. As much as she wanted to rest, they couldn't stop – not here. She jolted as Valli leaped from her shoulder and onto the thick chain lining the wall.

'Deodan?' she called.

'What is it?'

'Will the lure affect Valli?'

'No,' he said loudly, his voice echoing down the tunnel. 'I've not heard of any magic that could influence a creature like him, even as a hatchling.'

'Good,' Roh murmured. 'That's good …' She worried for Valli. He was a creature of the ancient deep, like her, and yet he had never seen the sea. She had robbed him of that joy. Was the fact that he was being raised on land interfering with his development? Was that why he behaved so moodily? Did he miss the sea? Did he miss his mother? She strained her eyes, trying to glimpse the little beast from wherever he'd got to, but there was no sign of him —

Roh's middle jerked as a firm tug of the rope came from ahead. 'Come on, we can't afford to slow our pace,' Deodan ordered them.

Behind Roh, Yrsa nearly barrelled into her. The Jaktaren stopped in her tracks and looked deeply into the dimly lit distance. 'I don't want to go,' she said, her voice sounding far away and frightened.

'We have to,' Roh told her. 'We have to get out of here.'

'I don't want to go without Finn.'

Roh frowned. 'Finn's right here.' She pointed to where he leaned heavily on his staff, his own brow furrowed as he surveyed his friend.

'I'm here, Yrsa,' he said, waving.

But Yrsa didn't look at him. She seemed smaller somehow, almost childlike. 'I won't go without him. I won't leave him with them again. *Do you know what they do to him?*'

Finn's eyes widened. 'Yrs,' he said more urgently. 'I'm right here. I'm here with you. You don't have to go anywhere without me.'

'Don't make me, Winslow. It's not fair. He's all alone. They've locked him up in the dark again —'

'Yrsa,' Finn snapped, tugging on her rope.

'She's under the spell now,' Deodan said quietly.

Still all tied together, they gathered around Yrsa, who looked straight through them.

Odi eyed Finn, whose hands were still on the rope between him and Yrsa.

'Be gentle with her,' Odi told him. 'Try to coax her along, but don't startle her. She might lash out if she's taken by surprise. It can be incredibly disorientating when the real world suddenly clashes with the one in your mind.'

'Was this what it was like for you?' Harlyn asked Odi. 'In Saddoriel?'

'Yes.'

Harlyn's face fell. 'For that I'm sorry.'

'Me too,' Roh added.

Finn glanced up at them. 'Me too.'

Surprise rippled across Odi's face, but he nodded stiffly. 'Hurry up.'

'Come along, Yrsa,' Finn said gently, his fingers lacing through his friend's. 'This way.'

'But I can't leave him, Winslow.'

'You're not,' Finn whispered. 'You never do. I'll show you where he is. Just follow me. Stay close.'

'Are you sure? What about Taro and Bloodwyn?'

'We've bested them before,' Finn said. 'We will best them again.'

Something shifted within Roh as she peered after the friends, Finn easing himself forward, supporting his weight on his staff as he held Yrsa tenderly. They were a family; there was no other word for it.

'Odi,' Deodan said. 'Remember to keep an eye out on the ground or in the antechambers for this cure. What does the parchment say?'

Roh watched Odi extract the torn page from his pocket and bring it closer to the light of his torch, doing his best to smooth out the paper single-handedly. On one side was the illustration of the Strothos vine and its star-shaped leaves. Roh had to stop her hand from going to her throat, remembering how the plant had tried to squeeze the life out of her in the hollow. Odi scanned the text she'd read a hundred times, before turning the page over. On the back was another sketch.

'It's a diamond-shaped leaf,' he told the others. 'Usually sprouting from a dense bush, identifiable by its white-and-grey flowers —'

'*Rohesia*,' a strangely familiar voice sounded in Roh's ear.

She whirled around, causing Harlyn to stumble at the jerk of the rope.

*There's no one there*, she told herself. *Stick to Deodan's path, hold onto the rope.* She chanted the instructions to herself, hoping they would somehow anchor her to the others.

'*Rohesia.*' Her name was a melody on familiar lips, as mesmerising as the currents of the sea. '*Go where the fear is darkest.*' The words were a song, stark in truth and warning. Roh took a step towards them.

'*Rohesia, I'm sorry ...*' At this, the scar across Roh's face burned. The white-hot pain lanced through her as it had the first time down in the depths of Saddoriel's Prison.

'*Rohesia, I'm sorry ...*' the voice said again.

'Cerys ...' Roh said aloud, trying to close the gap between her mother and her.

As the name left her lips, the others' heads snapped in her direction.

'Are you alright, Roh?' Odi asked from the back.

'I ... I'm fine.'

'You said your mother's name.'

'I … I know where I am,' she told them shakily, fending off whatever the enchantment had conjured to entrance her. 'I'm in the mountain pass,' she said, more to ground herself than to reassure the others. She could still hear the whispers. 'Any sign of the flowers, Deodan?'

'Not yet, but I think there might be some foliage up ahead —'

The group was wrenched to one side, and Roh went sprawling across the ground, her palms and cheek stinging, her torch extinguished in the dirt.

Finn darted from the line, pulling his crossbow in front of his body and loading it in one swift, blurred movement.

And pointed it right at Roh.

Roh leaped to her feet and threw her hands up. 'Finn! Don't —'

Deodan tackled the Jaktaren to the ground, holding his blade to Finn's throat.

'Deodan!' Odi shouted. 'What did I say about —'

'He was going to *shoot* Roh! Was I supposed to —'

But Roh's attention went elsewhere, to Valli, who was scurrying back and forth across an entrance to an alcove up ahead. Without thinking, Roh unsheathed her talons and sliced through the rope.

'*Go where the fear is darkest,*' Cerys told her again. Atop Roh's head, the topaz hummed, spreading warmth from the crown down to her toes. She left the angry words of warlocks and cyrens behind, walking towards her drakeling in a daze.

'What have you found?' she asked when she reached Valli. Inside the alcove was a strange little garden, with plants growing from elaborate garden beds, as though they were regularly tended to. But there was no sunlight here. Just like in Saddoriel …

Valli looked expectantly from Roh to the garden.

'You think it's in there?' she said quietly to Valli.

The poison and magic in Roh's body pulsed, filling her with a sense of urgency, of recklessness. She took a step into the alcove. She spotted the bush with the white flowers immediately and the diamond-shaped —

'Roh!' someone shouted a warning in the distance.

But it was too late.

Out of nowhere, an iron door slammed down, separating her from the others – locking them out, and caging her in.

# CHAPTER NINE

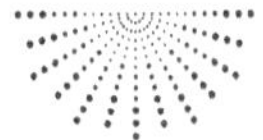

The alcove was instantly cloaked in darkness, and fear spiked through Roh, her heart hammering in her throat. In the pitch black, she fought to keep her rising panic at bay, reminding herself that she'd managed to escape the shrinking room back in Akoris easily enough. But this felt different, more sinister. She couldn't hear her companions on the other side of the iron door and not a single splinter of light made it through the entrance.

'*Rohesia.*' Her mother's voice was both in her ear and in her mind.

'*Rohesia.*' Another voice this time, deep and raw.

Roh's hands spanned the rough walls, brushing across all manner of flowers and herbs growing there, despite the darkness. That voice, she'd never heard it before, and yet somehow she recognised it. It did not have the melodic undertones of a cyren, but in those three syllables, she knew it in her bones. It was the voice of Eadric, her father.

*He's here.* The thought possessed her entirely as she blindly paced the alcove, half expecting a hidden doorway to open up and reveal her parents to her. Were they together? *How?*

But when her fingertips brushed against the cold of the iron door, she remembered: the mountain pass, the warlock enchantments, and the fact that she was trapped. She had severed her tie to the others.

She was completely alone.

Roh tried to contain her imagination and the lure of the pass as it attempted to drag her down a number of dark paths: starvation, her skeleton being found in this room centuries later … But as she wrangled with her innermost demons, a buzzing began. It was the sound of a swarm of insects, thousands of them, only … it was in her head. It rattled her mind, making her want to cover her ears with her hands.

She staggered beneath its weight. *What's happening?*

The buzzing was building and building, to the point of pain inside her head. No matter how hard she tried, she couldn't see past the darkness, couldn't mute the noise in her mind. She didn't know if it was Strothos' poison taking hold, the lure of the mountain pass, or her deepest, darkest fear – that madness ran in her veins, thick as the blood she shared with her mother. But Roh had passed the point of caring. Her head burned, threatening to split in two – or a thousand pieces. She fell to her knees, hands now pulling at her own hair, desperate to make it stop. The poison in her body seemed to answer the lure of the alcove, stirring to life wildly in her veins, pitting everything it had against her cyren magic.

The buzzing wasn't insects, she realised. It was voices. Those voices they'd heard at the mouth of the pass. Amplified. And now ... Now she could hear their cries clearly, hear their exact words. Hundreds of voices, begging for help, begging for mercy, praying to the goddesses. It only got louder and louder, piercing her mind —

*I can't take this, I can't take this*, Roh chanted to herself, her face wet with tears, as she rocked on her knees. She suddenly knew exactly what she was hearing – the victims of the Scouring, the water warlocks who had fled across the gorge of Csilla, trying to find a way through the mountain. Her ancestors had done that, had been on both sides, as she now knew. Cyrens, warlocks, humans ... how could they have inflicted so much upon one another? She could feel the sorrow of the past in every breath she took, a piercing, poignant agony of lives ruined and lost, of cruelties delivered. It was too much, the presence of history —

Her head dropped back and her mouth parted. At once, song poured from her. An all-encompassing, mournful melody, so rich, so pure, Roh could see the golden notes dancing before her in the same foreign script that Odi used when he wrote to his brothers. The pressure that had built up inside her eased at once as the music flowed from her body. It filled the strange dark room with magic, *her* magic. She could *see it*, in all its glory. It toyed with the flowers and leaves of the plants climbing the surrounding walls, and the little garden bed at the centre. Her song, her *magic* explored, played, as though it had all the time in the world, as though the enchantments of the pass and the poison in her veins hadn't just threatened to undo her. No longer did she feel weak and alone and helpless, no longer did she worry that she wasn't enough. The sound that poured from her was *hers* and *hers alone*, and it was rife with power. She could feel it in every inch of her being.

And that was when the names barrelled into her.

Cerys *Irons*.

Rohesia *Irons*.

But there had been another *Irons*, a missing piece of the puzzle she so desperately wanted to solve.

Memories came at her hard and fast.

In Akoris, she was sharing a bed with Harlyn.

*'Roh, Ames told me a tale about some Saddorien battalion leader who didn't find hers until her fifth decade. And hers —'*

*'Was the most powerful in all our history,' Roh finished for her. Ames had told her the same story. What had her name been? It was on the tip of Roh's tongue —*

Roh went back further, to a moment of despair, alone in the bone-cleaner workshop, until Ames had turned up.

*'Queen Delja sang her first note at eight years old! And she has the most powerful song in history.'*

*'Does she?' Ames tugged on his collar, as he usually did when he posed such questions. 'Queen Delja did sing her first note at eight years old, but she didn't sing her full song until*

*her later fledgling years. However, even then, it was not she who had the most powerful song in known history. That claim belonged to one of King Asros' battalion leaders, many hundreds of years ago, and if my sources are correct, she did not find her deathsong until long after her fifth decade. She was in the minority, that's sure enough. But when she did eventually find her song, Rohesia, it was something else entirely.'*

*Roh gaped at her mentor. She had never been told that story before. 'You heard it?'*

*Ames nodded. 'Once. And I'll never forget it.'*

*'Who was she?'*

*'Sedna Irons.'*

Roh nearly lost her footing as the memory rushed through her. She was the daughter of Cerys Irons, the Elder Slayer, but she was also the granddaughter of the great *Sedna Irons*, the cyren from whom legend was carved. There was no denying it, even with poison coursing through her, even up against enchantments, her magic was leagues above the rest. How could she have ever doubted it? Roh revelled in her power and strength, letting it pour from her and flow through the room as though it had a mind of its own and it answered only to her.

Golden rays burst through the cracks in the black walls, bathing the alcove in a buttery light, warm and comforting, shielding Roh from that heavy darkness that had cloaked her senses only moments ago.

She had suspected it after Valli had hatched, but now she knew. Her deathsong was unlike any other.

She stopped singing, but the light didn't fade.

With her magic still pulsing around her, her power so thoroughly alive and connected to her, Roh stood on steady feet. Forgetting that she was trapped, forgetting that the others were likely panicking outside, she went to the manicured garden beds and brushed her hands across the leaves there. A different sort of magic whispered against her skin. Warlock magic, she realised. It had the same imprint that Deodan's power had, a playful essence that would only grow stronger when it met sacred water. But another part of her recognised it … She was part cyren, but warlock blood flowed through her veins as well. She was her father's daughter. No wonder she had been drawn to Deodan's magic in the Gilded Plains. Did it explain Deodan's support for her? Slowly, it was as though the alcove recognised her as well …

*What is this place?* Roh wondered, pacing around the garden beds, not quite ready to pluck the foliage from its soil. A strange sense of calm had washed over her. She was not alone, not with her magic alive around her, not knowing where she had come from. And so she wandered around the alcove. Any notion of urgency had vanished completely. She knew she was safe here, she knew she would find her way out eventually, and so she surveyed her surroundings. In the fresh light, from the markings on the walls and the discarded belongings in the far corner, it looked like someone had stayed here long ago. It had been a refuge or camp of sorts.

Crouching, Roh calmly sifted through the items. A ragged blanket with holes bitten through by insects or rodents; a dented tin mug, several empty vials like the ones Deodan carried, a feathered quill, and several thick volumes —

A near-deafening *bang* sounded and Roh jumped back as the iron door flew into the alcove, clattering to the ground. The noise echoed off the walls and Roh's hands covered her ears once more.

'What in the realms …' Yrsa's voice cut through the commotion. 'Roh?'

'Over here,' Roh waved. 'I'm alright. Are you?'

The rope between the companions had been severed and Yrsa was at her side instantly. 'We're fine,' she told her. 'What happened?'

Roh frowned. 'I … I sang my deathsong. It created all this light …'

Yrsa was staring strangely at her. 'The entire door lit up from the other side,' she explained. 'We had no idea what was happening to you. And … something happened to Valli.'

'Is he —'

'He's fine. But he … he *glowed*, Roh. It was as though he was absorbing your magic, as though you could reach him, even from in here … He's the one who broke down the door.'

'*What?*' Roh couldn't believe what she was hearing. *That tiny little thing managed to cave in an iron door?*

Yrsa was nodding as though she could read Roh's mind. 'He seemed to light up, and then he sort of lost it? He kept ramming it and we tried to stop him, worried he was going to kill himself trying to get to you. It was like he could hear what was going on inside. I … I don't know *how*, but he knocked the door in … It was as though your magic powered him, Roh.'

Roh scanned the room for the drakeling. There he was, sitting in the garden bed, cheeks bulging, happily munching on several leaves at once as though nothing had happened.

Roh shot Yrsa a look of pure disbelief. 'Apparently, he was just really hungry.'

Yrsa simply shrugged. 'He's *your* drakeling.'

'At least we know the leaves are safe,' Finn said, frowning at Valli, who was still gorging himself. He then met Roh's gaze with a blush. 'I'm sorry,' he said. 'About before.'

'About trying to shoot me with your crossbow?'

'Ah, yes, that's the one.'

'Consider it forgotten.'

Harlyn and Odi pushed past the Jaktaren and rushed to Roh, both of them looking her over critically.

'I'm alright,' she reassured them.

Harlyn gripped Roh's shoulder as though she needed physical proof that she was indeed in one piece. 'Gods, there was all that light.'

Roh's attention snagged on Deodan, who was slowly pacing the perimeter of the room. He was unusually quiet, his brows knitted together, his hands rubbing his arms as though he was chilled.

'What's wrong, Deodan?' Roh asked, taking a step towards him.

Deodan started, like he'd forgotten they were all there.

'I can feel a presence here,' he said quietly, his eyes scanning the walls.

Roh nodded, shivering at the memory of the voices that had filled her head. 'I heard them.'

Deodan's expression was grim. 'The last of the water warlocks from Lochloria fled through here.'

A chill raked down Roh's spine. 'Yes, they did.' She moved aside, so Deodan could see the belongings at her feet. She could have sworn his hands trembled as he picked up one of the heavy books.

They were all quiet as the warrior warlock blew the dust from its cover and opened it. The pages within were yellowed and water damaged, ink bleeding from the parchment in several places. Roh heard Deodan's sharp intake of breath.

'What is it?' she asked, peering over his shoulder.

The text was handwritten in the common tongue, neat and precise on some pages, a scrawling mess in the final pages.

'They're journals … This one predates the Scouring of Lochloria …' Deodan's voice was raw. He picked up the other volumes and carefully tucked them under his arm. 'I'll be taking these,' he announced to no one in particular.

Roh didn't object. If Deodan wanted the extra weight in his pack, so be it. There was also a vague sense of comfort in that someone would read the last words of whoever had died here.

Without another word, the warlock left the alcove and the others all turned to her. Roh wanted to ask what had happened in the main tunnel, and how it was that her companions were free from the enchantment.

'Well?' Finn prompted with a pointed look at the garden bed.

A sleepy Valli lay sprawled in a bed of white flowers, surrounded by stems stripped of their leaves, his belly swollen.

Strothos' poison whispered in Roh's veins as she reached to pluck one of the remaining diamond-shaped leaves from the plant. Following Valli's approach, she peeled it from the stem.

'Here goes …' She popped several into her mouth. The taste was terrible, and bitter juice slid down her throat as she chewed, grimacing the whole time. 'Urgh.'

'It doesn't say how many to eat,' Finn muttered, taking the crumpled page from Odi and studying it carefully.

'We should take some with us,' Yrsa said, already pulling several plants from the soil, roots and all. 'That way if you don't feel any better, we've got some on hand. And if you do, well … Valli seems to like them.'

Roh nodded, desperate to get her water canteen to wash away the bitter flavour. But as she swallowed the last of her mouthful, she swayed on her feet.

Harlyn grabbed her elbow.

'Something's happening,' Roh muttered. 'I feel … strange …'

'Let's get you out of here,' Harlyn said, supporting her weight and leading them to the exit. 'This place sets my teeth on edge.'

In the main tunnel of the pass, they set up camp.

Deodan assured them it was safe. Whatever enchantments remained were no longer a threat, and there was no way they'd make it to the other side without resting, especially not while Roh felt so out of sorts. She sat with her back against the wall, watching the others share rations. Valli curled up in her lap, clearly content with the feast he'd had. Roh frowned as he huffed a sleepy sigh.

With exhaustion latching onto her bones, Roh glanced up at Yrsa. 'Is it just me, or is he bigger?'

Yrsa nodded. 'He grows every day. But what happened just now … Well, I can't say for sure. In any case, it won't be long before he doesn't fit in that pocket of yours.'

Roh stroked the diamond pattern on Valli's forehead, recalling the sheer size of the full-grown sea drake that had chased her through the currents. She couldn't imagine Valli getting to that size, not when he could still fit in her cupped hands. But then, he'd also just broken down a solid iron door for her and apparently glowed upon hearing her song … There was much of him that remained a mystery to her.

Roh's gaze fell upon Deodan, who sat a little further away from them, on the opposite side of the pass, his head bowed and eyes transfixed as he read one of the journals. His expression was unreadable. Curiosity piqued, Roh made to get up, to go to the warlock and ask him about it, but a wave of dizziness hit her.

She rested her head against the wall and closed her eyes, exhaustion barrelling into her once more. They hadn't stopped since they'd left Akoris, not really. A few hours of sleeping under the stars each night, plus that single sleepless night in The Thorn. The constant warring of magic and poison inside her had also taken its toll. And so, Roh forgot about Deodan and the journals, she forgot about Valli and the others, she forgot about Cerys and Eadric and Sedna Irons. She inhaled deeply, just before a deep slumber dragged her under.

When Roh woke, something was different. *She* was different – no, *stronger*. Blinking rapidly, her eyes adjusting to the torchlit pass, she saw that the others, except for Deodan, were all dozing. Sensing her movements, Deodan glanced up from the book in his lap; he hadn't moved since she'd fallen asleep.

His eyes filled with surprise as his gaze met hers. He opened his mouth to speak, but Roh pressed a finger to her lips, not wanting him to disturb the others. Not yet. Scooping Valli from her lap and settling him by her pack, she got to her feet, marvelling at the new sense of strength that rushed through her.

*It worked*, she realised. The plant from the alcove had cured her. There was not a whisper of Strothos' poison within her, only pure magic and power, unlike anything she had felt at her fingertips before. Whatever she'd felt before had been but a whisper compared to the magic that now surged through her.

Deodan hadn't taken his eyes off her. Roh tiptoed across the pass to him.

'It worked, didn't it?' Deodan whispered as she sat cross-legged beside him.

'How can you tell?' Roh asked.

The warlock studied her face. 'It's like a shadow has lifted from your eyes. After the rite, you had this haunted look about you, and now … You seem like yourself again, better even. How do you feel?'

Roh wished she had a looking glass. 'I feel good,' she told him. 'Better than good. I feel … powerful.'

Deodan nodded. 'That makes sense. The first time you sang your deathsong, you were already under the influence of that poison. You're experiencing what it is to be a full Saddorien cyren, without that tarnishing your magic.'

Roh gaped at him. 'Have my eyes changed to lilac?' she asked hopefully.

'No. They're still green.'

'Then how can I be a fully matured Saddorien cyren?'

Deodan shrugged. 'You're asking the wrong person there, Queen of Bones.'

When he had first called her by that name, it had bothered Roh. But now, she heard the note of fondness in the title. 'I suppose I am. How long have we been asleep?'

'A good few hours. By my estimate, it should be close to daybreak outside the pass.'

'How is it that we're no longer at the mercy of the warlock enchantment?'

Deodan shrugged. 'My guess is that the pass recognised you as one of its own. Your family falls under that protection.'

Roh nodded, the word *family* stirring up mixed feelings as she gazed upon her companions. 'Should we wake the others?'

Deodan appeared reluctant, but he gently closed the journal in his lap. 'The sooner we reach Csilla, the better.'

With their ropes discarded, Roh led the company through the second half of the mountain pass. With each step, she grew stronger and more eager to reach the cyren territory. She was ready to retrieve the next birthstone of Saddoriel, she was ready, *truly* ready for the first time in weeks, for this quest to continue. None of the others had commented on the change in her, but she could tell they'd noted it by the way their eyes lingered on her just a fraction too long.

Downing another vial of tonic, Finn left the staff he'd been using for support at their makeshift campsite. To Roh's relief, he moved with only a slight limp now; he too looked stronger and more himself, especially with his crossbow at his back.

Harlyn still wore her sling, the fall from her horse had set her healing progress back, but she was managing well enough. Roh made a mental note to go over her rehabilitation exercises with her the next time they stopped.

Valli sat atop Roh's shoulder as they continued on, just as keen to leave the passage behind as she was, it seemed. He felt heavier than before. There had always been a connection between the drakeling and her, but now ...

She could feel a defined thread between them, as though her song had solidified their bond into something almost tangible.

On the other side of the pass, the evidence from fleeing warlocks mounted. Artefacts from centuries ago lined the passage: weapons, pottery and to Roh's horror, skeletons. The bones of war victims were nothing like those that had been used to build Saddoriel. These were covered in spider silk, yellowed and chipped, still in the positions in which they'd died.

A sombre mood settled over Roh and her companions. Deodan was particularly quiet, his blue eyes full of sorrow as they passed adult and child skeletons, resting hand in hand.

'They were trapped,' he said quietly. 'Akoris to the south, Csilla to the north. There was no escape for these people. King Uniir wanted their kind completely exterminated.'

Roh didn't trust herself to speak. She knew there was nothing she could say to make up for the horrors inflicted by her race.

'They stayed here until they died …' Deodan's voice was but a whisper now.

'We never knew,' Harlyn murmured as they passed another group of skeletons. 'We were never taught about this side of it.'

Deodan stopped walking. 'Why would you be taught anything other than what feeds cyren lore and legend?' His words cut through Harlyn's like a knife. 'Haven't you realised yet? That nothing is what it seems? That the histories you've been taught are nothing but lies? I thought you'd know better after Akoris.'

The anger lacing Deodan's words was palpable. How long had he been carrying this resentment around with him? How could he stand to spend his days with a group of cyrens, the very kind who had nearly wiped out his ancestors? How had he pledged his loyalty to Roh and her quest, when this was what lay at his heart? Had something in those journals reignited his anger? Or had it been building from the first moment he'd laid eyes on them all?

Deodan seemed to gather himself. 'I wasn't born then. I didn't witness the depravity firsthand. But I have grown up in the shadow of all that was done to my people. I have lived through the burning hatred that spurs on our leaders and clans. For the first time I find myself understanding it, for the first time I feel the same rage coursing through my veins as the Warlock Supreme and all those who came before her ... I understand the drive for revenge ...' His voice broke. 'Innocents died here in this pass, children in their mothers' arms. Turned away from Csilla, hunted like wild beasts by the Saddorien Army. The Scouring of Lochloria brought an entire race to its knees.'

'I'm sorry,' Roh rasped.

Deodan looked at her in surprise.

'I wasn't there, either,' she said quietly. 'But I'm sorry for what was done to your people. I feel the pain of this place in my bones.'

Deodan's whole body seemed to sag. 'Thank you,' he

said. 'I have known the history my whole life, but reading a firsthand account … It's like witnessing it myself. I can imagine being in the writer's shoes, I can imagine what it must have been like to watch those I care for suffer, to see the world I love ripped apart.' And with that, he lit his pipe, inhaling deeply, and continued down the path.

The intensity of Deodan's words stayed with Roh for a long while as they journeyed through the mountain pass. No one else spoke, and Roh hoped that they too were reflecting on what this place meant to their friend and what it said about their ancestors. It seemed that every day, Roh's understanding of her own kind, of herself, changed. The version of events that had been painted for them, and carved into mosaics in the Passage of Kings, was exactly that: a version, one that didn't represent the whole truth. Ever since she had left Saddoriel, there had been many things that didn't add up, didn't make sense. Her mind wandered to the *Tome of Kyeos* back in the lair, locked away in the Vault. Every moment she spent away from her homeland she discovered more gaps in her knowledge about their own history and existence. But how could that be, with Delja having access to the tome for centuries? Surely the former queen held the knowledge, so why had she failed to share it with her people? Suddenly, Roh was back in a private wine cellar, surrounded by a clan of warrior warlocks, recalling what she'd concluded then: that the kings and queens of the past had ignored the gems, the very tools supposed to guide them towards a better Saddoriel.

Question upon question plagued Roh, dancing with her newfound power as she continued to lead her friends through the last stretch of the mountain pass, dreaming of what she would do once she obtained the *Tome of Kyeos*. She would learn of her history and share it with Finn as she had promised back in Akoris, and everyone else, too. Wasn't knowledge most powerful when shared?

At long last, the stuffy passage air changed, swept away by a crisp mountain breeze that played with the loose strands of Roh's hair and cooled her flushed skin. Up ahead, a pale beam of natural light sang from the end of the pass, and the smell of rain filled her nose.

For just beyond, the misty moors and plunging gorges of Csilla called.

# CHAPTER TEN

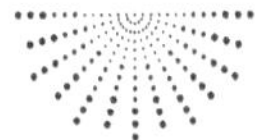

Long white clouds loomed low in the valley, a stark contrast against the emerald-green precipices on either side. An ice-blue river carved through the heart of the gorge, as formidable as the jagged cliffs themselves. Light rain fell from the grey sky, cold on Roh's exposed skin, and she gazed up in wonder. At her feet, Valli seemed to love the water running across his scales, scurrying across the ground and happily flapping his wings.

The group's exit and descent from the passageway had happened quickly, despite the slippery, uneven path, and it wasn't long before they had reached the base and were crossing the moors in good time, spurred on by Roh's eagerness to reach Csilla and Deodan's eerily quiet demeanour. They followed the edge of the cliffs north-west for a time, peering down into its jaws through the downpour.

Yrsa reached across and tugged the hood of Roh's cloak up over her head. 'It'll lose its novelty if you catch a chill,' the Jaktaren said, lifting her own hood, too.

Roh licked the fresh rain from her lips and took in the sight of the vast gorge below and its rapid, raging river. 'So, this is Csillan territory.'

'It is,' Finn said, brushing his wet hair from his face and following her gaze to the wonders below. He looked so different to the cyren who had aimed his crossbow at her only hours earlier, whose face had been lined with pain.

'The clans live in the cliffs, don't they? Any idea how to get down there?' she asked.

'Yes,' Finn replied slowly, his eyes bright and a grin spreading across his face. 'But you're not going to like it.'

Roh sighed. 'I'm getting sick of hearing that. Lead the way, then, Jaktaren.'

With each step Roh felt more and more like herself, as though a blanket had indeed been lifted from her senses. She could feel her deathsong humming within her, and from the pointed glances from the others, they could feel it, too. She had never felt so strong, so powerful.

Until Finn stopped at the very edge of the cliff and reached over the side.

'What are you doing?' she demanded, her stomach squirming at the sight of him being so close to the precipice.

'Showing you the way down.' He revealed a timber bar, which was attached to a thick wire that disappeared down into the gorge and beyond the clouds below.

Roh took a step back. 'You can't be serious.'

Yrsa's gentle hand found her shoulder. 'I'm afraid he is. Unless you want to wander the clifftops for the next five moons or so.'

'I … I can't do that.' The words were out of her mouth before she could stop them. There was no way she was leaping off a cliff. Absolutely *no way*.

'Just think of it as a bigger version of what we jumped from in the Akorian sea caves,' Finn said, still grinning.

'How can you be enjoying this?' Roh hissed.

'You would be too, if you could see your face right now.'

If he hadn't been standing so close to the cliff's edge, Roh would have shoved him.

'What about Harlyn?' Roh said instead, turning to Yrsa, who she knew would take her concerns more seriously. 'She can't be expected to hang on with one hand? And what about Odi? His hands aren't the strongest, either.'

She gave Odi an apologetic glance, but he waved her away.

'It's true. They can seize up at any time. And knowing my luck, it would be just as I leaped off a cliff into an unknown abyss.'

Harlyn snorted a laugh. 'Sounds about right to me.'

'It's a lot safer than it looks,' Yrsa said, clearly trying to soothe them. 'There's a belt, too. It works as a harness. But if you're really worried, Finn can take someone and I can take someone. We'll get in the harness and strap whoever it is to us.'

Roh stared at her in disbelief. 'Can it even *hold* weight like that?'

Harlyn put a pointed hand on her stomach. 'I don't know how I feel about that implication, Rohesia.'

Roh threw her hands up in the air. 'Why are none of you taking this seriously? It's a damn deathtrap!'

This time, Harlyn burst out laughing. A deep belly laugh, one that had her doubled over and clutching her middle.

'What?' Roh snapped.

Wiping the tears from her eyes, Harlyn shook her head in disbelief. 'For someone who has bested a sea drake, taken on the Arch General of Akoris and been wrapped from head to toe in bone-crushing pythons, *this* is what undoes you?'

Roh glanced at the others, all of whom were on the verge of laughing. Even Deodan. She rounded on Harlyn. 'You're telling me you're alright with this? With being strapped to one of the Jaktaren and thrown off a ledge?'

Harlyn's amusement didn't fade. 'It's not at the top of my wish list, but what needs to be done, needs to be done.'

Roh crossed her arms over her chest, determined not to be the only one refusing, and turned back to Finn. 'How does it work, then?'

His lilac eyes bright with satisfaction, Finn motioned for her to come closer. 'There's a ledge, just down here.' He crouched and to Roh's horror stepped down onto a small platform, just over the edge of the cliff. He took hold of the bar that looped over the thick wire. 'This is what we call a hang line. You hold onto these bars, there's another one to sit on, or you can use the harness. You hold on and push off from here, it follows the line back and forth across the gorge, ending down the bottom. It's simple enough.'

'And you've used one of these … hang lines … before?'

'Once or twice,' Finn said casually.

Roh looked to Harlyn, who was usually more than happy to go toe to toe with the Jaktaren.

But Harlyn simply shrugged. 'Who goes first?' she asked.

'Finn can go first,' Yrsa said confidently. 'And I'll go last. Finn, you take Odi and I'll take Harlyn.'

Roh couldn't help the slight satisfaction she felt at the sight of Yrsa strapping Odi and Finn together, both seeming equally uncomfortable at their proximity.

Roh glanced around, spotting Deodan a little way from the group, chewing on the end of his pipe as he paced the damp grass. Her amusement faded, noting the warlock's sunken shoulders and vacant gaze. Their venture through the pass had taken a toll on him, had unravelled something within. Sensing her gaze, Deodan glanced up and locked eyes with her instantly. Roh went to him.

'I won't pretend I know what that's like for you.'

'Good,' Deodan said softly.

'But I am here,' she told him firmly. 'If you want to talk about it.'

Still chewing the end of his pipe, Deodan regarded her thoughtfully. 'Another time, Queen of Bones.'

Roh nodded. 'Whenever you're ready.'

'They're not just my people, you know.' His voice was almost a whisper.

'I had the same realisation,' she replied. 'But how do you reconcile two warring parts of a whole?'

For a moment, their other companions faded into the background and Roh and Deodan stared out onto the breathtaking gorges of the Csillan territory, its colours bruised and moody.

'How do we get the harness back?' Harlyn asked loudly, focusing Roh on the present predicament, apparently realising that their single means of travelling down the gorge was about to disappear. Roh was glad to be distracted from the intensity of what hung between Deodan and her, and a glimmer of hope sparked within her. Perhaps she wouldn't have to launch herself over the —

Yrsa waved her away. 'There are at least ten stocked up here.' She checked and double-checked the harness that held Odi close to Finn.

'What about their packs?' Roh pointed at the discarded supplies.

Yrsa smiled gently. 'We can strap them to their own line and send them down after. Don't worry, Roh.'

'I'm not worried,' she said unconvincingly.

'You've faced worse than this,' Yrsa reassured her.

'And likely will face worse still,' Harlyn added cheerfully.

The voices of the mountain pass and its lure were a distant memory in the face of the cliff edges and their dizzying heights. Suddenly, there was nothing more to be done but watch Finn and Odi step off the ledge and shoot down the hang line. Odi's yelp echoed in their wake as they disappeared into the clouds below. They were gone.

Next, Deodan secured the warlock journals safely in his pack before shouldering the weighty load. Without so much as a sound, he stepped into a new harness, gripped the timber bar and jumped.

'He's not himself,' Roh told the others, watching his dark cloak vanish down into the gorge.

Harlyn and Yrsa nodded.

'Must be hard for him,' Yrsa said.

'There's something about those journals as well,' Roh added, running a talon down the scar on her face.

'We'll keep an eye on him and ask him about it later.' Yrsa stepped down onto the platform and offered Roh her hand.

Roh scooped Valli from the ground. 'You'd best stay in my pocket,' she told him. The drakeling seemed to understand what was going on and crawled into the safety of Roh's shirt. She then took Yrsa's hand and stepped down onto the ledge, her legs shaking uncontrollably. Clutching the rockface, digging her talons in deep, she stepped into the harness Yrsa spread before her. A loop around each leg that also connected to the timber bar she was to hold.

Yrsa squeezed her shoulder. 'We can send your pack separately, if you like? So there's less weight?'

Teeth chattering, Roh nodded numbly.

'And you should probably put this away.' Harlyn

swiped the crown from her head and tucked it carefully into her bag.

'Alright,' Yrsa said, her voice full of reassurance. 'We'll send the packs after you, so Harlyn and I might be a little longer, but don't worry. I've done this plenty of times before. Ready?' Yrsa asked, still holding onto Roh's harness.

'Not really,' Roh muttered, gripping the timber bar as tightly as she could. A dozen questions formed on Roh's lips and the urge to stall, to interrogate Yrsa about her Jaktaren travels nearly consumed her, but she felt Valli squirming in her pocket. Was he as scared as she was?

Yrsa smiled. 'On the count of three, then. One. Two —'

Roh's scream caught in her throat as Yrsa swung her out into thin air before the third count. She flew from the ledge, the wind whipping against her face as she shot across the wire, the gorge a green-and-blue blur beneath her. Tears streamed from her eyes as she built up momentum, plummeting down, down, down.

She was too terrified to curse Yrsa, who'd cast her off the ledge prematurely, unexpectedly. With her heart hammering in her throat, she was too terrified to do anything but hang on for dear life.

The hang line was endless, or so it seemed as she zigzagged back and forth across the gorge. She passed through the thin clouds, moisture clinging to her skin. Grateful that the harness distributed some of her weight from her hands, Roh finally gathered herself enough to take in her surroundings. The vast views were mesmerising. The cliffs were covered in a vibrant, emerald-green moss and wild thyme that looked like velvety carpet from above. Below, the ice-blue river roared through the valley, foaming over jagged boulders and lashing around various bends.

Roh's attention snagged. Carved into the rockface were great statues, spanning the entire vertical drop of the cliffs, figures of goddesses no doubt, their sandalled feet chiselled into the base of the gorge, their wings stretching up to the clifftops. They were absolutely huge. And it wasn't just goddesses, the statues were of wingless warriors, too —

Roh's stomach churned, and not from the dizzying height. But she swallowed the lump of fear in her throat. If she made it to the bottom alive, *then* she would worry about how fanatical the Csillans might be.

Her mouth dropped open. For coming into view was a great arched bridge spanning the width of the gorge. Valli must have sensed the shift in her, because he popped his head out of the top of her pocket and took in the view as well.

'It's the most majestic thing I've ever seen,' Roh murmured to the drakeling.

All at once, the bridge and the river grew closer and closer, and Roh gaped helplessly at the rapids. Where did the line end? Was she going to be slammed into the rock face at this speed? Or dropped into the raging currents below? It didn't matter if she was a Saddorien cyren or not, the impact would —

Someone was waving to her.

Odi.

*Thank the gods.*

Roh swayed in her harness as she lost speed. Something had changed in the wire and she slowed as she approached Odi, who was standing on a rocky path by the river. At last, her boots touched the ground and Odi caught her, bringing her to a complete stop.

Roh exhaled shakily, relieved to be back on solid ground as Odi helped her out of the harness.

'Pretty incredible, wasn't it?' he said, his face flushed with exhilaration, dragging the timber bar to the end of the line, where his and Finn's hung.

Roh turned slowly, heart still pounding, drinking in the sights of the looming cliffs and the majestic feat of architecture that was the bridge before them. She spotted Deodan sitting cross-legged beneath an overhanging rock, a journal in his lap, his unlit pipe between his teeth. Utterly transfixed on what he was reading, the warlock didn't look up at the sound of her footsteps.

Roh continued to scan the area and turned on her heel. 'Where's …?'

'He insisted on scouting ahead.' Odi shrugged.

Roh frowned in the direction that Odi motioned to. 'He should have waited.'

'In case you haven't noticed, Finn Haertel seems to do what *he wants*, not what *he should do*,' Odi told her.

Roh was inclined to agree with him there.

Moments later, her pack came shooting into view, flying down the wire towards them. Roh helped Odi catch and unload it, all the while wondering where Finn was and what awaited them in Csilla. All at once it hit her. *She was in Csilla*, with another birthstone at last within reach. Never mind that the leader from whom she'd have to pry it was called The Carver. Roh had focused on one task, one obstacle at a time and now … Now she was here, stronger than ever, with the brilliant bridge and cliffs looming overhead, and the kiss of the river's spray on her skin. For just a moment, she gave herself permission to dream, to wonder what it would be like to close her fingers around the Willow's Sapphire and see it to the rightful place in her crown. She imagined what it might feel like to have its power thrumming alongside that of the Mercy's Topaz … Her own power and magic surged through her, her deathsong rushing to the surface, as though answering the rhythm of the river at her side. Roh was still very much in this race. She had journeyed far and wide to reach this point. Hope flared hot in her chest and she revelled in it quietly, a rare moment of pride at all she had achieved, no matter what, or who, guarded the Willow's Sapphire ahead.

Odi and Finn's packs followed shortly after, and as they unloaded them, Roh found herself looking around for the Jaktaren again. The shadow of the bridge stretched along the rocks around them.

'Has he been gone long?' she asked Odi.

Odi gave another infuriating shrug.

'Helpful,' Roh retorted.

When Harlyn and Yrsa's packs appeared, Roh started to feel anxious. What was Finn playing at? Going off on his own in a foreign territory? And why did it feel like the others were taking so long? Roh tried to be patient, though it had never been a strength of hers. Yrsa had said this would happen, it would all be fine. Roh noticed that Odi was pacing the rocky path, rubbing his hands through his fingerless gloves. He appeared as aggravated as she felt, and for some reason that soothed her. It meant she wasn't alone. Deodan was still reading, ignoring them.

To distract herself, Roh went to her pack and took out her crown, placing it atop her head. There would be no hiding who she was when they met with the Csillans, and she had no doubt they would need the topaz's guidance along the way.

Odi's gaze lingered on the crown. 'If you become queen —'

'*When*,' Roh corrected him.

Odi rolled his eyes. '*When* you become queen, will you have a different crown made? One that isn't so … distasteful?'

Roh's fingers wandered to the bones. 'I hadn't thought that far ahead,' she told him.

A flash of anger crossed Odi's amber gaze. 'You *have so* thought that far ahead,' he countered. 'You're a planner, a schemer. You're *always* thinking that far ahead. But only for yourself. You don't care that it's made of bones, the bones of my people.'

'I *do* care,' Roh argued, recalling the shame she had felt when she realised she wasn't being presented with Delja's crown of coral. Heat flushed her cheeks, for it had indeed been a selfish shame, shame that her own people didn't think her worthy, not shame at what her kind had done to Odi's for centuries. Roh knew she had made many mistakes. The eerie mountain pass flashed in her mind, followed by the archway of bones, the entrance to the lair, and the worship halls of Akoris. Her deathsong stirred again, as though it too yearned for answers. A final image filled her head: the *Tome of Kyeos*, the all-knowing book of cyren history, floating in its beam of light in the Vault. One day it would be hers, and no longer would her kind live in the shadows of lies and mistold history. Purpose surged within her.

'When I am queen,' she said, fixing Odi with a meaningful stare, 'there are going to be a lot of changes to Saddoriel.'

There was a pause, brimming with questions, but it wasn't Odi who spoke next.

'Just Saddoriel?' Deodan's voice called from where he sat, still not looking up from the journal in his lap.

Roh inhaled sharply. Slowly, she was realising that along with dreams and purpose, came pressure. Immense pressure from within and otherwise to get it right, to make things better than before, and to please not only herself, but an array of others as well.

'How about I focus on winning the birthstones first?' she countered and stalked away to the water's edge.

At last, Roh made out the blurry, tangled forms of Yrsa and Harlyn gliding towards them from above. As they drew closer, she could see both cyrens had wide grins upon their faces, their eyes bright with exhilaration.

Harlyn even let out a gleeful *whoop* as they slowed upon approach.

*At least someone is having fun,* Roh grumbled to herself as she approached. She helped them out of the harnesses, which were far more complicated than the one she'd worn. But finally, they were free of them.

'Where's Finn?' Yrsa asked, looking around, the joy fading from her eyes.

'Odi said he went to scout ahead,' Roh explained.

To her surprise, Yrsa clicked her tongue in frustration, her brows knitting together in a frown. 'I told him *not* to do that.'

Roh was quietly glad that it wasn't just her whom Finn ignored. 'We'll catch him up,' she said.

The air was icy as they walked the narrow, rocky path alongside the raging river and it began to rain in earnest, a downpour in heavy sheets. Roh tried to tell herself that Finn wasn't far ahead, that perhaps he had decided to scout so he had a moment to himself. He had faced his own struggles since leaving Thornhill, so it was understandable that he might need time alone to regroup.

Yrsa pointed to his tracks in the muddy gravel. 'These will wash away before long.'

But Deodan insisted that they stop so he could replenish his vials with the near-freezing river water. As soon as he did, the warlock poured one into his palm. With the roar of the river and the rain, Roh couldn't hear his muttered enchantments. She only watched as he produced a water bird, like the one she'd seen in Akoris, and sent it flying downstream.

'What was that?' she called out to him over the noise.

'A sensor,' he replied, pocketing the rest of his vials. 'I thought we would have caught up to Finn by now.'

Roh ignored the dread that shifted in her gut and carried on walking. If Deodan was worried about the Jaktaren, it wasn't a good sign. They were in The Carver's territory, after all …

Together, they trudged along the narrow, stony path in silence, the relentless rain doing very little for their morale. Each time they rounded a bend, Roh hoped to spot Finn, but they had no such luck. She tried to distract herself with thoughts of the Willow's Sapphire and the *Tome of Kyeos*, but not even those dreams could warm her when she was soaked to the bone.

What felt like hours later, Deodan's water bird reappeared. It flew directly to the warlock and sat in his cupped palm with a contented chirp. Valli emerged from Roh's pocket, peering curiously at the water magic.

The group halted, watching the exchange unfold, eager for news of what lay ahead. After a moment, Deodan looked up at them, his brow furrowed in concern.

'Finn's not far off,' he told them, his voice low. 'But he's not alone.'

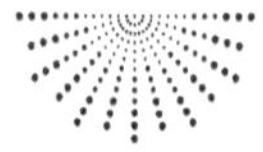

Fear sank its talons into Roh's heart and she realised that she would have leaped off the cliff again if it meant Finn was safe. He was one of them now, he was *her* responsibility. And she'd lost him. Fear and anger towards the Jaktaren entwined as she readied her sling, the others unsheathing their weapons, too.

'Did your sensor tell you how many he's with?' Roh hissed.

Deodan whirled his cutlasses, limbering up his joints. 'No.'

Gritting her teeth, Roh started forward once more, her whole body tense, ready to attack at a moment's notice. Yrsa stood to her left, and Deodan to her right, while Harlyn and Odi brought up the rear. The tension was palpable, and the anticipation had an energy of its own, flowing between them all. Roh tucked Valli into her pocket so he was fully hidden.

But as they rounded another rocky bend, Roh froze. *Am I hallucinating again?* She wiped the water from her eyes and blinked through the rain.

Under an overhanging rock, stretched a row of enormous garden beds, full of lush green plants and vegetables; even small fruit trees grew there. And kneeling at the foot of one of those trees, was Finn, a basket overflowing with vegetables in the crook of his elbow.

Roh stared, her mouth open. If she wasn't so furious with him, she might have laughed at the image, tried to burn it into her memory. Anger won, but just as she was about to spew a myriad of curses at the Jaktaren, something – no, *someone* – moved behind him.

There, waiting with her hands on her hips, was a seven-foot-tall female cyren with broad shoulders, wearing a dirt-smeared apron. The sheer size of her was intimidating enough, let alone the fact that she held a huge machete in her hand.

'It's about time,' the cyren said gruffly. 'We've been expecting you, Queen of Bones.'

But she made no move to attack and Finn seemed unharmed. Roh could have sworn she heard him grumbling something about her not being any sort of queen, but she didn't take her eyes off the woman.

'Who are you?' Roh demanded, closing the distance between them.

'She said if we want to eat in Csilla, we have to contribute,' Finn muttered moodily.

That was the last thing Roh expected, as was the sight

of the woman laying down the knife, wiping her hands on her apron and offering one to Roh.

'I'm Kezra,' she said. 'I cook for the Csillan clan.' She eyed the weapons the others still held at the ready. 'You can relax. I bear you no ill-will.'

Deciding that there wasn't much else for it, Roh accepted the handshake, feeling the topaz hum contentedly in her crown as the woman's surprisingly warm hand gripped hers. Kezra was sincere, it seemed to tell her.

'I'm Roh,' she said.

Kezra nodded. 'Finnicus here was just helping me gather extra supplies.'

Roh blinked. *Finnicus?*

As though he sensed the incoming ridicule, Finn winced, pink tinging his cheeks.

Roh heard Harlyn snort behind her and it took all of her willpower not to do the same, but she managed to gather herself. There were more pressing matters at hand.

'Is the Csillan Arch General in residence?' she asked Kezra. She deliberately made no mention of The Carver, hoping that by keeping the name quiet, it might not prove to be prophetic.

Kezra moved around the garden as though she hadn't heard Roh. Deodan fumbled with his cutlasses as the Csillan pressed a large basket of produce into his arms, pausing to size him up.

'It's been a long time since one of your kind entered Csilla, Warlock,' she said quietly.

Roh gaped at her. *How does she know what he is? How is she not surprised —*

'You know,' Yrsa spoke Roh's thoughts aloud. 'You know of the warlocks' existence?'

Kezra turned to her, frowning. 'We Csillans never believed they had all been killed.'

Deodan flinched at this, but Kezra continued.

'Their kind was too skilled, too clever, too resilient to fade away into oblivion.' She faced Deodan. 'I should warn you, your welcome here will be mixed.'

Deodan nodded stiffly before shooting Roh a baffled look. Roh simply shrugged.

'And you,' Kezra changed tact, locking eyes with Roh. 'Interesting choice … To align yourself with his kind. Some might consider it a statement.'

'I consider it a necessity,' Roh countered evenly. 'Now, about the Csillan Arch General —'

'You'll need more patience than that if you wish to be queen,' the cyren quipped, continuing to gather supplies and palm them off onto the Saddoriens. She surveyed what each of them now held, counting to herself.

Roh held her tongue, despite feeling as though she'd burst for all the questions bubbling to the surface. Was this the beginning of the Csillan games for power? Would the so-called Carver have them running circles before delivering his final blow? Though Roh expected nothing less, the constant guesswork did nothing to quell the sense of urgency within. The drive that desperately sought the Willow's Sapphire, longing to set it in its rightful place alongside the Mercy's Topaz.

At last, Kezra nodded at Finn. 'That'll about do it,' she said. 'Follow me.'

There were no arguments from Roh or her companions, just bewildered obedience at the sheer force of the new cyren in their midst. The Csillan led them over the short distance to the base of the mighty bridge, where in a towering column of rock lay a large door. With no ceremony, Kezra yanked it open.

Roh's stomach squirmed as she recognised what sat within. A crate-and-pulley system, similar to those she had used in Saddoriel to move between sectors. She recalled the queasy feeling she'd experienced.

'In you get,' Kezra barked. 'We don't have all day.'

Just as Roh had been herded into a similar apparatus in Saddoriel, so she was again, though the circumstances this time were vastly different. It was a squeeze, with their packs and baskets of produce. Roh found herself shoulder to shoulder with Harlyn and Yrsa.

'Is this a good idea?' Harlyn whispered in Roh's ear.

Not quietly enough, because Kezra stared right at her. 'I told you, I bear you no ill-will, bone cleaner. Though I can't say I enjoy repeating myself.'

When they were all loaded into the crate, before they were plunged into darkness, Kezra tapped the wall thrice. In an instant, light flooded the space above them, as hundreds of valo beetles awoke, glowing within numerous jars that lined the vertical chamber.

'Hold on,' Kezra instructed, just as the crate lurched upward.

Roh lunged for the railing as the movement caught her off-guard, in spite of Kezra's warning.

The group was quiet as they were pulled up into the hollowed rock. Though Roh couldn't see the height yawning beneath them, she only had to picture the towering bridge outside to guess at how far up they were. She swallowed her discomfort and glanced at Kezra, who seemed very much at ease, even as she escorted a handful of armed strangers into her territory.

*Why didn't she insist that we leave our weapons? Why the strange interest in Deodan? Why is she treating us as though we're nestlings to be scolded?* Roh bit back each question that found itself on her tongue. *Patience,* she told herself. *You have to have patience.*

As though sensing her discomfort, Valli stirred with a low noise, but Roh's hand flew to her pocket, willing him to remain hidden and quiet. He settled.

'Here we are,' Kezra announced as they slowed to a stop and a pair of doors swung outwards.

Momentarily blinded, Roh shielded her eyes against the bright light as she stepped out from the crate. She heard a sharp intake of breath from Harlyn at her side.

'The Bridge of Csilla is our pride and joy,' Kezra told them, sweeping her arms wide and gesturing to the feat of architecture upon which they stood.

Roh could see why. The bridge was flooded with warm light, despite that outside the gorge was grey and misty. Blue-veined marble covered the ground, the candlelight from the chandeliers above reflected in its glossy surface, while enormous floor-to-ceiling arches looked out onto the river on either side. There was no visible window in place, but somehow the warmth was trapped in.

They followed Kezra across the mighty bridge and Roh couldn't drink it in fast enough. She wished she hadn't wasted pages of her sketchbook on Akoris; this place was far worthier of her efforts.

Kezra spoke as she took long strides. 'The head Csillan clan resides in the eastern wing of the fortress, while the common clans reside in the western side and in the outer gorges. The bridge joins the two wings, but most importantly, the upper level is where we monitor the terror tempests.'

'What did you say?' Roh blurted.

Kezra frowned. 'What part of that confused you, Queen of Bones?'

Deodan's name for her on a stranger's lips unsettled Roh and her face heated. 'I'm not confused. I just ... You mentioned the terror tempests?'

'I did. Was that your question?'

Roh stared dumbly at the Csillan. 'I —'

'Be quick about it, girl. I have to get to the kitchens.'

'Well, the terror tempests ...' Roh struggled to string her words together. 'We have only just learned of their existence. I was told they haven't raged in over five decades.'

Kezra scoffed loudly, shaking her head as they reached the end of the bridge. 'Saddorien fools. You have a warlock in your midst and know nothing of the tempests? Are you daft?'

With a sideways glance at Deodan, Roh had to stop herself from putting her hands on her hips. 'There's been quite a lot happening,' she said testily. 'My apologies that I haven't thoroughly investigated every minor line of inquiry, all the while fighting off predatory leaders, suffocating pythons and debilitating poisons.' There was a beat of silence and more heat bloomed in Roh's cheeks. Gods, she'd said too much.

A grin crinkled the corner of Kezra's eyes. 'Good to see you've got some teeth, Queen of Bones. You'll need them,' she said at last.

Roh gaped at the cook. 'Right … well … can you tell us more about these tempests, then?'

Kezra waved her away, looking annoyed again. 'You'll find we are a much smaller community than you've seen in Saddoriel and Akoris,' she continued as though Roh hadn't asked her a crucial question. 'Though no less mighty.'

Roh huffed in frustration. *Fine, if that's how the Csillan wants to play it, that's how we'll play it, for now ...* But she sidled up to Deodan and hissed, 'And why exactly is it that you've not spoken of these terror tempests? Apparently, you're an expert?'

Deodan raised a brow. 'It's like you said. We've been a tad busy. Besides,' he said, nostrils flaring. 'It's not like you ever asked.'

Roh could have socked him with her sling. Of all the things she was contending with, Deodan's nonchalance infuriated her the most.

'How many cyrens live here, then?' Harlyn was asking, clearly sensing the need for a change in topic.

'There are thirty-eight cyrens currently residing in Csilla,' Kezra told her. 'The head clan consists of four, the Arch General and their family.'

Roh's head whipped back to her. 'That's it?'

'As I said, we're small but mighty,' Kezra replied proudly. 'And we have arguably the most important role of all the cyren territories. It is our work that protects Talon's Reach and Saddoriel, after all.'

She was clearly alluding to the terror tempests again – was she trying to bait them? Roh didn't press the matter. There was no point in interrogating the Csillan cook, not when she would sooner or later have an audience with The Carver.

'So this is the eastern wing, then?' she asked instead as they stepped off the bridge and into a cosy reception hall. With all the marble, Roh expected the place to be chilly, but she guessed it had been enchanted somehow, because even with her boots on, she could feel that the floor was warm beneath her soles.

'It is,' Kezra allowed, leading them across the room and into a hallway beyond.

Given that the territory was built into the rocky gorges, it should have had the same dark subterranean atmosphere as Saddoriel and Talon's Reach. But Csilla was well lit, warm and ... welcoming somehow. Despite the beauty and sheer size of the bridge, the rooms Roh and her companions walked through now were homely. There was something missing, though ... It took a few moments for Roh to put her finger on it, but when she did …

'Where is the music?' she blurted, her ears extra sensitive to the quiet surrounding them. They had gone from the rich melodies of fiddles and harps in Saddoriel, to the incessant drumming of Akoris, to this … Where no sound vibrated through the halls, no notes danced along their skin …

Kezra raised a brow. 'Music is meant to be appreciated and savoured, not lost in the background. We do not play music here all day, every day. We do not waste it. When we play it, we bow down to it, we want to be worthy of it.'

'But how do you power Csilla?' Harlyn asked. 'Is that why it's so small? The lack of music cannot support —'

Kezra silenced her with a single look. 'The entire eastern wing belongs to the Arch General.' Again, the Csillan continued as if the previous topic hadn't been broached. 'Within it are the private residences, the royal guest chambers, the formal dining room, the kitchens and the mirror Pool of Weeping, of course.'

The words caused Roh's heart to flutter. She couldn't help but glance at Deodan. During their time in Akoris, he'd explained the importance of the pools to her, that they acted as portals to the other cyren territories. More importantly, they were where the First Cry ritual took place. Only, the two of them suspected Roh had never taken part in the sacred rite of passage.

'— your packs in your rooms.'

Roh realised they had stopped outside a pair of open stone doors. She was at the back of the entourage and so couldn't see what lay beyond, but judging by the way the others were all unloading their packs, Roh gathered that the rooms inside were theirs. She shot Harlyn a questioning look, but her friend merely shrugged, seemingly bewildered by the Csillan towering over them.

Luckily, Valli had so far remained hidden in Roh's pocket, but she knew it was only a matter of time until the little beast's curiosity got the better of them all, but she couldn't think on that now.

She slipped her pack from her shoulders, groaning at the relief, and passed it to Odi, who placed it just inside the guest quarters. Roh massaged the back of her neck, wondering when she'd get the chance to bathe.

'Be quick about it,' Kezra said sharply, 'we've got a clan to cook for.'

'We ...?' Deodan frowned.

Roh had never seen him look so unsure of himself.

'Didn't you hear what Finnicus said in the gardens? If you want to eat, you have to contribute. I don't care if you're a warlock, human or future queen. Let's go.'

Roh's gaze cut to Finn. Challenge flashed in his eyes, almost daring her to make fun of his full name. She didn't take the bait; she'd save that morsel for later.

Between them, they carried the baskets of fresh produce and Roh found her eyes roving over the food, unable to recall the last decent meal she'd had. Her stomach gurgled as if in answer. To her surprise, Kezra didn't lead them to another storey; the kitchen was just at the end of the hall.

The Csillan pushed open the doors to the kitchen and

Roh nearly gasped aloud. She had never seen anything like it. It was a massive space, with several stone benchtops at the centre, pots and pans hanging from hooks in the ceiling. A woodfire oven blazed at the far end, though Roh had no idea how or where the smoke extracted to. An enormous vat sat atop glowing hot coals, the mouth-watering smell of slow-cooked meat wafting from beneath the rattling lid. Roh felt Valli stir in her pocket as the scent floated around them. She prayed he'd be able to control himself.

Shelving took up an entire wall, sporting all manner of dinnerware: plates, bowls, serving trays, cutlery and various utensils. There was also an entire section dedicated to knives of every size and shape.

Kezra followed her gaze. 'That's my favourite section,' she said deadpan.

Roh truly didn't know what to make of the Csillan cook. It wasn't just her stature that gave her a strong presence, she was a force of nature regardless – incredibly self-assured with a keen sense of purpose and direction. Roh got the impression that even if the Council of Seven Elders were here, she'd have them cooking their own dinner. Csilla was clearly different to Saddoriel. Roh remembered Ferron, the kitchen hand from the Queen's Tournament. There was no way he'd ever be privy to the workings of the Upper Sector; the hierarchy of cyren society did not allow it.

Kezra pushed something soft into Roh's hands. 'Here.' An apron.

'As for your earlier question about the Arch General,'

the Csillan said. 'They're not currently in residence. Their sister, Floralin, leads in their stead.'

Roh's mouth went dry. She could have sworn the warmth of the topaz flickered at Kezra's words, as though there was something *not* being said. But Roh didn't let on. She felt Harlyn's eyes on her, but Roh lifted the apron over her head and tied it at her back. *The Arch General, the one they called The Carver, wasn't in residence? When would they be back?* Roh didn't have time to waste thanks to Adriel's games back in Akoris. But she didn't voice her concerns. She'd learned, albeit slowly, that it was best to keep one's cards close to one's chest.

'Thank you,' she said to Kezra.

The Csillan's eyes brightened, as though she was pleasantly surprised to find that the future Queen of Cyrens had manners.

Roh decided to take advantage of the moment in another way. 'Do you mind me asking … How did you know we were coming? You said you were expecting me?'

Handing out the last of the aprons, Kezra fixed her with a knowing stare, her gaze flicking to the crown of bones atop Roh's head. 'A few weeks back, the Arch General of Akoris sent word that there was an underhanded, disloyal bone cleaner on the way, claiming to be our next queen. And that she was keeping company with a strange entourage. A warrior warlock known as Deodan, Finnicus Haertel and Yrsa Ward of the Jaktaren guild, Harlyn of the Bone Cleaners and Odalis Arrowood, the famous Prince of Melodies.'

Roh froze, her talons sliding free. She should have

known that her rejection of Adriel would haunt her across the realms. She should have known that he would try to slight her wherever she went. She'd made it personal with him, and now he wasn't going to stop until he'd engineered her fall from the throne. Around her, Roh could feel the others tense up, Finn going so far as to reach for the hidden dagger in his boot.

Kezra huffed a laugh in his direction, as though he was well out of his depth, and the sight of him in an apron did nothing for his warrior reputation.

'But Adriel's a letch,' Kezra said lightly. 'So, we'd never take his word, not without several grains of salt at least.'

Roh's whole body sagged with relief, the movement causing Valli to growl from her pocket.

Kezra shot her a curious glance, but luckily, Valli remained hidden. Who knew what the Csillan would do if she found out they were harbouring a stolen sea drakeling. But the cyren's attention didn't linger. Instead, Kezra dished out orders as though the group worked in her kitchen regularly, and to Roh's amazement, her friends obeyed. She tried not to stare openly at the sight of Finn and Deodan in their yellow aprons cleaning and peeling vegetables.

'You can do the potatoes,' Kezra told Roh, handing her a wooden chopping board. 'Nice big chunks, you hear? And we'll want to boil them first, so get on with it.'

There was a no-nonsense attitude about Kezra that Roh and her companions seemed to respond to. For the first time in weeks, Roh felt some semblance of peace creep in as she chopped up the potatoes and slid them from the board into a pot of boiling water. It felt good to work with her hands once more, to find a sense of rhythm in the ordinary. There was no way she could scout for the Willow's Sapphire from the kitchen, and besides, she was absolutely *starving*.

Beside her, Kezra was mixing several ingredients in a bowl. 'Stuffing,' Kezra told her, adding a generous handful of herbs. 'For the roast boar.'

Roh nodded. 'Where do you get a boar around here?' she asked.

The Csillan shrugged. 'Our territory works much the same as Saddoriel. We have our own gardens and livestock throughout the gorges, and cyrens who tend to them. Various enchantments help where we need them. Though I think as you've already found, things are a lot less formal here.'

'I'll say,' Roh agreed.

'It's true we live a simple life,' Kezra said, a note of fondness in her voice. 'But that doesn't mean we don't take pride in what we do and who we are.' She gestured to the various stations of preparation around them. 'For example, a fine meal is just as much an art as any oil on canvas.'

The next two hours passed quickly. Kezra ran her kitchen like an experienced captain on a war-bound ship. There was a system and a place for everything and the Csillan ensured everything was just so. The aromas of herbs and roast meat made Roh's mouth water, and from the way Harlyn was munching on a raw carrot, she knew the others were just as hungry as she was.

'Mama, Mama,' cried a small voice from the doorway.

Roh whirled around, halfway through turning the roasting potatoes on their oil-slicked tray. A nestling, no older than five or six, stood at the door, his bright eyes processing the sight of the strangers in his mother's kitchen. Roh hadn't seen many young nestlings – they were usually kept to the nursery or their parents' private residences, even in the Lower Sector. But it wasn't the child's youth that had her staring.

It was the gold circlet that graced his forehead.

# CHAPTER TWELVE

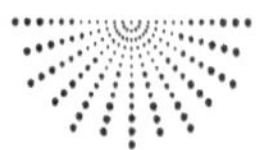

'Sol!' Kezra exclaimed, scooping the nestling up into her arms. 'You're early. Go and find your sister. By the time you do that, dinner will be ready.'

Sol blinked at the Saddoriens as he was placed back on the ground.

'Off with you,' Kezra gave him a nudge.

The little boy burst into a run and disappeared down the hall.

There was nothing Roh could do to hide her shock. She'd never seen another circlet-wearer before. She hadn't realised there *were* other circlet-wearers … She found Kezra with her hands on her hips, waiting expectantly.

'Questions?' the Csillan asked, her brows raised.

Roh just stared after the nestling. 'How …?' was all she managed.

'How *what?*'

Roh recalled how her own circlet had felt around her head; tight and unnatural, ever present. She remembered walking through the entrance of Saddoriel for the first time, during the announcement for the Queen's Tournament, her own kind staring her down like a pariah. How no one wanted to be near her, let alone touch her.

'How is a circlet-wearer allowed to run around where the head clan resides? Where the meals of the head clan are prepared?' she asked.

Kezra went about her work in the kitchen, setting up trays of food on one of the far benches, placing serving spoons in each and moving a stack of plates to one end. 'He is one of us, as much as any Csillan,' she told Roh. 'He should wear it with pride. It is a symbol of his strength, to overcome adversity and the unfortunate narrative surrounding his birth.'

Roh stared. She had never heard anyone say such a thing about circlet-wearers, not even her best friends, not even to combat her darkest days, when the band of gold was all too heavy. 'That's … progressive.'

Kezra met her gaze. 'I imagine you'd think so. We know of your *questionable heritage*, Queen of Bones.'

Roh refused to blush. 'Adriel?' she guessed.

But the Csillan shook her head. 'The council.'

'They told you when they brought the birthstone?' Roh asked carefully. It was her first mention of the gem and she knew she couldn't be too aggressive with her queries about it.

'They did.' The way Kezra confirmed her suspicions

was almost a challenge. Roh watched the cook walk to the far corner of the kitchen, her hand going to a thick cord. She tugged on it three times, a bell ringing loudly throughout the wing.

Running footsteps and an excited squeal sounded from the door. The circlet-wearer and another nestling skidded to a stop at the entrance to the kitchen, grinning openly.

'Told you there was a human!' the boy told the little girl at his side, pointing to Odi. 'Look!'

The girl's eyes went wide. 'Mama, Mama – why is there a human here?'

Kezra surveyed the nestlings, her sharp gaze softening with affection. 'He has a name. Odi is a friend of the cyren who might one day be our queen.'

Whatever answer Roh was expecting from the Csillan, it hadn't been that. However, the nestlings didn't seem all that concerned that they might stand in the presence of a future monarch.

Instead, the circlet-wearer frowned. 'Cyrens don't have human friends,' he said matter-of-factly.

Roh met Odi's gaze from across the kitchen. 'They do now,' she said clearly.

The two nestlings' heads snapped towards her. 'Who are you?' Sol demanded.

Roh's heart sang at the sound of his confidence. How different Csilla was, to raise someone like him to believe they had as much of a voice as any other cyren. Though, it was strange that only the boy wore the circlet…

'I'm Roh,' she replied, crouching so she was eye level

with the nestlings. 'Who are you?'

The boy shifted from foot to foot. 'My name is Sol. And this is Mora.'

Roh could feel everyone's eyes on her as she offered her hand. 'Nice to meet you,' she said.

'You're a Saddorien,' Mora announced, watching as her brother shook Roh's hand.

'I am,' Roh allowed, unsure of what came next.

Thankfully, Kezra swooped in, shooing the nestlings towards the bench that was fully stocked with freshly cooked food. 'You two know what to do. Don't let it get cold.'

Roh watched in shock as Sol fetched a small stool from a cupboard and placed it in front of the bench, then helped his sister up onto it. There, Mora took a plate and filled it, passing it down to her brother, before helping herself to another.

'The servants eat before the head clan?' Harlyn asked under her breath.

Kezra's laugh boomed across the kitchen. 'Servants?'

'Well … er … helpers …?' Harlyn shifted awkwardly, looking down at her sling.

The Csillan waved her away, amusement brightening her eyes. 'Help yourselves, Saddoriens and friends. Mora and Sol will show you to the dining room.'

Yet again bewildered by the strangely informal practices of the Csillan cyrens, Roh did as she was told. She piled her plate high with food, taking cutlery from a tin and a napkin from a stack of linens that Mora pointed to. When Roh and her companions were ready, they followed the two nestlings back out into the hallway and a few doors down. They were led into a large rectangular room, where several lounges had been pushed to the far walls and a long table had been placed in the middle.

Sol and Mora took the head of the table, and Roh became more baffled by the second.

'What in the realms is going on here?' she hissed in Yrsa's direction.

The Jaktaren somehow looked at ease as she put down her plate and pulled back a chair. Yrsa shrugged. 'Just go with it.'

But Roh's mind was spinning. Were the Csillans so unlike Saddoriens and Akorians that the cook and her offspring ate before the clan? One of which was a circlet-wearer no less? She eyed the ring of gold around Sol's brow – how was it that he wore one but not his sister? And did that mean that Kezra's partner had committed an unimaginable crime? That he was locked up in a cell of bones, somewhere near Cerys? Dazed, Roh sat down beside Yrsa, searching the room for any clues as to what to expect. But there were none. The room didn't even seem to be a proper dining room with its various lounges.

Roh felt eyes on her and looked up to find Sol staring.

'Why are your eyes green?' he asked, shovelling a forkful of potatoes into his mouth.

Roh blinked at him. 'I don't know,' she replied truthfully.

Mora straightened in her chair beside her brother. 'Can you sing your deathsong?'

'Yes,' Roh said, pride flickering at the fact that she

could now answer that question with the reply she'd always wanted to give.

Sol's brows furrowed. 'Then why are your eyes green?'

Roh shrugged. 'I told you, I don't know.'

The nestling turned to his sister. 'She's strange.'

'Uh-huh,' Mora replied.

Someone gave a snort further down the table and Roh's gaze cut to the Jaktaren. 'What's so funny, *Finnicus?*'

That shut him up.

At that precise moment, Kezra appeared in the doorway holding two plates, one covered with a silver cloche. She left the covered plate down one end of the table before taking up the empty seat beside Sol.

'Where's Mama?' he asked her as she eased herself into the chair.

Roh frowned. 'Aren't you "Mama"?'

'She's on her way.' Kezra wiped a smear of gravy from the nestling's face before turning to Roh. 'Sol and Mora have two mothers,' she explained.

'And none at all,' Mora added cheerfully, eating with her hands.

Kezra huffed a laugh. 'I suppose that's also true.' Noting Roh's confused expression, Kezra elaborated. 'Sol's father is in Saddoriel's Prison. His mother and Mora's birth parents died monitoring a terror tempest. My sister and I took them on as our wards when they were still infants.'

*Terror tempest, there it is again.* Roh glanced at the two nestlings, who were happily gorging themselves senseless. 'That was good of you.'

'It was the least we could do,' Kezra said sadly. 'An unconventional family now to be sure, but it suits us.'

'They're not siblings by blood, then?'

'If we were,' Mora interjected, 'I would wear a gold circlet, too.' She turned to Kezra. 'When can I get one?'

'We've been through this, Mora.' Kezra sighed. The Csillan went to a table at the far end of the room, bringing back a ceramic jug and several goblets. 'Help yourselves,' she told Roh and her companions after she finished pouring herself some wine.

Roh didn't make a move for the refreshments. Instead, her mind lingered on the two broken halves of her own circlet that lay somewhere at the bottom of her pack. She couldn't imagine what it would be like to *want* such a thing. Unsure of what to say next, she busied herself with her plate, a fresh pang of hunger hitting her as soon as she took her first bite. Around her, the others were silent too, as they ate their fill.

'It's been some time since you last had a meal, then?' Kezra asked, scanning the group.

Roh nodded, ripping a roll of bread in two and mopping up the thick gravy. 'We thank you for your hospitality.'

While she ate, Roh's mind continued to spiral as she sifted through all the tactful ways she could potentially broach the topic of the birthstone and when she might meet the Csillan clan leader. Hopefully whoever they were, they had the same opinion of Adriel as Kezra apparently did. She could only imagine the lies that bastard had spun about her. Or truths.

'Kezra,' Harlyn's voice sounded from the other end of the table. 'What else can you tell us about Csilla?'

'There is much to know about this territory,' Kezra began, pushing her plate away and dabbing the corner of her mouth with her napkin. 'But as I said, our most important role is monitoring the tempests and assessing the risk they pose to Talon's Reach and Saddoriel. I shouldn't be surprised really, that you know nothing of them.'

Roh cleared her throat. 'Even the Jaktaren had never heard of them,' she added with a glance at Yrsa.

Yrsa nodded in confirmation.

Kezra grimaced before turning to Deodan. 'And what of you, Warlock? What do you know of such forces?'

Roh's gaze went straight to the warrior. Even after his betrayal in Akoris, she had trusted him, enough to allow him on their quest, enough to allow him to use his magic to disguise them, to guide them through the mountain pass. Had the topaz been wrong about him?

'What makes you think I know anything?' Deodan replied coldly.

Roh's breath whistled between her teeth. 'More than you let on,' she said. 'You were there when the Warlock Supreme spoke of them, when she was plotting against Saddoriel. You spoke of them yourself when you were leveraging my promise against me, to rejoin our quest. It's time to share that knowledge, Deodan. What do you know?'

Deodan glanced from Roh, to Kezra, to the rest of their group; all eyes were on him. Giving a heavy sigh, he sat back in his chair and took a long drink from his goblet. 'Only what my people have passed down. Sybil, my mother —'

'The Warlock Supreme.'

'Yes,' Deodan said tersely. 'She told me that the tempests are all-powerful storms, capable of tearing through the protective enchantments around Talon's Reach, of making it vulnerable for the first time in centuries.'

'How can they be stopped?' Roh asked.

'My kind used to weave water magic through the enchantments, strengthening them for our cyren brothers and sisters.'

Roh knew that the alliance they had once shared was long dead. The symbol of wings etched into the stone walls of her mother's cell came to her.

'In our adapted forms, the warlocks of today are incapable of wielding such power,' Deodan said. 'Even if we wanted to help. Which we don't.'

'I gathered as much,' Roh muttered before turning back to Kezra. 'So it's inevitable?'

'My sister will show you the bridge tomorrow, where the work is carried out. You will have a better understanding of such things then.'

'Does Delja know?' Roh found herself asking.

Kezra looked up sharply. 'The former queen knew all she needed to. The *Tome of Kyeos* tells all.'

Roh's song stirred within her at the mention of the great text. 'Then why does no one in Saddoriel know of these storms? Why are we not taught —'

'I will not speak for *Delja the Triumphant.*' Kezra's words were suddenly cold.

Roh glanced across at Yrsa, who was seemingly fascinated with the scraps left on her plate, while the others did their best to appear busy as well. This would go down as one of the strangest meals Roh had ever shared with her fellow cyrens.

But Kezra's attention snagged once more on Deodan. 'Are our discussions not entertainment enough for you, Warlock?' she asked.

Roh saw that rudely, Deodan had opened up one of the journals they'd found in the mountain pass and had his head bowed, completely immersed in it.

Finn elbowed him roughly. 'For Thera's sake,' he cursed, nodding to where the rest of them awaited Deodan's response.

Deodan looked up at last, dazed, as though he'd forgotten where they were. 'Sorry?'

'What is it that has you so engrossed?' Kezra asked.

Deodan closed the journal and pinched the bridge of his nose, as though the very question exhausted him. 'History,' he replied, reaching for the wine.

A shriek of delight made Roh jump in her seat and she whirled around to where Mora and Sol were standing on their chairs, pointing at their plates in wonder.

Heart in her throat, Roh's hand went to her breast pocket. Which was empty. Cursing silently, she followed the nestlings' pointed fingers.

Valli was on the table, his face buried in their leftovers.

'Ah,' Roh managed, getting to her feet. 'That ... that's my Battalonian gecko,' she said, reaching for the drakeling, who promptly hissed in her direction.

'That's not a gecko,' Sol declared. 'He has *wings*.'

Roh winced. Valli's little wings were indeed outstretched for all to see as he devoured every scrap on Mora's plate.

Running her fingers through her hair, Roh sighed. 'You're right,' she admitted. 'He's a sea drakeling.'

Sol and Mora's jaws dropped.

'Whoa,' Mora said, looking from Valli to Roh with wide eyes. 'And he's your friend?'

Roh studied the moody creature who had moved onto the next plate. 'Most of the time.'

Someone cleared their throat. 'I'd advise that you keep that little fact to yourselves ...' A female cyren, even taller than Kezra, entered the dining room wearing a floor-length waxed cloak, her wet hair scraped back into a knot atop her head.

'Mama!' Sol leaped from his chair and threw himself at the cyren's legs, clinging to her.

'Hello, my boy,' she said, her voice softening. 'I missed you, too.'

Mora seemed less inclined to greet her other mother, determined not to leave the drakeling, watching him with eager eyes.

Kezra stood, retrieving the cloche-covered dish she'd brought earlier and placing it before the other cyren. 'Flo, meet Rohesia of the Bone Cleaners and her entourage.'

Something prickled at the back of Roh's mind. She

turned to Kezra, the question catching in her throat. 'Flo?'

The new cyren disentangled herself from Sol and offered her hand. 'Floralin, Kezra's unfortunate sister,' she said.

Roh shook her hand and slowly it dawned on her. She gaped at Kezra. 'But ... Floralin is the *clan leader's* sister. Which means ...'

Kezra sketched a mock bow. 'Kezra Wisehand, Clan Leader of Csilla.'

'You're ...' Roh couldn't believe it. 'You're The Carver?'

Kezra barked a laugh. 'They're still calling me that?'

Roh stared at the cyren, her hand drifting to the hilt of her dagger. 'So, it's true?'

'That a bunch of butchers used to call me The Carver because I could slice up a whole boar in three minutes flat? Yes, it's true. I can gut a man as easily as I can gut a pig, but that nickname seems to have morphed into a legend of its own as they travelled the lands.'

A chair scraped back and her sister, Floralin, rolled her eyes as she sat down. 'You've been tormenting the guests with your theatrics, I see.' She removed the silver cloche from her plate and leaped from her seat with a curse as Valli shot across the table, scenting the fresh food.

Roh lunged for him before he could stick his face in it. 'Sorry,' she muttered, wrangling with the little beast and forcing him back in her pocket, ignoring his gnashing fangs.

Floralin sat back down, warily eyeing Roh's bleeding fingers. 'Like I said before, I'd keep his existence quiet for now. It'd work in your favour if the Saddoriens don't know about him.'

'I want to play with him!' Mora shouted from the other end of the table.

'Maybe tomorrow,' Kezra said, lifting her daughter from where she still stood on the chair and placing her firmly on the ground. 'Get ready for bed, we'll be in shortly.' She gave the little girl a gentle push. With a huff, Mora grabbed Sol by the hand and dragged him from the room.

Roh met Kezra's gaze. 'So, you're the clan leader, after all.'

Kezra grinned. 'I am.'

'And you're not a blood-lusting murderer who likes to carve up humans and cyrens alike?'

Kezra shrugged. 'Depends what day you ask me.'

Roh didn't bother to hide her frustration. 'Well, if we're done with the games, perhaps you'll show me where I can find the Willow's Sapphire?'

From where she sat eating her belated dinner, Floralin gave a dark laugh. 'Perhaps you'd best put the bone cleaner out of her misery, Kez ...'

Kezra insisted on escorting Roh without the others, even insisting that Valli remained with Yrsa. Roh didn't know what to make of the unconventional leader as they took the crate-and-pulley system down the other side of the gorge.

'What was the point of all that?' Roh asked, walking

briskly to keep up with the long strides of the clan leader.

Kezra raised a brow. 'Wasn't it obvious? I wanted to see what kind of cyren our potential queen is.'

'And?'

'I'm reserving my judgement.'

Roh shook her head in disbelief. 'So, was it all a ruse? The gardening, the cooking?'

'A ruse? Not at all. I like cooking for my family, and when I am doing so I am not the Arch General of this place,' Kezra said simply as they rounded a bend. 'All Csillan cyrens live a self-sufficient, simple life.'

Roh chewed her lip as she followed the clan leader down a narrow set of stairs. The rest of Csilla had been bright and warm and welcoming, but where they walked now … It was cold and dark, reminding Roh of the passageways in the Lower Sector of Saddoriel.

Kezra brought her to a stop in front of a huge glass window of what looked to be an enclosure of sorts. The space within was vast, dense and dark foliage covered a rocky outcrop, and it was impossible to see beyond the undergrowth.

The clan leader pointed to a small door on the far right. 'The birthstone is through there.'

Roh turned to her. 'What *else* is in there?' she asked.

'That's the real question, isn't it?' Kezra lifted a silver chain from around her neck and held it out to Roh, a key dangling on the end. 'This unlocks the door. But please, shut it behind you.'

'Kezra …'

Kezra shrugged. 'It wasn't my idea, if that's what

you're asking. The council only updated the ... security ... a few weeks ago.'

Taking the key, Roh peered past the glass, trying to find whatever lurked beyond. 'What does that mean?'

'I imagine it means they learned something about you and have used it against you to defend the stone.'

'That sounds about right,' Roh said, toying with the key chain and not taking her eyes off the enclosure. 'Does sunlight reach inside?' she asked.

'Not much.'

Roh paced the length of the window, trying to make out any detail within other than plant life. When she reached the end closest to the door, she spotted something just beyond in the dirt. Pressing her face to the glass and shielding her eyes from the glare of the torchlight behind her, she peered desperately inside.

*Is that a ...?*

A carcass. Of what animal Roh couldn't tell, it lay discarded in strips. Any remaining flesh was covered in dirt, while bones peeked from bloodied fur. Roh's chest grew heavy with dread as she scanned for whatever beast had inflicted such damage. Her mind went to the pythons Adriel had claimed he'd imported from Csilla for her challenge against Orson in Akoris; they were from the jungle, he'd said. But Roh recalled the squeeze of the serpent around her ribs, the bruises that had stayed on her skin for days after ... Tearing something to shreds was not how those creatures killed. They killed slowly, wringing the very life from their prey, breath by breath. They wouldn't leave a body behind.

Kezra was quiet as Roh combed through her memories from the past few months. She had met all manner of beasts in the first trial of the Queen's Tournament, but the scene before her didn't suit the backahast, the great water horses that hailed from Lochloria, which was arguably the most powerful creature she'd faced in that first trial. But that didn't make sense, nor did a sea drake or serpent in this context. She racked her brain, knowing the answer lay in her previous experiences. The council and Adriel wouldn't have gone to the trouble for something ordinary. This decision had been calculated, a deliberate move to not only scare her physically, but derail her mentally.

With her fingers tracing the cut of the key, Roh went to the glass door at the end of the enclosure. She slid it into the lock but didn't turn it.

'Queen of Bones, think about this,' Kezra warned, her eyes bright with alarm.

But Roh did not turn the key. It was the sound, the vibration of the act that she sought. That pit of dread inside her yawned wide as movement flickered amidst the trees and Roh's suspicions were confirmed.

A silvery-black coat shimmered. And a giant, claw-tipped paw crushed the soft earth.

Roh stepped back from the door in terror as a massive teerah panther stalked towards her, growling between its yellowed fangs.

A thick, gold collar was clamped around its throat and the second birthstone of Saddoriel, the Willow's Sapphire, shone at its centre.

# CHAPTER THIRTEEN

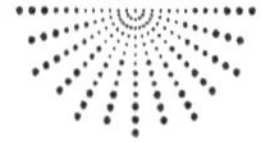

Unease gnawed at Roh's insides as she took in the sight of the beast before her, its dark coat littered with scars, its yellowed fangs bared as it snarled.

Even Kezra took a step back from the enclosure, watching intently as the teerah panther prowled towards the glass.

'The Willow's Sapphire,' Roh murmured. 'The gem that helps its bearer endure and have faith.' As the words left her mouth, Roh wondered if they were true, as the gem's current bearer gave no such indication. Its gaze was *vicious*, full of an unnerving awareness that Roh had thought impossible for a beast. But her gaze trailed along its powerful torso, the scars there both fresh and old, brutal webs of marred flesh.

'What was done to you …?' she whispered, pressing a palm to the cold glass.

The teerah panther flung itself at the barrier with an

enraged roar that rattled the ground beneath Roh's boots, spittle flying, its hackles raised.

Roh scrambled backwards. 'Is this safe?' She gaped at the creature within. Its eyes locked onto hers as it leaped up, dragging its claws down the glass, creating an ear-piercing screech. Roh shuddered. Was the beast marking her as a target?

'The enclosure is reinforced with magic, if that's what you mean,' Kezra told her, not taking her eyes off the teerah panther. 'It cannot get out, unless you let it out.'

Roh snatched the key she'd left in the lock and looped the chain around her neck. A new measure of madness would have to descend upon her to let that thing loose upon Csilla. It now stalked the length of the glass barrier with an increasing intensity, clouds expelling from its nostrils as it growled.

'What does the creature mean to you?' Kezra asked quietly. 'They wouldn't use it unless it had some significance.'

Roh pinched the bridge of her nose, Harlyn's scream in the Gilded Plains echoing in her mind and the vision she'd had of her friend during the Rite of Strothos, her arm nothing more than a bloody stump. Roh could taste the raw panic and desperation at the back of her throat at the mere memory.

'Harlyn …' she managed, clearing her throat. 'The one with the sling? She was attacked by one not long ago. We … we almost lost her.'

'I see,' said Kezra.

'But this … this isn't the same one,' Roh realised aloud,

trying to peer past her panic. As large as the panther was, it wasn't as big as those they had encountered in the plains, and its temperament … While the other panthers had been wild, territorial and instinct-driven, the creature before her held deep knowledge of human cruelty in its eyes, in the markings across its body. There was an awareness to it, a fury that knew its targets.

'You're right.' Kezra heaved a loud sigh. 'This one isn't from the south. It's from the Upper Realms. There is a magic wielder there who breeds these beasts in a pit of torture and unleashes them upon her enemies. I was told by one of the council elders that this one here was the most savage of the pride.'

'Gods …' Roh loosed a shaky breath. They had put the most dangerous teerah panther in all the realms between her and the Willow's Sapphire. Of course they had.

'And what are the rules for the gem's retrieval?' Roh asked, running a hand through her cropped hair.

'Rules?' Kezra raised a brow. 'Get the sapphire by any means necessary.'

It was Roh's turn to show her surprise. 'Was that what they told you?'

Kezra met her gaze. 'That's what *I'm* telling *you* … We have a saying here in Csilla.'

'Oh? And what's that?' Roh was doing her best to remain standing upright.

Kezra gave a sad smile. '*Through the strongest of currents you shall swim.*'

Roh turned back to the teerah panther, noting the

scratches in the glass from its ragged claws. 'And you think that beast is akin to a strong current?'

The Csillan Arch General huffed a dark laugh. 'More like a terror tempest.'

Roh pushed open the thick stone doors to the royal guest chambers and Valli was instantly at her feet. Relieved to see the little beast, she scooped him up in her hands and tentatively stepped inside, hearing the quiet murmur of familiar voices within. She had entered an informal hall of sorts, where marble floors were covered in luxurious rugs and massive vases, and white tree branches lined walls of emerald green, mirroring the hues of the grassy cliffs outside. Arched windows revealed the gorge beyond, where the moon was full, illuminating the rushing river and the chalky rock faces.

'There you are,' Harlyn appeared from an arching doorway and pulled her into a lounge suite, where the others all sat waiting on the plush sofas. 'How was it? What did Kezra say? Where's the gem?'

Roh let her friend push her gently into a giant armchair, noting the crackling fire and thinking abstractly of Orson, who used to manage the fire in their chambers back in the Lower Sector. Valli curled up in her lap, nuzzling her until she began to stroke the top of his head.

'I …' But the words got stuck in her throat and the key to the enclosure felt like a brand against her skin. How was she meant to tell Harlyn of the viciousness that awaited them in the bowels of the Csillan gorges?

Harlyn perched herself on the arm of Roh's chair. 'How bad is it?'

'Look at her face,' Odi pointed out. 'It's bad.'

Roh's gaze flicked to the human in annoyance. 'Thanks.'

Sensing her mood, Valli lifted his head and growled in Odi's direction, flaring his wings. That helped, somehow.

Odi crossed his arms and glared at the little creature.

Roh steeled herself, squaring her shoulders. 'It's the Willow's Sapphire,' she said. 'And it's set in a collar around the neck of a teerah panther.'

Roh heard Harlyn's sharp intake of breath. The others merely blinked at her.

'I'm sorry,' she heard herself say to her friend. 'I never wanted you to have to face one of those beasts again. And you won't have to. This is just me —'

'It hasn't been "just you" for a while now, Roh, in case you hadn't noticed.' Yrsa gestured around the room to her fellow Jaktaren, the water warlock immersed in his books, Odi and Harlyn, who had risen to her feet and now paced the border of the thick rug across the floor.

'I know,' Roh replied. 'And I'm grateful for you all.'

'Good,' Finn said gruffly. 'So, let's figure out how to get that stone.'

Roh's hand stilled over Valli as she looked up at Finn. 'Kezra says that this beast is the most dangerous one of its kind.'

'I'd expect nothing less,' he told her, his lilac gaze steeled in a light of challenge. 'Can it be killed?'

Valli stirred in Roh's lap and she considered the drakeling, her fondness for him swelling in her chest. 'I don't know,' she admitted. 'But is that the best course of action? To slay the poor tormented thing?'

'You might put it out of its misery,' Yrsa interjected.

'I just … I can't help but feel it's wrong, somehow?' Roh managed, trying to process and understand her own feelings as she spoke them aloud. They were wild, vicious creatures to be sure, but to do what had been done to them? For a moment, she imagined Valli being subjected to the same treatment —

'Wrong?' Harlyn snapped testily. 'I could have died thanks to its kin.'

Discomfort squirmed in Roh's gut. 'I know. And I will never forget that, Har. I'll never forget the terror I felt in those moments.'

Harlyn's fiery gaze found hers. 'But?'

'But … was it their fault? From what Deodan said in the plains, and from what Kezra told me about the one in the enclosure, they have been tormented into that existence.'

'That's not our responsibility,' Harlyn argued.

'Isn't it?' Roh challenged. 'After Akoris, I decided I wanted to be a queen of action, of change.'

'That you did.' Deodan's voice carved through the tension.

'*Cyrens* are your responsibility. Not wild beasts who

roam foreign lands.' Harlyn clutched her slinged arm as she spoke, her words sharp and void of compromise.

'The beast we speak of is not in foreign lands. It's in Csilla, beneath these very residences.' Roh heard her voice rise to match Harlyn's, but she reined in her temper. 'I would seek an alternative solution, if we can,' she said more gently.

'What if we drugged it?' Odi offered. 'I believe we have an expert in our midst? Someone with a fondness for lacing wine with coral larkspur, if I'm not mistaken.' He gave Finn a pointed look.

A grin split across the Jaktaren's face. 'No idea what you're talking about.'

Roh failed to hide her smile. 'We could try? Lace whatever they're feeding it with a sedative? Once it's unconscious, I could slip into the enclosure and take the gem.'

'It's not the worst idea I've ever heard,' Harlyn allowed begrudgingly, walking to a cart on the far side of the room and pouring herself a generous splash of amber liquid.

Roh nodded, still stroking the sleeping drakeling in her lap. 'Let's start with that, then. The sooner I get my hands on the gem, the better. After our time in Akoris, I expect to be challenged here, too.'

Yrsa followed Harlyn to the refreshment cart. 'I think you're right to prepare yourself for that. There are too many highborns with an axe to grind, I'm afraid.' Yrsa poured a splash of amber liquid into several glasses and started to hand them around to the others.

Roh accepted hers gratefully, until she caught a whiff of the sharp liquor within.

'They'll have a greenhouse here,' Finn was saying. 'No doubt they'll have some sort of plant we can use.'

'The question is, do we trust Kezra?' Odi asked. 'I know she seemed friendly enough, and granted, unlike all the other cyrens I've met …' He seemed to wait for someone to challenge him; no one did. 'But I've learned the same lesson time and time again.'

Roh nodded. 'We should learn as much as we can about Csilla and its Arch General, but keep everything important just between us. Agreed?'

Yrsa raised her glass. 'Agreed.'

The others followed suit.

Roh took a measured sip, and as soon as the liquor hit the back of her throat she choked, coughing violently. Whatever it was burned with a vengeance. Valli looked up at her, unimpressed with being woken.

'What *is* this?' she rasped, her eyes watering.

Yrsa laughed quietly. 'The Csillans are known for their river whisky – it's one of the strongest blends in all the realms. They have a distillery down in one of the smaller gorges.'

Grimacing, Roh placed her glass on the floor beside her armchair and sat back, willing the taste from her tongue. She glanced across at Odi. 'I prefer rum,' she said with a shudder.

'Same,' Odi replied, but knocked back his glass regardless. 'But I'll take what I can get.'

To Roh's surprise, Finn was watching the human with

an unmasked expression of respect. 'Cheers to you, then, Prince of Melodies,' he said, and downed the rest of his drink as well.

Harlyn nudged Roh, nodding towards the Jaktaren and musician. 'Whatever *that* is,' she muttered, 'I find it disturbing.'

Roh opened her mouth to agree, but a flash of light from the gorge had her shooting to her feet, disturbing Valli as she rushed to the arched window. 'What was that?' she murmured, looking out onto the surging river below.

Deodan was at her side, clutching one of the warlock journals. 'Could be one of the terror tempests they mentioned.'

Roh peered out onto the moonlit crevices of the gorge. 'It's no storm,' she realised, spotting cyrens emerging from hidden alcoves, holding lanterns of glowing valo beetles. There were perhaps fifteen of them, stationed along cliff ledges.

'What are they doing —' But Finn's words were cut short as *music* filled Csilla.

Roh darted for Odi, her fingers snatching at his shirt front until she caught sight of the protective shell token around his neck. She sagged with relief. But as she turned back to the window, she realised it was no deathsong the Csillans were singing. It was something else entirely.

Less than two-dozen voices came together, but the sound was that of a hundred: rich and balanced and harmonious, threading through the valley and dancing with the river. The singers' heads were tilted to the stars as they sang, each note coming from an individual, but joining together as the heart of the entire choir. They sang in Old Saddorien, but it didn't matter that Roh couldn't understand the lyrics. The voices enveloped her, every breath, every word woven into a colour before her very eyes, until the gorges themselves became song.

As Roh watched on, her magic stirred within her. She had felt it growing stronger with each passing day, but this … This music seemed to feed her power. She could feel it stretching and testing its reach inside her, wanting to unleash itself and play with the magic swimming around her. Both she and her magic were enraptured by the Csillan choir, their sound nothing short of celestial. Roh was in the semi-floating state between awe and utter surrender to the song. This was not a mere gathering of voices, but a sonic event.

'I don't understand it,' Odi whispered at her side. 'But I *feel* it.' His hand was pressed to his chest, his eyes lined with silver.

'Yes,' Roh said, resting her palm against her own heart.

As the music built, as the warmth of each note wrapped around Roh, her own magic threatened to burst free in an explosion of colourful power. For the first time since she'd sung her deathsong along the banks of the Endon River, she allowed herself to wonder, just for a moment …

Could it be that her own song would one day rival that of the great Sedna Irons?

# CHAPTER FOURTEEN

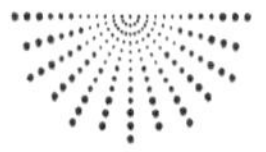

R oh woke to the bright sound of youthful laughter. From her top bunk in the sleeping quarters, she could see through the open arched doors to the living room, where Sol and Mora were playing with Valli on the floor. Buttery rays of sunlight washed over the two nestlings, who had a ball of twine which they rolled to one another across the carpet while Valli darted from one to the other, trying to intercept. Mora shrieked with delight and reached for him as the drakeling pounced, his little wings flaring as he caught the twine between his fangs.

'Careful,' Yrsa's voice sounded from out of Roh's sight. 'His teeth are razor sharp.'

Sol's gaze shot to the other side of the room in alarm, but Mora carried on playing.

Roh rubbed the sleep from her eyes and stretched, her elbow making contact with something hard. Frowning, she dug beneath the quilt and retrieved the volume of *The Law of the Lair*. She smoothed her hand over the leather-bound cover, which was in almost pristine condition. Just before they had departed Akoris, in the early hours of the morning, Roh had found herself tugged down the deserted corridors by the Mercy's Topaz, through the shrinking room and into the library, straight to the shelf with the law volumes. A surreal warmth had directed her to a particular tome: *Volume Seventeen*. In the silence of pre-dawn, she had taken the book, swapping it with her old tattered edition from Saddoriel, vowing she'd have it returned to its rightful place when she was queen. She didn't know why the birthstone had brought her to that particular volume, but she had learned to trust the gem and had been scouring the text for any hint of help in her limited free time ever since.

She must have fallen asleep reading it again. Whenever she wasn't planning the next stage of her quest, she was combing through its pages, determined to leverage whatever knowledge she could glean from it in her favour. The laws of cyrenkind were complex, full of contradictions and loopholes, usually designed to favour the ruler, the council elders and the highborns, and Roh needed as many of them up her sleeve as possible. She sighed. Not that she'd been able to absorb any of the information last night; her head had been too full of the memory of the Csillan choir.

Something knocked against her sternum as she pushed the sheets back and she looked down between the laces of her nightshirt. *The key*. It had left an imprint on her skin, a reminder of the dreaded task at hand. The very sight of it bringing the roar of the enraged beast to the forefront of Roh's mind, she shuddered.

As she descended the ladder from her bed, the harmonies from last night filled her mind and her skin tingled, her power whispering in her veins. She had never heard anything like it. Scanning the rest of the sleeping quarters, Roh realised that everyone else must be awake – the beds were all made. She had opted to ignore the enormous bed in the 'queen's' private chamber and stay with the others, though she couldn't pinpoint why. She caught sight of her reflection in a mirror hanging from a wardrobe and winced. Her dark hair stuck out at all angles and her still moss-green eyes blinked dumbly back at her.

'Gods,' she muttered, doing her best to run her fingers through her messy tresses and flatten the bits that stuck out. She didn't have much luck and the rest of her wasn't any better. Somehow with her short hair, the scar down her face seemed more prominent, but there was little she could do about that. Still wearing the matching cotton night pants and shirt Kezra had supplied, Roh padded across the carpets into the living room.

'Bone Queen!' Mora exclaimed. 'Mama says you're going to fight a teerah panther, is that true?'

Roh stopped short, not even noticing Valli scale her leg and arm to perch himself on her shoulder. 'What?' It was too early to relay her plans to a bunch of nestlings. 'Something like that,' she muttered, waving Mora away as she spotted a basket on one of the side tables.

'That's breakfast —'

'Or what's left of it,' Deodan interjected from an armchair in the corner, a journal open in his lap. 'We ate without you.'

'I didn't mean to sleep late.' Roh sifted through a variety of freshly baked goods and decided on a scone.

'You needed it. First decent sleep you've had since the rite, I imagine.' The warlock turned back to the book.

'What have you discovered in those so far?' Roh asked, jutting her chin in the journal's direction.

'Nothing I didn't already know.'

'Which is?' Roh pressed.

Both Mora and Sol seemed to sense the tension that had gathered around them and the two nestlings slipped from the room without a word.

Valli exhaled a hot puff of air on Roh's neck as she frowned, looking from the doorway back to the warlock.

A muscle twitched along Deodan's jaw and he closed the journal with a frustrated snap. 'The basket came with a note,' he said. 'We're to meet Floralin at the stairs to the bridge at the ninth hour.'

Roh nearly choked on her scone as she spotted a clock on the mantle. 'But that's in thirty minutes. Why didn't you —'

Deodan had already resumed reading.

Roh muttered a curse in his direction and returned to the sleeping quarters to find a fresh set of clothes and the bathing chamber.

'Oh good, you're up,' Harlyn said from behind her.

'Where have you and the others been?' Roh asked.

'Wandering around the bridge, exploring. Yrsa is carrying on about finding us a place to train, but I thought I should come back and help with the bathing system.'

'What?' Roh gaped at her. 'I'm perfectly capable of washing myself.'

Harlyn laughed. 'Obviously. Though, you wouldn't know it from the look of you at the moment. Come on, I'll show you.'

Baffled, Roh followed her friend into the bathing chamber and realised immediately what Harlyn was talking about. There was no bath inside, nor any buckets or basins of water. Instead, a strange tray of pebbles sat in the far corner, with a metal hose of sorts positioned above it.

'What is that?' Roh asked, wondering how on earth she was going to scrub days of travel from her skin without a decent tub.

'They call it a "falls bath",' Harlyn explained, reaching for a pair of knobs jutting from the wall. She turned them and a spray of water shot down from the hose. 'You stand under it and wash. You can adjust the temperature, like so.' She twisted the handles and pulled Roh's hand under the stream of warm water. 'See?'

'I suppose the name is … apt,' Roh murmured, picturing herself washing underneath a waterfall. 'But it's … odd.'

'I'll say,' Harlyn agreed. 'But I quite liked it. You just turn the handles this way to shut it all off.' Harlyn demonstrated and the water ceased to fall. 'Anyway, you'd better hurry up. There are fresh towels and soaps over there.' She pointed to a pair of neatly organised shelves in the opposite corner.

'Thanks.'

Harlyn laughed. 'Looks like someone wants to keep you company.'

'What?' Alarmed, Roh followed Harlyn's pointed finger to Valli, who was waiting eagerly on the wet pebbles beneath the hose.

'Gods. What are you doing here?' Roh hissed. 'Go with Harlyn.'

But the little drakeling merely plonked himself down on his rear and flared his wings expectantly.

Harlyn snorted. 'I guess he's staying.'

Once Harlyn had left, Roh made quick work of washing herself beneath the 'falls bath', all the while trying not to step on Valli, who kept darting in and out of the water stream with leaps of delight. As Roh scrubbed at her hair, she wondered what it was like for him to not have seen the sea, where he belonged. The usual pang of guilt hit her low in the gut for taking that away from him. As though sensing the emotions roiling within her, he blinked up at her with those molten-gold eyes and flapped his wings beneath the water.

'One day,' she told him. 'One day I'll take you to the waves.'

Roh wished she had more time to stand beneath the spray of hot water, the heat easing the ache in her muscles, the design of the contraption inspiring the creator in her, but they were all due to meet Floralin soon, and then there was the small matter of figuring out how to drug the teerah panther. She shut off the water with a heavy sigh and towelled herself dry. Tugging on her spare pair of black pants and her linen shirt, Roh combed her butchered hair with her fingers as best she could, swearing softly at the sight. With Valli at her heels, she padded into the sleeping quarters and found her pack at the foot of her bunk. Unsure why she felt compelled to do so, Roh strapped the sheath with her father's quartz dagger around her thigh.

*Perhaps with everything swirling around my head, I need something to remind me where I come from. Birthed by a cyren, fathered by a warlock, named for a human girl ...* Ames' words rang in her mind, like a bell echoing in a tower.

Checking the buckle of the sheath, Roh sighed as she scooped Valli up and went to find the others.

She didn't have to go far. They were all waiting for her in the living quarters.

'Shall we?' Yrsa said, motioning towards the door.

Roh adjusted her crown, pulled on her boots and nodded. 'It's time we learned once and for all what in the realms these terror tempests mean for Saddoriel.'

As promised, Floralin waited for them at the foot of the spiral stairs to the upper bridge. She wore the same clothes as she had the night before, a heavy waxed coat and sturdy boots.

'You'll find spare outerwear in that cupboard.' She

pointed to a hidden door behind Odi. 'It's windy up there, so rug up.'

Roh exchanged a bewildered glance with Harlyn but did as the leader bid, shrugging a thick treated cloak over her shoulders and pulling up the hood. Valli nestled in between her neck and the fabric, his claws gently scratching at her skin.

The others donned their cloaks as well. Finn looked particularly menacing in his, still insisting on carrying his crossbow over his back.

Floralin started up the metal stairs. 'My sister said you didn't know much of the terror tempests?'

'No,' Roh told her. 'Not even the Jaktaren among us have heard of them. Though,' she added. 'Deodan hasn't said much.'

'Likely because his kind often gets the blame for them,' Floralin said.

'Often?' Deodan's voice was low. 'My kin are held responsible for creating the savage storms and directing them to the cyrens. It was one of the excuses used for the genocide of our kind.'

Roh started. She hadn't realised that the water warlock was right behind her. She turned in surprise, the whirlpools of water he'd created in the Gilded Plains flashing before her, whirlpools strong enough to obliterate *teerah panthers* —

'Don't even think it,' he practically growled, reading whatever horrified expression had crossed her face. 'That was in *your* defence. That was to *save your friend*.'

'I know.'

'Then don't give me that look.'

Roh felt her magic flinch at his tone; there was a threat laced between his words, of what she didn't know, but she didn't like it, not one bit. There was something going on with him … He hadn't been his usual self, not since they'd left the mountain pass.

*Not since he started reading those journals*, Roh realised, continuing up the stairs. What did they contain? Was something in them making him regret his decision to join her quest? The questions started to churn, but there wasn't time to delve further into the complicated inner workings of Deodan's motives, not now. Roh reached the final steps and Floralin pushed open a heavy iron door, cold air blasting inside.

'This way,' the Csillan called, leading them onto the upper bridge.

The wind was bone-biting, a powerful force that stole the breath from Roh's lungs as she strode out onto the vast bridge. Valli buried himself deeper into her neck and the collar of her shirt with a quiet growl of protest. It was incredibly exposed up here, but completely mesmerising as well. For either side of the stone railings, was a sheer drop into the gorge, the river swelling with white foam below. All along the bridge were large apparatuses that Roh didn't recognise and a number of Csillans layered in cloaks shielding themselves against the wind, hunched over and scribbling across thick wads of parchment. She didn't miss the glares some of them shot Deodan. Word had clearly got around about the warlock's arrival and Kezra had been right – his welcome was certainly mixed.

'What are they doing?' she shouted to Floralin, who waited as Roh and her companions huddled around her.

'They're taking readings,' Floralin replied, projecting her voice over the lashing of the wind. 'Our devices can detect the traces of pre-tempest magic in the air currents. We constantly monitor these for high readings, should we need to prepare for an incoming terror tempest.'

'But what *is* a terror tempest?' Harlyn asked loudly.

Floralin glanced momentarily at her workers before turning back to the group, her brows raised. 'You truly know that little?' She didn't keep the dread from her tone.

Roh cleared her throat. 'We only heard of them a matter of weeks ago. In passing.' She made a point of looking at Deodan then, for no matter his objections to warlocks' responsibility for the storms, it had been his own mother, the Warlock Supreme, who had alerted Roh and Finn to their existence.

'We were *also* told that they hadn't occurred in over fifty years,' Finn added.

'Good gods.' Floralin actually put her head in her hands. 'That is what they teach you in Saddoriel?'

'No,' Yrsa corrected. 'They teach us nothing in Saddoriel, *literally nothing*. Saddoriens have no knowledge whatsoever of these terror tempests and what they do.'

Floralin glanced around them, shaking her head in disbelief before she gathered herself. 'Follow me.'

They walked briskly across the bridge, and to Roh's relief, they entered a large room at the far end, sheltered from the wind. At the centre was a large oak table covered in maps and charts with chairs around it.

'Take a seat,' Floralin said, sinking into the chair at the head of the table. 'Shall I start at the beginning, then?'

Roh cupped her hands before her face, trying to bring the warmth back into her fingers. 'Please do.' Her gaze trailed along the walls, where framed works of art depicted great storms across the seas, and to her surprise, a sea drake battling a cyren amidst a tempest.

Floralin followed her stare. 'For the longest time, cyrens believed that the great sea drakes caused the terror tempests.'

As if in answer, Valli emerged from the folds of Roh's hood, leaped onto the table and promptly sneezed, the force of it sending him skidding backwards across the maps. Though Roh herself had been at the mercy of a fully grown sea drake, it was hard to imagine the drakeling before them posing such a threat.

'But that has never been true,' Floralin continued.

'Nor is it true that the warlocks are responsible,' Deodan added coldly, his eyes bright with anger.

'I never said they were,' Floralin replied evenly. 'The truth is, we don't know what causes them. Some say they represent the anger of the goddesses. Some say they're enchantments from magical beings in another world. Here in Csilla, we say they're simply unfortunate instances of nature. The realms are forever changing and evolving, and the terror tempests are only one part of that. But Deodan is right, they were used against the water warlocks, who in fact, did everything in their power to *contain* them, to prevent them from destroying Saddoriel and Talon's Reach, which is where the tempests hit hardest.' She eyed Deodan. 'I want you to know *that* is what we teach here. We do not spread unfounded hate in Csilla, but sadly, old superstitions are hard to kill when they're passed down the generations. Hence the looks you may have noticed on the bridge.'

Suddenly, Roh was back in the outer passages of Talon's Reach with Odi and Yrsa's human, Tess. The entire lair had shaken, stalactites had dropped from the ceiling and cut into her skin, and they had shattered all around her feet. Roh remembered the spike of fear in her chest as she tried to picture what could have caused such a tremor. It had been no creature of any kind, not even a sea drake … It had been a terror tempest.

'You implied that they've been occurring without our knowledge?' Roh prompted.

Floralin nodded. 'I don't know who started to spread the rumour that they hadn't raged in fifty years. That's completely inaccurate. The terror tempests are ongoing. Saddoriel hasn't been hit *hard* in about fifty years, but that doesn't mean the storms have ceased. And like anything inevitable, the longer Saddoriel goes without one, the more likely it is to occur, and the worse it's going to be.'

'What exactly happens?' Yrsa asked.

'It starts as a wild storm of thunder and lightning, before it progresses to wind and water tunnels of unstoppable force. They usually occur over bodies of water, more often the seas than anywhere else, though as we've learned, rivers serve just as well for a starting point. A terror tempest that is strong enough will cleave through the protective enchantments that have seen Saddoriel stand for thousands of years. It will carve through spells and passageways and sectors, no matter Upper or Lower. In doing so, it leaves the cyren territory vulnerable to attack.'

Harlyn straightened in her chair. 'From water warlocks?'

Floralin tilted her head as she met Harlyn's questioning gaze. 'Do you think water warlocks are the only race who wish ill upon our kind?'

Goosebumps rushed across Roh's arms, despite the warmth of the room. 'Humans.' It wasn't a question. There was no doubt in her mind that humans had been biding their time since the Age of Chaos. Had there ever been a true victor of that war?

'Could you blame us?' Odi asked quietly.

Roh looked from the human to the water warlock sitting before them, who'd taken up her quest alongside her, whose kin had been through so much at the hands of her ancestors. 'No,' she replied, her voice equally soft. 'I couldn't.' She turned back to the Csillan. 'So, what can be done about the tempests?'

'We monitor them, try to predict the force of each one with the equipment you saw out on the bridge. Those devices can measure the saturation of magic in the air. As Csilla is typically exposed to all sorts of climate, it's the perfect spot for monitoring such things. From our work here, we report back to Saddoriel if and when it's threatened.'

'And the former queen, the council, they all know of this?'

'They do. Saddoriel is weaker than ever before, as is cyrenkind,' Floralin told them. 'It has withstood decades' worth of tempest battering, but the enchantments that protect it are old, and cracks have begun to form in its armour. It is only a matter of time before it is cleaved wide open and attacked for real.'

'But there's a council elder in charge of Saddoriel's defence.' Harlyn turned to Yrsa. 'Isomene Sigra, right?'

Yrsa nodded.

'Well, surely she knows of this? Surely, it's her job to replenish the enchantments somehow? What in Thera's name has she been doing all this time?'

Roh found she couldn't swallow. A lump had formed in her throat at the thought of her home and her people being ambushed.

'How is it that the *Jaktaren* know nothing of this?' Finn asked, smoothing his palms across the map before him. 'Surely, this is something our guild should be aware of?'

'Both questions only Delja and the council can answer,' Floralin replied.

'Is it simply a matter of protecting the concept of our own strength? That the council likes Saddoriens thinking we're far less vulnerable than we are?' Roh wondered aloud. For what other reason could there be for hiding such a threat from the cyrens of Talon's Reach? Was that why Csilla was such a small, isolated territory? Was the idea that the less who knew about the weaknesses of their kind, the better?

'Yet in doing so, in keeping this secret, they make us weaker still —' But her thoughts were interrupted by Valli leaping from the table to a shelf beneath the paintings. His little wings stretched out, as though he might try to fly, but he went sprawling into the books on the other side. When he'd recovered himself, he scrambled up a small set of drawers, so that he was at eye level with the artwork of the sea drake.

Without thinking, Roh got to her feet and went to him, following the little creature's intense stare to his painted, matured counterpart. It was a battle scene ... Human warships surrounded the fully grown drake, its body suspended above the crashing waves between a pair of great wings. A cyren hung from a dagger embedded in its chest, the beast roaring in pain.

'That's King Asros' consort, Freya,' Floralin told her. 'The one the Saddoriens called *ramehra*.'

Roh found herself nodding. It had only been weeks ago that she'd found reference to the beloved Saddorien in a library book when she'd been attempting to research how to raise a drakeling.

'She threw the dagger at it?' she asked, not taking her eyes from the thick whorls of paint. 'Brought it down?'

'So they say.' Floralin stood. 'Come, I will show you how the devices work and how to take the readings.'

Soon, they were back out on the bridge, the wind stinging their faces and cracking their lips. Valli buried himself deep in the folds of Roh's cloak as they wandered out onto the exposed structure, following Floralin to an unmanned apparatus. It was made of some kind of metal and stood on three long legs. The main body of it was cylindrical in shape and could be manoeuvred to point in any direction up at the sky.

'We take readings every half hour from the north, the south, the east and the west,' Floralin was explaining. 'Usually within one of those four points, the storm magic is detected, as we take a more refined approach in that particular direction. If a reading is over a certain level, the team alerts the principal, if the reading remains high, Kezra and I are alerted and thus we go through the chain of command at Saddoriel from there.'

Roh frowned. 'How do you communicate so quickly with the lair?'

'We have special permission to use our mirror Pool of Weeping.'

'I see ...' Roh let that piece of information sink in, toying with the key on the end of the silver chain at her neck. She was still in the process of understanding the living beast that was the interconnected mirror pools of the cyren territories, and not only the pools themselves, but her relationship to them. In Akoris, she had started to question whether or not she had participated in the great cyren rite of passage – the First Cry. But there had been no time to investigate further and no one to ask who might have answers. Perhaps she could visit the Csillan pool ... Perhaps she could try to communicate with Delja ... The thought was fleeting.

Floralin had moved onto another piece of equipment and was explaining to an intrigued-looking Finn and Yrsa how it worked. Deodan was watching too, albeit with a faraway expression etched on his face. Roh had never seen the warlock turn so inwards. His usual quips and suggestive comments had evaporated and in their place was a sombre man who was quick to anger.

'Is there any way to contain the storms?' he asked, tugging his cloak tighter around him.

Floralin eyed him knowingly. 'The warlocks used to help with their enchantments. It's their magic that protects Saddoriel and Talon's Reach in the first place, after all.'

'But the Saddoriens killed us off.'

Floralin didn't shy away from the intensity of his gaze. 'They did. Thus cutting themselves off from the very source of their protection. In order to reinforce the enchantments, there would need to be a call for magic across the lands, a gathering of power that no longer exists in the realms as we know them today.'

Something unpleasant slid around Roh's gut, like a viper through oil.

Deodan's nostrils flared. 'Then tell me, tempest master, what is the point in all this monitoring if there's no way to prevent the storms from tearing the currents and the lair apart? Why not let nature succeed in its purpose? Wipe out the Saddoriens and start afresh —'

'Deodan!' Roh gasped, lunging for the warrior.

But Finn beat her to it. In a blur of movement, he slid Roh's dagger from the sheath at her thigh and had it pressed to the soft skin at Deodan's throat. '*Say that again.*'

Deodan's gaze was hollow. No fear, not even anger

flickered in his blue eyes. Perhaps he was used to having blades at his throat by now. 'You would use my own kind's weapon against me?' he asked softly.

'The tool itself matters not,' Finn hissed.

Roh's heart thumped against her sternum; her talons unsheathed and pierced the soft flesh of her palms. 'Stop it,' she said, 'stop this *now*.'

But Finn's grip didn't loosen. His gaze trailed from Deodan's empty eyes to the quartz blade, where a fine trickle of blood ran from the crease in his neck. 'I'll use *anything* against you, if you threaten my people like that again,' he spat.

Roh's skin prickled then flushed. Every Csillan on the bridge was staring at them. Was this the sort of leadership she was presenting to the world? Would this be what the cyrens of other territories remembered when they left? That Rohesia of the Bone Cleaners couldn't keep her companions in line enough not to kill each other during a demonstration?

She was moving before she'd thought it through. She shoved herself between the Jaktaren and the water warlock, the blade now at *her* throat. Fury surged, causing her power to awaken within. Magic pulsed around her, a force field to be reckoned with. 'That's enough,' she said. She didn't raise her voice. She said no more than that, but instead allowed her magic, her deathsong to reach out and briefly touch both idiots on either side of her.

They broke apart instantly, shock slackening their faces.

Finn's eyes snapped to hers and he baulked at

whatever he saw there. He flipped the quartz dagger between his fingers, offering her the bone handle wordlessly.

After a moment's pause, her deathsong poised at her lips, Roh let her magic retreat and she took the blade from the Jaktaren, sheathing it at her thigh once more.

The tension around the group and across the bridge dissipated as quickly as it had seized. With a wary glance in Roh's direction, Floralin returned to her lecture on the various measurements of the tempest readings.

Roh couldn't contain the heavy sigh that escaped her then. Gods, she had thought that the group was starting to meld together, in spite of their differences. They had overcome so much already, she thought they shared a certain bond, a mutual respect for one another now. But perhaps there were some prejudices that ran too deep, that no matter what one did to fill the cracks, they were always there …?

Roh found Deodan leaning in, his words only audible to her. '*A gathering of power that no longer exists in the realms as we know them today,*' he said. 'Do *you* think it doesn't exist, Rohesia?'

Roh's head snapped to his, the final traces of her magic still lingering between them. 'What are you implying?'

'You know exactly what I'm implying.'

'That my magic is powerful? I know that, Deodan. But powerful enough to stop a tempest?'

'Perhaps not alone. But with help …'

Roh stared at him. 'You think it could be done?'

Deodan used the toe of his boot to draw something in the film of dust on the bridge and frustration flared within Roh. *Half a pair of wings*, the symbol of the long-dead alliance between warlocks and cyrens.

'It's not that easy,' she hissed. 'Stop trying to force that on me. I can't just form some sort of treaty with you on a whim. I'm not even queen yet, and there's still so much I don't know.'

'It *is* that easy, Roh. You either believe in our cause, or you don't. I thought you'd have made up your mind by now. I thought you would have seen the truth for what it is.'

'Deodan —'

He gave an infuriating shrug. 'What would I know? Apparently, everything's my fault anyway.'

'Roh.' Harlyn nudged her with her elbow, looking pale and perturbed as she pulled Roh away from the warlock.

Her anger and Deodan's words were forgotten as a pang of worry hit Roh low in the gut and she leaned in close to her friend. 'What is it?'

'The wind,' Harlyn murmured, looping her arm through Roh's, as though she needed the physical contact to reassure her. 'The wind whispers her name to me.'

A rush of goosebumps raced along Roh's arms and that pang of worry became something more. Fear.

'Whose name?'

'*Orson's*, Roh. It whispers *Orson's* name to me.'

What little heat Roh had retained vanished and an icy talon dragged down her spine, causing her to shudder.

She met Harlyn's gaze, whose eyes were wide with horror.

'Do you think Adriel slipped me some of that rite poison?' her friend asked quietly.

Roh had to strain to hear her amidst the wind. 'I … I don't know,' she admitted. 'It's *possible*. And it's certainly not above Adriel's usual tricks.'

But atop Roh's head, the topaz in her crown gently pulled her away from such an idea. As though sensing its magic change, Valli stirred in her cloak and huffed hot air against her skin. Full of fear, Harlyn's gaze was darting around to wherever she heard this voice.

'I don't think he poisoned you,' Roh told her. 'Do you think … Do you think it might be guilt?'

'Guilt?' Harlyn's expression darkened. 'What do I have to feel guilty for? I've done nothing wrong.'

'I didn't say you had,' Roh soothed. 'But guilt doesn't always follow reason. Is it possible that you feel bad for how things between Orson and us ended? And that no matter how angry we were at her, seeing her banished into those passageways is not something we would ever have wished upon her?'

Harlyn muttered something Roh didn't hear. 'So, you think I'm making it up? In my own head?'

Roh sighed. 'I believe you're hearing what you say. But it might be some trick of your mind, brought on by guilt. Don't you think there's a slight chance that's possible?'

'I guess,' Harlyn admitted begrudgingly. 'I wish she'd just leave me alone. I've had enough of her lies.'

While Harlyn's tone was hardened, it was easy enough

to see the gleam of hurt in her eyes. Roh felt it too, the gaping hole of Orson missing from their lives. She knew in her heart that the image of Orson walking into the darkness plagued the dreams she couldn't remember, that emptiness was there upon waking. But in the muted light of day, she packed away the thoughts of her former friend, locked them safely in a box of iron and pushed it to the darkest corner of her mind, tempted to discard the key. Perhaps one day she would be ready to delve into all that had occurred between them, but not now, not when she had teerah panthers, terror tempests and councils to defeat.

She gave Harlyn's good hand a gentle squeeze. It was the only comfort she could offer. No words would bring Orson back, no words would undo what she had done, in the same way that Roh couldn't take back the choices that had led them all down this path. All they could do was push on and live with the consequences of her actions.

Roh found herself scanning the faces on the bridge, those she was beginning to know and those who were still strangers to her. Just as there were dangerous fissures in her group of companions, so too were there cracks in the legend of cyrenkind. She had learned long ago that not all was as she had been taught, and slowly but surely, she was beginning to unlearn the narrative that she hadn't questioned for so long. A fresh wind whipped through the gorge, icy and forceful. The Csillans scurried from device to device, scribbling in their books, some still watching Deodan warily.

This was what she had fought for, so far. For the

knowledge that cyrenkind was not as formidable as she had thought. They were struggling for survival, amidst terror tempests and fading magic. Roh's crown of bones flashed before her eyes, a vision of it with all three birthstones in their proper places. The Mercy's Topaz, the Willow's Sapphire and the Gauntlet Ruby. Would it matter if she obtained them all? Was her magic a match for all that sought to destroy them?

Or was she to inherit a broken throne? A broken kingdom?

# CHAPTER FIFTEEN

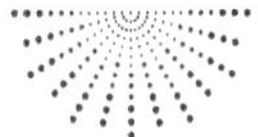

Roh's despair stayed with her long after they had retired from Floralin's teachings on the Bridge of Csilla. It followed her back to their quarters, stirring up all manner of dismay and magic. Her power was restless beneath her skin, uncomfortably so, and she couldn't bear the thought of more tension between the others. She slipped away quietly, taking *The Law of the Lair* and retreating to the teerah-panther enclosure in lower Csilla. The strain of the morning had knotted itself tightly in the muscles of her back and neck, causing them to burn no matter which way she stretched, no matter how often she rolled her shoulders. At the former, Valli protested with a sharp nip to her earlobe, clearly irritated at being disturbed so often.

'How much sleep do you need?' Roh muttered to him, massaging her bleeding lobe between her thumb and forefinger as she sat cross-legged on the floor before the glass.

The drakeling simply snorted as if to say it was none of her damn business.

Floralin and Deodan's words had stayed with Roh. *A gathering of power that no longer exists in the realms as we know them today* ... She knew she was strong, but *how strong* was another question entirely. She was yet to test her power and its limits in any truly meaningful way, if that was at all possible without the suffering of the human she cared about. With everything building up inside her, Roh desperately wanted to *talk* to someone, but who? The fleeting thought of using the mirror pool returned to her, not to find Ames or Delja, but to talk to Cerys. Perhaps she would find her mother in a state of lucidness, so she could ask about the magic that had been passed down to her ... Roh dismissed the thought nearly as soon as it had entered her head as she recalled the nightmare she'd had on the way to the mountain pass; the pleas of the council elders, the blood pooling at her feet ... *Cerys the Slayer* ...

Sighing heavily, Roh opened the book in her lap but didn't start reading. Instead, she gazed into the enclosure, trying to spot a sign of the enraged beast within. There was no flicker of movement, not even the skeleton of a devoured carcass, and Roh wondered just how far back the enclosure went, how much space the poor creature had.

'I don't want to kill you,' she murmured. She didn't know why that had suddenly become so important to her. Was it her relationship with Valli? Or was she just simply tired of violence and cruelty? The vicious memory of the Queen's Tournament trials sank its talons into her once again, a near-crippling reminder of what cyrenkind was capable of, their bloodlust, their ruthlessness. Roh didn't take her gaze from the enclosure. Whatever her reason, she was adamant – she would not kill the panther, it didn't feel right, and perhaps that was reason enough.

She watched as Valli tentatively approached the glass, his little wings flared at his back, his chest puffed out. He strutted the length of the window, peering within, his gold eyes bright with curiosity.

*I wonder what it is to be fearless*, Roh mused while Valli started another patrol of the glass. *To know that when your time comes, you will be an unstoppable force unto the realms, that not a single creature could rival you ...*

A flash of silvery-black fur came flying at the window, a roar echoing through the enclosure, through Roh's very bones. The impact was strong enough to rattle all of Csilla.

Valli darted back with a terrified screech, trying to bury himself in Roh's pocket, despite the fact that he was now a little too big to do so. Roh herself had leaped back, heart pounding in her throat.

'I guess you're not so fearless, after all,' she muttered to the drakeling.

'Well, they're right: that's no ordinary teerah panther,' a familiar deep voice said from the door. 'He – or she – is definitely from up north.'

'What are you doing here, Deodan?' Roh asked, not bothering to stand.

The panther now prowled the edge of the enclosure, snarling aggressively, spit hanging from its yellowed fangs.

'I wanted to see you,' he told her, dropping to the floor beside her, a journal clutched in his hand.

'Well, here I am,' Roh said, trying to keep the anger from her voice. While she had prevented the near-throat slitting between Finn and him, she was still furious that he'd voiced what he had, in a cyren territory of all places.

'I came to apologise,' he said, as though reading her thoughts.

'Oh?' she prompted, fishing the squirming drakeling from her pocket where he'd managed to get stuck.

'I was out of line. I should never have said what I said. And I know it put you in a difficult position.'

'That it did.' Roh only faintly remembered the press of the quartz blade against her skin. She glanced at Deodan's throat, where a very thin line of scabbed, red skin showed.

'I know it's no excuse, but ... I've been struggling with myself lately. I think you've noticed that.'

'I have. I didn't think you wanted to discuss it. Particularly not with a cyren.'

'I didn't want to, not at first. But you're not just a Saddorien, Roh. You're one of us as well.'

*Birthed by a cyren ... Fathered by a water warlock ...* Even as the words echoed in her mind, Roh didn't interrupt her friend; she could feel the pain pouring from him.

'These journals,' he continued, offering her the one he held. 'They've been harder to read than I thought. They're written by a prominent water warlock, who assisted the Warlock Supreme hundreds of years ago.'

'An ancestor of yours?'

'Very possibly. The warlock leadership is usually passed down through generations, but that doesn't mean there isn't the occasional exception. Warlocks aren't as rigid in their traditions as other races. Where there is a need for change, change occurs. So, I can't be sure if I'm related to this particular leader. I'd have to ask —'

'Your mother?'

'Yes. Sybil would know. She takes great pride in such things.'

'And you don't?'

Deodan shrugged. 'I don't think we are always a mirror of those who came before us.'

'I'd like to believe that.' Slowly, Roh took the journal from him, its weight heavier than she expected. 'How many of these are there?' she asked.

'Seven that I managed to carry from the mountain pass. Though I'd wager there are more there.' He grasped her hand around the leather-bound book. 'I want you to read these,' he told her, a note of desperation sharpening his voice.

'I got the opposite impression when I asked you about them earlier today.'

'Was that only this morning?' Deodan murmured, more to himself than to her.

'It was.' Though Roh knew what he meant.

Deodan's hand released hers. 'Will you read them?' he asked quietly.

A tidal wave of thoughts threatened to barrel into Roh, but she kept them at bay by thumbing through the thick pages of the journal. 'If it's important to you, then I will,' she heard herself say.

Deodan's whole body sagged and he looked more at ease than he had in weeks. 'Thank you,' he said, getting to his feet. 'I'll take my leave, then.'

A moment later, Roh was alone with the teerah panther and drakeling once more. Behind the glass, a pair of vicious eyes blinked at her from the darkness and Valli watched the beast warily. Roh pushed aside her tome of laws and instead opened the warlock journal to the first page ...

*Spring has opened Lochloria like one of its numerous blooms. After such a brutal winter, it's a relief to see the sun peeking through the canopies and warming the garden beds. It also means a new influx of students, for which I am grateful. I was sad to see them go, so many of them determined to make an impact in Saddoriel ... Though I'm loath to admit it, I missed the inane questions and our lessons by the stream. Workers have begun the restoration of the quadrangle – ridding it of the vines and dust from disuse. Its pavers shall be golden once more before long —*

·   ·   ·

Roh paused, a memory of her own swimming to the surface. No, not a memory … A vision she'd had during the Rite of Strothos. The scent of pine and mountains wrapping around her, the quiet notes of timber wind chimes … A quadrangle of sandstone pavers lining gardens of emerald grass and trees of yellow wattle, and a babbling stream at its centre. The heart of the scholar's city, flowing with arching walkways and breathtaking architecture … Though Roh had never been there in the flesh, she knew it for what it was – Lochloria in its glory days, a place of peace and learning.

She swallowed the lump in her throat. How could she be homesick for a place she had never been? How could she subdue this haunting desire for what was gone? Her hands traced the words scrawled on the parchment before her and she turned the pages, drinking in the images of the scholar's city. But it wasn't long before the prose that was rich in luxurious detail and patience faded away, and in its place were short, sharp entries and incomplete sentences.

Roh frowned. Had a new author taken over? No, the name was the same, signed in a loopy scrawl at the end of each passage: *Killian*. No, it was news of the lair of bones that darkened the entries, a shadow from afar, sweeping in to swallow the golden sun.

*A former student of mine has been brought to the infirmary in Lochloria. He was a sickly nestling, but after the Warlock Supreme intervened, he recovered for a time. For the protection of his privacy, he will hereon be referred to as Patient Blue. After many years of good quality of life, it seems that Patient Blue has relapsed: tremors rack the whole body. Blotches of skin discoloured.*

*Treatment is ongoing. Confined to infirmary. Too unwell to be moved to more comfortable personal quarters. Will he live?*

*What will forever be known as the Age of Chaos is at last at an end. The Saddorien cyren army has returned to the lair, though who holds victory is unclear to all of us here in Lochloria. What a waste of life. What a horrific piece of our history —*

*It appears we have swapped one tyrant for another. Uniir the Blessed defeated King Asros in The Dawning today. It is a dark hour. Our community in Lochloria fears for the peace here, knowing Uniir's stance on our kind.*

*A small reprieve. Old students – friends, really – returned to our glorious basin here, from the bloody seas of battle. Though their joy was short-lived upon seeing the state of Patient Blue. They deserve happiness after all they have been through.*

*There are rumours about the tempests growing hungrier, more frequent, putting our allies in Saddoriel at risk. One of my former students sent word from the lair that there is talk of the warlocks being behind this change. Why would anyone say such things?*

. . .

*Rumours have reached Lochloria. There are whispers everywhere about the source of the terror tempests and who is to blame. This cannot be the work of water warlocks. These phenomena are bigger than us, they are the will of the gods. At His Supremeness' bidding, I sent word to our scholar counterparts in Csilla. They may have answers for us yet.*

Roh read until her eyes were sore. Her stomach gnawed at her insides as she stood, her spine cracking in several places. She felt weakened, hollowed out from reading, emotionally depleted. No wonder Deodan had behaved the way he had. And she was only a quarter of the way through the first volume. How had Deodan ploughed through so many in such a short amount of time? Even if she had the hours in the day to devote to reading the journals, she wasn't sure she'd have the emotional capacity. With a heavy sigh, she picked up the *Law of the Lair*, that she'd barely touched, suddenly buckling under the weight of all she had to do. She knew the Mercy's Topaz had led her to that book for a reason and she'd abandoned it for the journals.

'*A queen must know the law of the lair better than she knows herself ...*' Delja's warning was never far from Roh's thoughts and she knew she needed to keep the law close, because sooner or later, she would need it to come to her defence. With a final glance at the enclosure, no longer any sign of the teerah panther within, Roh left, the weight of both the past and the future heavy on her shoulders.

Somewhat numb, Roh followed Valli as he scurried up to the eastern wing of Csilla. Night had well and truly fallen, and a trail of laughter echoed from the dining room. Feeling unsteady, Roh pushed open the doors to find Finn Haertel sitting on the floor, with Mora and Sol behind him, plaiting his hair.

His lilac gaze shot to Roh and flashed a warning: *Don't you dare*, he seemed to say.

But at the sight of Valli, the two nestlings abandoned their current task and rushed towards the drakeling, chattering excitedly between themselves. Finn ran a hand through his hair, teasing out the damage the youngsters had done, and got to his feet.

'Not a word,' he muttered to Roh, as she tried to contain the grin on her face. But gods, it felt good to smile in the face of everything she worried about. And Finn being subjected to the whims of the Csillan nestlings was apparently the wholesome remedy she needed.

Harlyn pressed a plate into Roh's hand. 'Come, sit. Have something to eat,' her friend ordered, not unkindly. She took the tomes from beneath Roh's arm and frowned. 'Deodan let you have this?' she asked curiously.

Roh nodded. 'He asked me to read them.'

Harlyn slid the books onto the table, pointedly out of Roh's reach. 'Well, I'm asking you to eat. You look like you're wasting away.'

'She's right,' Yrsa added, pushing a tankard of something in front of Roh.

'Where is Deodan?' Roh asked, scanning the room. It was a common area more than a formal dining one, a place where the head Csillan family could spend time in private. That they were included in its use was an honour, Roh realised. She found that she enjoyed the small, simple joys of Csilla, rather than the stiff formality of Akoris, or the rigid hierarchy and oppression of Saddoriel.

'He's back in the sleeping quarters,' Harlyn supplied, swiping a piece of bread from Roh's plate and munching on it thoughtfully. 'I think he's embarrassed, about earlier, I mean.'

'So he should be,' Finn muttered from where he watched Mora and Sol play with Valli by the crackling fire.

Roh didn't respond. Instead, she sipped at the mead in her tankard and craned her neck, scanning the room for Odi. He was there, in the far corner, hunched over a pile of papers, scribbling away.

'More music for your brothers?' she called.

'Yes,' Odi said, surprised, as he paused to massage his hands. 'Though I don't know if it'll be any good. It's hard when I don't have a piano to test the sounds.'

Roh simply nodded and returned to her food. She knew there was little she could do to help Odi, except to get him through this extended part of the tournament.

'I asked Kezra about a sedative,' Yrsa offered, taking a long draught from her own tankard.

'And?' Roh asked between mouthfuls of pie.

'She said there's a greenhouse in the western wing, and we can help ourselves to whatever we need there. She offered to take us there after we have finished eating.'

Roh raised a brow. 'Did you happen to ask her why she's being so accommodating?'

'I did actually,' Yrsa replied, amused. 'She said that changes need to be made amongst cyrenkind. And perhaps you're the one to make them.'

'Right,' Roh muttered, pushing her plate away. What little appetite she'd had was gone, stolen by the mounting pressure.

Soon after, Kezra appeared and showed them to the greenhouse as promised. Roh didn't know what she'd been expecting, but the large glass house on the edge of the cliff had not been it. Moonlight and jars of valo beetles illuminated the humid space, where rows and rows of garden beds lined the ground, protected from the wind and cold.

'You're after some sort of sleep-inducing herb?' Kezra asked as she led Roh towards the back of the greenhouse.

'Yes,' Roh replied. 'Though herbology isn't my strength. If there's something more effective, by all means let me know.'

Finn cleared his throat. 'There's also another option.'

Roh turned to him. 'Oh?'

'I still have the Strothos vine,' he ventured. 'We could use it to —'

'No.' The word was out of Roh's mouth before she had even thought it. 'No,' she said again, more gently this time. 'I don't want us handling that poison. And I wouldn't inflict that substance on anyone, even a beast.' She took a breath, trying to force away the memory of the drug racing through her body. Roh sought Kezra's gaze again. 'We'll take whatever sedative you have.'

Kezra made a thoughtful sound at the back of her throat. 'Well, are you sure about this?'

Roh paused mid-step, meeting the Csillan leader's gaze. 'Sure? I'm not sure of *anything*, Kezra. I haven't been for a long time now. But the fact is, I need to get the sapphire, and sooner rather than later. So, if you know something I don't …?'

'I wish I did.' Kezra came to a stop before a wall of shelves at the back of the greenhouse. She took a jar from the bottom row and handed it to Roh. 'There's your sedative, a herb called silver boxweed. We only have dried stores, we can't grow it here.'

'Thank you,' she said. 'How do you feed the panther?'

'There's a much smaller door to the enclosure. We slide the food through there.'

Roh nodded. 'When is its next feed due?'

'Tomorrow morning.'

'I'll lace the meat with the boxweed then.'

'Very well,' Kezra said. 'Meet me in the kitchen at dawn.'


Roh didn't sleep that night. Every time she was on the verge of sinking into unconsciousness, she was struck with a new worry, a new fear that sent her spiralling into a whirlpool of chaotic thought. In the dark and early hours of the morning, she left the warmth of her bed and stoked the fire in the living quarters to life. There, she curled up in one of the armchairs before the crackling flames and opened Killian's journal again ...

*Patient Blue continues to decline. We have sought healers from all over the realms. Ashai folk have been permitted to enter our sacred grounds to tend to him. Will continue to monitor his progress.*

*Returned to the little greenhouse today to tend to the herbs and growing enchantments at the bidding of His Supremeness. The marigold flowers are wilting – due to conditions of the greenhouse? Or other variant?*

*Official visit of Uniir the Blessed tomorrow. His Supremeness is anxious, though he will not admit it aloud. Tension is high, though no one will say why. My former students have not left Patient Blue's side until news of the king's visit spread. They departed for Saddoriel this morning, though they have promised to return.*

*I don't know how much longer Patient Blue will be with us.*

*His Majesty arrived via the mirror pool with an entourage. The first thing that struck me was their fashions – he has implemented some mandatory change there. Exposed-backed robes, revealing a new trend sweeping the cyrenkind – tattooed wings at their shoulderblades. Strange.*

*He insisted on visiting our 'temple' before all else. Was displeased to discover Lochloria has no temple; it is a city of scholars, not religion. He has demanded this be rectified immediately, lest we anger the gods further and they rain more terror tempests upon the lair.*

*His Supremeness insisted I keep to the shadows. He is convinced the king will not approve of my treatments on Patient Blue – warlock magic used upon a cyren is sacrilege according to our new king.*

The watery golden light of dawn pulled Roh reluctantly from Killian's harrowing words. Careful not to wake the others, she tugged on her clothes and a light cloak. Valli was waiting for her by the door. Seeing him now, proud and alert, she realised how much he had grown. When he'd hatched from the egg, he'd been the size of a lizard and now … Well, now he was the rough size and weight of a kitten, almost too large for her pocket.

'Come along, then,' she said, opening the door to the hallway.

The drakeling dashed out, wings flaring, far more eager than Roh was to take on the new day.

Together, they made their way to the kitchen, where Kezra stood carving a giant slab of venison from a carcass, her apron spattered with blood.

'You brought the boxweed?' she asked, intent on her task.

Roh approached the workbench and placed the jar by the chopping board.

Kezra wiped her hands on a rag and examined the jar. 'How much were you thinking we'd use?'

Roh raised a brow. 'All of it.'

'All?'

Roh ran a hand through her dishevelled hair. 'Have you seen the size of that thing?'

'And if it doesn't work? Then you've used up all our stores.'

'Then it wouldn't have worked in smaller doses anyway,' Roh countered. 'And I'm assuming silver boxweed isn't the only sedative in your greenhouse? You have things healers would use, if need be?'

'I will not have you empty our supplies entirely, Queen of Bones.'

'Let's hope it doesn't come to that, then,' Roh replied evenly. 'Now, what I was thinking is that we'd cut a sort of pocket or hole in the meat, where we could lace it thoroughly. That way, the panther won't detect it, at least not until it's already halfway through eating. What do you think?'

'I think it sounds like you've done this before.'

'Not quite,' Roh murmured.

They made quick work of lacing the drug throughout, Kezra going so far as to season the cut with sea salt.

Roh shot her an incredulous glance.

But Kezra simply said: 'Everyone eats well if the meal comes from my kitchen.'

It wasn't long before Saddorien and Csillan found

themselves standing before the enclosure of the teerah panther, the beast nowhere in sight, but the claw tracks through the glass deeper than ever.

'There's the door for feeding.' Kezra pointed to a small slot in the larger window, by the main door. 'The key you have unlocks that, too.'

'And I just slide the food in?'

Kezra baulked. 'Not with your bare hands! Gods, have you lost your mind?' She went to the corner of the room and retrieved a long-handled spade of sorts. 'Use this.'

Roh went about positioning the venison on the flat blade and crouched by the smaller hatch. Valli eyed her curiously, but she ignored him. Taking the key from around her neck, she slid it into the lock. The click that sounded as she turned it in place seemed incredibly loud, but nothing moved within the enclosure. Not a breath of air disturbed the foliage within.

Biting her lower lip, Roh lifted up the flap of the door and slid the game inside on the spade, not taking her eyes off the jungle-like trees and shrubs. He or she was in there somewhere … watching. Roh could feel it. She manoeuvred the venison off the blade and —

Roh jolted with a cry as Valli darted inside the enclosure, intent on the meat.

'No!' Roh shrieked. 'Valli, *no!*'

But the foolish drakeling seemed to have forgotten his state of terror from the previous day. He trotted around the game, sniffing delicately, as though he had all the time in the realms.

'No, no, no,' Roh muttered, trying to pull the venison

back in her direction, but she'd already half shucked it off the blade. 'Valli,' she hissed. 'Get back here!'

The damned creature wasn't moving. He paid her cries of dismay no heed.

'Gods,' Roh cursed, lurching to her feet, snatching the key from the smaller hatch and putting it to the lock in the main door —

'Don't be brash!' Kezra cried, making a lunge for her. 'Don't open —'

Roh slid the key into place, and fully intent on charging into the enclosure to seize the idiotic drakeling, she began to turn it.

Without warning, Valli was on the safe side of the glass again.

'What in the realms …' He stood by her boots, stretching his delicate wings, to where he'd been mere seconds ago, inside the deathtrap. 'You little …'

There was a scraping sound as Kezra pulled the empty spade back out, closed the hatch firmly in place again and dabbed the perspiration from her brow with the back of her sleeve.

'Lock it,' she commanded, her voice tight.

Roh did as the Csillan leader bid, a bead of sweat trickling between her shoulders. The armpits of her shirt were damp.

Kezra stared at her in disbelief. 'You were truly going to charge inside there?'

Dazed, Roh looked from the key still clutched in her hands and shrugged sheepishly. 'I … I suppose I was.'

Shaking her head, Kezra made to leave.

'What now?' Roh called after her.

'Now? Now, you wait.'

Without her books or Kezra's comments to distract her, time passed slowly in front of the panther enclosure. Roh was doing her best to ignore Valli, who seemed determined to gain her affection in light of her scoldings. She still couldn't believe the little fool had done that, nor could she believe what she herself had almost done to save him. There had been no sign of the teerah panther, not a flicker of movement. The slab of venison still sat in the dirt untouched.

*Is it watching me?* Roh wondered, straining her eyes as she tried to peer through the dark leaves and dense foliage within. *Does it know what we did?* Roh knew the notion was foolish; there was no way the beast could tell what they'd done.

As she watched the enclosure, her eyelids began to feel heavy and her head began to nod. The sleepless night was catching up with her, as were the draining journal entries she'd burned through.

*Gods, there's just so much ...* Roh blinked, fighting to keep her eyes open. A massive yawn shook her whole body, and before she knew it, sleep dragged her under.


'Roh.' Someone was shaking her. A large, gentle hand on her shoulder. 'Roh, wake up.'

*Finn.*

Her eyes flew open.

'What are you doing?' he asked, his brows knitted together in concern.

Roh pulled herself upright, realising that she'd fallen asleep with her back against the cold wall. 'I …' She spotted Valli with his face pressed to the glass.

The bait was gone.

Heart surging, Roh lurched to her feet and staggered to the enclosure. 'He's taken it,' she said, fumbling for the key around her neck with shaking hands.

'The drugged meat?' Finn asked, following her to the window in two long strides and scanning the enclosure. 'How long ago?'

Roh fitted the key to the lock of the main door. 'It … it can't have been long,' she said. 'This is my only chance.'

'Roh, you don't know how long you've been asleep, do you?'

'I … not long, I swear.'

But Finn was already shaking his head. 'It's too dangerous.'

'That's all the silver boxweed Kezra has. The panther will be unconscious for *hours*.' Roh could hear the desperation in her voice. How could she have let herself fall asleep like that? The gods-damned *Willow's Sapphire* was at stake. How many more mistakes would she —

'I'm not letting you —'

'You are not my keeper, Finn Haertel.' Her words were hot with anger, both at him and herself.

'I was going to say, I'm not letting you go in *alone*.'

'Oh.'

Finn swung his crossbow from his back and loaded it. 'Yes, *oh*.'

Roh's mouth went dry as she turned the key. 'Are we really doing this?'

Finn met her gaze, his own eyes brimming with challenge. 'You tell me.'

Roh steeled herself, and unlocked the door.

It was cooler inside than she expected, the crisp air kissing her skin in a wave of goosebumps. Valli barged past her feet and went to the spot where the bait had been laid, sniffing vigorously before creeping into the dense foliage.

Roh motioned to Finn to follow, not daring to speak aloud. She forced one foot in front of the other, her knees threatening to buckle beneath her. There was still no sign of the teerah panther.

*This is either genius or the stupidest thing I've ever done,* she thought as she crept after her drakeling, leaves crackling beneath her boots.

The enclosure was larger than she'd imagined. It stretched back as far as she could see, lush with deep-green leaves and the rich scent of fresh earth. But Roh wasn't sure it mattered. She knew better than most that a large cage was still a cage.

Something snapped up ahead and Roh froze. Finn instantly halted behind her. She heard him adjust his grip on his crossbow, but she held up a clenched fist as he'd done during their journey from Akoris.

*Where's Valli?* Roh scanned the dark patches of leaf litter, her heart hammering in her throat.

Finn's arm came over her shoulder and he pointed silently, as though he'd read her thoughts. Her eyes latched onto Valli, whose tail poked out from behind a large rock. Slowly and quietly, Roh and Finn approached him, careful not to disturb the branches around them as they moved deeper into the dense foliage.

A shuddering breath escaped Roh.

Valli stood before the cut of venison.

Which was utterly whole; untouched.

The click of Finn's crossbow sounded, but Roh turned, her vision blurring as she gripped his arm. *'Run.'*

As the word left her lips in a ragged gasp, a roar tore through the enclosure, rattling the very ground beneath their feet, flooding her insides with icy terror.

The teerah panther had been waiting for them.

It had *known.*

Without even latching their eyes on the beast, Roh and Finn crashed through the trees and bushes, in a burst of primal survival instinct. *Run.* It was the only way they'd survive the beast. Fallen sticks and reaching branches clawed at their exposed skin as they hurled themselves back towards the exit.

'Faster,' Roh hissed, her hand still clamped over Finn's arm, almost hauling him through the underbrush herself.

Heavy paws pounded the ground behind them and the Jaktaren's crossbow bounced uselessly on his back as they sprinted.

Roh glanced back, nearly sending herself sprawling to her death in the process. She caught a glimpse of a blue shimmering reflection. The sapphire. But there was no way she could stop, no way she could retrieve it without certain death.

Had it been a stupid moral clause to let the beast live? She wasn't sure Finn's crossbow bolts would bring it down, even if she allowed him to fire.

She staggered through the jungle, shoving the Jaktaren in front of her. Roh could only pray that Valli was close.

A powerful rush of wind swept behind her, and she could feel the cold air on her exposed back —

The panther had taken a swipe at her; she could feel the two halves of her shredded shirt flapping over her skin.

The glass barrier came into view and Roh nearly sobbed at the sight, fear erupting through her like the raging river in the gorge.

*Nearly there*, she told herself as the teerah panther let out another enraged roar, the sound rumbling in Roh's body.

The door was open.

And Roh and Finn threw themselves through it, slamming it closed behind them with all their might. An enormous *bang* echoed through the enclosure and the chamber as the teerah panther slammed against the glass.

Roh lunged for the lock with her key, turning it just in time.

Finn was already on the far side of the chamber, his back to the wall. 'Gods,' he huffed, sliding to the floor.

Roh spotted Valli on the safe side of the glass and heaved a sigh of relief. His head was tilted in curiosity, calmly watching the teerah panther tear through the enclosure, swiping entire branches from trees, snarling viciously, its spittle foaming at its fangs.

With her pulse still pounding furiously, Roh went to Finn on wobbly legs and slid down the wall to sit beside him. She rested her elbows on her knees and let her head fall into her hands.

'You're bleeding,' Finn said quietly.

As he spoke the words, Roh felt the warm trickle down her exposed back and the sting of a fresh cut. She leaned forward, exposing the wound to him. 'Is it bad?'

'You'll live,' he told her.

Roh ran a hand through her hair and huffed a dark laugh. 'Thanks for your concern.'

'It's a scratch. You've had worse. Best get it cleaned though, can't have it getting infected like Harlyn's.'

But Roh's whole body felt like stone and she couldn't seem to force herself to move. She stared at the enclosure, the teerah panther still prowling within, mad with rage. There were new scratches down the glass and the foliage within looked like it had been ravaged by a terror tempest.

'What do we do now?' she murmured, her voice as small as she felt.

Finn got to his feet and offered her his hand. 'We try again,' he said.

# CHAPTER SIXTEEN

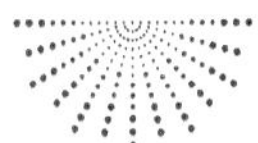

'Flo told me there's a mead hall, just north of the bridge,' Harlyn announced in their chambers later that evening, watching Valli bask in front of the fire yet again.

'And?' Roh asked, brows raised. Her recent defeat had left her feeling raw and hollow. Finn had filled the others in while Deodan had seen to the gash on her back. It stung badly enough to make her breath whistle between her teeth, but the Jaktaren had been right – it was just a scratch.

'And I think we should go,' Harlyn finished, demanding Roh's attention by placing her good hand on her hip.

'Har ...' Roh started, readying herself to launch into a lecture on how time was of the essence, how every waking moment that she spent not trying to retrieve the sapphire was a moment wasted, but … The words died on her lips. She was exhausted, down to her very bones.

'What's one drink?' Odi interjected from where he was mending yet another hole in his gloves.

Roh scanned the faces of her companions, each as eager as the last for a reprieve. Even Haertel. Perhaps they *could* all use a night, just one, where they could escape this quest of hers?

A grin broke out across Harlyn's face as she saw Roh's expression soften. 'Is that a yes?'

Roh caved. 'One drink,' she said, a smile tugging at the corners of her mouth.


The mead hall the Csillans frequented was indeed north of the mighty bridge, located in a large cavern of sorts that overlooked the gorge. Dozens of fire pits blazed, surrounded by comfortable chairs and convenient side tables, while the hum of warm conversation buzzed in the air. At the centre of it all was a circular bar where a young Csillan boy, one Roh had seen during the tempest monitoring, was serving tankards of foaming, cold mead.

Floralin spotted them from across the way and waved them over. 'Glad you could make it, Saddoriens. Kez and I thought you might need to see the lighter side of Csilla.'

'You're right about that,' Yrsa said, accepting the tankard being offered and taking a long draught from the foamy top.

Roh murmured her thanks to the Csillan who handed her a drink as Floralin introduced them to one of the more prominent clans. The cyrens eyed her crown of bones warily, but peppered Roh with questions and observations about Saddoriel. She listened politely, answering where she could.

*These will be my people one day*, she told herself, doing her best to listen to their stories and laugh at their jokes. However, after a time, she took a few steps back, allowing Harlyn to take over the centre of attention. She did it so easily and with much more joy in her heart than Roh could manage at the moment. As the evening wore on, Roh herself was happy to fade a little into the background and watch the night unfold as she indulged in the crisp mead that flowed freely from the bar. With the Csillans suitably engaged, Roh found a free fire pit and sank into one of the comfortable chairs, the woody scent of smoke drifting around her, the glow of the flickering flames warming her cheeks. From there, she watched her companions fondly, unable to stop herself reflecting upon just how far they had come since crossing the threshold into the realms beyond Talon's Reach.

The scrape of a chair sounded and Yrsa was beside Roh, handing her a fresh tankard.

'Harlyn's enjoying herself,' she said by way of greeting, jutting her chin towards Roh's fellow bone cleaner, who had amassed an eager audience to her wild tales.

'She's always been able to make friends quickly.'

'Friends, is it?' Yrsa wiggled her brows, and nodded to where Harlyn was unwrapping her bandages and showing off her scar to a rather handsome Csillan.

Roh couldn't help grinning. 'She likes having a lot of friends.'

'Good. She should enjoy herself.' Yrsa clinked her tankard against Roh's, so that mead sloshed over the side. 'Here's to Harlyn's many friendships.'

Roh laughed.

'What are we toasting?' Odi asked as he approached, holding his half-gloved hands to the fire to warm his fingers.

Roh drank deeply. 'Harlyn's admirers,' she told him.

*Was that hurt that flashed in Odi's eyes just now?* she wondered. She'd known that the master musician had become close with her childhood friend, but she hadn't realised … She shook her head. Perhaps she was reading too much into it.

'And what about you two?' Odi asked Roh and Yrsa. 'Any admirers in your sights?'

Roh felt herself slide down into her chair slightly, but luckily, Yrsa chuckled.

'I only have eyes for one cyren, and she's back in Saddoriel,' she told him.

'Piri, right?' Odi said. 'You haven't told us much about her.'

The Jaktaren raised a single brow. 'You haven't asked.'

'Point taken,' Roh replied. 'How long have you been together? What's she like?'

Yrsa's entire face softened as she considered Roh's questions. 'Six years,' she said quietly. 'A drop in the ocean of a cyren's lifetime, and it still won't be enough.' Yrsa took a long swig from her tankard.

'A first and last love, I know it in my bones. As for what she's like, she's *stubborn*. More stubborn than me, even more stubborn than Finn —'

'*That's* saying something,' Odi quipped.

Roh snorted. 'I'll drink to that.'

'What exactly are we drinking to?' came a familiar voice.

Finn slipped into the vacant seat on the other side of Roh. His hair had come loose from its tie, hanging messily about his face, and he slouched back in the chair, holding his mug of beer casually in his lap. Roh had never seen him look so relaxed in all their travels together.

'Oh this and that,' Yrsa replied.

Finn didn't press the matter, seeming content to sip his mead and stare into the flames blazing from the pit, crossing his legs at the ankle.

'What about you, Odi?' Yrsa nodded to the human. 'Any admirers?'

He huffed a laugh. 'You mean on this swoon-worthy quest, surrounded by the realm's most cunning cyrens? I think not.'

Yrsa shrugged. 'For what it's worth, I think Tess might have had a little crush on you, back in Saddoriel.'

'What?'

Yrsa wiggled her eyebrows again. 'She was always talking about you. *Odi this, Odi that ...*'

'Nonsense,' Odi said.

'Don't believe me, then.' Yrsa sighed. 'Do you have someone back home?'

Odi's expression turned far away for a moment. 'Not

anymore.'

That piqued Roh's interest. 'So there was someone?'

Odi gave her a hard look. 'There were a few people, if you must know. I'm actually quite the catch where I'm from.'

Yrsa laughed again and stood to knock her tankard against Odi's. 'Of course you are. The *Prince of Melodies*, chased by Jaktaren and girls alike.'

Odi simply drank.

Roh and Finn watched their exchange, thoroughly amused. But as though sensing the questioning might head in their direction, Finn asked Roh, 'Where's Valli?'

'I left him sleeping in front of the fire in our chambers,' Roh told him. Her drakeling's name on the Jaktaren's lips sounded oddly comfortable, and she was reminded with a strange swoop of her stomach that it was Finn who had found the name that the little beast was content with.

'He's sleeping a lot,' Finn observed, taking another swig of his drink.

'It's because he's growing,' Yrsa explained. 'Haven't you noticed?'

Finn shrugged. 'I don't know. It's hard to tell when I see him every day.'

Roh knew what he meant, but she had been determined to watch the drakeling carefully as time passed, mindful of anything that might tell her he missed the sea or needed something she couldn't give him. She had noted the small changes in him, how as each day passed, his claws didn't seem too big for him.

'He's growing alright,' Yrsa declared. 'Who knows how big he'll get.'

Roh was transported back to the Gilded Plains when Yrsa had first discovered she'd stolen the drake egg. *'Can you imagine ...'* the highborn had said, her voice full of wonder. *'Having a sea drake at your side ...'* Remembering those words now, Roh's chest swelled with a hopeful sense of pride. Who knew what the future held for them all, but the image of her with a fully grown Valli at her side was a powerful one.

Roh and the two Jaktaren sat in comfortable silence for a time, while the revelry of the hall continued around them, the conversations growing louder with each passing moment. Eventually, Harlyn stumbled up to them.

'Guess what?' she said eagerly, her good arm linked with that of the handsome Csillan she'd been with earlier.

From the corner of her eye, Roh saw Odi stiffen slightly, but she couldn't help the grin that broke across her face. 'What?'

'Mattias says there are hot pools just beyond the hall.' Harlyn glanced up at the broad-shouldered Csillan, almost batting her lashes.

'Did he now?' Roh ventured, sizing up the poor sod. If Harlyn had him in her sights, he had no chance.

But the Csillan nodded enthusiastically. 'Only a ten-minute walk or so from here, if you care to join, Queen of Bones.'

Roh frowned. That was Deodan's title for her. Just how many cyrens had he been speaking to? And what about? She scanned the hall. *Where* is *the warrior warlock?* Roh spotted him instantly; he stood out with his hands resting on the cutlasses as he spoke to Kezra. They were too far away for Roh to catch anything they were saying, but they seemed to be in deep, serious discussion.

'Roh?' Harlyn prompted.

'Hmm?' she replied, dragging her eyes away from Deodan and the Csillan leader.

'The hot pools?'

'Oh. Right.' Roh started, looking to the Jaktaren for input.

Finn simply shrugged. 'So long as there's more mead there.'

'There is,' Mattias reassured him.

'I'll give it a miss,' Yrsa said.

'Fair enough,' Roh replied. 'Let's see these pools, then.'

Swiping a bottle of liquor from the bar, Odi agreed to join them as well. It wasn't long before he was swaying on his feet as he spoke to one of the Csillan choir singers. He loudly invited her and her friends along and they happily agreed.

Mattias led the group up several narrow, rocky paths.

As they walked, something fluttered by Roh's ear and she jumped, her hand instantly shooting up to bat whatever it was away.

Finn caught her by the wrist. 'It's just a bird,' he said with quiet amusement.

And it was; a *tiny* bird at that, with bright stripes of yellow beneath its wings. It was a dainty little thing, darting between their group, soon joined by two – no, three – more. Roh watched them curiously as they followed the small entourage up the path.

Mattias glanced back at them and his face fell.

'What's wrong?' Roh asked.

'Those are harvester canaries,' he told her, his voice low, as though the tiny creatures were listening. 'When they follow someone …' he trailed off.

'When they follow someone *what*?' Roh pressed.

'It means death is near,' Mattias finished, his throat bobbing.

Roh blinked at him. 'Says who?'

'It's Csillan lore. The harvesters have graced our gorges for millennia. It is said that they're the shepherds of death, of its god.'

Beside Roh, Finn snorted.

Mattias shot him a glare before continuing up the path, putting as much distance between the harvester canaries and him as possible.

'What?' Finn caught Roh's stare. 'You don't actually believe such superstitious nonsense?'

Roh shrugged, ignoring the goosebumps that had rushed across her arms at Mattias' words.

Finn shook his head in disbelief. 'They're scavengers,' he said with a light laugh. 'They're hoping we drop food.'

But Roh couldn't help watching the little birds flit between them, a darker feeling, a foreboding of sorts, seeming to beat along with their wings.

It wasn't long before she spotted ribbons of steam rising beyond the rocks, into the night air. Pools of dark water greeted them, and as Roh dipped her fingers to the surface, she realised. 'We-we don't have spare clothes,' she stammered.

'Doesn't matter,' one of the Csillan singers declared, already stripping off her outer layers. 'Just keep your small clothes on.'

Roh shot Harlyn an incredulous look, but her friend was easing her arm out of her sling and Mattias was helping her.

Finn's shirt slipped from his shoulders and every thought emptied from Roh's head. The moonlight cast a soft glow across Finn's tanned skin, highlighting the savage letter *C* marring the flesh of his bicep and the thick slash across his carved abdomen. Roh's mouth went dry as she remembered the heat of his skin under her touch back in the alley of Akoris.

For a moment, Finn's eyes lingered where her fingers had stilled at her buttons, an intensity to his gaze that made Roh's toes curl. She'd never undressed in front of a man before ... A thrill rushed through her at the thought and she wished she'd paid more attention to the stories Harlyn had told her in the past. But Finn looked away, considering the pool. Roh bit her lip, her mind racing. He *had* been staring at her, hadn't he? She chastised herself. Why did she care? She had bigger things to worry about than some male cyren – than *Finn Haertel* – watching her.

'Are we getting in or what?' he asked, pushing his trousers down over his long legs, revealing dark undershorts and muscular thighs.

Roh forced her gaze elsewhere, praying he hadn't noticed her staring. She heard a splash and gathered that he'd got in, as everyone else had, she realised. She'd almost forgotten that the others were there. Roh made quick work of her shirt and pants, leaving her undergarments on, before easing herself into the heat-soaked water.

'Careful,' Finn cautioned from a ledge. 'It's slippery there.' He held out a hand for her, and without thinking she took it, a charged energy shooting through her as their skin touched. He guided her into the pool with care, and soon she found herself sitting beside him, submerged up to her neck. A deep flush crept up Roh's face and she was desperate to look anywhere but at Finn. All around her, Csillans were laughing and passing around flasks of more liquor. Odi and Harlyn weren't far away, but each of them was more than occupied with their respective groups of admirers. So it was just her and the Jaktaren.

'I've been thinking,' Finn said quietly.

'Sounds dangerous,' Roh quipped.

An elbow gently nudged her side. 'I was thinking I'd like to read these journals that you and the warlock are obsessed with.'

Whatever Roh had been expecting Finn to say, it hadn't been that. 'Why?'

Finn twisted to face her, the ends of his hair damp and droplets of water glistening on his exposed shoulders. 'Is that so surprising to you?'

'No ... I just ...' Roh stammered. They were so incredibly close that she couldn't think straight. 'Why?' she asked again, wincing inwardly at how stupid she sounded.

'You promised to share the knowledge of the *Tome* with me,' Finn said. 'Why not the journals?'

'That's not an answer,' Roh replied, training her gaze on his.

Finn sighed, letting his fingers trail across the surface of the water, ignoring the laughter around them. 'I think it's important to learn from the mistakes of the past. And the Scouring of Lochloria, despite whatever I feel about the warlock, was a mistake. A cruel, unnecessary mistake.'

'It was once a haven,' she said, watching the patterns Finn was making in the water.

'You truly saw it, didn't you? During the rite?' he asked.

'I did. It was beautiful.'

'All the more reason for me to read the journals. I want to understand what they lost.' A soft determination lined Finn's face.

'Very well,' Roh said. 'Though, you should ask Deodan first.'

'Aren't you the leader of our entourage?' Finn asked, his brows raised.

'Not that you'd ever admit it,' Roh quipped. 'But the journals belong to Deodan's people. It would be respectful to ask his permission first, don't you think?'

To Roh's surprise, Finn nodded. 'You're right.'

Roh nearly fell off the ledge she was sitting on. 'Can I get that in writing?'

Finn huffed a laugh. 'Absolutely not.'

Roh hadn't realised how much she liked the sound of his laugh, nor how much more she liked it when she was the cause of it. She was still thinking about it when she noticed how few cyrens were left in the pools around them. As time had ticked by, more and more of them had retreated back to the hall, or their own quarters, it seemed. There was no sign of Odi, nor the Csillan choir singers he'd been with. Roh was surprised to find Harlyn in the process of leaving.

'You're going?' she called.

'I'm turning into a prune,' Harlyn retorted, holding her dry clothes against her, her teeth chattering. 'You coming?'

Roh swallowed the lump in her throat, careful not to look at Finn at her side. 'I'm going to stay a little longer.'

'Suit yourself.'

One by one, the remaining cyrens left and Roh became increasingly aware of Finn's presence as he pushed off the ledge and swam lazy laps. His toned arms carved through the water effortlessly and for a second, Roh was back in Akoris, as those same strong arms pulled her from the drug-laced hollow. A ball of nervous energy settled in the pit of her stomach as she watched him. They had never been alone before, not like this. She didn't know why it mattered so much to her, but it did. Unsure of what to do with herself, Roh peered up. And gasped at the sight before her.

Darkness blanketed the sky, but for the glimmering smatter of stars across its canvas. During their travels, Roh had marvelled at the night's sky often, at all the wonders it held, but now ... The view of the realms from Csilla was somehow more vibrant, purer. There were millions more stars in the sky tonight, a shining streak of them right down the centre of the world. She didn't remember getting to her feet on the ledge, but there she was, her chin tilted to the moon, her undergarments clinging to her, water dripping from her hair.

Water surged around her and suddenly Finn was there on the ledge beside her. 'Beautiful, isn't it?' he said, following her gaze into the night.

'It is,' she breathed. All at once, she was aware of every single inch of her own skin, wet and chilled against the cool air, and she was aware of him, so close their arms almost brushed against one another. *Does he realise it, too?* She didn't dare look at him, didn't dare drag her gaze away from the shimmering stars, lest he read the thoughts plain on her face.

The reach of a hand was all it would take to close the gap between them, a single step.

Roh turned to him, ready to —

'Roh!' Harlyn shouted from somewhere down the path. 'You *have to see this!* Mattias is opening a bottle of Vallian wine!' Her next words slurred slightly as she continued to yell. 'Dunno what it is, but apparently it's *really* good!'

Roh caught Finn's eye. 'I suppose we'd better go.'

Finn held her gaze for a moment longer before he nodded, a muscle twitching in his jaw. 'Or Harlyn will bring the gorge down.'

Roh could have sworn she saw a shadow of disappointment cross his face.

# CHAPTER SEVENTEEN

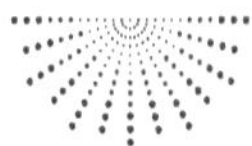

The next day, Roh visited the teerah-panther enclosure again. She didn't know for which reason: to rid herself of thoughts of the half-naked Jaktaren or to figure out how to obtain the Willow's Sapphire. She sat before the scratched glass, watching the enraged beast within stalk up and down, the gem gleaming in its gold collar, taunting her.

'If you're just going to sit here and mope, you may as well train,' Yrsa said from the doorway.

Roh noted the determined gleam in her friend's eyes.

'We can do hand-to-hand combat and self-defence down here,' Yrsa said. 'And there's a clearing by the gorge that would make a decent sling-practice spot. But I'll not allow you to lose the skills you gained in Akoris.'

'Yrsa …' Roh started reluctantly.

But Yrsa shook her head. 'You must *always* be ready

for anything. Learning, bettering yourself, it never stops. As future queen, you should strive for that.'

Roh motioned to the enclosure. 'In order to be queen, I need to deal with this first.'

'And you will,' Yrsa countered. 'But staring at the glass won't do you any good. You need to move, you need to get your blood pumping.'

Grudgingly, Roh got to her feet. 'You're a Jaktaren through and through, aren't you?'

Yrsa grinned. 'I like to think so. Now, feet apart, fists up. Let's go.'

Roh hated to admit it, but Yrsa was right. It was good to get her body moving, to draw herself out of her shell and relish the physical contact of blocking blows and sidestepping attacks. Yrsa ran through several drills and exercises with her, each harder and faster than the last.

'Good!' the Jaktaren exclaimed as Roh successfully dodged a punch to the kidney and returned the attack with an elbow to Yrsa's face, which she blocked easily, of course. 'Again.'

Roh's shirt was damp with sweat and she tried to stay light on her feet as they circled each other.

'Don't wait for me to attack, don't hesitate,' Yrsa encouraged.

Roh lunged for her, feinting a blow left and swinging right.

'Good!' Yrsa beamed.

Roh mopped her brow with the sleeve of her shirt. 'Who taught you all this, anyway?' she panted.

'You know we go through numerous stages of

training,' Yrsa said, pausing to let Roh catch her breath. 'But it was my aunt who really instilled in me the importance of constant practice, constant improvement.'

'The same aunt who taught you the sling?'

'The very one. Aunt Winslow.'

Roh was grateful that Yrsa had the foresight to bring a canteen of water with her. She passed it to Roh, who took several large gulps, the cold liquid sliding down her parched throat.

'I've been meaning to ask you for ages,' Roh said, handing the canteen back. 'Why were you raised by your aunt? Where are your parents?'

Yrsa took a measured sip. 'They died when I was young.'

A pang of pain hit Roh's gut. 'I'm so sorry.'

'I was only three, so I don't remember much of them. It was an accident. They were overseeing a remodel of the music theatre and part of it collapsed. Three other cyrens died as well. There was an inquest and such, but there was no one to blame. The scaffolding gave way and … Well, you can imagine the rest. My mother's sister, Winslow, took me in. She had no family of her own.'

'I get the sense that she's different from the rest of the elders,' Roh ventured.

Yrsa smiled. 'She's the youngest on the council, but old enough to have witnessed much during her time there. Since I was little, she's told me of the corruption within the council, about their system that rewards those at the top and crushes those at the bottom.'

'Finn told me of your original plans, back in Akoris, to

win the tournament,' Roh said. 'Was that your aunt's idea?'

'Finn and Winslow's, yes,' Yrsa replied. 'But I want you to know, that's not what I wanted. And certainly not now. My duty is to you. I signed the contract, I gave you my word.'

'Your word is your bond, I remember.' Roh reached out and squeezed her friend's shoulder. 'I trust you,' she told her. 'I doubt you'd be in here harassing me to train if you had some ulterior motive.'

Yrsa laughed. 'Good. Now quit stalling. Your left hook needs work.'

Later, with their slings in hand, Yrsa took Roh to the clearing by the gorge she had mentioned. They were surprised to find Finn and Odi already there, hunched over Finn's beloved crossbow.

Odi glanced from Finn to Yrsa. 'You two are definitely cut from the same cloth. Not all of us live to train, you know.'

Finn clapped Odi on the shoulder. 'You'll thank me later.'

'Where's Harlyn? And Deodan?' Roh asked.

'Harlyn is off with one of her many Csillan suitors,' Odi announced, his voice slightly strained. 'And Deodan's still reading those journals somewhere.' He turned to Finn. 'How's this?'

Finn stepped back and eyed Odi's stance critically. 'Not terrible,' he said.

'So I'm getting better, then?'

Finn shrugged. 'If by "getting better" you mean you

can hold a crossbow more upright than one of my dead ancestors, then yes.'

Yrsa laughed. 'High praise indeed, Odi,' she offered.

The human simply rolled his eyes and aimed the weapon.

For the next few hours, they lost themselves to the rhythm of training. Roh was pleased to find that her sling skills continued to improve under Yrsa's guidance. The Jaktaren made for a patient teacher, that was for sure. Throughout their lessons, Roh couldn't help but glance across at the other Jaktaren, who remained fully clothed, much to her disappointment. Though that didn't stop her watching him direct Odi through a range of drills. There was an easiness between human and cyren that warmed Roh's heart —

'Are you listening?' Yrsa demanded.

Roh's head snapped back to her instructor. 'Yes. Absolutely.'

Yrsa snorted.

'I'm done,' Odi called out, dropping to the ground, sweat gleaming on his brow.

'Just as well,' Finn quipped. 'You're hardly helping me stay in shape. Yrs, want to go a round?'

Yrsa gave Roh a friendly shove towards Odi before bounding towards Finn, snatching Odi's discarded practice sword from the ground.

With a sigh of relief, Roh sat down beside Odi. 'Let them have their fun.'

Odi peeled off his half-gloves and began massaging his hands.

'Are you in a lot of pain today?' Roh asked.

'A little. Sometimes the exercise is good, other times it aggravates them. The condition has a mind of its own.'

'Are you out of the treatment Incana made for you?'

'Nearly. There's a bit left.'

Roh nodded. 'I'll ask Kezra if she has something.'

'No need.' Odi smiled. 'Harlyn already did. She uses something similar on her arm. Kezra said she's having some made for us.'

'That's good of her.'

'Harlyn's a good person.'

Roh hid a smile. So she hadn't been reading into things at the mead hall. 'I was talking about Kezra,' she said.

'Oh.'

'Your secret's safe with me.' Roh elbowed him playfully.

'I don't know what you're talking about.'

'You're a terrible liar, Odalis Arrowood.'

Odi laughed. 'You'd think I'd have learned a thing or two, surrounded by so many cyrens.'

'Perhaps you're just a slow learner.'

'Perhaps.'

Roh glanced across the clearing to where Yrsa and Finn sparred viciously. 'Should we leave these two hot heads to it?'

'Definitely,' Odi said, getting to his feet and offering Roh a hand up. 'Any longer and you might start drooling again.'

Roh glanced at the cheeky grin on Odi's face, an

answering smile tugging at the corners of her mouth. 'I don't know what you're talking about,' she said.

With the help of the others, Roh attempted to drug the beast with other supplies from the greenhouse three more times over the following days, but each try was a failure worse than the last, only succeeding in aggravating the creature further. And yet, she still didn't want to kill him, if that was even possible. She couldn't explain it any more than that. There was something within her that was outraged at the very suggestion, which was floated aloud more than once by her companions. With Kezra, she had discussed the gold of the panther's collar, remembering her own circlet breaking in two so long ago now. Kezra had told her the same sort of power had soldered the collar, so an ancient sort of magic is what it would take to break it.

As each new day dawned, Roh was all too aware of the time passing. She couldn't stay in Csilla forever; another gem awaited her in Lochloria. On the cusp of another evening, after training with Yrsa all afternoon, Roh sat with Valli in front of the teerah-panther cage again, one of the warlock journals open in her lap as she stared into the enclosure. Valli patrolled the glass, taunting the beast within by flaring his wings and bursting into sudden runs across the open space. Roh watched him with a distant sense of amusement. Yrsa was right, the little menace was certainly growing. In a matter of weeks, he'd gone from the size of a small gecko, to that of an overfed house cat.

Though the drakeling didn't seem overly aware of his change in size, still insisting on sitting upon Roh's shoulder.

With a sigh, Roh returned to the heavy journal.

*His Supremeness is hiding something from me. I know he means to protect me, to spare me from pain, but the ignorance is killing me. I thought I would feel relief to be home, but the same darkness clouds across our scholar's city. There are rumours of lessons being outlawed and warlock children being smuggled from the territory. Something is coming, I can taste it in the air ...*

Roh read on.

*He's gone mad. He came rushing into my rooms in the wee hours of the morning, sprouting absolute nonsense about the Pool of Weeping. I tried to soothe him, but he was too incensed. I've never seen him in such a way before. I made him a calming tea, which he threw out the window. A flask of His Supremeness' best liquor went untouched as well. He was making such noise I feared he would wake the whole city, and if His Supremeness saw Eadric like that —*

Roh froze. All she could do was blink at the name that had been mentioned so casually.

*Eadric.*

She traced her trembling fingers over the letters, unsure if she was imagining such a thing. But there it was again, a few paragraphs down.

*Eadric has not relented with his ramblings about the pool. The others are encouraging him, which is not helpful —*

'It can't be you,' Roh murmured, her talons still on her father's name. This Eadric was not her father. Warlocks didn't live that long, and if he was alive at that time, then it couldn't be the same Eadric who fathered her. That sound, practical knowledge didn't stop her skin from crawling, and didn't quell the compulsion to read on.

*If what Eadric says about the pool is true, then to expose the truth would be dangerous to our kind, given how much power the cyrens already have —*

A deafening roar shook the entire enclosure, and Roh jumped, dropping the journal to the floor. Her head snapped up, immediately spotting the teerah panther pacing aggressively within, white foam at its fangs, snarling as though it was in agony. Anticipation seemed to brew around the beast, as though it was waiting for something, something Roh couldn't sense. With a final glare in her direction, its silvery-black coat disappeared into the foliage and left a trail of carnage in its wake – trampled branches and broken trees, its snarling still echoing through the cage and the room beyond.

Almost as soon as the last flick of the panther's tail had vanished, a ground-shaking tremor rocked the entire wing. Roh's hands shot out to her sides as she staggered with the movement. Valli shrieked, flapping his wings manically. Roh scooped the drakeling and the journal into her arms and darted for the door. As she raced up the stairs, she could hear the shouts of Csillans from the gorge. She panicked as her boots pounded the stone steps and she at last reached the bridge. Not knowing what else to do, Roh made for the upper level. When she burst through the doors at the top, rain lashed her face and a sharp, powerful wind tore through her clothes.

*A terror tempest.*

'What are you doing here?' Floralin shouted from across the way, wrangling with a piece of equipment and struggling to point it at the sky. Kezra wasn't far from her, shouting orders at the tempest workers, wildly waving her arms about.

Roh turned to face south-east. 'Gods,' she breathed, her eyes latching onto the towering, swirling column of wind and water in the near distance. Heart hammering in her chest, she made a dash for the room at the other end of the bridge. Ignoring Valli's vocal protests, she dropped him and the journal on the oak table and left them in the shelter, which she prayed to Dresmis and Thera would hold.

Her hair and clothes already soaked and plastered to her body, Roh found Floralin. 'What can I do?'

'Gods, get out of here,' Floralin half yelled. 'You'll just get in the way.'

'I can help. Give me an order,' Roh shouted back, struggling to be heard over the roar of the incoming storm.

Floralin hesitated, just for a moment, before she thrust her finger in the opposite direction. 'Get to that meter over there, help Kezra hold it in place!'

Roh didn't wait for further instruction. She sprinted across the bridge, careful not to slip in the puddles pooling. The rain only poured harder from the skies as she reached the Csillan leader and gripped the handles of the device.

'Hold it steady,' Kezra called. 'We have to point it at the heart of the tempest.'

Roh did as she was told. 'There's nothing we can do to stop it?'

'Not at this stage,' Kezra told her with a grimace, swinging the contraption around. 'Our readings missed this one late last night. We could have attempted to steer it away when it was smaller, but now ...'

'Now we hold fast?' Roh's knuckles were already turning white from holding the device so hard, the wind threatening to drag it from her grip.

Kezra met her gaze with steely determination. 'We hold fast.'

Roh trained her eyes on the incoming tempest, the roar of its viciously spiralling wind and water blocking out all other sound. She and Kezra still struggled to keep the measuring device in place, as the wind grabbed mercilessly at it, threatening to send it and the two cyrens over the railings, falling to their doom.

'Kezra!' Roh shouted, keeping her feet apart and bracing herself against the maddening strength of the wind. 'Why aren't these working?' She gestured to the contraptions and the tempest workers all around them who were struggling with their own. It wouldn't be long until they were swept away. Surely, they were stronger than this?

'I don't know!' Kezra yelled back. 'Something's wrong!'

'Here!' Deodan was suddenly at Roh's side. 'I'll hold, you figure out what's messing with it.'

There was no time to argue. Squinting through the downpour, Roh knelt at the foot of the contraption. As she studied the design of the device, the chaos of the terror tempest around her muted and she retreated into the depths of her mind, imagining what the blueprint of such a piece might look like. Wiping the rain from her eyes, Roh ran her hands along the metal legs and the bolts in the stone floor. She examined the weight of the contraption and where the wind seemed to want to pull it.

'You've used the wrong bolts, Kezra,' she yelled over the storm.

'What?'

'You've used the wrong bolts – that's why they're not holding in place.'

'Can they be fixed?'

'Not in the middle of all this,' Roh called back to her. 'Your best bet is to take all the equipment you have and get to shelter.'

'But the readings —'

'Your equipment won't survive taking these readings. Nor will you or your people! We need to get under cover, *now*!'

Kezra began to argue, but Floralin skidded to a stop before them. 'Roh's right. We can't hold out against this.'

As if in answer, the towering whirlpool gave a massive surge, funnelling towards them, sending a wave of icy water cascading down on them all.

'We'll be swept away,' Floralin yelled. 'The bridge will hold, but the rest of us won't!'

'Hurry!' Kezra screamed. The hurricane was heading straight for them.

'Roh!' Deodan yanked on her arm. 'Help me with this.'

Together, cyren and warlock wrenched the contraption from its flimsy bolts. 'Make for the stairs!'

'I can't,' Roh moved in the other direction.

'Roh! Don't —'

'Valli's in there!' She pointed to the shelter at the far end of the bridge. 'So's one of Killian's journals.'

Something changed in Deodan's face. 'Then we go together.' He hauled the contraption up and Roh dived for it, helping him with its weight. The pair went against the current of cyrens fleeing for the shelter of the lower wings of Csilla, instead, racing towards the little room.

'Where are you going?' Kezra cried.

But Roh waved her away. 'Go! We'll be fine.'

The reluctance was clear in the leader's eyes, but she had a territory to guide and nestlings to look after. Roh saw each consideration cross her face before she gave a stiff nod and darted for the doors, Floralin crying out to her.

Roh and Deodan staggered towards the shelter on the other side. The wind was like a thousand tiny knives biting at Roh's skin and the rain was near blinding. She gasped beneath the weight of the Csillan contraption and Deodan's unsteady gait. Her heart caught in her throat as she saw the churning waves of the tempest draw close.

They burst through the door, panicked shouts strangled in their throats.

Roh lunged for the door and slammed it closed, then bolted it and threw all her weight against it, lest it fly open. Deodan helped by slamming his back into it, panting.

Valli was instantly at Roh's feet, something akin to rage gleaming in his molten-gold eyes.

'I'm sorry,' she rasped. 'I was trying to protect you.'

Without another sound, the drakeling took up its place beside her, pressing against the door.

Outside the wind screamed and the tiles of their small shelter tore away from the roof. A window shattered, sending glass flying.

Deodan took a vial of water from the pouch of his belt, his hands trembling. Roh watched in shock as he poured the liquid into his palm and whispered his warlock enchantment to it. A small shield formed there, and floated towards the window where it blocked out the storm raging outside.

Roh cupped her hands around her mouth. 'You couldn't have done that out there?'

'Were you looking at the same tempest as I was?' Deodan asked, incredulous. 'One little vial of water wasn't going to stop that thing.'

The room shook uncontrollably as the terror tempest thundered. Deodan poured another vial into his palm and sent his magic water to reinforce the little room, but it didn't stop the small building from being battered.

'All we can do is wait,' Deodan told Roh, reaching for the journal she'd left on the oak table. 'How far through this are you?'

It wasn't lost on Roh that without him, she might have been swept away with the shelter.

'I'm at the part where he mentions a warlock called Eadric,' Roh replied, gritting her teeth against the shriek of the wind beyond the thin walls.

'Ah.'

'It's strange,' she admitted. 'Seeing my father's name in ink. I know it's not him, that it can't be … But …'

'It still feels like a loss?'

Roh nodded. How could she miss what she'd never had? How could she long to read about this man, just because he and her father shared the same name? As though sensing her inner turmoil, Valli crawled into her lap and curled up there.

'Do you think everyone got inside?' she asked, eyeing

the strange shield that shimmered at the broken window. All she could see beyond it was a blur of grey.

'I hope so,' Deodan said. 'We need to learn more about these tempests, Roh. I'd never seen one firsthand before, but if this is what my mother intends to wield against Saddoriel …' he trailed off.

'Do you think they can be controlled?' Roh asked, listening to the howl of the wind outside.

'I don't know. But if they can – if Sybil discovers how – then Saddoriel is done for. You realise that, don't you?'

Roh nodded slowly. 'Deodan …?'

'Hmm?'

'Why do you care if Saddoriel is destroyed? After all cyrens have done to your kin? After reading those journals for yourself?'

Deodan gave a soft laugh. 'Sybil called me a dreamer, like my father, because I do not want war, or to obliterate another race. And I do not want my own kin to become the monsters people say we are. We were always a peaceful people – healers and scholars. We do not lust for battle and blood. Or we didn't, back then. Roh, I just want to go home, to Lochloria. I want to see it stand as it once did: glorious and full of life.'

'I understand,' Roh told him. 'Can I entrust a task to you, then?'

'You may.'

'While I deal with the teerah panther, find out everything you can about the storms and their origins. Learn all you can about defending against them and … and if there's a way to *call for magic across the lands*, to *gather power that no longer exists in the realms as we know them today.'*

Deodan bowed his head. 'I'll do my best, Queen of Bones.'

There was a moment of quiet between them as Deodan thumbed through the pages of the journal he'd already read. 'Finn came to me,' he offered.

'Oh?'

'He asked permission to read these.'

'And did you agree?'

Roh sensed a hesitation in Deodan, but at last, he nodded. 'I did. He made some valid points. And perhaps if he understood our history better, he wouldn't be such a single-minded bastard sometimes.'

Despite their circumstances, Roh huffed a laugh. 'He's not so bad,' she murmured.

Deodan raised a single brow. 'My Queen of Bones ... I do believe you've just done the impossible.'

A long-suffering sigh escaped Roh. 'And what's that?'

'You've surprised me.'

'Well, if we manage to survive this tempest, I'll aim to surprise you more often,' she quipped.

It was one of the longest nights of Roh's life. The storm continued to rage for hours on end, and just when they thought it had moved on, it started up again, more savage than before. Deodan sent his water birds out into the fray to report back, but more often than not they didn't return. Those that did chattered to Deodan in a language Roh didn't understand, but he relayed to her that there was no one on the bridge, that the foundations of the structure remained sound, by some miracle.

The pair spoke little, and Roh wondered where her other companions had found themselves during the tempest. Were they together? Were they okay? Were they worried about her?

Roh woke to an eerie quiet that had settled like a fine mist throughout the gorge. At long last, a watery dawn broke across the sky outside and the tempest was nowhere in sight.

'Is it over?' she mumbled, hauling herself upright from where she'd slipped to the floor by the bolted door. Valli gave a soft growl in protest as she disturbed him.

Deodan stood at the window packing herbs into his pipe. His shield was gone, the crisp air drifting into the shelter. 'I think so.'

'Why didn't you wake me?'

'I've only been up for a moment myself.'

Roh got to her feet and went to the window. The bridge outside was barren but for the piles of debris that had hammered it throughout the night. Branches, chipped pieces of stone … Either all the equipment had been saved before the tempest hit, or it had been swept away in the winds. Roh tucked Killian's journal under her arm and unbolted the door. Valli was instantly clambering up her leg to sit on her shoulder, no doubt with a newfound hunger for breakfast.

'Are you coming?' Roh asked Deodan, who was still at the window, his gaze fixated on the carnage outside.

Deodan inhaled deeply. 'I'll meet you later. I have some research to do.'

Roh hesitated. 'Deodan?' she said.

'Hmm?'

'Thank you.'

With Valli clinging to her shoulder, Roh searched all over the eastern wing for the others. They weren't in the kitchens, they weren't in the guest chambers, and she doubted they would have opted to go to the mead hall after all the chaos.

'They're at the enclosure,' a voice said from behind her. Kezra looked exhausted. Her hair was loose and messy around her face, she wore the same clothes from last night, as Roh did, and the deep smudges of purple beneath her eyes told Roh she hadn't slept at all.

'Are you alright?' Roh asked, taking a step towards her. The towering Csillan leader was almost swaying on her feet, as though she might topple over at any moment.

But Kezra held up her hand, waving Roh's concern away. 'Find your friends. I have much to do.'

'Is everyone alright?' Roh pressed, barring Kezra's way as she made to leave.

'A few cuts and bruises, but thankfully everyone survived. Largely thanks to you.'

Roh's brows furrowed. 'What are you talking about?'

'If you hadn't checked the bolts, we might have stayed out there.'

'I'm sure you wouldn't have,' Roh offered. 'Hasn't this happened before?'

Slowly, Kezra shook her head. 'That's the thing. It hasn't. Someone changed the bolts.'

'What?'

'Someone tampered with the bolts, replaced them with the wrong ones, ones they knew wouldn't hold in a larger-scale tempest. We were sabotaged. And my people nearly died for it.'

A cold shiver raked down Roh's spine. 'I'm sorry,' she murmured, knowing how much this would hurt Kezra and her sister. 'Do you have any idea who?' The Csillan clan was small. Surely it wouldn't take much to reveal who had wronged them so cruelly?

'Not yet, but when I do … gods help them.' With that, Kezra strode off, each step more determined than the last.

Roh didn't linger, she headed straight for the teerah-panther enclosure. Sure enough, Harlyn, Odi, Finn and Yrsa were all there. Harlyn sat with her back to the wall, massaging her bad arm, a discarded bowl of breakfast at her side. Odi was hunched over and scribbling on a piece of parchment, no doubt writing more music for his brothers, while Yrsa and Finn had their heads together, in deep, hushed conversation.

Valli gave a squawk from Roh's shoulder and their heads snapped towards her.

'Roh!' Harlyn practically leaped to her feet. 'Where in the realms have you been all night?'

'I've been on the bridge. Do you know about the tempest?'

'How could we *not* know about the tempest?' Odi chimed in. 'The whole wing rattled.'

'Why in the realms were you on the bridge?' Harlyn chastised her before pulling her into a crushing embrace.

'That doesn't matter right now,' Yrsa interrupted, standing at Roh's side, her body taut with anticipation. 'We know how to get the gem,' she said.

Roh blinked at her. 'What?'

'We figured it out,' Yrsa told her excitedly, her bright eyes darting from the enclosure back to Roh. 'Well, Finn did, actually.'

Slowly, Finn approached them. 'We all did. We've been up all night.'

'And ...?' Roh pressed, unable to contain the hope flaring within.

Finn nodded eagerly. 'We have to —'

Someone cleared their throat from the doorway and a long shadow cast across the floor. 'I'm so sorry, Rohesia,' Floralin said as she approached, her face full of regret as she held out a weathered envelope.

Roh's knees buckled as she recognised the wax seal.

'The council will be here within the hour,' Floralin told them as Roh's shaking hand accepted the envelope. 'You've been challenged.'

# CHAPTER EIGHTEEN

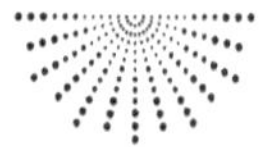

Challenged. The word barrelled through Roh just as the terror tempest had raged through the gorges of Csilla. It tore down everything in its path: visions of the future, hope, and any semblance of joy, leaving the debris of dread and fear in its wake. She had known it was coming, had known it all along, and yet it still shocked her, right to her core.

'Roh?' Floralin was saying. 'Roh, you must get ready. They'll be here soon.'

Roh blinked, trying to tether herself to the present once more, to find focus in the familiar faces around her, all etched with concern and outrage. Roh turned to Finn.

'Can we retrieve the gem before they get here?'

Regret shone in his eyes. 'No, it's too risky. Regardless if we got the gem, you'd still have to face the challenge. Attempting anything now would only leave you unprepared for that.'

The gleam of the panther's silvery-black coat caught Roh's eye from inside the enclosure, nearly invisible against the dark foliage and shadows. 'So we just abandon whatever plan you came up with?' she asked her companions.

'Not abandon, just postpone,' Harlyn offered.

Frustration and fear swept through Roh, but she refused to give in. She had won a challenge before, despite what it had cost her. And now … Things were different now. She was a cyren *with a deathsong* this time, and she was more powerful than she had ever been. She broke the wax seal of the envelope and opened the worn parchment, scanning its contents, fully expecting the council's usual cryptic explanations. She frowned.

'What is it?' Harlyn asked, trying to read over her shoulder.

Roh read the letter again, to be sure. It was right there on the page. 'I've … I've been challenged to a battle of strength,' she said.

Yrsa clicked her tongue in frustration. 'The thing is, that could mean anything.'

Roh nodded, her stomach churning. 'I know.' She turned back to Floralin, who was still waiting anxiously by the door. 'You mentioned something about getting ready?'

Floralin motioned for them to follow. 'The council have requested a gala in their honour,' she explained as they climbed the stairs. 'With an hour's notice, no less.'

'A gala? They think quite highly of themselves don't they,' Roh muttered.

'Yes, they always have,' Floralin said. 'And you need to be dressed for the occasion.'

A dark laugh burst from Roh's lips. 'You think I've got a ballgown hidden away in my pack?'

'Not quite, but you've got some options, courtesy of Delja the Triumphant.'

Roh faltered on the final step. 'What?'

'Apparently, she gathered you'd run into this slight snag.'

Roh could feel her companions' eyes on her, trying to work out how she felt about it all. She saved them the trouble. 'That was kind of her,' she told Floralin.

The Csillan made a non-committal noise and shooed them into their chambers. 'Be ready within the hour. The Saddorien elders are nothing if not prompt.'

Deodan was waiting by the fire inside, smoking his pipe with great intensity. 'I heard,' he said, shaking his head.

But Roh's attention went to a large rack of clothes in the centre of the room, where various shimmering fabrics draped from hangers. A note was pinned to the gown at the front.

*Rohesia,*

*I imagine you have been caught unawares by the upcoming event. Please choose something from my collection. Your companions are welcome to it as well. Though I'm sorry for the circumstances of our reunion, I will be glad to see you.*

*Faithfully,*

*Delja*

Roh exhaled shakily, a strange sense of relief flooding her body. The former queen, and the cyren who had known her mother best, had comforted Roh a great deal at the end of her previous challenge. Now, she would be at Roh's side once again and that was a great source of comfort. Roh let Harlyn take the note from her as she trailed her fingers through the luxurious fabrics.

'That's generous of her,' Harlyn muttered, passing the note to Yrsa.

'A little too generous,' Deodan added from where he still stood smoking before the fireplace.

Roh's gaze snapped to his, her hands dropping from the clothes. 'What do you mean?' Valli leaped from her shoulder then, as though sensing the tension surging through the air, and retreated to the sleeping quarters with a flash of his small wings.

But Deodan simply sucked on his pipe, his cheeks hollowing, expelling a thick stream of smoke.

He was in one of his moods again and Roh didn't have time for it. She turned back to the rack of gowns and started sifting through them, while Harlyn did the same from the other end.

While the letter from the council had specified the nature of the challenge, it had failed to disclose when and where it would take place. Surely, they couldn't expect her to submit to a challenge mid-gala? All the same, she pushed aside the billowing skirts that Delja seemed to favour, as well as the skin-tight gowns, searching for something more practical.

'How about this?' Harlyn offered Roh a hanger. The silken fabric was the colour of deep slate, with a slight purple hue in a certain light. Roh took it from Harlyn with a confused frown; it wouldn't be what she usually picked for herself. But then she saw why Harlyn had suggested it. Instead of a skirt, the material separated into pant legs. Roh had never seen such a thing before.

'Hurry up,' Harlyn waved her hand towards the sleeping quarters. 'Go try it on. We don't have much time.'

Roh made quick work of changing into the strange formal wear in privacy. She stepped into the pant legs that swept across the floor, while the top half grazed her collarbone as she slipped her arms through the long bell sleeves. However, it was the back of the garment that caused her to linger before the mirror. There *was* no back. The material gaped open, revealing her shoulderblades and the length of her spine. Roh found herself staring at her reflection. She had never seen herself look this way before ... Elegant. And the colour and cut of the strange suit made her seem ... *fierce*. As she had done back in Saddoriel, even for these fine events, Roh tugged her boots on, letting the cascading fabric fall over them, hiding them from sight, before placing her crown of bones atop her head.

Roh returned to the common area to find Finn kneeling on the carpet, helping the little nestling, Sol, button his formal jacket.

'There you go,' the Jaktaren said, sitting back on his heels to survey the boy. 'All done.'

To Roh's surprise, the nestling reached for Finn. 'Now, you.'

A tender smile tugged at the highborn's mouth. 'Thank you,' he said, his voice soft as the youngster closed his buttons painfully slowly with chubby fingers.

At the sight of Finn's smile, Roh found herself back in the hot pools, the Jaktaren's skin glistening in the moonlight beside her. Her throat dry, she forced herself to swallow.

*Gods, this is the last thing I need right now*, she chastised herself, all too aware that she'd merely been standing there staring. Perhaps if she wasn't about to face only the gods knew what in this challenge, she might talk to Harlyn about it. Harlyn knew about such things. But with everything ahead, there was nothing to do but force whatever her feelings were, way down.

Roh made to rejoin Yrsa, Harlyn and Odi across the room, but something caught her eye as Sol moved to Finn's final button. Around one of his sleeves was a band of bone. Without thinking, she closed the gap between them and knelt at the nestling's side.

'What's this?' she asked him, pointing to it.

With a massive grin on his face, Sol said, 'It's for you.'

'Me?' Roh repeated dumbly.

'Yep!' On that final note, the nestling darted from their rooms.

Roh exchanged a confused glance with Finn, but he merely shrugged. There was a tug on Roh's arm and Yrsa pulled her onto a chair, a small paint brush angled towards her face.

'What are you doing?' Roh baulked.

'Just close your eyes and hold still.' Yrsa rested the heel of her hand against Roh's cheek and applied light pressure to the lids of her eyes with the brush.

'I thought Saddoriens were too beautiful for cosmetics,' Roh muttered.

'This is just one tiny detail,' Yrsa said.

Roh supressed a snort. 'I'm sure it'll make all the difference in the challenge.'

'Hush.' When Yrsa was done, she handed Roh a looking glass. 'There.'

She had lined Roh's eyes with a dark kohl, making her moss-green irises all the more vibrant. 'It's like war paint,' Roh murmured. She'd read about such things in the Akorian library books she'd borrowed.

From across the room, Harlyn gasped. 'You … you look like a queen.'

'And just as well,' Kezra's voice sounded from the hallway. 'The council have arrived, and it's about time they started seeing you that way. Hurry up, everyone.'

But Roh darted back to their rooms. There, she belted her father's dagger at her waist. It had served her well once before, perhaps it would do so again now. Never mind that it was a warlock artefact, it belonged to her and she would no longer deny who she was, not for anyone. At last, she turned to Valli, who was waiting on one of the beds, alert, with his wings flared.

'You have to stay here, my friend,' Roh told him, trying

to keep the note of regret from her voice. While she would have loved to walk into that gala with a sea drake hatchling on her shoulder and see the shock on the elders' faces, she agreed with what Floralin had said on her first night in Csilla; that it was best the council didn't know about the drakeling. No doubt they would find some rule to use in their favour, and at this size, they could take him from her.

Kezra was tapping her foot against the marble floor when Roh emerged, ready at last. The Csillan Arch General eyed the quartz dagger belted at Roh's waist, but said nothing. She led Roh and her companions through the familiar halls of the east wing. Roh hadn't had the chance to see what the others were wearing, but as they walked, she scanned their attire, surprised to find all of them equally formally dressed for the occasion, bar Deodan, who still wore his weathered clothes and his cutlasses at his hips and his pipe between his teeth, as always. Harlyn had chosen a close-fitting floor-length gown in cobalt blue that seemed to make her unusual blonde hair stand out even more. It showed off her bare shoulders and the tops of her breasts. She didn't wear her usual sling, but rather a compression bandage around her arm, which she still held close to her body, as though she feared getting knocked. Yrsa wore a much looser gown that fell to mid-calf, covering up much of her skin. A jewelled belt in Saddorien fashion cinched in her waist and she had managed to attach her weapon of choice and her pouch of stones there. Odi walked at Roh's side in a crisp, tailored three-piece suit, befitting of the human fashions she'd seen his brothers in back in the lair, although their garments were far worse for wear. Delja must have included it especially for him. Roh noticed that the human kept stealing glances at Harlyn, his gaze lingering on her bare skin. Before Roh could glance across at Finn, Kezra rounded a corner and Roh nearly stopped in her tracks.

The Bridge of Csilla was magnificent. Illuminated by hanging jars of valo beetles and hundreds of candles, the marble floor glowed and the archways looking onto the gorge seemed more vibrant than ever. It was a brilliant hall of light. And the music … Roh's breath caught in her throat as the sound of the Csillan choir drifted up onto the bridge. Her magic stirred against its call, desperate to explore, begging to be unleashed. Long tables of food and drink lined the edges of the bridge, while Csillans and Saddoriens alike gathered at its heart.

'How did you pull this together so quickly?' Roh murmured to Kezra.

'Piri,' Yrsa gasped from behind Roh, pushing through their group and darting onto the bridge. The Jaktaren collided with a pretty cyren wearing the uniform of the Saddorien Army. They embraced hard, burying their heads in each other's necks, both crying out in relief.

In a different context, Roh would have loved to approach the pair and embrace Piri herself, to thank her for her patience and to be properly introduced to the cyren who meant so much to her friend. She also wanted a glimpse at this stubborn streak that supposedly rivalled

Finn Haertel's. But at the far end of the bridge, the Council of Seven Elders waited.

Roh's entourage remained behind. But with Kezra at her side, she made her way through the throng of cyrens dressed in all their finery, who all parted before her, making way. Several glimmers of ivory caught her attention. Roh had to look twice. For the Csillans … they wore the same armbands of bone that Sol had. As Roh passed, they bowed their heads in acknowledgement. Her mouth must have fallen open in shock, for Kezra leaned in.

'They're for you,' she whispered. 'In support of the Queen of Bones.'

'But … why?' Roh asked as she approached the end of the bridge. 'Why would they want to exchange a queen with six hundred years of experience with one who has not even twenty?'

'Because a fresh perspective might be the exact change cyrenkind needs,' Kezra said. 'They're not human, by the way,' she added. 'The bones. Given the master musician in your court, we opted for animal bones.'

*Your court.* The words made Roh's magic thrum beneath her skin.

'Thank you,' she managed.

Kezra simply nodded. 'This is where I leave you.'

All too soon, Roh realised she stood before the Council of Seven Elders, who stared down at her from upon a small dais.

*Of course they needed to be above everyone else,* Roh mused as she scanned their faces: Finn's parents, Taro and Bloodwyn Haertel, whom Roh now despised even more than she had before, recalling the C one of them had carved into their own child's flesh; Yrsa's aunt, Winslow Ward; Erdites Colter; Arcus Mercer; Koras Rasaat and Isomene Sigra, dressed in their best finery, their wealth and power on clear display in the form of silver, jewels and horned serpents around their necks.

She expected them to say something, but they merely gazed down upon her and it became clear to Roh that they did not intend to make any life-altering announcements just yet. As was their prerogative, she knew they would attempt to wait until she was as least prepared as possible. So she decided she would waste no more of her time here. She dipped her head in a show of respect.

'Council,' she said, turning on her heel.

It was as though the entire population of the bridge let out a sigh of relief. Suddenly, movement flowed and a relaxed rhythm found its way into the crowd of Saddoriens and Csillans. Roh held her head high as she made her way to a table of refreshments. She took up a goblet of wine, more so she had something to do with her hands than to drink. She knew now more than ever she would need a clear head for what came next, whatever it may be. As she walked slowly through the guests, she scanned their faces with a growing sense of unease.

*Where is Delja? Where is Ames? Surely as my official guardian, he will be in attendance again?*

But the next familiar face she spotted was not one she had sought out. Neith, the water-runner fledgling, was still as scrawny as she had always been, but her face seemed older, more hardened than before.

'So, you had poor Orson banished,' she said by way of greeting, sipping on her drink, knowing exactly which nerve to press. She stood before Roh, straight-backed and chin raised, as though she was trying to take up more space than she needed.

'It wasn't a choice,' Roh replied between gritted teeth, surveying the cyren. 'She forced my hand by challenging me.'

'Perhaps you forced *hers* by cheating your way into the tournament,' Neith bit back.

Roh stood her ground. 'Where did it go wrong between us? Why do you hate me so much? What did I ever do to you?' she couldn't help asking. 'We were from the same place. We could have helped one another.'

Neith scoffed. 'Like you helped Orson? We are *not* from the same place. Not even close. You're an *isruhe* – the *Elder Slayer's daughter*, no less. Your presence here is a stain on our history. It might not be me who gets to take you down, but believe this, bone cleaner. You will fall, in one way or another.'

'Is everything alright, Rohesia?' At the sound of the melodic, silken voice, Neith retreated.

Roh would know that voice anywhere. 'Delja,' she said, turning to face the former queen.

Delja was resplendent in a turquoise gown that hugged her hips and flared out halfway down her legs. Her iconic wings were nowhere in sight, but it was clear she didn't need them to command attention.

Wings or not, everyone knew who Delja the Triumphant was.

'Are you alright, Rohesia?' she asked again.

Roh found herself nodding, trying to shake the skin-crawling effect that Neith's words had on her. She was used to being threatened and insulted, but somehow at the hands of a fellow lowborn, it always cut deeper than she expected. Delja's presence, however, soothed Roh's churning gut and she gave her a grateful look.

'Thank you for the garments,' she said, gesturing to the silk she wore.

'Of course.' Delja smiled. 'I wanted to offer whatever armour I could. I understand that these past few weeks have not been easy. I would like to hear about them, if you care to tell the tale?'

Roh felt the reassuring pulse of the topaz from her crown, forever guiding her towards sincerity. Delja truly cared for her, truly wished to know of her struggles. Together, former and future queen walked the length of the bridge, sipping wine as Roh told Delja of their journey across the Gilded Plains, of how they had been set upon in Thornhill and just how badly the Rite of Strothos had affected her. She told Delja of their perilous travels up and through the mountain pass, and how they had discovered a herb to counteract the poison she'd been subjected to during the rite.

'I imagine that would have been an eye-opening journey,' Delja said carefully. 'Through the pass. I have heard tales of what went on there.'

A sudden lump formed in Roh's throat as she

remembered all she had seen in those passageways. 'There were skeletons. Of every age,' she replied. 'And remnants of the half-lives those poor people had lived there. We found journals, too,' she told Delja, wondering if the former queen had ever read firsthand accounts of what had occurred at the hands of Uniir the Blessed, the king she had overthrown.

'Journals?' Delja asked, her head tilted in curiosity, not pausing to acknowledge the Csillan who had just refilled her goblet. 'Those must have made for harrowing reads.'

Roh nodded. 'They're awful … And I'm only on the second one.'

'The second? How many are there?'

'Seven.' Roh frowned. 'I think?'

'If I may offer some gentle advice, Rohesia?' Delja said.

'I need all the advice I can get.'

A kind, knowing smile curved Delja's lips. 'While there is much to be learned from the past,' she said quietly, 'your current situation begs that you focus on the present. There are many here who care for you deeply and long for you to succeed.'

Roh's gaze skimmed across the throng of cyrens on the bridge, the impending threat of the obstacle to come gnawing at her insides. 'Do you know what the challenge is? Or who?'

Delja shook her head. 'I wish I could tell you.'

Of all the faces that stole glimpses at Roh, it could be anyone. Anyone could be waiting in the wings, readying themselves for their chance to unseat her from her would-be throne.

Out of the corner of her eye, Roh spotted Finn a few yards away. He wore fresh Jaktaren leathers, his crossbow strapped across his back and his expression cold and calculating. Moments later, Roh saw why: Taro and Bloodwyn made their way towards their son, cornering him. Not for the first time, Roh realised just how different Finn was from his elder-council parents. Although he could be rough around the edges, there was a warmth to him, a hidden brightness honed by humour and worldliness, whereas his parents were nothing but cruel.

*'I don't like enclosed spaces …'* Only a matter of days ago – or was it weeks? – he'd told her why. Because of them. Parents who wouldn't accept their son for who he was, parents who had been more concerned with their positions of power than their own child's wellbeing. Roh tensed up, watching them. Their faces were so close, Finn looked like he might push his father away. An argument was about to break out. Panicked, Roh tried to make her way towards them, but Yrsa caught her eye. She gave Roh a subtle nod; Yrsa would take care of it. Someone was waving at Roh. The talon-less hand motioned to her in an overtly enthusiastic manner, with no thought for the social decorum the current gala called for.

Jesmond.

The fledgling didn't stop waving, making it impossible for Roh to continue her conversation with Delja. But if Jesmond was here, that meant …

'Excuse me,' Roh said to Delja, ducking into the crowd towards Jes.

'What?' she hissed when she arrived at the youngster's side. 'Is Ames here?' she asked, craning her neck to scan the surrounding cyrens.

'Good to see you, too, Rohesia. I'm well, thank you so much for asking. Your concern moves me.'

'Jes!' Roh hissed.

'Tcha,' Jesmond snapped, pointing across the bridge. There he was. Her mentor, Ames, wore his usual grey robes, which billowed about his arms as he waved them, speaking animatedly to Kezra and … Deodan. But for all of his hand gestures, which were very much unlike the understated cyren she knew, Ames looked wildly uncomfortable.

'What's that about?' Roh wondered aloud.

Jes shrugged, swiping a pastry from a nearby tray. 'I'd get over there if I were you.'

'Why do you say that?'

Infuriatingly, Jesmond simply shrugged again. 'Just a feeling.'

As someone whose 'feelings' usually resulted in a pile of gold, Roh decided to heed the fledgling's advice, and with her hand gripping the bone hilt of her father's dagger, she started towards her mentor, the Csillan leader and the warrior warlock.

Only to have something else catch her eye.

Zokez Rasaat, one of the tournament's previous competitors, the highborn who Finn had punched in the face at the end of her last challenge, was cutting through the crowd, making his way straight for her. Roh's whole body tensed. It had to be him who was challenging her this time, the utter loathing in his glare told her there was no alternative. He came to a halt before her, his nostrils flaring.

'I hope you're ready to be banished like your lowlife friend, *isruhe*,' he said.

Roh had been expecting the insult and it didn't bother her, not from the likes of him. 'Have you finally found the courage to face me, then, Rasaat?' she asked coldly. 'Last time I saw, you were forfeiting, too scared to face a sea serpent. And yet somehow, a lowly bone cleaner found the courage … The next time you were flat on your arse, crying about a bloody nose.'

A dark cloud passed over the highborn's face. 'I was biding my time.'

Roh scoffed. 'You mean hiding? Hiding until it was safe to show your face again?'

Zokez ignored the barb; instead, he made a mockery of searching the crowd. 'Where's your new protector, then? Off finding some other way to shame the Jaktaren guild?'

'He's not my protector,' Roh snapped.

'No?' Zokez smiled nastily. 'Oh, that's right. He couldn't be, could he? Wasn't he the one who spread all that support for that pathetic water runner?'

Roh froze, her stomach dropping to the ground. She bit back her retort, but her shock must have been obvious on her face.

'You didn't know?' the bastard said in mock surprise. 'Our dear Finn put up all those signs and ribbons for that stupid lowborn. He even sent her flowers and gift baskets … All to mess with your mind.'

*Neith, Spirit of the Water Runners.*

*Neith for Queen.*

*On Neith's swift wings …*

Roh remembered every single banner. She remembered tearing them apart with her talons as she came undone in the dark passageways of Saddoriel. *Finn did that?*

'There was never any true support for that fool,' Zokez whispered smugly, watching as his words found their mark. 'She's almost as detestable as you.'

But Roh would not come undone again, not at the hands of a coward, of someone who thought he was infinitely better than the rest simply because of the circumstances of his birth. Her deathsong sparked fire in her veins and she lifted her chin, allowing her magic to dance around the highborn, to toy with what little power he possessed. It was no longer a mere flicker, but a forceful current that coursed through her, an unparalleled dominance, the birth right she hadn't known was hers, until now.

Zokez's eyes widened and he took a step back. 'But you don't …'

All around her, Roh could feel the power of the Saddoriens and the Csillans mingling, and for the first time, she noticed the lingering magic of the terror tempest, suspended in the air around the bridge. It seemed to coax her own power into the open and stirred the song deep in her chest.

'I don't *what*, Zokez? I don't have a deathsong?' Roh let herself smile. 'Think again.'

She revelled in the shock on the highborn's face, relishing the way his mouth hung open and his feet shuffled backwards.

*So this is what it is like to be feared*, she thought.

But it wasn't only Zokez who had noticed her magic pulsing in the atmosphere. The mood of the entire bridge had shifted. Roh looked around, self-conscious of the darker side she'd allowed to breach the surface.

The music of the choir ceased and a sharp elbow from Jesmond had Roh craning her neck towards the far end of the bridge once more. There, Kezra struck a gong and Saddoriens and Csillans alike fell silent. All at once, Roh's heart was thick in her throat. She'd let herself get carried away —

Kezra didn't speak. She simply moved aside once she had the crowd's attention, making way for Elder Erdites Colter, who took to the dais with his hands clasped behind his back. There was no fanfare or flourishing hand movements as there had been when Adriel announced the last challenge. Erdites Colter made no efforts to charm the crowd or create some spectacle of entertainment. He simply stood before them, his very presence commanding the crowd's attention. He smoothed a hand over the zigzag pattern shaved into the side of his head, the one that matched Yrsa and Finn's.

'The council and I see no need to prolong the inevitable,' he said, his voice as gravelly as ever. 'You know we have been brought here to bear witness to a challenge of strength against Rohesia of the Bone Cleaners.'

Roh's skin prickled. She felt all eyes home in on her, assessing her.

'Rohesia,' Erdites called again.

All Roh could do was step forward as the crowds parted for her once more and she made her way to the platform. Closing that gap seemed to take forever and a chill swept over her as she took the last few steps. Then, all too soon, she was upon the dais, next to the Council of Seven Elders.

'You have been challenged by Izan Rasaat,' Elder Colter said, 'cousin to former competitor Zokez Rasaat.'

Roh followed Elder Colter's outstretched hand, to where a cyren who bore an uncanny resemblance to the highborn stood, his hand on the hilt of a sword at his belt.

Roh managed to swallow. 'And what is the challenge?' she asked, fighting to keep her voice steady.

'The challenge will be a trial by combat.'

# CHAPTER NINETEEN

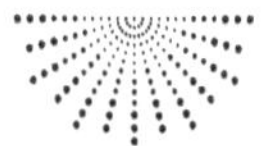

Elder Colter was still speaking, explaining the stakes of the challenge and the rules, exactly what Roh and her friends had to lose: *everything*. But the world around Roh had slowed and muted. She couldn't hear what he was saying; she didn't dare move lest her legs gave out beneath her.

Only three words echoed in her head: *trial by combat*. And they threatened to carve out her pounding heart and crush it to a pulp.

She knew little of the ancient tradition save this: it was a physical fight, usually to the death, and while Roh had learned self-defence and how to use a sling from the Jaktaren, she knew she was no warrior. The silver pommel of Izan Rasaat's sword glinted in the candlelight and Roh was under no delusions about whether or not the highborn could use it. She found her hand moving towards the quartz dagger at her thigh as her mind whirred. With that longsword against her, there was no way she'd be able to get close enough to wield it or her sling, nor would Izan stand idly by, allowing himself to be a long-range target, allowing her to line up her sling from afar —

'Roh?' said a familiar voice at her side. Harlyn.

Dazed, Roh found that Elder Colter had finished speaking and the "festivities" had recommenced. She stared at Harlyn. 'What's going on?'

'You have thirty minutes to prepare,' Harlyn told her, whisking her away from the dais towards the east wing beyond the bridge.

Roh nearly laughed. 'Thirty minutes to prepare to fight to the death with a trained killer? Sounds reasonable.'

'Well, you won't be fighting, will you?'

Roh stopped in her tracks, causing Harlyn to lurch forward.

'What do you mean?' she asked.

Harlyn's brows knitted together in concern as she studied Roh. 'Weren't you listening? You can select a champion to fight in your stead.'

Harlyn didn't wait any longer, she pulled Roh along after her, towards their chambers. Numb, Roh followed her, barely aware of her legs moving beneath her. When they reached their rooms, the others were all waiting.

Odi's expression was grim, while Yrsa, Finn and Deodan's faces were hardened with determination. Yrsa stepped forward, grasping Roh's hands in hers.

'Which of us do you choose?' she asked, her eyes

brimming with purpose.

Roh pulled her hands away and stepped back in horror. 'I can't choose *any* of you,' she said, panic bubbling. All that magic and power she'd felt earlier had been snuffed out the moment those words had been uttered.

*Trial by combat.*

'Roh, you can't be serious,' Deodan implored, taking Yrsa's place before her. 'As talented and strong as you are, you're no fighter. I am. Yrsa is. Finn is. Let one of us duel in your stead.'

'What …' Roh stammered. 'What sort of queen would I be if I let someone risk their life in my place?'

'A smart one,' Odi interjected. 'You won't be queen at all if you go out there and try to wield a sword against that cyren. A true queen knows her strengths, but knows her weaknesses better.'

'Roh,' Deodan said again. 'You have two Jaktaren and a warrior warlock to choose from. Those are strong odds. That Rasaat bastard is a nobody —'

'He comes from one of the *oldest families* in Saddorien history,' Roh countered. 'You don't think he would have received the training of one of the elites? Don't underestimate him, we have learned that lesson thoroughly enough already.'

'Please, Roh,' Harlyn implored. 'You can't win this one alone. Let them help you.'

Roh paced the living quarters, ignoring Valli, who had emerged from the bedroom and was growling from the back of an armchair, the tension in the room no doubt agitating him. Roh raked her trembling fingers through her hair and bit her lip as she walked the length of the carpet and back again. There had to be another way, had to be an alternative to offering up someone else's life —

A warm hand closed around her forearm and brought her to a stop. Finn. He waited until her eyes met his.

'*Sometimes being strong means knowing when to accept help,*' he told her, echoing her own words back to her.

'I can't …' It came out a near sob, the realisation washing over her like an icy wave. 'I can't,' she said again. What couldn't she do? She couldn't win against Izan; deep in her aching heart, she knew that much. But she also couldn't ask one of her friends to risk themselves for her. They were too good, too precious to lose. They all had others depending on them, who loved them, who —

'Let me go,' Finn said quietly.

Roh shook her head. 'You? The highborn who supported *Neith* from the start?' It bubbled out of her, raw and unfiltered. She hadn't realised how much it had bothered her until this moment and she clung to the anger, preferring it to the despair that threatened to overwhelm her.

'What's she talking about?' Harlyn demanded.

'I believe one of the Rasaats divulged that I was the one to drum up false support of the water runner during the Queen's Tournament,' Finn answered evenly.

'So you don't even deny it?' Roh gaped.

Finn's brow furrowed. 'Why would I?'

Roh threw her hands up. 'Why? Because *now* you ask to fight for me.'

'Now is *different*,' Finn snapped back. 'I did what I had to do before. I used my cunning, as any Saddorien would do, as *you* would do. Don't tell me otherwise.'

Roh couldn't breathe. If she couldn't trust him, she couldn't send him into battle. If she couldn't —

'Let me do this,' Finn said softly this time, gripping her hands in his, forcing her to look at him. 'Using Deodan will send the wrong message – a warlock cannot take your place, not now. Yrsa is an incredible warrior, but her prowess lies with her sling and I'm sure you realised that's not the ideal weapon for the circumstances.' He didn't break eye contact. 'Let me do this,' he said again.

'Why?' Roh managed. 'I'm not your queen.'

'No, you're not,' Finn agreed, his eyes boring into hers. 'But you're my friend.'

Roh felt herself falter. The betrayals of the past faded into nothing. She knew he was right, that they did not matter. That his actions back then had no bearing on them now, just as she hoped the same for her own decisions. But that meant a choice had to be made, one that she did not want to make.

Finn's resolve only seemed to intensify. 'I will not let you face this alone.'

Roh couldn't find the words, or she didn't want to, as the reality of it all sank in. She knew that Finn was an extraordinary warrior, one of the best Jaktaren Saddoriel had produced in centuries, but *this*? She opened her mouth, to say what, she didn't know. Instead, she found herself dropping Finn's hands and reaching for his sword. Deep amidst the fear, understanding settled in the pit of her stomach. She knew the others were right: there was no other way.

Roh handed the Jaktaren his weapon. 'Then, so be it. Finn Haertel, I choose you as my champion.'

Finn bowed his head as he accepted the blade. 'So be it.'

All too soon, they were on the Bridge of Csilla once more. The crowds had been corralled to either end, leaving the length of the bridge clear and open for combat, the grand arches revealing the gorge below, creating a dramatic, ominous backdrop.

Winslow Ward found Roh and ushered her towards the dais, which had been moved temporarily to the centre of the bridge. Roh found herself standing alongside Izan Rasaat, utterly exposed to the world, clasping her hands together to hide their trembling.

'Don't worry,' Elder Ward whispered in her ear as her gentle hands positioned Roh at the front. 'All will be well.'

Roh wanted to lean into that reassurance, that kindness, but Elder Ward ducked away, bowing her head to Elder Colter as he moved to the dais, his eyes gleaming with unchecked excitement.

Silk robes brushed against Roh's arm as an elder took their place beside her.

'It sickens me to see you here,' said a quiet voice, laced with death. 'You're a disgrace to Saddoriel, a disgrace to all our kind.'

Taro Haertel didn't look at Roh as the poisonous

words left his mouth. 'You bring chaos and disorder wherever you go, tainting each of our precious territories with your dirty blood and grandiose ambitions.'

Roh realised she was shaking, not with fear, but with fury. 'Me? Tainting our territories? You must confuse me with someone else. Perhaps the Arch General of Akoris? The cyren who drugged his people into submission?'

'You want to speak of Akoris?' Taro sneered.

'Only of how I liberated its people from the claws of a predator.'

A dark laugh sounded. 'Liberated them? Is that what you call it? Burning their fields and letting them suffer and die from withdrawal?'

Roh's blood went cold.

Taro continued, clearly enjoying himself. 'Chaos rules Akoris now. Its people are dead or dying as a result of your brash actions.'

Each word pierced Roh deeply, finding its mark in the weak spots of her mental armour. *It can't be true … This is part of the manipulation, to mess with my mind in the face of the trial, to unnerve me …*

'The healer, Incana, she would have told me were the consequences so dire. She had sound knowledge of —'

'I'm sure she did. But as a warlock sympathiser, do you think she cared what fate awaited the good cyrens of Akoris?'

Roh's stomach turned, recalling the winged symbol of alliance the healer had drawn in salt on the refectory table during Roh's first night there. But surely … surely that didn't mean —

'You brought terror down on an entire territory. And you think you're fit to rule? You're as mad as the Elder Slayer, bone cleaner.'

*It's not true,* Roh chanted to herself. Incana was a *healer.* She would never have put innocent people at risk. Besides, they would have heard the news from someone. They would know. She had *freed* the Akorians, she had unchained them from Adriel. *That* was the truth.

'We are about to witness a trial by combat,' Elder Colter announced, his voice loud and clear, effortlessly projecting across the length of the bridge. 'Rohesia.' He turned to her. 'Do you wish to select a champion to compete in your stead?'

'I …' Roh's chest threatened to cave in and there wasn't enough air in her lungs. Her breaths became short and shallow as the faces in the crowds blurred. 'I …'

'Well?' Elder Colter pressed coldly.

Roh heard a steady rhythm of footsteps across the marble. 'I do,' she said, forcing her voice to remain even.

'Whom do you wish to select?'

Roh found the source of the steps, her eyes meeting a familiar lilac gaze. 'Finn Haertel,' she said loudly. 'Finn Haertel of the Jaktaren.'

An audible gasp sounded from the crowds and excited chatter broke out across the bridge as Finn approached the dais and took up his place at Roh's side.

*A Jaktaren defending a bone cleaner in a trial by combat?* History was being made. The anticipation was palpable, the whispers growing louder and louder with each passing moment.

'That's enough,' Elder Colter's gravelly voice cut through the noise like a hot blade through butter. With his brows raised in disbelief, the elder turned to Finn. 'Do you accept?'

'I do.'

Roh didn't miss the look of shock Elder Colter shot at Taro and Bloodwyn Haertel, who stood at the foot of the dais, their expressions unreadable. 'Very well,' he said, motioning to several Csillans who came forward to manoeuvre the dais elsewhere.

Before Roh could say anything to Finn, she was ushered away, to where the Council of Seven Elders and Delja the Triumphant stood, ready to watch the trial unfold. Yrsa, Harlyn, Deodan and Odi made their way towards her. When they reached Roh, Harlyn's cold fingers laced through hers, an attempt at reassurance, but Roh could feel her friend shivering. A chill had settled over the bridge.

Ames was nowhere in sight, nor was Jesmond, Roh realised abstractly. She returned her gaze to the marble floor, where Finn stood opposite Izan and unsheathed his sword, tossing his belt aside.

Izan Rasaat stood with his feet apart, clutching his sword as he sneered at the Jaktaren. Roh was just close enough to hear the poisonous words he uttered.

'You made a grave mistake striking my cousin trying to defend an *isruhe*'s honour,' he murmured, shifting on the balls of his feet, readying himself.

'Your cousin made a grave mistake insulting her,' Finn said, his tone equally threatening. 'He was a coward then, just as he was a coward when he forfeited in the tournament. He should have slinked back to whatever hole he came from and licked his wounds in private, but instead he sent you. A coward then, and a coward now.'

Unleashed fury flashed in Izan's eyes and he twitched, almost making a premature lunge towards Finn. 'You —'

'Champions, at the ready!' called Elder Colter, as though sensing the duel might begin without his say-so.

*Gods, I might be sick.* The contents of Roh's stomach turned watery and saliva filled her mouth as she watched Finn centre himself. Whatever happened next, it was her doing. She had allowed this to happen, had allowed Finn to take her place at the end of Izan's blade.

'Begin!'

The word was still echoing through the bridge when the first clang of steel rattled Roh's entire being. Izan lunged viciously, his eyes glazed with a venom that told Roh just how deeply she'd wounded the Rasaat family by refusing to forfeit back in her third trial against the sea serpent. And now, Finn Haertel had insulted them further.

Roh flinched as the impact of steel on steel reverberated across the bridge. Her heart pounded mercilessly in her throat as she watched on, clutching Harlyn's hand so hard that she could no longer feel her fingers.

Finn blocked Izan's blows confidently, never hesitating. His footwork was like a choreographed dance beneath him as he conceded ground, stepping back, allowing Izan to attack wildly, fuelled by rage and indignance. Izan struck hard and true. Each blow had the full force of his weight behind it and yet Finn blocked and blocked again, his cool demeanour only seeming to feed Izan's anger.

'Fight me,' Izan growled, beads of sweat shining at his hairline.

Finn blocked another strike.

'I said, fight me. What are you waiting for?' the highborn panted, lunging forward again with a precise jab of his blade.

The Jaktaren knocked it aside with his sword. 'This.' His boot collided with Izan's ribs, sending him sprawling across the marble floor, a cry of surprise escaping him.

Izan leaped back up, breathing heavily as he brandished his sword. 'Fight like a Saddorien, Haertel. Not some *isruhe*-loving fool.'

Finn stalked towards Izan like a predator approaching its prey. This time, he attacked. His blade was a blur of silver as he rained blow upon blow down on Izan, who scrambled to block.

A yelp of pain followed.

Red splattered across the pristine marble and Izan slowly gazed in shock from the gash on his arm to the Jaktaren advancing upon him. Finn didn't hesitate. He struck again, causing his opponent to stumble clumsily. Izan only just raised his sword in time to block what might have been a fatal blow.

Roh bit the inside of her check, tasting the coppery tang of her own blood as the two Saddoriens fought on. The duel spanned the length of the bridge and back again, the sharp sound of clashing blades ringing in Roh's ears. Finn had the upper hand and Roh couldn't help the embers of hope that flared as he delivered yet another debilitating blow to Izan, this time the blade slicing him across the shoulder.

To Roh's left, Yrsa was shifting from foot to foot, her gaze latched on her fellow Jaktaren.

'He's doing well,' Roh ventured in a whisper. 'Isn't he?'

Yrsa didn't take her eyes off the duel. 'He is,' she replied. But there was something about the set of her jaw and her rigid stance that only fuelled the uneasiness within Roh. Wind whipped across the bridge in a sudden gust. Whatever enchantment that had kept the warmth inside was gone and Roh realised with horror that the drop to the raging river in the gorge below was real.

Cursing, Izan threw himself at Finn with reckless abandon, slashing wildly. The Jaktaren parried and returned the attack with several precise thrusts of his blade, aimed at Izan's middle. Izan managed to deflect the blows – just. The edge of his sword skittered across Finn's forearm, cutting through his leathers.

Roh desperately craned her neck, trying to see if he'd drawn blood. But a flurry of movement followed, each strike and feint and parry more vicious than the last. They fought beneath one of the open grand arches now, beams of moonlight gleaming against the flashing silver of their blades.

Roh was transfixed, struck by the absurdity of this trial by combat. Was there meant to be some code of honour here? Were clashing swords supposed to be a symbol of fairness?

The taste of blood shocked Roh from her reverie and she realised with a start that both duellers were on the edge of the bridge. Finn blocked Izan's lunge and retaliated with a series of quick, precise slices, the final one finding its mark in Izan's bicep.

Izan let out a groan of pain, blood running down his arm and between his fingers around the grip of his sword. He doubled over, overcome by the numerous slashes Finn had delivered to his torso.

Finn took a step back, whether to deliver his final blow or to give Izan a reprieve, Roh didn't know —

A ragged scream escaped Yrsa. 'Finn!'

Talons of terror carved through Roh's heart as she whipped her head from Yrsa's horror-stricken face back to Finn.

Izan unsheathed a curved dagger from his boot, dripping with a shimmering green substance, and sliced it across Finn's ankle.

Agony rippled across Finn's face. It was his bad leg. And Roh watched in horrified disbelief as he crumpled inwards, a silent cry of pain on his lips. The magic supporting his limb vanished, leaving the left leg of his pants flapping loose below the knee.

Finn's eyes went wide and his arms flailed.

'No!' Roh screamed, lunging forward.

But it was too late.

Finn Haertel fell, plunging soundlessly into the raging waters below.

# CHAPTER TWENTY

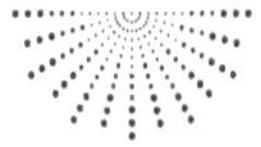

A scream ripped from Roh's throat.

Chaos had erupted, the crowds surging forward, trying to glimpse over the deadly edge. Saddoriens and Csillans were shouting, but Roh couldn't make out the words. Everything was moving too fast and she was too slow, or she couldn't move at all. She didn't know which.

Someone's arms banded across her chest, hauling her away from the bridge.

'You have to go, *now*. Take the crown and the topaz and *run*.'

It was Ames, dragging her away from the madness.

Roh didn't register her feet moving. Numb, she allowed herself to be hauled through the throng of bodies, barrelling into others, stumbling when Ames got too far ahead and wrenched her forward.

Finn's look of surprise flashed before her. He couldn't be gone, he just couldn't —

'Rohesia, *hurry!*'

Roh had never heard that note of panic in Ames' voice before, and it spurred her on. She couldn't remember the last time he'd actually touched her. His grasp was rough around her wrist and she spotted a patch of discoloured skin peeking out from the sleeve of his robes. She staggered again. The whole realm around her was a sensory overload; so many sounds, so much movement, so many things pulling her attention in the opposite directions —

Something bulky was pushed hard into her. Her pack. 'You have to get out of here.' It was Kezra speaking this time. She put her arm behind Roh's back, shielding her from the jostling crowd. 'This way.'

Roh didn't turn to look at Ames as Kezra led her from the bridge to the east wing, towards the kitchen. She put one foot in front of the other, with no idea how, and her thoughts, which were usually so loud and voluminous and scrambled in her head, were eerily silent.

'They'll be coming for you.' Kezra burst into the kitchen and opened a hatch in the floor Roh had never noticed before. All she could see beyond it was darkness.

'Let them come,' Roh said, her first words in a long while sounding like those of a stranger's.

'You're not ready,' Kezra said, forcing Roh's arms through the straps of her pack as though she was a nestling and settling it on her shoulders. 'Not yet.'

'He's …' But Roh couldn't get the words out, couldn't say Finn's name aloud.

'I know,' Kezra said, her voice softening. 'But you cannot stay here.' She pushed Roh towards the open hatch. 'Follow the ladder down. Take the blue-lit path. The others will be waiting for you at the end.'

'Others?' Roh said dumbly.

'They had to flee immediately. The Jaktaren would have taken your human friend and Thera knows what they would have done with the warlock. Keep the crown and the gem safe. *Through the strongest of currents you shall swim.* Now, *go*, Rohesia. May we meet again.'

Roh didn't fight Kezra as the Csillan Arch General guided her to the hidden ladder. The chaos of the bridge was getting louder and Roh heard footsteps pounding against the marble floors outside.

'Hurry!' Kezra urged.

As soon as Roh's head was clear of the hatch opening, the lid slammed and darkness swallowed her. She heard a strange hissing sound and tiny specks of light rained down around her shoulders as a magical seal was put in place around the hatch.

*More warlock enchantments?* Roh wondered abstractly as her feet found the rungs below her. Her body felt weighted as she moved down the ladder, as though it didn't belong to her. She focused on each rung, hoping that singular concentration would keep everything surging within her at bay.

*Follow the ladder down. Take the blue-lit path … Follow the ladder down. Take the blue-lit path …* She repeated Kezra's instructions like a mantra, but with each step, her hands began to tremble more and more. The ladder was longer than she could have imagined, and for a time she wondered if she was in a dream, a surreal part of her subconscious that would have her descend a never-ending ladder into darkness.

*Follow the ladder down. Take the blue-lit path ...*

Just as Roh started to truly question her sanity, her foot hit solid ground. As did the other. For a moment, she clung to the ladder, refusing to let go of the thing that physically tethered her to Csilla, to the bridge and what had happened there.

A ragged gasp escaped her and she would have doubled over, but for her grip on the ladder.

*Follow the ladder down. Take the blue-lit path ...* Kezra's voice stayed with her and Roh took a deep, steadying breath. In the darkness, she saw a faint blue glow in the distance, and without giving herself a moment to hesitate, she heaved her pack high up on her shoulders and started towards it.

The path beneath her feet was smooth, unlike the outer passageways of Talon's Reach. She wondered how many cyrens frequented these paths to warrant a paved path, or if it was something only known to Kezra's inner circle. Likely the latter, Roh decided as she trudged on, her chest tight and her talons unsheathed at her sides.

The image of Finn threatened to swim before her eyes, but she pushed the sight of him aside and muted his words in her mind.

*Follow the ladder down. Take the blue-lit path ...*

The cool, crisp air told Roh that the blue-lit path was taking her deep below the gorge, away from Csilla, perhaps to the north, though she couldn't be certain. The path itself wasn't lit so much as it was punctuated with generously distanced jars of blue valo beetles; they didn't do much in the way of illuminating her surroundings.

The terrain began to incline. Slightly at first, and then steeply enough to make Roh pant and her legs burn with effort, the satin of her slate-grey suit sticking to her clammy skin. Still, she climbed, knowing nothing but Kezra's instructions, unwilling to know anything else. All at once, she realised that the light ahead was no longer blue.

It was the yellow orb of the moon.

The passage opened up, revealing the inky night sky beyond and the chilled air of the Csillan clifftops.

'Roh!' Someone crashed into her and she didn't have the strength to stay upright. They toppled over onto the dew-drenched grass.

'Har?' she croaked.

Harlyn was already on her feet, wincing as she adjusted her sling. She offered her good hand to Roh, helping her up.

'You're all here?' As the words left Roh's mouth, she instantly knew how stupid they were. Of course they weren't *all* here. Finn was gone. Finn —

A reptilian shriek sounded and something else collided with Roh. Soft scales brushed against her cheek as Valli scrambled up her side, as big as he was, and settled on her shoulder.

'Thank the gods.' She hadn't spared the drakeling a single thought as she'd fled Csilla, hadn't spared anyone a single thought, but now she was here ... 'Thank the gods,' she said again, reaching for the creature and stroking his forehead.

Roh surveyed her companions. They were all still dressed in their gala attire, save for Deodan, who hadn't bothered to dress up in the first place. All were dishevelled and shocked.

'Did it really happen?' Roh asked, turning to Yrsa. As she drew closer, she could see that the Jaktaren's eyes were red-rimmed, hollow.

Roh's heart splintered.

Yrsa looked around, dazed, as though she was trying to find her words in the space around them. 'Yes,' she said at last, her voice raw. 'It happened.'

The next breath Roh took didn't fill her lungs with enough air, nor did the next. Atop the Csillan cliffs beneath the waning moon, she fell to her hands and knees. Her talons sank into the damp earth and she gasped raggedly.

Valli growled beside her, pawing at her arms, trying to reclaim her focus, but she couldn't ... she couldn't breathe. Finn was gone. Dead. She had sent him to his death.

'It ...' Roh wheezed. 'It should have been —'

A large warm hand found her back, rubbing wide circles. 'One breath at a time, Roh.' Deodan's voice sounded at her side. 'In,' he commanded. 'And out.'

Roh clung to his words as though they were a lifeline, and perhaps they were. She did as he instructed.

'In,' he said, 'and out.'

Somehow, air made its way into Roh's lungs and her breathing steadied; she let out a strangled sob.

'That's it,' Deodan soothed her. 'You're alright.'

She met his gaze for the first time since she'd emerged from the tunnel. 'Am I, though? Are any of us?'

Deodan glanced at the others and then faced Roh. 'No. None of us are alright, Roh. But we don't have any other choice but to keep moving.'

Roh wanted to curl up in the darkness and block out the rest of the realm.

'They'll be coming for you, for all of us,' Yrsa said quietly from the shadows. 'Do you think they'll let you keep the topaz and the crown in exile? Do you think they'll let the Prince of Melodies wander the lands freely?'

'No,' Roh murmured, the truth of Yrsa's words sinking deeper and deeper into her fractured heart. She wiped her nose on the back of her hand and stood, feeling unsteady on her feet.

Odi spoke for the first time. 'Can someone please tell me what in the realms happened back there? What happened to Finn's leg? I know he injured it back in Thornhill, but … I don't understand. How did this happen?'

Roh stared for a moment; she hadn't realised that he was holding Finn's crossbow.

Odi followed her gaze and shrugged self-consciously. 'Roh?'

Roh chewed her bottom lip and pain lanced through her. Finn wouldn't want her telling the others, telling his story, but … Finn was gone. Harlyn and Deodan were watching her, too, waiting for an explanation. But no spilling of secrets would explain what had happened. There was no sense to it. Yrsa remained quiet. Roh inhaled the crisp night air. The passage had brought her to a grassy cliff that overlooked the gorge and the rushing waters below, similar to the cliff from which they'd taken the hang line.

Roh told the others about Finn's leg, leaving out the details about his upbringing. That was private, even in death. The others stared at her as she spoke of the tonic, of the withdrawal he'd suffered from after Thornhill, and yet she still couldn't make sense of the trial, of how Izan Rasaat had won.

'Gods,' Deodan muttered when she'd finished. 'That stubborn bastard, keeping a secret like that.'

'How could we not have known?' Harlyn wondered aloud, her voice laced with regret.

'He didn't want anyone to know,' Yrsa said from where she stood at the edge of the cliff, gazing outwards.

'We all have our secrets,' Deodan offered. 'Parts of ourselves we want hidden from the world.'

Roh struggled to swallow the lump in her throat. She knew more about that than anyone, she'd wager.

It was Odi who spoke next, running his half-gloved fingers through his hair, his expression weary. 'So, what do we do now?'

Deodan crouched by a nearby rock, spreading the

map – *Finn's map* – across its surface. 'We don't have much time,' he said. 'But we need to get as far away from here as possible. I'm thinking we should go north?'

Yrsa rubbed her bleary eyes. 'I don't know,' she said, a note of anger in her voice. 'I have no idea where they might expect us to go. And therefore, I have no idea where to avoid.'

Deodan nodded. 'They might expect us to take Odi home, to the Isle of Dusan.'

'They know we're not that stupid,' Roh interjected.

Harlyn frowned. 'Do you mean we should double bluff and actually go there, then?'

Roh shook her head. 'No.'

Deodan huffed an impatient sigh. 'So, we know where we're *not* going. Great.'

'What's your plan, then?' Roh snapped.

'North-east,' Deodan said, pointing to the map.

Roh crouched beside him and narrowed her eyes in suspicion. 'Why?'

'Well, if we head south, we risk being trapped between Csillan and Akorian forces, just as my people once were. We won't find aid in Lochloria, which is north-west.' He pointed to Lamaka's Basin and the scholar's city. 'All I know is that there is a river we can follow to the north-east, that there aren't many human settlements, and … that's all. But it's better than nothing and it's better than being caught by the council or the Jaktaren. They're likely to join forces with the Saddorien Army at this point, too.'

Out of the corner of her eye, Roh saw Yrsa take a step towards the warlock. 'Finn would ask why you're even still here,' she said coldly, the words sounding foreign coming from her. 'You've not been banished. You can go home. So *why* are you still here? What do you want?'

Deodan's fists clenched at his sides. 'I gave Roh my word. That *means* something to me. Besides, do you think my mother would have me back now? After allying myself with cyrens and trekking across the realms with a bunch of Jaktaren?'

'You had plenty of support from your clan from what I heard.'

'Support for a better world,' Deodan bit back.

Yrsa sneered. 'Well, that's gone now —'

'Yrsa,' Roh cut her off. It was like watching the beginning of a terror tempest form. 'It's not Deodan's fault.'

'Then whose fault is it?' Yrsa snapped, her eyes full of rage, of grief. No longer was she the peacekeeper of the group, no longer would she soothe their conflicts and bring them together. That cyren was gone. 'Whose fault is it?' she demanded again.

'It's mine,' Roh said softly. 'It's all my fault.'

Yrsa didn't meet her gaze then, which only confirmed what Roh knew in her heart already. That it truly *was* her fault. That she had been the one to send Finn Haertel to his death.

Roh shoved the thought down and turned back to Deodan. He was right. Their options were limited and those that seemed favourable were where they were only slightly less likely to be killed or captured. 'North-east it is,' she said. 'Let's put some distance between us and them, then we can assess our supplies and re-evaluate if need be.'

'Agreed,' Deodan grunted, folding the map and tucking it into his jerkin.

Roh ignored the pain that lanced through her, having seen Finn do the exact action so many times before. Instead, with trembling hands, she took the crown of bones from her head and tucked it safely away in her pack. What was the point in wearing it now?

Roh steeled her voice, eliminating the tremor, the uncertainty in it before she spoke. 'Let's move.'

As the company crossed the clifftops in the dark and early hours, the raging river below drowned out any sounds of their escape. All that Roh could hear was the echo of loss, reverberating through her, just as her scream had echoed between the cliffs as Finn fell. The outer gorges of Csilla were wet and cold, and rain began to fall in a steady downpour, drenching Roh and her companions to the bone. There was a solemn vastness to this place that matched the depth of her sorrow, and the colours of the moss and the wild thyme were somehow muted, as though anything vibrant had been sapped from the realms.

Movement caught Roh's eye – a flock of tiny birds fluttering in dips and swirls amidst the cliffs.

*Harvester canaries*, she remembered the Csillan, Mattias, telling them. The shepherds of death. Finn had laughed in the face of such superstitions, but a shiver had passed through Roh's body, as it did now. She tried to rub the chill from her arms and she kept walking.

Roh couldn't help glancing at Yrsa, whose expression was blank. Her chest hurt anew at the thought of having ripped the Jaktaren away from Finn and Piri all in one night.

The sense of purpose and power that had filled Roh so thoroughly only a few days earlier had completely disintegrated. She found herself following Deodan listlessly, allowing him to take the lead without question, grateful that she could remain silent in the cold, dark night.

The warrior warlock took the lead as though it was second nature to him, and Roh supposed it was; he was the leader of his clan, after all. Roh's mind was in the throes of chaos, and to distract herself from the pain of losing Finn, it clung to a different pain: the moments before the trial, when Taro Haertel had told her of the Akorians.

'Deodan,' Roh said quietly, catching up to walk alongside him.

'Hmm?'

'Back in Csilla, I was told something before … about Akoris …'

Deodan didn't stop, but Roh noticed his body stiffen.

'Have you received word from Incana since we left?' Roh asked.

Deodan fished his pipe from his pocket and stuck the end between his teeth, chewing. 'No, I haven't. Why?'

Roh's stomach roiled. 'It's nothing,' she said, brushing

him off with a forced nonchalance. 'Just something one of the elders told me, trying to unnerve me before the trial.'

Deodan did stop then, meeting her gaze. 'What did they say?'

Roh's throat was suddenly dry.

'Roh,' Deodan warned.

She took a breath. 'That Akoris was in ruin. That the cyrens were dying from withdrawal from the drugs I burned …' She watched Deodan's face fall. 'That can't be true, can it? Incana wouldn't have advised me …' She was practically begging him; she could hear the desperation in her voice. How could she live with herself if it was true? That not only had she sent Finn to his death, but an entire territory of innocent cyrens as well?

Deodan wrenched his gaze away, instead staring out into the misty gorge. 'Anything can be true at this point, Roh.'

*Roh*, not *Queen of Bones* as he usually called her.

'What do you think?' she pressed, stepping in time with him once again as they continued on.

'I think you made a rash decision in Akoris,' he said bluntly, his words cutting into her, as sharp as any blade.

'But Incana … She was the one who told me that burning the fields would get rid of the draketail and monke's thorn …'

'And how well do you know Incana?'

Roh started. Incana and Deodan were friends, *weren't they?*

'She was an ally, she drew the —'

'Your decision was hastily made, Roh. Had you

consulted me, I would have told you so, warned you to be careful, to consider the consequences. In any case, we cannot know the events that transpired as a result.'

A sour taste filled Roh's mouth. 'But we can,' she argued. 'You can. Send one of your water birds.'

'You would have me waste precious magic? On this?'

'You would have us remain in the dark? On *this*?' she countered. 'I need to know, Deodan. I need to know what I have done, what I am responsible for.'

Deodan's expression softened. 'As you wish, then.' He reached for one of his vials.

Deodan directed them across the cliffs, setting a gruelling pace. Roh was glad for it. The burn between her shoulders and the aches in her feet stopped her mind wandering too far.

Valli went ahead of them, more restless and moodier than ever, even as the rain eased. Roh noticed that when anyone but her called to him, he reacted aggressively, snarling and snapping his growing fangs. His molten-gold eyes sought her out and he sniffed the air in her direction, as though he could taste the sorrow welling within. Roh paused to stroke his head, trying to reassure the drakeling, but he was no fool. He flared his wings and scurried ahead once more.

On they pressed, the wind whistling between the cliffs, stinging Roh's cheeks and whipping through her hair. She donned one of the cloaks they'd bought in Thornhill, not because she could feel the chill of the air, she couldn't feel anything, but because her teeth were chattering.

When dawn broke blood red across the sky, the company kept moving. The borders of Csilla were nearly in sight and the sooner they crossed the threshold into neutral territory, the better off they'd be. That was more than fine with Roh; she didn't want to stop. She wanted to walk until she could walk no more, until she could think no more.

Halfway through the morning, the rain set in again. Deodan shielded his eyes, squinting into the downpour. 'It should be somewhere around here,' he muttered, more to himself than to the others.

'What should?' Harlyn asked, trying to follow Deodan's line of sight.

'Shelter.'

'We're in the middle of nowhere, Deodan. There's nothing out here,' Odi said gently.

But the warrior warlock shrugged him off and started forward again, the terrain declining slightly. He brought them to the cliff's edge.

'Tell me it's not another hang line,' Roh muttered.

'Follow me,' Deodan said, swinging his legs over the edge and hopping down to a hidden ledge.

Roh's stomach plummeted at the sight of the foaming river and the deadly drop.

*The last thing Finn would have seen ...* The thought caught her off-guard and sent her head spinning.

Harlyn gripped her elbow. 'You alright?' she asked, peering into Roh's face with concern.

Roh couldn't find her voice, but she nodded weakly.

Harlyn glanced from Roh to the drop beneath them. 'Deodan?' she called out. 'Have you got Roh? She's a bit shaky.'

Roh let Harlyn push her gently to a sitting position atop the wet grass, letting her legs hang over the side of the cliff.

'Deodan?' Harlyn called again, this time her voice laced with command.

'I've got her,' Deodan's voice sounded. Large hands reached up and guided Roh's legs down, planting them firmly on the sturdy ground just below.

Roh was paralysed. All she could think of was Finn and how his eyes had widened in shock, as though he too couldn't believe he was falling.

Arms wrapped around her. She was carried from wherever they'd ended up into the warmth of a small alcove. She was placed gently on the ground, where Valli was instantly curling up in her lap, nuzzling her limp hands, trying to bring her back from the brink of going under.

'I'm here,' she croaked to him. 'I'm here.'

Roh hadn't realised how cold she'd become until all five of them and Valli were huddled inside the small cave.

'I think it's safe to light a small fire here,' Deodan was saying as he scraped together any debris lying around them. 'We need to dry off, get warm.'

'How did you know this was here?' Roh asked.

Deodan met her gaze. 'The journals,' he told her. 'I read an entry where the warlocks took shelter in a small cave on the outskirts of the Csillan gorges. It had quite a detailed description.'

'How'd you know it would be here after all this time?' Odi asked, peeling off his cloak and going to the mouth of the cave to wring it out.

'I didn't,' Deodan said, shaping the bits of kindling he'd found into a pyramid. 'But it was worth a try. I didn't think we could go on much longer without rest and I didn't want us to make camp out in the open. Not when we have no idea how many are on our trail or how close behind they might be.'

'Aren't you wise,' Yrsa jeered quietly.

Roh's gaze shot to her, surprised and hurt. The Jaktaren was not herself.

But Deodan shrugged. 'You're not the only one who knows how to move through the realms like a nomad.' He set about striking his flint.

'I know.' Yrsa turned her gaze to the entrance.

'Sorry,' Deodan said, realising his error. He reached for Yrsa, but the Jaktaren pulled away.

'It's fine.'

Roh felt her own heart fracture anew alongside Yrsa's, snatching her breath from her lungs again, but she made no move towards her friend. Instead, she pulled her pack in front of her and Valli made a squawk of protest as she disturbed him. Roh scooped him up and placed him by the fire that Deodan had brought to life.

'How long until we hear from your water bird, Deodan?' Roh asked.

'Akoris is a long way from here, Roh,' he said gently. 'Not for some time. Try to push it from your mind.'

'Fine,' she said, her voice devoid of any emotion. 'We should take stock of our supplies.'

Deodan grunted in agreement, rummaging through his own pack.

Roh lost herself in the practicality of her task. Separating the items in her pack into different piles: rations – *Kezra must have packed as a precaution* – clothing and miscellaneous items. She paused halfway through unpacking and stared blankly at the items … Her broken circlet, her crown of bones and the topaz … What was she to do with them? She wasn't queen and never would be. And Finn had died because of it.

'Roh?' Odi's hand rested on her forearm.

Roh hadn't realised that her cheeks were wet. Flushing, she wiped away her tears roughly and shook him off, returning to the task at hand. With a start, she realised that *The Law of the Lair* wasn't there. It had been under her pillow back in their sleeping quarters, so no wonder it hadn't been picked up by whoever had gathered her things.

'What does it matter,' she muttered. The topaz had led her to that book, but she was out of the tournament and banished from the lair entirely. Its laws no longer applied to her or anyone else in her company. She shook out one of her crumpled shirts, feeling desperate to get out of the soaked satin suit. Roh trudged further into the cave for a bit of privacy. There, she stripped out of the formal wear, her teeth chattering. As she found the arms of her shirt, something cold and hard bumped against her sternum —

The key.

The key to the teerah-panther enclosure, wherein was the Willow's Sapphire, yet another item the council would be scrambling to retake. Roh toyed with the key between her fingers, recalling the eagerness in her friends' voices when they told her they'd figured it out. But they never got to explain the plan to her. *Finn's plan.* Once, curiosity would have prickled at her until she demanded that the others tell her how exactly they'd intended to get the stone from the panther. But now … Now she didn't want to know. Not when Finn wasn't here to tell her himself. She tucked the key beneath her camisole and buttoned her shirt over the top, trying not to think of Finn falling, or the poor creature trapped in the cage back in Csilla.

'What else do we have?' Yrsa's voice sounded hoarse.

Roh returned to the group, finding Deodan pulling an extra pack into the light of the fire.

Roh gaped at him, recognising it at once. 'You brought Finn's?' How had she not noticed before now?

'Kezra's idea,' Deodan offered, untying the laces at the top. 'She packed these as soon as the challenge was announced … Extra supplies …'

A strange sensation rolled through Roh, as though they were doing something wrong. She glanced at Yrsa, half expecting her to object to them rummaging through Finn's belongings. He wouldn't want them doing this, surely? But Yrsa remained silent.

Kezra, it seemed, had seen to filling Finn's pack to the brim with rations of flatbread, cured meats and hard cheese. There were three additional canteens of water and a compass wrapped in waxed parchment. Next, Deodan retrieved one of Finn's daggers and a sob lodged in Roh's throat. A small shaving kit and blade were next, then Finn's tonic, a plain black cloak with a Jaktaren pin and …

'It's your sketchbook, Roh,' Deodan said, frowning as he held a thick pad out to her.

Roh took it without thinking.

'Why does he have your sketchbook?' Harlyn asked.

'Did …' Yrsa corrected quietly. 'Why *did* he have her sketchbook.'

But Roh was frowning herself, pulling her half-unpacked bag towards them and rummaging through it. 'Mine's here,' she said, dropping her sketchbook onto the ground before them and returning her attention to the one Finn's pack had revealed. She flipped through its pages, all blank, the parchment of far higher quality than her own, and she realised with a start as she closed it that it was leather-bound.

'Maybe Kezra put it there?' Harlyn offered.

'Maybe,' Deodan said, disinterested, trailing off as he hunched over his own pack once more. His entire arm disappeared into it, rummaging wildly. Cursing, he stood and tipped the entire thing upside down, shaking it violently.

'What is it?' Roh asked, unease yawning within her as she watched him.

His gaze locked on hers. 'Do you have the other journal?'

Roh picked up the journal that had been in her pack. 'This one?'

Deodan shook his head. 'No, the seventh one.'

Roh's brows furrowed. 'Why would I have the seventh one? I'm not nearly up to that one.'

Deodan scanned their belongings that now littered the cave. 'It's missing.'

'What do you mean, missing?' Odi asked.

'What do you think *missing* means?' Deodan snapped. 'It was with the others. Actually *tied* to them —' He gestured wildly to the neat stack of books that were tied together securely with string.

'Maybe Finn had it?' Roh said, his very name made her insides ache.

'He had just returned the first one to me,' Deodan said. 'Same as Roh, he wasn't up to the seventh.'

'Someone's taken it, then,' Yrsa surmised.

'No one else knew about them,' Deodan said, his face crestfallen.

Discomfort stirred Roh's empty stomach. No one else except … *Delja*. Roh had told her about them on the bridge.

*'Those must have made for harrowing reads … How many are there?'*

But what cause would Delja have for stealing one? Roh remembered the former queen's comfort after Orson's banishment, and her thoughtfulness before the challenge in Csilla. There was no way she'd steal one …

and she'd been on the bridge the whole time … Hadn't she?

Roh kept quiet. There had to be an explanation, and until she had one, she wasn't going to say anything.

There was nothing to be done about the missing warlock journal, and so the company counted their rations and tried to make themselves comfortable.

'No more than three hours' rest,' Roh heard herself say. Something had clicked within her as they'd sorted through their belongings. Her losses were her friends' losses, too, and she needed to steel herself against them. She had the crown of bones, the Mercy's Topaz and the key to the Willow's Sapphire. She was a target and that made her friends targets, also. She would not allow someone else to die because of her. It was up to her to get them as far away from Csilla, the council and the Jaktaren as possible. She would not allow Odi to fall into their clutches, nor Deodan … And who knew what they'd do to a defected bone cleaner and Jaktaren. No, her company was her responsibility and she would see them to safety, whatever the cost.

Roh had pushed things to the dark corners of her mind for her entire life and now she would use that particular skill to her advantage. Ever so carefully, she boxed up her thoughts of Finn, of Akoris, and tucked them away in the recesses of her mind. There would be time enough to grieve him later, but first, he would want her to get Yrsa and the others to safety.

. . .

When they woke, the day that greeted them beyond the warmth of the cave was wet, grey and dreary. They ate little before wrapping themselves in their waxed cloaks, and shouldered their heavy packs, with Deodan carrying Finn's as well. The warrior warlock guided them from the mouth of the cave back atop the grassy cliffs and onwards, north-east. They trudged across the lands in silence, with only grief and weariness for company.

After several hours of trekking, the gorge of Csilla met a far greater ravine, the sheer size of which was staggering. If ever Roh had felt like a tiny drop in the ocean, it was here.

Deodan pointed. 'If we followed it west, it would lead us to the seas —'

A pang of dread pulsed low in Roh's gut. How long had it been since she'd thought of the sea drake that had followed them along the coast weeks – or was it months – ago now? *She must still be out there, perhaps too distracted with her hatched brood of drakelings, Valli's siblings, to take up the hunt again.* There was no doubt in her mind that she had not seen the last of Valli's mother, and that however much time passed, the sea drake would take up her hunt once more to find her missing drakeling.

Deodan cleared his throat. 'And eventually, the Isle of Dusan.'

Odi looked wistfully to the distance, and Roh could tell that he was yearning for the comforts of his homeland.

'But we're going north-east,' Deodan added, pointing in the opposite direction. 'A river follows the ravine quite closely. It'll be good to stay close to a freshwater source, at least until we have a more solid plan.'

Roh nodded, adjusting her pack on her shoulders as she surveyed the forked ravine before her, her heart hammering in her throat as Valli strutted right up to the edge and peered over. 'Then lead on, Deodan,' she said.

With aching hearts and the warrior warlock at their helm, Roh and her company left the cyren territory of Csilla far behind.

# CHAPTER TWENTY-ONE

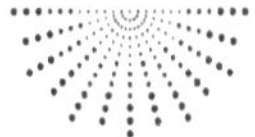

As the company headed north-east, following the river running parallel to the great ravine, the lands opened up into vast moors of heather, cloaking the grass with a distinct purple hue. At last the rain eased, only for the chill to set in as they wandered through the knee-high flowers. Roh gritted her teeth against the cold, trudging onwards across the heather with Valli taking refuge down the front of her cloak. She didn't mind the extra weight or the discomfort of him wriggling every few moments. If she could offer him the slightest bit of reassurance, she'd give anything to do so. She pushed a stray bit of hair from her eyes, scanning the endless horizon. Roh had no notion of the days or nights that had passed, only that it already felt like a lifetime since that fateful moment on the Bridge of Csilla and that no amount of travel could put enough distance between her and that place.

Deodan seemed to be thinking along the same lines,

because he turned back to face Roh and the others, the map in his hand and said, 'In a day or so, we should reach a redwood forest. That'll provide us with some proper shelter and the opportunity to make a decent plan.'

'Good,' Roh replied. The fact that they were still trekking out in the open didn't sit well with her. She knew the council would do anything to have the topaz and the key back in their possession, and that the Jaktaren guild felt the same way about the Prince of Melodies. They wouldn't be far behind, and who knew what resources they had at their disposal … If Roh had one purpose in life now, it was to ensure the safety of her remaining friends. She had already failed one of them.

Valli poked his head out of her cloak and pushed off from her, leaping to the ground. He scurried ahead, disappearing into the heather out of sight.

'I think he's sensitive to all the emotion,' Yrsa said, pausing at Roh's side and following her gaze after the drakeling. 'My viper, Disree, gets the same way sometimes. It's like they can sense the energy in the air.'

'You think it's too much for him?' Roh asked, continuing after Deodan, who wasn't far in front. She spoke tentatively – she knew that Yrsa walked a fine line between rage and sorrow, her moods swinging viciously between the two.

'It's too much for me,' Yrsa admitted, 'so I couldn't blame him.'

Roh let a ragged sigh escape her, her whole body sagging. 'No, nor could I.'

There was a heavy pause before Yrsa spoke again. 'The

group feels much smaller without him, doesn't it?' she ventured, her red-rimmed eyes meeting Roh's.

Roh hadn't dared to look properly at the Jaktaren since that first night, but she did now. Yrsa's eyes were bloodshot, the purple shadows beneath them deep, giving her face a skeletal appearance. Her movements were akin to that of the elderly human Roh had seen in the early stages of the Queen's Tournament; slow and pained.

'You look just as bad,' Yrsa managed, a tired flicker of amusement in her lilac eyes.

'I feel like it,' Roh told her.

Yrsa linked her arm gently through Roh's and they walked on huddled together like that for a time.

'Izan cheated, didn't he?' Roh asked after a while. It had been playing on her mind over and over: the strange shimmering green substance that had covered the curved blade of his dagger.

'There was no rule against what he did,' Yrsa said. 'But there was no honour in it, either.'

'Are Saddoriens known for their honour?' Roh couldn't help the note of bitterness that laced her words. Cunning, cruelty and victory at all costs, that's what they had always been taught.

'Some,' Yrsa replied.

Roh took a moment to gather herself. 'I didn't think anyone but you and the Haertels knew about Finn's leg.'

'Zokez found out during the first round of trials. I've never seen the bastard so gleeful. He pretended that he understood, that he was supportive, but Finn and I knew he was just biding his time, waiting for the right moment to use it against Finn.'

Roh remembered what Zokez had spat at Finn after she'd beaten Orson in Akoris: *A new queen won't make you whole, Haertel ...*'

'That snake,' she muttered, shaking her head. 'So he told his cousin about it ...'

'And he found some sort of counter tonic to treat his dagger with, to undo the support magic,' Yrsa finished. 'Otherwise, a strike to Finn's leg from a normal dagger would have done nothing. Finn would have won. Easily.'

'Gods,' Roh muttered, her voice cracking.

'I know.'

Roh and Yrsa's arms remained linked as they walked on, and the sound of Odi and Harlyn brushing the heather aside grew closer behind them. Roh suspected that her other friends had fallen back to give Roh and Yrsa privacy during their exchange, though Roh got the distinct feeling that Odi wouldn't mind the extra time alone with Harlyn. But Yrsa wasn't done.

'It was for you, you know,' Yrsa told her quietly.

Roh stumbled over an uneven patch of terrain. 'What was?'

'The sketchbook.'

Roh felt her chest cave. 'What?'

'The one in his pack. He got it for you. In Thornhill. Said he'd seen yours was out of pages.'

'He ...' Roh tried to swallow, but her throat was too dry. 'He never gave it to me.'

'No, I know.'

'He changed his mind?' Roh's voice was small.

Yrsa gave her a sad smile. 'I think he was waiting for the right time.'

The day ebbed away and the company didn't stop to rest. All Roh could think of was the sketchbook hidden in the spare pack that Deodan carried and that it had been meant for her, that Finn had bought it *for her*. Why? And if what Yrsa said was true, what was the *right time* he'd been waiting for? Roh wanted to ask her friend a dozen more questions, but it didn't seem fair. If Yrsa wanted to talk about Finn, she would. Who was Roh to force the conversation on her? And so she remained silent, the thoughts of the dead Jaktaren and the sketchbook whirring in her mind like a swarm of insects, loud and incessant.

Somewhere along the journey, Odi developed an allergy to heather. His sneezes punctuated their travels at an alarming rate, until Harlyn made him a face mask out of her spare sling to cover his nose and mouth.

'This stinks,' he grumbled, his voice muffled by the fabric.

Harlyn gave him a hearty slap on the back. 'It's either that or sneeze your brains right out of your skull.'

Odi wore the mask begrudgingly after that.

Valli continued to dart away from them, disappearing for long stretches at a time before burying himself back in Roh's cloak, as though he needed to soak up her warmth, her affection, in bursts before fleeing. Roh didn't know what to make of it, didn't know what she could do to ease whatever burdened the not-so-little creature. She certainly couldn't alter the current of grief that poured through her, through them all.

At long last, Deodan brought the group to a stop by the river's edge. 'I think we camp here for the night,' he told them. 'The redwood forest is less than half a day's walk, so we can reach it by noon tomorrow. No fire, though.'

Roh nodded in agreement. Were they to light a fire, they'd be a beacon to whoever was hunting them. And despite their lack of encounters so far, she knew in her bones that the Jaktaren, the council and perhaps even the army, were out there, somewhere. There was no sign of Deodan's water bird, either, no word of the fate the Akorians had met after Roh had burned their fields. Every fibre of her being wanted to believe that Taro Haertel had lied, a poor attempt to make her doubt herself before the trial. She had tried brushing the issue aside, telling herself that there were more immediate concerns at hand, but Akoris and its people bled into her thoughts nonetheless, as did the sinking feeling that her actions had been rash, as Deodan said, that she'd carried them out in the heat of the moment, without pause for thought of their consequences.

As dusk greeted them, Roh scanned the orange sky for any sign of the warrior warlock's magic. How long had it been since she'd ordered him to send the water bird across the gorge back down south?

Deodan followed her gaze across the sky streaked

with red clouds.

'We won't hear for a while yet,' he told her gently.

Roh sighed. 'I know. I just … I hate the waiting, the not knowing.'

Deodan nodded. 'It's one of the hardest things in life, I've always found.'

Roh glanced at the others, checking they were out of earshot. 'What if it's true?' she asked, raw fear cracking her voice. 'What if I've sent an entire cyren territory to its ruin?'

Deodan rummaged through his pockets for his pouch of pipe herbs. 'I don't know,' he said at last. 'I suppose we face it when it comes.'

'I'd be responsible.'

'You would.'

Roh let their words settle around her. She had nothing to offer Akoris now, no crown or power, nothing to undo what might have been done. She was a wanted cyren. A dead cyren walking, perhaps.

*We face it when it comes …* That would have to do.


It wasn't long before they had huddled together, resting against their packs and handing around rations. Roh took a long drink from her canteen, grateful that she didn't need to measure her sips with a source of fresh water so close by. The same heavy quiet that had kept them company these past nights fell once more, and one by one the companions turned their backs to each other to find what little comfort they could in sleep.

Not Roh. She waited until the others were out cold, knowing the deep rhythm of each of their sleeping breaths well enough by now, and went to the spare pack. Valli followed her, seeming keen to have her to himself for a change. Roh slipped the sketchbook from the bag and wandered a little way from the others, finding a dry patch of heather by the water to sit upon. With Valli sitting stoically by her side, she traced the soft leather of the cover beneath the moonlight, trying to imagine Finn at a market stall surveying the options and choosing something specifically for her.

*Why?*

She thumbed through the pages, as she had done in the cave, marvelling at the thick, creamy parchment, the quality so much higher than her own sketchbook. How could she bring herself to draw upon these pages? As she flipped to the very front, Roh froze.

Precise, neat handwriting, two lines of it, stood out on the otherwise blank page.


*Roh,*

*I thought*


Roh stared at Finn's incomplete words. 'Thought *what?*' she whispered, brushing her fingertips against his handwriting. 'Thought *what*, Finn?' This time, it came out angrily. What had he intended? What did this gift mean? Why hadn't he finished the inscription? Each question barrelled into her with more force than the last and Roh felt herself come undone. She hadn't known Finn, not as she should have, not as she had wanted to, and now … Now she never would. Her face was wet, the hot tears streaming down her cheeks freely, her aching sobs catching in her throat. Her magic whirred within her, building up as sorrow took a relentless hold of her.

Roh tilted her head back to the inky night and sang.

The next morning, no one said anything to her about her song, even though there was no way they hadn't heard it. Roh knew in her heart that the music she'd created last night had been more powerful and more poignant than ever. But it had done nothing to ease the raw agony within, nor the flicker of irrational anger at Finn for the gift she'd never understand.

As they readied themselves for the journey, Roh searched for Valli. She'd fallen asleep with him nestled against her, his gold scales glowing in the moonlight, but when dawn broke, there had been no sign of him.

'He's probably just gone ahead,' Yrsa said, patting Roh's shoulder. 'He was doing it all day yesterday.'

Roh chewed her lower lip. 'I know …'

'So let's go.' Deodan shouldered his pack. 'We'll either catch up with him, or he'll find us.'

Roh didn't miss the glare that Yrsa shot the warlock. She wondered if Yrsa had taken on Finn's disdain for the warrior in the hopes of keeping her friend close. Deodan's lack of acknowledgement of the Jaktaren's moods made Roh think that he suspected as much as well.

As they made to start the next leg of their journey, Roh couldn't help feeling hesitant. Since the drakeling had hatched, they'd rarely been apart, especially on long journeys. Now, it felt wrong. He was as much a part of her as the talons at her fingertips and the scales at her temples. But after scouring the heather for the little beast for over half an hour, the others were insistent that they leave.

'We've already been here too long,' Deodan argued. 'We want to get to the woods by noon, remember?'

'I remember,' Roh muttered, still scanning the moors. Cursing Valli softly, she reluctantly pulled her own pack high on her shoulders and followed after the warrior warlock.

The tight ball of worry in Roh's gut did not ease, and hours later there still had been no sign of the drakeling. Roh couldn't concentrate on anything the others were saying, she just kept scanning the heather for a flash of his golden scales.

'Keep up, Roh,' Deodan called.

Roh made a show of hurrying after them, but her heart wasn't in it. Where could he be? Had her sorrow grown too much for him? Or had he finally realised that he didn't belong with her? That his place was in the deep currents of the sea with his kin? Roh didn't think it was possible for her heart to ache any more than it already did, but with each question pain bloomed anew within her and she didn't know how to keep it all contained.

'There!' Odi shouted, his long finger pointing to something on the horizon.

For a second, Roh's heart soared, waiting to latch eyes on the golden scales of her drakeling. But it was not Valli that Odi had found. Trees. Hundreds and hundreds of trees as far as the eye could see.

'The redwood forest,' Deodan said, with no small sense of satisfaction.

While Roh was glad that they had made it so far, and that they must be leagues ahead of whoever hunted them, the absence of Valli was something she could not fathom, not after everything else. And so she said nothing as she started after the others, who moved with a newfound eagerness towards the shelter of the forest.

When they reached the start of the woodland, an awed breath whistled between Roh's teeth as she craned her neck to gaze up at the ancient giants before her. Enormous trunks of rich red heartwood stretched up into the sky, easily over three hundred feet high and surprisingly close together.

'Wow.' Odi turned in a circle with his head tipped to the entwined canopy. He still clutched Finn's crossbow.

'Shall we?' Yrsa was waiting impatiently.

With a final glance over her shoulder for Valli, Roh nodded and went to her friend.

'He'll find you,' Yrsa reassured Roh with a squeeze of her hand.

Roh forced a smile, which she knew must have looked more like a grimace. 'I hope so,' she replied.

They entered the forest with an air of awe and

trepidation. The presence of the giant redwoods bore down on them eerily, as though Roh and her companions were being watched by gods of old. The intoxicating scent of fresh rich earth filled Roh's nostrils as they moved deeper into the woods, and she marvelled at the sheer density of the trees and how she could no longer see the moors or the river behind them.

Harlyn fell into step alongside her. 'Did you ever think we'd see such a place?' she asked, almost whispering.

Roh surveyed their surroundings, so vastly different to the dank, wet passageways of Saddoriel's Lower Sector. 'No,' she said. 'No, I didn't.'

'Sometimes, I thought we'd never leave Talon's Reach. That we'd die amidst the bone shavings and dust,' Harlyn told her quietly. 'You never thought that, though, did you? You always knew we would do bigger things.'

Roh didn't reply, for the truth of Harlyn's words hit her square in the chest. She *had* always believed they would leave the lair behind, that they were more than lowly bone cleaners. But look at what it had cost her ... What it had cost Orson and Finn and the loyal friends at her side.

'Roh?' Harlyn prompted.

'I ... I don't know, Har —'

'No, look.'

Roh followed Harlyn's pointed finger to something that lay in the dirt before them. They all gathered around the glint of silver. Roh frowned. She'd recognise that piece of equipment anywhere – a bone scraper, from the very workshop they had just spoken of. Roh crouched, kneeling in the damp earth. It even had the initials for Talon's Reach engraved in the handle. She reached for it —

'Don't!' Yrsa's voice cried. But it was too late.

A trap fell from the canopy and snapped into place around them.

A cage.

A cage treated with some kind of magic that instantly snuffed out Roh's song.

A wave of nausea rolled through Roh as her power was trapped inside her, with no outlet. The others rattled the bars of their cage, desperately seeking a weakness in it, while Roh scanned the surrounding woods for their captors. *Are they here?*

'Remember what the old woman said in Thornhill?' Harlyn whispered. 'Do you think this was what she was talking about?'

The words came back to Roh. *'Strange, dangerous folk up there ...'*

Roh's stomach roiled at the thought, and with a trembling hand, she picked up the bone scraper, studying it as she turned it over between her talons, examining the engraving. This was no ordinary trap. It had been set specifically for cyrens, *Saddorien* cyrens ...

'I learned that little trick from you,' said a strangely familiar voice.

Roh heard an intake of breath from behind her and she saw what Odi had seen first.

Tess, the human girl from the Queen's Tournament, emerging from the redwoods.

# CHAPTER TWENTY-TWO

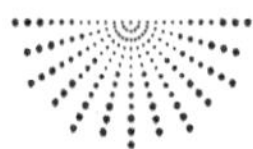

Gone was the trembling, stuttering teenager from the lair of bones; here was a huntress, with an arrow nocked to her bow, flanked by half-a-dozen armed men.

'Is it really you?' Odi pushed past Roh, his hands curling around the bars of their cage as he stared at Tess. 'I thought you were dead.'

'Not dead,' Tess replied, 'not the last time I checked, anyway.'

'How?' Odi gaped open-mouthed at the girl, as though he didn't dare believe what he was seeing.

Roh saw Tess' eyes dart to Yrsa, the cyren who had been her keeper during the trials of the Queen's Tournament. There seemed to be a question there.

Yrsa gave the human a subtle nod and Tess' gaze returned to Odi's.

'They helped us escape,' she said, lowering her bow and arrow. 'Yrsa and the other – what do you call them?'

'Jaktaren,' Roh answered quietly.

The word hung between them, trying to fill the hole Finn had left.

But Odi beamed. 'I can't believe it. You're alive after all this time.'

Although Tess gave a small smile, Roh remained on edge. They were still in a cage, after all, one that was treated with an enchantment no less.

'What are you doing out here?' she asked bluntly.

'I could ask the same of you,' Tess said, her sturdy voice and confident stance continuing to be a surprise to Roh. 'You Saddorien cyrens are a long way from home. And ...' Tess peered over Roh's shoulder to where Deodan stood gripping his cutlasses. 'It seems you've made an unusual friend.'

'Quit toying with them, Tess,' one of the armed men at Tess' side growled. 'They're cyrens. They need to be eliminated.'

'Stand down, Alek.' Tess didn't even look in his direction as she barked the command.

Roh gaped, watching the man fall silent and bow his head in a show of respect. Where was the girl Roh had dragged from the quicksand? Where was the stammering mess who'd cried out for her mama in the lair's twisting tunnels?

Tess' mouth quirked to the side, as though enjoying Roh's shock. 'We usually do execute cyrens ... Cut their heads clean off,' she said, seeming to savour the image. 'They have tormented our kind for centuries, longer even. I was not the first from our township to venture across the seas, only to be snatched away from my family, and I won't be the last.'

Roh's body tensed up and her talons slid free once more. Slowly, she placed a hand on the sling tucked into her belt.

'However,' Tess continued as she moved to one of the redwood trees, her fingers searching for something there. 'I owe more than one life debt to this company.' She found a rope behind the tree and coiled it in her hands, beginning to pull. The man she'd called Alek took up the slack behind her and drew the rope towards him without question.

The trap around Roh and her friends lifted.

The physical relief Roh felt was immense. Her magic was no longer suffocated, and while she did not sing, she felt it radiate from her, free.

'Thank you,' Roh said, stepping out from beneath the shadow of the cage still looming over them.

Tess grinned, refitting the rope to wherever it hid around the massive trunk. 'It's hard to forget someone who pulls you from a stinking bog of quicksand.'

'I did think about leaving you there,' Roh replied carefully, still unsure what to make of the human.

'Oh, I'm well aware,' Tess said, grinning. 'Lucky for me you had the Prince of Melodies with you.'

Odi baulked at that. 'You knew who I was?'

'Of course. I was only a child when I saw you play in Angove once, but I'll never forget it.'

'Why didn't you say anything?' Odi blurted.

'For the same reason you told her,' Tess jutted her chin towards Roh, 'to save me. We had to have each other's backs in there.'

Roh let that little revelation settle between the humans before she spoke again. 'Do you live in the forest?' she asked.

Tess motioned for her men to lower their weapons. 'We live in a township called Serratega, just south-west of here.'

'Then why the traps here?' Deodan interjected. 'Were you expecting us?'

Tess studied the warlock, her eyes narrowing slightly.

'He's trustworthy,' Odi interjected.

That seemed to be enough for Tess. She gave a stiff nod, returning her arrow to her quiver. 'We weren't expecting *you* specifically. But there are strange companies about these days, cyrens hunting cyrens, or so we've heard.'

Roh's stomach lurched.

'They're not the sort of folk we want near our home, so we've gone on the defensive in that regard.'

'But this trap was set for a cyren of Saddoriel,' Roh said, waving the bone scraper at Tess.

'It was. We've had reports that your guild of musician hunters —' another pointed glance at Roh, Harlyn and Yrsa — 'are scouring the realms for the Prince of Melodies. Have been for weeks now, longer. Since the tournament ended, I think. Ever since I returned home, we've come across cyrens in the most unlikely of places, so we started laying traps for your kind. Not too long ago, there was talk of a performance in Thornhill. I knew it had to be you, Odi. The Saddoriens … Well, they saw it as a taunt, a challenge to them. The news of it spread far and wide.'

Roh's skin crawled.

'So, we've increased our traps, our patrols. After everything I've been through, after everything the cyrens *still* put our kind through, we'll happily dispose of any Saddoriens that come our way,' she said with a wicked smirk. 'Except you.'

Deodan huffed a laugh. 'I like her,' he declared.

'That makes one of us,' Harlyn muttered.

Luckily, Tess didn't hear her. The human critically surveyed their company, noting the dark circles beneath their eyes, their ragged clothes and their general dishevelledness. 'By the looks of you, you could use a place to regroup …?'

Roh didn't realise how much she needed that understanding until the words had left Tess' mouth. 'Yes, if you know somewhere?'

'I can do one better,' Tess replied. 'I can take you there.'

True to her word, Tess led them through the redwoods, navigating without consulting a compass, as though she knew every ancient giant that stood within the forest.

Roh couldn't help but glance back every so often, praying that she would hear the scurry of a drakeling across the earth. But there was nothing behind them.

*Where is he?*

A dozen horses stood grazing at the treeline to the south-west and Roh raised a questioning brow.

'Why so many horses?' she asked, watching as the men went about retrieving them.

'We had intended on hunting – game, not cyrens, that is,' Tess replied, biting back a smile. The human turned to her men. 'Alek, you stay with me. The rest of you, try the clearing by the brook, there should be a few elk —'

One of the men interrupted as he mounted his horse. 'Your pa said he wanted hog —'

Tess cut him off. 'My pa isn't here. And there are more mouths to feed now.'

The man began to argue, but he caught the challenge in Tess' gaze and clearly thought better of it.

Satisfied, Tess mounted her own horse. 'The newcomers can ride double,' she declared. 'That'll still give you a few spare horses for whatever you catch.'

No one argued. Roh begrudgingly decided that she too liked Tess, especially this new version of her.

They quickly sorted out their pairs. Roh rode with Deodan, Harlyn rode with Yrsa, Odi rode with Alek, while Tess took the lead, riding solo.

As Deodan's arms closed around Roh's waist, she sucked in a breath. The last time she'd ridden a horse, it had been with Finn. It had been his arms around her waist, his body against her, his jokes and stories in her ear.

'Are you alright?' Deodan asked gruffly. Roh could smell the faint sweet scent of his pipe herbs.

'I'm fine,' she replied, gripping the saddle horn as they lurched forward.

'Keep telling yourself that, Queen of Bones,' Deodan said. 'One day you might just believe it.'

Tess set the pace at a canter across the yellowed grasslands. Roh fell easily into the rhythm. It felt good to ride again, even with Deodan crowding her saddle. She glanced across at the others; Harlyn was wincing with every step, her bad arm held close to her chest, while Yrsa controlled the reins from behind her. Odi looked equally uncomfortable with the stranger at his back, but Tess … Tess was a born rider. She barely moved her reins, directing her mare with subtle movements of the lower half of her body. Either the human had come a long way since they'd first met in the dank passageways of Talon's Reach, or she'd been wearing a mask all along.

As they rode, uneasiness grew in Roh at the thought of Valli. It was one thing for him to have fallen behind or scurried off searching for food while they were on foot, but now … Could he follow her scent across the lands when she was on horseback? What if the horses covered up her scent altogether? She closed her eyes momentarily. All of this assumed that Valli *wanted* to find her. It was entirely possible that he had left, the emotions of the group reaching breaking point for him. Perhaps he longed for the sea. She had promised to take him one day, and maybe he'd grown tired of waiting. The thought saddened her. She had wanted to be the one to show him the rush of the waves and the rhythm of the tides.

It wasn't long before Roh saw a settlement on the horizon.

'Welcome to the village of light,' Tess called over her shoulder.

Roh frowned as she read the script in the common tongue across the weathered sign they passed. To her surprise, Tess hadn't taken them to some barebones shelter in the middle of nowhere. She had taken them to the township of Serratega, her home.

They slowed to a walk, their horses forming two side-by-side lines as a dirt road opened up before them. Roh gazed ahead in wonder. At its heart was a sprawling village of simple buildings, larger than Thornhill, surrounded by farmlands and strange fields lined with rows of wooden boxes.

'What are those?' Harlyn beat Roh to it.

'Apiaries,' Tess said with a note of pride.

'Api-what?' Harlyn frowned.

'Apiaries,' Tess repeated. 'Bee yards.'

'Bees? What in the realms do you want with those nasty things?' Harlyn blurted. Deodan snorted and Roh nearly laughed too, for several weeks back on the way to Thornhill, Harlyn had been stung for the first time. Her hand had swelled up to the size of a sea-drake egg and she'd caused more fuss than when she'd been attacked by the teerah panther. The number of creative curses that had streamed from her mouth had been extraordinary.

'What do we want with them?' Alek burst out laughing, the sound sudden and deep, nearly startling Roh right out of her saddle. The human struggled to keep a hold of the reins in front of Odi as he wiped a tear from his eye. 'Gods,' he muttered, shaking his head as he shared a grin with Tess.

Harlyn scowled. 'What?'

Tess' eyes were bright with amusement. 'Let's just say, they have their uses.'

That brought on a new wave of laughter from Alek, who was slapping his own thigh as he howled.

'Come on,' Tess said, still grinning as she urged her mare into a fast trot. 'We'll be out here till dusk otherwise.'

The rest of them followed suit, and soon they were riding down the main street of the township. People going about their business paused to wave eagerly at Tess before they froze, realising who – or what – she had in her company. But Tess took everything in her stride, waving back reassuringly without stopping to explain herself. Roh had to admire her.

They rode right through the town centre, towards a massive farmhouse on the other side. An older man stood at the front steps, his arms folded over his torso, his eyes trailing suspiciously over Roh and her companions as they approached.

'Tess …' His tone was all warning.

But Tess brought her mare to a stop and swung easily from the saddle. 'Calm down, Pa,' she chastised. 'You'll give yourself another ulcer.'

'Care to explain yourself?' he said, looking down on the cyrens from the top of the stairs.

Tess laughed, tying her reins to a post and greeting

her father with a kiss on the cheek. 'That's Roh.' Tess pointed. 'The cyren who saved me from the quicksand. And that's Yrsa, the cyren who freed me from the lair.'

The man's harsh expression instantly softened.

'And this,' Tess waved her hand in Odi's direction, 'is the Prince of Melodies himself.'

Tess' father's jaw dropped. 'Odalis Arrowood?' he gaped. 'In the flesh?'

Odi dismounted after Alek and sketched a bow. 'At your service, sir.'

'Well … I never …' the man muttered, shaking his head in shock. But his attention snagged on Deodan, who was helping Harlyn down from her horse.

'What about him? And her?'

Tess frowned. 'Actually, I don't think we've been introduced.'

Deodan stepped forward, doing his best to look non-threatening despite the cutlasses swinging at his hips. He wiped his dirt-lined hand on the side of his jerkin before offering it to Tess.

'Deodan,' he said. 'Warrior warlock.'

Harlyn winced as she stretched out her legs. 'And I'm Harlyn.'

'They're friends,' Odi added quickly, moving to stand beside Harlyn.

While Tess didn't descend the steps and shake Deodan's hand, she seemed to be amused at the sight of a human, a warlock and a cyren standing side by side, but she said nothing about it. Instead, she patted her father on the arm.

'This is my pa, Nicholas.'

Roh nodded stiffly at the man, unsure what the etiquette here was.

Alek was gathering the horses and leading them towards what Roh figured were the stables. She cleared her throat. 'If you'd permit us to camp on your land, we'd appreciate it, Nicholas.'

Nicholas snorted. 'If you think I make the rules here, you don't know much, girl.'

Roh frowned; she was definitely missing something.

Tess laughed. 'You can stay in the barn. I'd offer you rooms, but we're full at the moment. My brothers are just back from their travels.'

'And friends or not, I'm not sure how your mother would feel about a house full of cyrens ... No offence,' Nicholas added, limping down the stairs. 'Come, we'll show you to the barn. It's actually quite warm in there.'

Somewhat dazed, Roh and the others followed Tess and her father across the grounds towards a large wooden structure not far from the main house. Dusk was falling around them and Roh saw the lanterns in the town centre being lit.

'Why did you call it the village of light?' she asked suddenly.

Nicholas threw his daughter a look of surprise before turning to Roh. 'You've never heard of Serratega?'

Roh shook her head.

'Our township is the biggest exporter of beeswax candles in all the realms.'

'Oh.' Roh blinked at him. She knew all there was to know about cleaning bones, but candles …?

'Oh?' Nicholas laughed, throwing an arm around Tess' shoulders. 'It was my clever daughter who put us on the map. It was she who started mass producing beeswax candles rather than tallow.' He spoke with unchecked pride. 'Tomorrow she can show you her empire.'

'Oh shush, Pa.' Tess' cheeks were tipped pink, but there was a note of affection in her voice. 'Here we are,' she said, sliding open the enormous barn door.

The space inside was huge. Crates were stacked against the walls from floor to ceiling, along with big square bales of hay. Various farmyard equipment hung from hooks in the timber beams and Nicholas was right, it *was* warm.

'Thank you, Tess,' Roh managed. 'Truly.'

Tess shrugged. 'I owed you one … or several,' she said, with a wink at Yrsa. 'I'll have one of my brothers bring you some food.'

'No need,' Roh insisted. 'We have enough rations for the moment. We don't want to take your supplies.'

'Nonsense,' Tess replied. 'We have an abundance of supplies. No one goes hungry in Serratega. The candle business is good, cyrens.'

Nicholas chuckled at that. 'Very good indeed, thanks to you.'

Tess waved him away. 'In any case, if you want to stay a while, there's plenty that needs to be done around here if you're wanting to earn your keep.'

Roh let her pack drop to the floor at last. 'Thank you,' she said. 'We'll think on it.'

'You do that. In the meantime, it's settled. Food will be with you shortly and I'll see you in the morning.'

Roh and the others murmured their thanks again as father and daughter departed. For the first time since they'd been captured in the redwoods, they all turned to each other in disbelief.

It was Odi who spoke first, his gaze shooting straight to Yrsa. 'How?' he demanded. 'You had me believe that you'd killed her.'

Yrsa raised a brow. 'I did no such thing.'

'You knew what I thought,' Odi pushed.

'I can't control your thoughts. You chose to think the worst of me.'

'But —'

'But nothing,' Yrsa cut him off. 'Finn and I agreed that we'd tell no one about freeing the humans from Saddoriel. We suspected it was a test of our loyalty to the Jaktaren already, we couldn't risk the truth getting out.'

Finn's name on Yrsa's lips sent a bolt of pain through Roh. For the briefest moment, with Tess and Alek at their sides, with a sense of purpose, she had almost forgotten. She had nearly laughed at the memory of Harlyn's bee sting, as though nothing had happened to Finn. How was that possible?

'What of the others? What of Aillard, the Battalonian? He had a wife ...' Odi was asking.

Yrsa sighed. 'He's safe. On a ship on his way back to

the fire continent. He might even be back home by now. Finn and I made sure that whoever could get out, got out.'

Roh watched, frozen in surprise as Odi strode across to Yrsa and embraced her firmly, nearly lifting her off the ground. 'Thank you,' he breathed.

A sad smile broke across the tense lines of Yrsa's face. She squeezed Odi and patted him on the back.

Half an hour later, there was a knock at the barn door and a young man holding a large basket cleared his throat awkwardly.

'You must be Tess' brother,' Harlyn said, getting to her feet and approaching him.

The man grew increasingly terrified as Harlyn drew closer. 'Ye-yes.'

Harlyn's head tilted to one side, as Roh had seen her do many times before when she was sizing up her opponent. Roh rushed to her friend's side, trying to plaster a friendly smile on her own face as she reached for the basket.

'Thank you,' she said quickly, before Harlyn could do any damage. 'I'm Roh, this is Harlyn. What's your name?'

'P-Pe-Peter,' he replied.

'We don't bite, Peter,' Harlyn told him sweetly. 'Unless you want us —'

Roh elbowed Harlyn roughly and her friend shot her a look of annoyance.

'Ignore her,' Roh told Peter. 'You need not fear us. We're friends of your sister.'

Peter's eyes narrowed then. 'Cyrens ... cyrens are no

friends of a human.' And with that, he turned on his heel and practically sprinted away.

'For the most part,' Odi said from where he was perched on a bale of hay. 'He's got a point.'

Roh rolled her eyes. 'We know, we know.'

'We haven't killed you yet, have we?' Harlyn quipped, collapsing against the bale beside Odi's.

'Yet,' Odi muttered begrudgingly.

Deodan snorted a laugh as he went to the doorway and leaned against the frame, lighting his pipe between his teeth.

Roh and Yrsa were quiet as they unpacked the basket, which was full of fresh, hot bread, a knob of butter, a jar of golden honey and two canteens of cold mead. The familiarity in the way they all gathered around and shared out the food and drink sent an acute ache through Roh. There was so much that was unchanged. The silly quips of banter, the ease of sharing what they had between them, even the smell of Deodan's damned pipe, but … There was so much that was different. There was a gaping hole in their group where Finn had once been, a missing energy that had filled their company, volatile at times, but always there, always strong. Without thinking, Roh's hand went to her side, to stroke Valli's head. Her fingers cut through thin air and she remembered with a jolt that Valli too was gone.

For the rest of the meal, Roh was silent. She could smell the delicious aromas of the food, which was clearly made with love and care, but she tasted nothing when she chewed. The others chatted quietly, but Roh couldn't follow their conversations, she merely stared blankly at the fast-emptying basket, numb. Finn was gone. Valli was gone. Both were her fault.

'I'm going to check the loft,' Roh said to no one in particular. She went to the ladder in the far corner and climbed. The flooring covered less than a third of the length of the barn, but the far end was open, with a view of the entire township and the surrounding lands. There, Roh sat, with her legs dangling over the edge, surveying Tess' kingdom beneath the moonlight. She breathed in the crisp night air, her deathsong stirring within her as it often did now, eager to explore, to play in the realms around her. She could almost see it, every note yearning to break free.

The floorboards creaked behind her. She had known it was only a matter of time before one of her companions sought her out, the only question was who had drawn the short straw …

Sweet smoke drifted out into the night. *Deodan.*

'Come to trade secrets and fears in the dark?' she asked, echoing the words he'd once spoken to her on their first night in Akoris.

Deodan groaned as he lowered himself to the floor beside Roh, swinging his legs over the side as well. 'I think you know all my secrets now,' he said.

Roh scoffed. 'I very much doubt that.'

Deodan merely shrugged and repacked his pipe with his strange herbs.

'Fears, then?' Roh pressed.

Deodan raised a brow at her. 'You don't have enough of your own?'

'Most of what I feared has already come to pass.'

'That's not true,' Deodan said. 'When we met, the thing you feared most, was never finding your deathsong.'

'And you were grappling with swearing fealty to the wrong person.'

'I was,' Deodan allowed.

'And now?'

'Now I am here.'

'Have you not made the same mistake again?' Roh hated that her voice trembled as she spoke.

Deodan met her gaze. 'I don't believe so, no.'

Roh gave a dark laugh. 'This is what it is to fail, spectacularly, Deodan.'

'No failure is the end, Queen of Bones,' the warlock replied.

'Stop calling me that.'

'Why should I?'

'You know why.'

'You don't remember what I said about failure? When we were on the balcony in Akoris?'

Roh looked coldly at him now, remembering his words well. 'I have failed harder and faster than most,' she told him. 'And the cost was a friend's life. How can I grow from that? Why would I want to?'

Deodan was quiet for a time before he offered her his pipe; the herbs in its bowl were different. 'Smoke this. It'll help you sleep.'

Ordinarily, Roh would have refused. She'd had more

than her fair share of mind-altering substances, but at that moment … Every part of her was weary, aching with a sadness from which there was no relief.

She took the pipe.

Deodan lit it for her and got to his feet, the floorboards creaking once more.

'No failure is the end, Queen of Bones,' he said again, before he left.

Roh inhaled deeply, the sweet smoke filling her lungs. She wished she could believe him.

# CHAPTER TWENTY-THREE

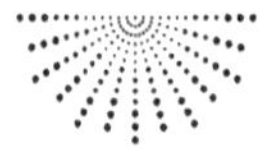

Roh awoke to a phantom stirring on her shoulder. Halfway between dream and consciousness, just for a moment she believed that Valli was curled up in the crook of her neck. Bleary-eyed, she sat up. But the space beside her was empty. He wasn't there.

Feeling hollow, she realised that she'd fallen asleep in the loft. Someone had moved her away from the edge and had covered her with a heavy blanket, possibly Deodan, because his pipe was nowhere in sight. Whatever he'd given her had worked. She couldn't remember the last time she had slept so deeply.

Wincing at the stiffness in her body from a night on the hard floors and the ride the day before, Roh got to her feet and started down the stairs. For the first time in months, she had no sense of purpose. There was nowhere to be, nothing she had to do. She was no longer in the Queen's Tournament, no longer fighting to obtain the birthstones of Saddoriel. For the moment, they were safe from the Jaktaren and the rest. They certainly wouldn't think to come here of all places.

Familiar voices snatched her from her reverie.

'— let her sleep, she's nearly falling apart,' Odi was saying.

'She needs to keep busy. If we leave her long enough to her devices, she'll spiral —' That was Harlyn.

Yrsa cut her off sharply. 'Give her time to process what has happened. Gods, she hasn't had a moment —'

'Here's an idea,' Roh said flatly, descending the ladder and landing deftly on the straw-covered ground. 'Why don't you ask her?'

Silence fell and a few of the faces flushed pink.

'Roh,' Harlyn started, reaching for her. 'I'm sorry, we're just worried.'

'It's alright,' Roh said, taking her hand. 'I know you're worried. I understand. I know I look like a wreck.'

'It's not about how you look, Roh,' Odi said. 'You're different.'

'Aren't we all different?' she countered. 'How could we not be different after everything? *After Finn?*' Roh said his name if only to feel that lance of pain through her again. If she felt it, it meant she couldn't forget him, no matter how much she wanted to.

'Yes, we are,' Yrsa replied firmly. 'But we're still here, we have to live on. So it begs the question … Where to now? What next?'

The Jaktaren waited for an answer, but Roh had none. She was done with making decisions. Her last had sent their friend to his death. So she shook her head and gestured to the others.

'You should vote,' she told them. 'Do we stay here a while? Do we pack our bags with supplies and continue to flee? It's up to you now.'

'Roh ...' Harlyn's voice was gentle.

'I can't,' Roh replied. 'I can't make another choice that might mean life or death for one of you, or all of us. Vote and leave me out of it.'

A wave of quiet shock washed over the group before Yrsa nodded. 'I vote we stay and regroup for a few weeks. Recover, as best we can.'

'I vote we leave,' Harlyn countered. 'The Jaktaren are no doubt on our tail and we need to put more distance between us and Csilla.'

Odi stepped to Yrsa's side. 'I vote we stay. I can't keep going at that pace without a decent rest.'

Roh sought Deodan's gaze. 'And you?'

Deodan seemed to weigh up the options, his brows furrowing and his knuckles paling as he gripped his cutlasses. At last he surveyed the group. 'We stay. No more than three weeks. Then we move on.'

'So be it,' Roh said.

'It's settled,' Yrsa agreed. 'Come to the apiaries with us,' she told Roh. 'Tess is showing us the grounds.'

Roh nodded, pulling on the cloak Yrsa offered her. What else was there to do anyway?

. . .

Outside, the morning was all buttery light and dew-soaked grass, the air crisp on Roh's face. There were plenty of humans already up and about, tending to their daily chores on the farms, bustling down the main street of the township, each moving with a clear sense of purpose.

Tess took them to one of the apiaries on the edge of the nearby woods. The human gestured to the dozens of wooden boxes, each painted a different colour, as she explained with pride how they harvested both beeswax and honey from the hives within, making her enterprise twice the profit.

'Beeswax burns more cleanly than tallow,' Tess said. 'There's no smoky flame, no smell of animal fat.'

'And you came up with that?' Odi asked, impressed.

Tess laughed. 'Well, I didn't invent beeswax candles, if that's what you're asking. But I did see a gap in the market for a better product. I already knew how to harvest honey, so I thought – why waste the wax?'

'Why indeed,' Deodan said, his hand resting on his cutlasses.

As Tess spoke, Roh realised just how badly she had misjudged her. Here was a woman of business, a person who, regardless of her age and gender, had dared to imagine outside the confines of what she had been taught. Because of her, an entire township flourished and prospered, and the girl that Roh originally had deemed weak and pathetic, was fiercely admired. Roh remained quiet as they walked across the wet grass, her regrets collecting like dust on old furniture while Tess guided their small group around the hives.

Roh was brought out of her trance-like state by Harlyn's elbow to her ribs. Her friend shot her a questioning look, her brows knitted together in concern. Roh smiled reassuringly and turned her attention back to Tess, though she could still feel Harlyn's eyes on her.

They spent the day with the human, who showed them around the farms and the township with a great sense of pride. Roh found herself wondering what the place had been like before Tess' contributions. But the girl didn't boast, she simply seemed happy to tell them of her business and how the rest of the town ran. She introduced them to farmers and shopkeepers, all of whom were tentative at first, but at Tess' encouragement, warmed to the cyrens and the warlock as though they were simply human neighbours from across the way.

Odi was in his element at last, no longer amidst a nest of vipers, Roh realised. And she was happy for him. It was nice to see him chat openly with the townsfolk, the colour returning to his cheeks as he answered their questions about his music and travels. Flushing furiously at the requests, he even signed his name to several pieces of parchment for a number of young women. Roh chanced a glimpse at Harlyn.

'They love him,' her friend muttered, watching on with strange fascination.

'Of course they do. He's the Prince of Melodies,' Tess offered. 'What's not to love?'

'I ...' Words failed Harlyn.

Roh had never seen her speechless before.

As the second evening in Serratega fell, Roh asked for Deodan's pipe again. He hesitated for a moment before he handed it to her. With a murmur of thanks, she climbed the ladder to the loft. Up there, she sat with her back against a bale of hay and smoked, letting the events of the past weeks and the tension in her body drift away with the streams of sweet smoke.

Roh slumped to the floor, at last submerged in a deep, dreamless sleep.

As the days wore on, Roh began to appreciate the rugged, rural beauty of Serratega. Its vast lands and tight-knit community thrived and she'd never seen a more content people. By day, she and the others helped Tess with whatever chores needed tending to. Roh was all too eager to take direction, whether it was from Tess, Nicholas or one of Tess' brothers. It was a relief not to think for herself, not to make decision after decision. If she was asked to wash one hundred dishes, that's what she did. If she was asked to don protective clothing and see to the honey in the hives, that's what she did. The fatigue that had clouded her senses so vividly before was gone and in its place was the comforting familiarity of working with her hands. It was easy to lose herself in the rhythm of the work, to numb herself against thoughts of Orson, Finn, Valli and the possible ruin of Akoris. The crown of bones and the topaz remained hidden away in her pack; she hadn't looked at them since fleeing Csilla, nor would she ever again. The key to the sapphire remained around her neck, though. For whatever reason, she'd become accustomed to its weight against her sternum and she did not want to face feeling like another piece of her was missing.

At Tess' urging, each evening, Deodan, Harlyn and Odi went to the local inn to eat and drink with the townsfolk. There was a lightness to their steps as they headed down the hill towards the double-storey structure, a soft glow escaping from the windows, illuminating the street. Yrsa went too, though her steps were far from light. A cloud of anger hovered over the Jaktaren. In the blink of an eye, her demeanour would change from quiet and thoughtful, to a wild, nasty rage about something that seemed insignificant. And yet she went to the inn all the same. No matter how much they insisted, Roh couldn't bring herself to join them. Instead, she stayed in the barn, often scanning the darkening fields for Valli and reading Killian's journals, in search of what, she didn't know. She had long ago given up on finding any answers to her lifelong questions. After all that had transpired in Akoris and Csilla, Roh had come to terms with the fact that she and her life would forever remain a question mark.

After that first morning when she'd interrupted the others discussing her welfare, they had left her to process her thoughts and grief alone for the most part. Each day, she expected one of them to lose their patience with her, for what right did she have to mope, when it was she who had put all of them in this position? But none of them ever said anything of the sort. They watched her with wary eyes and always pushed second helpings of food in her direction. They were kind. So kind that Roh couldn't stand it. She was being selfish, she knew that much. They were all mourning in their own ways, for Finn, for the hope they had lost, for their homes. But Roh couldn't help keeping her distance, worried that her pain would make theirs worse. So each night, she stayed in the dark with the warlock journals.

Roh didn't know why she continued to read them, especially now that she knew the seventh volume was missing. Every now and then she would wonder who had taken it, and if Delja was to blame. The former queen's interest didn't sit right in hindsight, but what did it matter now? And so Roh read, even though she would never know the end of the story.

*Several master scholars have gone missing, their lifelong research burned in piles in the quadrangle for all to witness. Lessons have long since been suspended and the few families remaining are fleeing Lochloria. The territory itself seems to be affected by the despair; the buildings have begun to crumble and the land wilts around us. The crops no longer flourish and the livestock weakens each day. Warlocks and cyrens alike who voice their concerns are escorted to Saddoriel, never to be heard from again ...*

*His Supremeness begged that I abandon my patients and flee. But I cannot leave those in my care, especially Patient Blue. He needs constant treatment. Tremors rack his body daily and the discolouration of his skin continues to spread. I have tried all known remedies, but there has to be more I can do …*

Roh sat back against the hay, staring out into the star-littered night. She felt like she knew Killian, that she shared his fears, both for the cyren called 'Patient Blue' and for Lochloria. It was heart-wrenching to read, knowing what became of the warlocks and their scholars' city. Maybe she continued to leaf through the journals because she believed she deserved to bear the pain of it. It was her kind who had done this to them.

Roh ran her talons across the text, wondering what it had been like for Patient Blue, whoever he was. To be bed bound and largely unaware of the storm brewing outside, preparing to sweep in and obliterate everything in its path.

She froze, staring at where her talon met Killian's messy scrawl.

*The discolouration of his skin continues to spread …*

The strange sensation of recognition stirred and her skin prickled. All at once, she was back in Akoris, in the poison-soaked hollow, visions swimming before her. A female cyren sitting at the stream's edge in what Roh now knew to be Lochloria. In the cyren's arms was a nestling. Blankets were pulled back, revealing a tiny body racked with tremors, and a patch of discoloured skin …

But the recognition didn't end there.

As though in a dream, Roh was pulled from one memory to the next … She, Odi and Ames had been in her chambers in the Upper Sector, and because of Odi's snitching, Ames had made her promise not to visit Cerys. With his eyes full of his usual frustration, her mentor had adjusted his collar, as he often did, hiding … hiding …

Roh and Odi had visited Ames' study, to ask for his help with the second trial. Reluctantly, he'd fished about for his keys to a secret forest-felling site.

*'What's wrong with your hand?'*

*Ames looked down and saw what she was seeing: an uncontrollable tremor. 'Oh, that,' he allowed, turning his shaking hand over to examine it himself. 'The lasting effects of an illness I had as a child,' he told her. 'It flares up now and again, particularly when someone causes me stress,' he added pointedly, shoving his hand in his pocket.*

Roh exhaled a shaky breath, staring at the lines of scrawling text. Killian's words from a previous volume came to her …

*A former student of mine has been brought to the infirmary in Lochloria. He was a sickly nestling, but after the Warlock Supreme intervened, he recovered for a time.*

'But,' Roh said aloud. 'It can't be him …' Patient Blue in Killian's journals would be hundreds and hundreds of years old by now, there was no way he was still alive. Delja, and apparently Cerys, were the only cyrens of their kind who had lived so long. There was no way that *he* could be …

Roh was on her feet before she realised it, fumbling her way down the ladder, Killian's journal tucked under her arm. She had to talk to Deodan. Deodan would know. The warrior warlock had read ahead of her, he had a much deeper understanding of such things. He would know, *he had to.*

Snatching a lantern from the barn, Roh didn't bother with a cloak as she burst out into the fresh evening air and raced down the hill towards the township. The lamps had been lit, but the main street was mostly empty. She knew most of the townsfolk would be at the inn. She headed straight there, trying to think of ways to signal to Deodan from outside – she didn't want to enter the revelry. As luck would have it, the warrior warlock stood outside the inn, smoking his pipe and talking to one of the farmers. Upon spotting Roh, he excused himself from the conversation and met her on the street, his hands gently gripping her upper arms.

'What has happened?' he asked instantly, reading whatever shock was etched upon her face.

'This,' she said, pressing the journal into his chest.

'What about it?' Deodan asked, frowning.

'You've read this one? Haven't you?'

'At least twice. Why?'

'Patient Blue,' Roh began, wondering if what she had to say now sounded utterly insane. 'It's not … it's not *Ames*, is it?'

'Roh …' Deodan said.

'I know,' she replied. 'I know how it sounds, but … Deodan, Ames was sick as a nestling. He has patches of discoloured skin on his neck. His hand trembles …'

'An illness often plagues more than one person, Roh.' But there was something off in Deodan's tone, something that told her he didn't quite believe his own words.

'I know,' she said, her voice steadier in the face of challenge. 'But … doesn't it seem unlikely? That he would have everything in common with that cyren? And that when I undertook the Rite of Strothos, I saw that nestling by the stream in Lochloria?'

'You saw it?'

'You know I saw Lochloria, from my drawing.'

'I know that, but I didn't know you'd seen … A nestling? A sick nestling?'

Roh nodded. 'I didn't know why. It wasn't a nightmare like some of the other visions. And later when I thought on it, the topaz … The topaz told me it was sincere, that it was true.'

Deodan seemed to realise it at the same time as she did.

*The topaz.* Why hadn't she thought of it sooner? Surely the birthstone could determine the truth of things?

'Let's go,' she said, tugging Deodan's arm.

As they started back up the hill to the barn, she turned to the warrior warlock. 'Is it … is it even possible?'

Deodan made a noise at the back of his throat. 'Well … there's Cerys … there's Delja …'

'Delja's a descendant of the gods.'

Deodan made the noise again. 'Is she?'

It was enough to make Roh stop in her tracks. 'What do you mean? Of course she is. She has the wings of Dresmis and Thera.'

'I know,' Deodan said. 'But does that give her a longer life than a regular cyren?'

'Yes? How else would you explain —'

'Then what about your mother?'

'We don't know about my mother.' In truth, Roh had continued to push the question of her mother's lifespan to the back of her mind with all her other unanswered questions.

'It was something I was discussing with Kezra before we left,' Deodan said slowly, as though he wasn't sure if it would upset Roh.

'Go on,' she told him.

Deodan sighed, motioning for Roh to continue walking as they spoke. 'There were rumours in Csilla … about Delja's long life. Kezra and Floralin seemed to think there was more to it than being blessed by the goddesses.'

'How?'

'Kezra told me that … Well, there was talk of Delja buying years.'

Roh scoffed. 'How in the realms can you buy years of life, Deodan? That's ridiculous.'

Deodan gave her a look. 'Perhaps not, Roh. There are other magic wielders in the realms besides cyrens and warlocks. You know that much, surely?'

Roh's nostrils flared at the condescending tone. In truth, she knew very little about magic outside of her own kind's songs and enchantments, but she wasn't a fool. 'I'm sure there are, but —'

'There are people in the human territories that have all manner of powers,' Deodan pushed on. 'They call themselves Ashai folk. Some have control over elements, some can see into the future, some can move objects with their minds and some can even read your thoughts.'

Roh gaped at him. 'And these are humans?'

'Of a sort.'

'Alright,' she said, not quite believing him. She opened the barn door. 'And what do these folks have to do with Delja?'

'There were rumours of an Ashai who could take and bestow years of life upon those he favoured.'

Roh frowned. 'But why would Delja want —'

'Longer life?'

'Well, yes. Cyrens are already gifted with longer life than any mortal being.'

'I'm aware,' Deodan said. 'Only Delja can answer that.'

'But it doesn't explain my mother.'

'No,' Deodan agreed. 'It doesn't.'

'Nor does it explain …' Roh trailed off, gesturing towards the journal Deodan held.

Deodan turned it over in his hands. 'We don't yet know if that needs explaining.'

'Don't we? Deodan, how can it be someone else?' Every instinct inside Roh was screaming that at last she had stumbled upon some strange kernel of the truth and now she was desperate to make sense of it.

'It seems unlikely, I'll admit. But, Roh, this would mean that Delja, your mother *and* Ames have outlived every other cyren in history. Why?'

'Well … my mother and Delja, they knew each other. They were childhood friends … Perhaps something happened to them when they were together.'

'That's all very well and good, but what of Ames? The mentor of the bone cleaners? How does he fit in? Why would *he* be given eternal life?'

'I don't know,' Roh said as they entered the building, the warm air wrapping around her instantly when Deodan shut the door behind them.

'How does it work with the topaz, then?' Deodan asked.

Roh went to her pack, which had remained mostly untouched since their arrival but for rummaging for clean clothes. She took up a place beside Deodan and retrieved the crown of bones from the depths of the bag, the topaz gleaming from its apex. A rush of emotion flooded her. She'd told herself that she'd never again look upon it. That her quest for power had been the most brutal failure of her life.

'It doesn't belong to me,' she whispered, her hands shaking slightly. 'Not anymore.'

'It is yours as long as you hold it, Roh.'

Roh didn't argue with him. She could tell Deodan was up for a verbal brawl and she didn't think she was. Instead, she held out her hand for the journal, which Deodan passed eagerly to her.

'Perhaps I should read the passage while holding the topaz, but exchange the name "Patient Blue" with "Ames"?' she said, wondering if it was more ridiculous than she realised.

But Deodan merely shrugged. 'It's worth a try.'

Roh nodded stiffly and flipped to the page she'd finished on, scanning the text until she found the entry she was looking for. Holding the crown of bones and topaz in her other hand, she cleared her throat awkwardly.

'*But I cannot leave them, especially Ames, he needs constant care. Tremors rack his body daily and the discolouration of his skin continues to spread. I have tried all known remedies, but there has to be more I can do …*'

Nothing happened. No pulse of warmth spread to Roh's fingers, and there was no glimmer from the gem. No recognition of sincerity or truth. Nothing.

'Well?' Deodan asked.

Roh shook her head. 'It's not true. It can't be.'

The warrior warlock's expression mirrored her own disappointment.

'That would have been something,' he said.

'It would have,' Roh agreed. 'To think that Ames was *that* old … And had been through all of that. I guess part of me is glad it's not true, is glad to think he didn't experience all that suffering.'

The barn door slid open and the others tumbled in.

'Roh!' came Yrsa's voice, sounding pleasantly surprised. 'You're still awake.'

'I am,' Roh replied, realising with a start that it had been days – or was it a week? – since she'd been conscious when the others returned from the inn of an evening.

Yrsa smiled.

Roh stared. *Yrsa was smiling.* And Roh couldn't remember the last time someone had looked at her that way, with … pride. It was enough to get Roh on her feet and approach the Jaktaren.

'Have I been that bad?' she asked quietly.

But Yrsa just squeezed her shoulder. 'It's good to see you. Good to have you back. Shall we share a drink?'

Still reeling from the dispelled revelations about Ames, Roh found herself nodding. 'I'd like that.'

The pair sat in the loft, their legs swinging over the edge as Roh usually did.

'I'm sorry,' Roh said, when Yrsa passed her Odi's flask.

'Sorry? What for?'

'For my behaviour. He … Finn … Well, Finn was your friend, your family. If anyone had the right to fall to pieces, it was you. Not me.'

'Grief is complicated, Roh. No one has the right to grieve more or less than someone else.'

'But how have you stayed so strong? Is that a terrible question to ask?'

'No, I don't think it is,' Yrsa said. 'I don't feel strong. I'm sure you've noticed my moods, my anger …? I feel like pieces of my broken heart are rattling around inside me. But … I don't want to block out the world. There is good that still remains, no matter how hard it is to appreciate it at times. And I have a lifetime of memories with Finn. So many things to reflect on and be grateful for.'

Roh took a swig from the flask, surprised to learn that Odi had found a new supply of rum somewhere, the drink they both liked best. 'Sacred is the ledger, right?'

Yrsa huffed a laugh. 'Since Finn and I were fledglings,

our goals have been one and the same, goals that mirrored those of my Aunt Winslow: create a better Saddoriel. Not the lair our ancestors created with bones and terror. Not a place where Finn was caged for being different. Finn always thought that I was the path forward, that with me as queen, we could achieve what we wanted.'

'I'm sorry,' Roh said, passing the flask back. Her mind drifted to an alternative reality, where Yrsa had claimed victory at the Queen's Tournament. There would have been no quest for the birthstones. Harlyn would never have been attacked by a teerah panther, Orson would have never challenged her and been banished, and Finn … Finn would never have fought in her place …

'I never shared that particular sentiment,' Yrsa told her. 'I want you to know that, even now, even after everything.'

'Even now that you can't see Piri?'

'Even now. This won't be our forever, Roh. We will find a way through the darkness.'

'Thank you,' Roh said. 'But what of the Jaktaren pledge? In the sea caves by Akoris, you said you'd repurposed it, as your own code.'

'We had. The ledger we spoke of was a book of ideas we kept on how to improve Talon's Reach and all the cyren territories. A book of dreams.'

'Oh.'

Yrsa smiled sadly. 'He was more of a dreamer than anyone realised. More so than you and me put together.'

The pain that had been so tightly knotted in Roh's

chest had been slowly loosening as Yrsa spoke of their friend. It hadn't eased, but it was a different sort of pain, something more bearable, perhaps. Roh stared out onto the darkened lands of Serratega and the stars that glimmered against the inky night's canvas.

'Will you tell me about him?' Roh asked.

And Yrsa did.

# CHAPTER TWENTY-FOUR

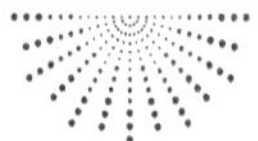

The next morning, Roh felt different, as though a blanket had been lifted from her senses. She and Yrsa had stayed up well into the early hours, talking of Finn and Piri and a better Saddoriel. Instead of finding the conversations harrowing, they somehow rejuvenated Roh, as though she *needed* to hear Yrsa's tales of their friend and home. When the sun had hit the loft and Yrsa had offered Roh a hand up, Roh had taken it and followed Yrsa out into the grounds to train.

Roh hadn't realised Yrsa had kept up her training all this time, but as soon as they began to spar, it was abundantly clear that she herself had not. Within minutes, Roh's body was slick with sweat and her limbs burned from the effort of whirling her empty sling as they ran through practice drill after practice drill.

'Gods,' Roh panted. 'Can't we take a break?'

Yrsa gave her a savage grin. 'Already?'

'Yes *already*, I'm about to collapse.'

'Ten more minutes.'

'Ten?! Try one.'

'Try fifteen.'

Roh gritted her teeth and advanced on the Jaktaren. 'You're going to regret it.'

'Prove it,' Yrsa quipped, blocking Roh's next blow easily and sweeping her feet out from under her, sending her sprawling across the dew-soaked grass.

Roh cursed. 'Is this how you treat all your friends?' she muttered.

Yrsa only laughed and waited for Roh to get up.

The two cyrens practised close combat for some time, with Yrsa pausing every so often to show Roh a new manoeuvre or correct her form. Roh wasn't surprised to find that despite all her complaining, she relished the physical exertion, that the crisp morning air felt divine in her burning lungs and that Yrsa's company was like applying salve to an aching wound. And so she followed the Jaktaren's every instruction, ignoring her fatigue and pushing through.

'How long have you two been at it?' came Deodan's voice. The warrior warlock sat on a nearby fence, two slices of bread between his hands.

'A few hours,' Roh replied. 'Care to join? Yrsa could probably do with more of a challenge.'

'True,' the Jaktaren retorted.

Roh made to elbow her, but Yrsa blocked her effortlessly.

Deodan chewed thoughtfully. 'An interesting offer, but I think we should discuss a different form of training.'

'Oh?' Roh said warily.

'It's time we figured out how to train you and your magic, Roh.'

Roh stared at him. 'What do you mean?'

'We've all felt your power. You need to train to contain it, to —'

'Why?' Roh said bluntly. 'It's one thing to keep myself in shape,' she gestured to Yrsa. 'But what good can come of my magic now? I'm no longer a Saddorien cyren, no longer the future queen. What's the point?'

To Roh's surprise, Yrsa turned to her in shock. *'What's the point?'* she repeated. 'You've been given a gift.'

'Not to mention something you always wanted and never thought you'd have,' Deodan added.

'I realise that,' Roh said. 'But —'

'There is no "but" here.' Yrsa gripped her by the shoulders, suddenly. 'Deodan is right, Roh. A cyren's power is chaos, and our deathsong is the very fabric of that power. And yours … Yours is unlike any we have witnessed before. You have to harness it, master it, lest it undo you.'

Passion and determination shone in Yrsa's lilac gaze, unrelenting.

Roh found herself nodding. 'Alright, then,' she said. 'But how? And who? Who can train me in that way?'

'I can teach you what I know,' Yrsa told her. 'But your power is so different, so much more than mine.'

'Verbal lessons only,' Deodan said sharply. 'Given

Roh's heritage, it's very possible that her deathsong could pose a threat to you, Yrsa, to us all. I'll think on it, Roh. We need to be careful. But I'm glad we're all in agreement for a change. We will find someone to help you. You *will* master your magic.'

Later in the day, with her mind reeling from her conversation with Yrsa and Deodan, Roh joined Harlyn, who was heading out to make candles with some of Tess' friends. Previously, Roh would have slept late and followed the nearest person around the farms, so it had slipped her attention that each of her friends had found a specialty in Tess' business to attend to.

'It's good exercise for the muscles in my bad arm,' Harlyn explained as they approached an outdoor workspace, where half-a-dozen or so humans worked on makeshift benches covered in drop cloths.

Harlyn led Roh to a double boiler. 'We melt the wax here,' she said. 'And shape the wax around the wicks here …' She gestured to a workbench, where a human woman gave her a broad grin, which Harlyn naturally returned.

*Harlyn has been working her charms here, too,* Roh mused. She didn't begrudge her friend that joy. That spark had always been a part of Harlyn, a part that flourished in the presence of others. In the past, on more than one occasion, Roh had found herself envious of that trait, to be at ease wherever she was in the world. But at the genuine smile on her friend's face, she could be nothing but glad, glad that Harlyn had found a flicker of light in the dark, and had found a reason to bring that smile back into the world.

'Then we hang the candles here to dry. The colour fades in the sun, too,' Harlyn finished happily, pointing to where dozens of candles hung suspended from their wicks between two sawhorses.

'Beats bone cleaning, no doubt,' Roh said.

'You're not wrong there,' Harlyn agreed. 'But I wouldn't be mentioning our former profession in the present company.'

Over the course of the morning, Roh found a quiet joy amongst the humans. There were no acts of cunning or betrayal, just everyone working and chatting peacefully. She could see why Harlyn had been drawn to this particular aspect of Tess' work – the women were welcoming and kind, there was a whisper of pride between each station and they clearly revelled in the visible progress of the candles hanging to set at the end of the production line.

As Roh watched the villagers shape the candles by hand, inspiration struck for the first time since she could remember. As the simple idea formed, she relished using that part of her mind again, the part that yearned to design, to build. She took it upon herself to create moulds to pour the hot wax into. The villagers monitored her movements, fascinated by the device she made.

'That could double production,' one woman said, impressed. 'We'll get you some more materials.'

And so they did. Roh spent the morning lost in her own rhythm, glancing at the rest of the production line for opportunities to improve. The morning passed in a blur, almost allowing her to forget why it was they were here at all. Almost.

A few hours later, when they broke for a meal, Harlyn wrapped some food in a cloth and tied it to the end of a stick, resting it on her shoulder.

'Come on,' she said. 'I'll show you my favourite lunch spot.'

'You have a favourite lunch spot?' Roh nearly laughed.

'Of course I do.' Harlyn led Roh across the fields, past several herds of cattle and up a round, green hill. 'Up here,' she called.

Roh followed.

At the crest of the hill, Harlyn dropped unceremoniously to the grass and started unwrapping their spread. 'Well, don't just stand there,' she said. 'Look around.'

Roh turned back to face the way they had come. Breathing in the sweet, crisp air, she marvelled at the expanse of open space. No matter how far she travelled, that feeling never grew old to her. The cloudless sky met the verdant fields in smooth lines around the hills. Livestock dotted the lands, grazing happily. There was a peacefulness here that Roh had never encountered, a leisurely slowness to life that allowed one to drink it in, to savour its rich taste. For the first time since leaving Csilla, she allowed herself to wonder if she could have lived again in Saddoriel after all of this, to be confined to the lair once more, even as queen.

'It's beautiful,' Roh said at last, sitting down beside her friend.

'I know,' Harlyn replied as she drizzled honey over a slice of fresh bread.

'You come here every day?'

'Pretty much since we first arrived.'

'I can see why.'

Harlyn made a satisfied noise as she ate and took in the view.

'Har?'

'Hmm?'

Roh pushed her hair back from her brow. 'I'm so sorry it's taken until now for me to ask, but … how have you been?'

Harlyn gave a sad smile. 'I'm alright, Roh. Managing. It's strange, being here and not knowing where we're heading next, but … I'm glad in a way.'

'Glad?'

'I have seen so many things. Learned so much … We're here with *Yrsa Ward* of all cyrens, and Odi …' she trailed off.

'What about Odi?' Roh pressed gently.

Harlyn raised a brow. 'What are you suggesting?'

'Nothing.'

'Uh-huh,' Harlyn said sarcastically. 'You know, you're not half as subtle as you think you are, Rohesia.'

'Well, tell me, then.'

'There's nothing to tell.'

'You've always got something to tell.'

Harlyn sighed. 'He's human.'

'Does that truly matter?'

'I'm not sure.'

'He's been looking at you,' Roh told her, thinking of all the times she'd seen their friend steal glances at Harlyn.

Harlyn grinned. 'Everyone looks at me, I'm amazing.'

'Well, that's true,' Roh replied, seeing the response for what it really was: a deflection. She let the matter rest.

The friends sat in silence for a while, watching the shadows of the clouds pass over the green fields below. But wrapped in quiet, Roh felt the all-too-familiar flicker of guilt.

'Har?' she said again.

'What now?'

'Do you resent me?' Roh asked, wondering where she'd plucked the courage from. It was one of many questions that plagued her day in, day out; the paralysing fear that Harlyn secretly couldn't stand her, for all she'd done to bring them here, for all they had lost. 'I haven't apologised to you yet,' she heard herself say.

Harlyn handed her a piece of bread and sighed, looking out onto the paddocks and the township beyond. 'You know ... I was so angry at you for cheating in that game of Thieves,' she said, her voice sounding far away. 'It was like you'd taken the life I had planned away from me. But ... I look at you now and all that you've endured ...' Harlyn paused, her face lined with her own guilt.

'And what?' Roh asked quietly.

Harlyn met Roh's gaze. 'I look at all that ... and I selfishly think: *thank the gods that's not me.*'

Roh let the words sink into her, like a hot brand into

flesh. But she found that they didn't burn as they once might have, that Harlyn's honesty did not chain her to her past actions, but rather, they freed her from them.

Roh put an arm around her friend's shoulders. Harlyn leaned into her, resting her head against Roh. Perhaps Harlyn had been right back in Akoris …

*'Maybe some things need to be broken before they can be welded back together, to be stronger than ever before …'*


Days in Serratega turned into weeks. The passing of time meant little to Roh now that she was no longer competing for the crown, racing against the clock to find the birthstones of Saddoriel. The panicked intensity of her quest had ebbed away, replaced by pockets of silence and quiet moments with her friends. There had been no sign of the Jaktaren hunting Odi, nor of any cyrens who were likely seeking the Mercy's Topaz. As Roh went about her daily tasks, she wondered if it was pure dumb luck, or that amongst the renowned candlemakers of the realm, was the last place cyrens would think to look. There was also no sign of Deodan's water bird, no word from Akoris … During a moment or two when Roh felt daringly indulgent, she pretended she'd imagined the conversation with Taro Haertel. But she never let her thoughts linger there for long. She missed Valli intensely, still waking to a phantom imprint at her side, still half expecting to find him buried in her dinner. She told herself she'd made peace with it, though, his leaving. He was a wild creature, a legend of the ancient deep, he didn't belong at the side of an exiled cyren. He belonged in the magic of the current, where he would grow to be a king of the vast seas. That thought gave Roh comfort in his absence, that Valli had somehow found his true place in the world.

Roh no longer used Deodan's pipe in the evenings, but she had yet to venture into the local inn with the others. There was something about it that made her want to retreat to the loft in the barn and stare out onto the fields alone. Each night, the others took turns asking her to join them, and each night she politely declined. She didn't know why. Perhaps it was because when the last rays of the sun dipped behind the hills and the moon rose to take its place, she allowed herself to sink into her thoughts, her memories, her questions … The ones she kept at bay all day, but that like a garden, needed tending to. As much as she told herself she wanted to forget, that she wanted to move on from everything that had happened with the Queen's Tournament, she couldn't. There came a point during every night where these thoughts and memories demanded her undivided attention, and for that she wished to be alone.

Cocooned by her own solitude, Roh thought of Orson and Finn, of Valli and Ames, of everyone she had lost. She missed them all terribly, as though a part of her had been taken and she would never be whole again. In her darkest moments, she thought of Cerys … She wondered if anything had changed for her mother, she wondered if Cerys had realised that her daughter hadn't stepped foot inside Saddoriel's Prison for months. Did she know that they would never see each other again? Had Delja told her?

One evening, Roh was midway down this particular thought spiral when she heard something. A sound that had every nerve in her body alert and thrumming.

A note of music.

Roh didn't remember getting to her feet or climbing down the ladder from the loft. She was halfway down the hill towards the township before she noticed she'd left the barn at all. However rough around the edges it was, the music called to her: a lone fiddle in the night.

Roh found herself on the doorstep of the inn, the melody pouring from the windows around her, the sound of contented chatter and laughter within. But she was in a trance … How long had it been since she'd heard music? Since her cyren magic had awakened so wildly within?

'Roh? Is that you?' Tess appeared in the doorway, a foaming jug of mead in hand. 'Aren't you coming in?'

Roh opened and closed her mouth, but the words didn't come.

Tess tugged gently on her arm, and with the human at her side, Roh at last went inside.

Her eyes went straight to the source, unable to see anything else but the small girl who held her fiddle to her chin. She couldn't have been older than ten. She stood on a chair at the centre of the bar, so all could see her, so the song drifted across the crowd.

Her chords were not as finessed as the Eery Brothers, but the sound that flowed from her instrument had heart. Each note that cascaded around Roh coaxed her magic from where it had buried itself within her. She felt it rushing through her veins.

'You're here,' said a familiar voice. Odi. 'Come sit with us.'

'I …' Roh wanted to say that she didn't know if she should, with her cyren magic swirling so strongly around her. But she also couldn't walk away, not from the human-made magic that flooded the inn.

Odi looped his arm through hers and brought her to a table where Harlyn, Yrsa and Deodan sat. It was achingly familiar.

*'Vallius,' Finn had declared, naming her drakeling before a crowd of eager humans. 'Valli for short.'*

The memory hit her swift and sharp, like the slice of a blade to exposed skin. But with a sudden start, Roh spotted an old piano in the far corner and remembered what had happened the last time they'd all been in a tavern together.

'They haven't forced you to play, have they?' she asked Odi. She wasn't sure she could bear it if they had.

But Odi shook his head. 'No, not at all. They have asked me about music and my travels, but no. No one has tried to make me do anything.'

Roh loosed a breath. 'That's good.'

'They're good people,' Odi replied, easing back into his seat and returning his attention to the youngster with the fiddle.

Harlyn poured Roh a mug of mead and pressed it into her hand. 'I'm glad you're here,' she said.

'I didn't know there was music,' Roh murmured, her eyes still on the performer.

'We told you there was,' Deodan interjected.

'Did you?'

'Only about fifty times,' Harlyn replied.

'Oh.'

'You weren't ready.' Yrsa gave her a small smile.

'I guess not.'

'But you are now?' Odi asked.

'I must be …' Roh relaxed back into her seat. 'Gods, I missed it.'

Odi seemed to nod to himself and slowly he stood. 'Good.'

Roh frowned. 'What's he doing?' she asked the others, watching her friend stride across the tavern as the final note of the fiddle fell silent. He made straight for the piano.

'No —' Roh started in alarm.

But Harlyn's hand fell atop hers. 'He's been waiting for you.'

'What … what do you mean?' Roh managed.

'A few times I've seen him looking at the piano, like an old friend he missed dearly,' Harlyn told her.

Roh didn't take her eyes off Odi, who had settled himself on the stool, the entire inn falling silent around him.

'But he said that when he first played of his own free will, it would only be when you were there for it,' Harlyn finished.

Hot tears burned Roh's eyes, but she didn't allow them

to spill. From across the room, Odi met her gaze and smiled.

The Prince of Melodies ascended his throne, and at last Odalis Arrowood lifted his long fingers freely to the keys and began to play.

Roh was swept away on a current of Odi's making. The piece burst into being, a ballad of thriving chords and delicate dips; it filled every inch of the inn and every hollowed heart. Odi's fingers danced across the keys, at one with the instrument, as though he possessed it and the music it made.

Roh was hardly breathing as the song wrapped around her, as it coaxed whatever remaining power of hers lay dormant, out into the wild. She felt her magic surge, felt it flourish as the vibrant chorus began anew.

'Roh ...' Deodan whispered, nudging her.

Roh tore her eyes away from the Prince of Melodies and saw what Deodan pointed to. Ribbons of shimmering gold streamed from her unsheathed talons, drifting into the air, slowly exploring the space in time to Odi's song.

Roh gasped, a fist clenching around her heart. Deodan's words about her magic being a threat echoed in her mind. This was what he'd been talking about. She had no mastery of it. She'd lost control, she'd put them all at risk.

'Easy,' Deodan said to her, gripping her arm. 'It's alright.'

'But —'

'You're not hurting anyone.'

Roh's eyes darted around the inn, expecting to see

humans falling to the ground, for screams to slice through the beauty of Odi's playing. But the gold light simply explored, and the humans … Something shifted in the humans … Their faces were bright with joy as they watched it, fascinated, not fearful. Children at their parents' sides let out small shrieks of delight, darting from beneath tables and behind skirts to chase the light across the room, a wonderful new game. The adults let them, their eyes wide with awe, with appreciation for something beautiful.

'What's happening?' Roh asked.

'You know what's happening,' Deodan told her, releasing her arm and looking from the ribbons of light to Odi.

'My magic … It likes the music …'

Deodan smiled. 'So it would seem.'

'And it's not dangerous …?' Roh stared, watching on in wonder as her magic floated in streams amidst the beams of the ceiling, each one inching closer to where Odi played. He smiled; the Prince of Melodies was not afraid.

Tess' father, Nicholas, waved to Roh from across the room, no suspicion in his gaze, only utter elation.

'No,' Deodan said quietly to Roh. 'Tonight, it's not.' The water warlock beamed at her. 'It was your darkest fear not so long ago, that you would not find your power. Do you remember what I told you? Back in Akoris?'

At last, Roh let herself return his smile. 'That there was no such thing as a songless cyren.' Brimming with relief, she sat back, leaving her palms upturned on the table, more gold pouring from her talons as she closed her eyes and let the music wash over her again. She felt it deep in her empty chest, shifting shards, knitting together that which had fractured so many times and broken apart. The sound was the creation of a true master, a never-ending hymn, a celebration of life itself that spoke directly to Roh. And so Roh stayed, into the darkest hours of the night, and she listened.

She listened with every fibre of her being and drank the music in.

Just as Odi's music had started to knit Roh back together, so too had it begun to mend the fractures between them all. Roh remembered the words Odi had once spoken to Finn: *'If that's not power, I don't know what is.'* She had agreed with him then, as she did now. With the entire township buzzing about the Prince of Melodies' performance, the next morning, Roh and her friends retreated to the southern apiaries to harvest wax and honey for Tess.

That poignant sadness still lingered in Roh, but it was lighter somehow, lighter when they all bore the weight of it together. She breathed in the crisp, fresh air and turned her chin to the sky, allowing the distant warmth of the sun's rays to kiss her face.

When they reached the apiaries tucked away in a small valley, Odi helped Roh into a protective suit and mask, so she could harvest the wax without being stung.

'I'll just stay back here, out of the way,' Harlyn called

to them, making a show of her sling which had made a sudden reappearance that morning. 'I'll be no use. Can't move my arm all that well for harvesting,' she added.

Odi huffed a laugh and Roh shared his grin. 'Whatever you say, Har,' he called back to her.

At a hive a few yards away, Yrsa and Deodan were deep in conversation over a frame, about to start extracting the wax.

'You ready?' Odi asked Roh.

Roh nodded. 'So we just take out the frame, like they have,' she gestured to the others, 'then use the hot knife to scrape the wax into the container? That's it?'

'Basically,' Odi said. 'Then I'll deal with the honey.'

'Right. Where are the knives?'

Odi pointed to a steel bucket as he pulled on his own gear. 'In there, they're kept hot with coals, so be careful. Use the protective gloves.'

'Got it,' Roh said.

Together, they removed a thick frame from the hive, and while Odi held it in place over an empty vessel, Roh used the hot knife to scrape the wax away from the honey.

'It's sort of soothing,' she murmured, watching the wax curl away from the heat of her blade.

Odi laughed. 'I know. Why do you think I've been out here every day since we arrived?'

They moved from hive to hive, doing their best not to disturb the queen and her swarm within as they removed the frames. Roh enjoyed the work and being in Odi's company again.

'You seem good today,' Odi observed as she continued to scrape away the wax.

'I suppose I have you to thank for that,' she replied. 'Thank you … for what you did.'

'It was my pleasure.' Odi smiled.

'We can't stay here forever, though,' Roh said, cursing herself at the same time. Why couldn't she ever just enjoy a nice moment?

But to her surprise, Odi nodded. 'I know. Do you have a plan?'

'Not yet … I just know we can't stay, can't continue to put Tess and her people at risk.'

'I agree.'

'Perhaps … perhaps tonight we can talk to the others, maybe brainstorm together and find a solution. What do you think?'

'I think that's the best idea you've had in a long while.' Odi was grinning.

*We make a good team*, Roh realised. *We always have.*

However, halfway through the day, while the sun was still high and the fields were still abundant with movement, Roh's skin prickled.

She froze, her hot knife suspended in midair.

'What is it?' Odi asked, frowning beneath his mask.

Roh thought it would pass, that it was just a drop in temperature or a change in the direction of the gentle breeze around them. But her magic stirred beneath her skin, as though it sensed something she couldn't yet see.

A shadow passed over the verdant field, dark and swift.

'Did you see that?' Roh searched the skies for the source. She saw nothing.

Odi removed his mask and squinted to the crest of the northern hill. 'I did … but what —'

The shadow cast across the lands again and a strangled noise escaped Roh.

Large gold wings flared above the rise.

Roh took an unsteady step forward, towards the young sea drake that flew over the cresting land.

'Valli?' she croaked.

An ear-piercing shriek sounded and a hard gust of wind hit Roh in the chest as the beast flapped its wings, hovering above the land, as though he was waiting for something.

Before Roh could run to him, another cry sounded.

Yrsa was running across the field, towards the hill.

Roh's hand went to her mask, drawing it away from her face. A ragged gasp escaped her and her knees buckled.

For a figure had appeared on the rise, just beneath the drake.

He leaned heavily on a staff, his broad shoulders sagging with the effort, something tucked under one arm.

He lifted his hand in recognition.

Roh's heart quickened. *I know you*, her song seemed to say.

And she did.

For Finn Haertel had returned from the dead.

# CHAPTER TWENTY-FIVE

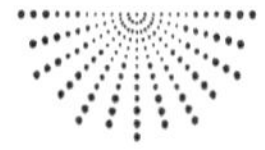

Roh dropped her mask.

*How is this possible?*

She took a step towards the figure on the horizon, hands trembling at her sides, not allowing herself to hope. *This has to be some sort of trick, an illusion …*

But there was nothing false about the forceful wind that whipped through the air as the drake flew towards her, nothing false about the beat of those golden wings, the bone structure visible through the membrane, and the clumsy landing that nearly sent the creature sprawling before her.

'Gods,' she murmured as she reached Valli, her heart in her throat. 'You've gotten big.' She launched herself at the creature, who was now the same height as a large horse, the barb protruding from the end of his tail looking deadlier than ever. Roh wondered if it was poisonous yet. The spikes along his spine had hardened and his scales were warm from the sun as he nuzzled her with his long snout. Roh didn't miss the new rows of razor-sharp teeth that lined his mouth now.

Relief rushed through her, relief so pure it was overwhelming. She hadn't scared him away. He hadn't returned to the seas. Valli was back. And so was —

Roh watched Yrsa and Finn collide in a fierce embrace. Yrsa's feet actually left the ground as Finn's arm wrapped around her. They buried their faces in one another's necks, holding each other tight, a family reunited.

Staring at the Jaktaren, Roh still wasn't sure she believed it. She had watched Finn fall, had seen his death with her own eyes —

Valli nudged her and Roh ran her hand over the drake's forehead, relishing the feel of his soft, warm scales, something she had thought she'd never do again.

'Well, there's no hiding you now, is there?' she told him, resting her brow against his.

Valli huffed.

Slowly, Roh allowed herself to turn to where Finn and Yrsa were approaching the rest of the group, arm in arm. Roh looked Finn over critically. His clothes were dishevelled and worn, his hair was messy, strands coming loose from its tie. The dark shadow of a beard graced the lower half of his face, making his square jaw even more angular and his gaze sharp. Roh's eyes went to the staff he leaned heavily on and saw that the fabric of his trousers flapped loosely below the knee of his left leg. Finn met her stare as she glanced back up at his face, which was lined with pain and weariness. His lilac eyes locked on hers, and Roh was desperate to say something, anything, to tell him —

Words escaped her, so she threw herself at him instead, nearly knocking him over. She pulled him to her tightly, savouring the feel and smell of him. He was *real*. *This* was real. Finn dropped whatever he'd been holding and closed his arms around her, returning her embrace, hard. They didn't let go of each other. For a moment, it didn't matter what Roh had thought she wanted to say. As she stood wrapped in Finn's arms, her grief, her guilt, her questions, and everything in between, all fell away.

Then she became aware of the others, and how long she and Finn had been holding onto one another. Reluctantly, she stepped back, reached for the staff he had dropped and handed it to him.

Finn tore his gaze away from Roh. 'What's a cyren need to do around here to get a chair?'

A laugh burst from Harlyn and she rushed forward, hugging the shocked Jaktaren firmly. Odi followed after, wrapping his long arms around them both. A sight Roh never thought she'd see.

Even Deodan came forward and shook Finn's hand. 'Gods, it's good to see you,' he said gruffly.

'Can you make it back to the barn?' Roh heard herself say. 'It's about two miles ...' She flushed. *That's what I chose my first words to be to him, after all this time?*

But Finn simply nodded. 'If someone takes this damn

book, I can manage well enough.' He reached for the other object he had dropped.

Roh recognised it instantly. It was *The Law of the Lair*, the one she'd taken from the Akorian library.

'How did you get that?' she breathed, taking it from him. As she did, her knuckles grazed his, and for a moment they were connected once more.

'It's a long story,' Finn replied, easing his weight evenly between his good leg and the staff. 'One I'd care to tell from the comfort of a decent seat, and a flask of something strong in my hand.'

Yrsa was beaming beside him. 'I think we can manage that.'

'Good.' Finn grinned back at her. 'Now, can someone tell me what in the name of the gods you're all wearing?'

The others laughed, closing up the hives and peeling off their protective layers. But Roh just stared, her hand finding Valli once again.

*He's back*, she told herself, as though she still didn't believe what she was seeing. *They're back. They* both *are.* But the drake shifted beneath her touch, his powerful muscles bracing before he launched himself skywards, flying in a lopsided way towards the woods.

The group started towards the township and Roh felt a piece of herself go with him. *Don't leave*, she wanted to scream after him. But she kept quiet, at last pulling off her own protective suit.

'He'll return,' Finn said quietly. 'We haven't eaten in a while, so he's probably just gone to find food. He was eager to get here, to see you.'

*Was he the only one?* Roh was desperate to ask, but instead, she just nodded.

As they entered the township, Tess spotted them, and to Roh's surprise, the human thrust aside the basket she was carrying and lunged at Finn, throwing her arms around him, nearly toppling him over, as Roh herself had almost done.

'They said you were dead!' she cried, her face alight with joy.

'Not quite,' Finn replied, smiling down at her.

'Pa,' Tess called over her shoulder. 'This is the cyren who led the escape through Talon's Reach! This is Finn.'

Nicholas came forward, offering his hand. 'Then I owe you a great debt.'

The tips of Finn's cheeks flushed pink. 'There's no debt,' he said gruffly, waving Nicholas away.

'Finn led us through the tunnels,' Tess gushed. 'And he found a ship for Aillard, the older man I told you about, one bound direct for Battalon so he could get back to his wife.'

Finn looked immensely uncomfortable and for that, Roh was selfishly grateful. It was the first *normal* thing that had happened since the Jaktaren had crested that hill.

'We've left the wax with your brothers,' Roh interjected, drawing the attention away from Finn. 'But if you've got no objections, we'll take the afternoon to ourselves?'

Tess was already shooing them away. 'Of course, of course, take whatever time you need.'

Roh went to leave, but Valli flashed in her mind. The

townsfolk of Serratega were surprisingly accepting, but she didn't think they'd take kindly to the shock of her scaled friend flying overhead, casting shadows over their crops and livestock. She hugged *The Law of the Lair* close and shifted from foot to foot. 'Ah … Tess?' she ventured.

'Hmm?'

'Don't be alarmed if you … if you see a young sea drake flying about.'

Tess' mouth dropped open. 'What?'

'A sea drake,' Roh said clearly. 'He's … he's a companion of ours. He won't harm anyone.' *I don't think,* Roh added mentally. 'But if you see him around the barn later … well, he's with us.'

'A sea drake,' Tess repeated.

'That's right.'

Tess shook her head in disbelief. 'Don't suppose you're going to tell me how *that* happened?'

'Perhaps another time.'

'Whatever you say, Roh,' Tess said, smiling.

Yrsa went ahead to the main house to stock up on food, while Roh and the others led Finn back to the barn. Deodan and Odi went to work manoeuvring bales of hay and stacking pillows to make Finn a decent chair and somewhere he could rest his leg. While he looked tired and dishevelled, the rugged appearance suited him, perhaps more so than that of the stoic Saddorien.

'Thank you.' Finn sighed as he sank back into the makeshift seat. He pulled his stump up, massaging the end of it with a pained wince.

Roh ached for him. She'd been there the first time he'd

gone through the withdrawal of his tonic. To have to go through it all over again in such a short space of time was horrific. Putting down the book she still clutched, she went to his pack, which they'd kept, rummaged until she found the vials and brought them to him. She had to ground herself with practical tasks, lest the tidal wave of feeling come crashing in.

'You'll be wanting these?'

Finn stared at them in her palm, almost as though he didn't recognise the tonic he had depended on for much of his life. 'I don't know,' he said, more to himself than to her. The uncertainty in his voice was more foreign to Roh than any of the unknown lands they'd crossed.

Roh frowned. 'What do you mean?'

Finn took the vials, pocketing them, but he did not take a dose. 'It doesn't matter.'

Roh opened her mouth to argue that *yes*, it very much *did* matter, but Yrsa appeared at the door, her arms laden with food. Deodan rushed to help her, so Roh and Odi pushed two more bales of hay together to create a table for their feast.

Yrsa pressed a large flask into Finn's open hand. 'You've got a chair and something strong,' she said. 'So start at the beginning.'

Roh and the others sat around the makeshift table and turned their attention to their friend. Each of their awed expressions mirrored what roiled within Roh. None of them could quite believe that he sat before them, but they didn't want to question it, lest he vanish before their eyes again.

Finn's gaze skimmed across them before he lifted the flask to his lips and took several large swigs. 'Alright, then …' He ran a hand through his hair. 'I'm assuming you worked out that Izan's dagger was coated with an enchantment to interfere with my leg?'

They nodded.

'Well, my leg vanished and I stupidly lost my balance as the agony of it hit me. It wasn't like the slow withdrawal of missing doses of tonic. This was like any magical support, both physically and mentally, was ripped from my very being, like part of me was torn open. I went into shock instantly and then … Well, then I was falling. I thought I was going to die.' Finn cleared his throat and took another long drink. The memory of it was raw for all of them, but Roh couldn't imagine how it must have felt, to have those moments of freefall, to understand that what awaited you was death.

But Finn continued. 'I saw the flash of the jagged rocks below, but I couldn't for the life of me manipulate the water. I intended to have it rise up, to break my fall so I didn't splatter on the boulders, but … I couldn't do it. The water didn't listen, it wanted nothing to do with my will. From what I've gathered afterwards, that's something to do with the power of the terror tempests. They render water they touch immune to our influence, our magic. But by some miracle, I missed the rocks … I don't remember hitting the water.'

Roh's talons dug into the hay beneath her. That exact image had seared itself into her mind. It replayed in both her waking and dreaming hours, a cyclical nightmare she would never be rid of.

*But he's here*, she told herself. *He survived and he's here.*

'I don't know how much time had passed between then and when I woke upon the rocky shore ... I still don't understand it, even now.'

'What don't you understand?' Deodan asked, pouring himself a very generous serving of wine, the red liquid kissing the rim of the glass so Deodan had to slurp it before it spilled.

'Something brought me out of unconsciousness. A song.'

Roh's skin prickled.

'Someone was singing to you?' Yrsa frowned.

'Yes ... and no,' Finn said, as though he himself was still working it out. His gaze went to Roh. 'I heard you ... your deathsong.'

'My ...?' Roh's breath caught in her throat. 'That's ...'

'Impossible?' Finn finished for her. 'Did you sing it? Did you sing it after you thought I'd died?'

'I ...'

'You did, Roh,' Harlyn said gently. 'Right after you found out —'

'I did,' Roh cut her off. She knew exactly when she'd sung it, right after running her talons along Finn's neat handwriting in the sketchbook, his inscription incomplete. 'But that doesn't explain ...'

'I know what I heard,' Finn told her sharply. 'There was no mistaking who that song belonged to. There's nothing like it.'

Roh swallowed the thick lump that had formed at the back of her throat. 'Well … what happened after that?'

Finn studied her a moment longer. 'I passed out again,' he said. 'The current must have swept me away, because when I woke next, I was much further down river, the rocks were different, the moss … Anyway, by then, I was in complete withdrawal from my tonic. I found shelter in a small inlet, and several days passed. It was worse than the first time – I don't know if it had something to do with whatever Izan had used on his dagger. But … I thought I'd survived the fall, only to die from fever in some dank little cave. I had no idea what had happened to any of you. At best I thought you'd be turned out into the realms as your friend had been.' He gave Roh an apologetic glance at the mention of Orson. 'At worst … well, I couldn't fathom that as I lay dying.'

'But you didn't die,' Odi offered.

Finn raised a brow. 'How observant of you, human.' He grimaced as he adjusted his position on the hay bales. 'When the fever broke, I crawled to one of the war beacons I could see from the cave. I thought there might be a loyal Csillan guarding it. I saw how they'd rallied with Roh at the gala …'

Something sparked in Roh at the sound of her name on his lips. She could probably count on one hand how many times he'd said it; she never thought she'd hear him say it again. Roh pinched the bridge of her nose, trying to bring herself out of whatever useless state she was in. Finn was *here*. And he was telling his story. She needed to hear this, needed to take in every damn word.

Finn continued. 'There was no one there. I must have collapsed at some point because the next thing I knew, Kezra was shaking me awake. And Valli was there … The little beast could *fly*,' he said as though he still couldn't believe the fact himself. 'He was glowing again, not as strongly as he did in the mountain pass, but … His scales, they were definitely … alight …'

Roh stared. She still hadn't seen this side of Valli herself … and she had no idea what it meant.

Finn continued. 'He led Kezra right to me. She told me not to return to Csilla, that she'd helped you all escape. She was in shock, I think, that it had all ended in the way it had. Shocked that I was still alive, no doubt. She apologised that she had nothing for me, not supplies or weapons, save for that …' Finn pointed to the volume of *The Law of the Lair* that Roh had discarded.

Roh went to collect it, turning it over in her hands. 'What does this have to do with anything?'

'They didn't pack it amongst your things because they thought it was too heavy to take on the run. But they spent days poring over it after I lost the challenge. When they found me, Kezra gave it to me … One last weapon … She told me to find you, to tell you that it's not over.'

Roh's grip on the book slipped, and she nearly dropped it. 'What's not over?'

Finn held out his hand, motioning for her to pass him the volume. Dazed, Roh did as he bid.

Finn opened the book and flipped through the pages to one of the final chapters, where an emerald-green ribbon marked the spot. 'Kezra and Flo found a clause,' he explained, scanning the text. 'Kezra said it was likely included as a failsafe for the council, in case things didn't go their way. But now … Now we can use it against them. Here.' He passed the volume back to Roh, their hands brushing as he reached to point to the paragraph of text.

'A clause that could see you back in the running for the throne,' Finn said.

Roh's blood went cold. It wasn't possible. She had lost, well and truly lost. *The council had won.* There would never be a bone cleaner on the cyren throne. She thought she had come to terms with that, thought she had made her peace with it. But Finn's words chilled her to the very core and then reignited something anew within her. The Mercy's Topaz had brought her to that very book, as if it had known it contained what she would need …

Roh took a deep breath. If there was a thread of hope, an ember of a chance that she might still wear the crown, that she could right the wrongs she'd caused … Would she take it? Her gaze went to the text.

Finn cleared his throat. 'They insisted that there's always a loophole, if you look hard enough. It's the very heart of cyren nature.'

His words washed over Roh as she read aloud. '*Clause seven hundred and forty-one: In respect to formal competitions and tournaments, should a competitor be eliminated at the hands of a fellow cyren, grounds for reinstatement are as follows: proof of an unjust trial, the consequential or immediate death of the competitor's opponent, or a sacrifice of the highest order …*'

Roh stared at the clause. 'Can we prove that Izan's antics were unjust?'

Finn shook his head. 'What he did was what any cyren worth his cunning would have done to best me. There was no rule against using such a tactic. I was just too stupid, too arrogant to see it coming. The fault lies with me.'

'If there's any fault, it's with me,' Roh said sharply. 'I sent you to go in my stead. I should never have done that.'

Fire flashed in Finn's gaze. 'You were never going to best —'

'It doesn't matter. It was *my* responsibility —'

'What was? To die for no reason?' Finn shot back.

Roh's blood heated. 'No. *You!* You were my responsibility and I let you —'

'You don't *let me* do anything!' Finn was half out of his chair now. 'I *wanted* to fight. I wanted to fight for —'

'Enough!' Yrsa shouted. 'This isn't helping one bit. Sit back down, both of you. Finn, tell us about this clause. What was Kezra implying?'

Roh hadn't realised how heavily she was panting, nor Finn – his chest was heaving. She clicked her tongue in frustration and shoved the book at Finn. He had been back in her life mere moments and already he was under her skin.

Finn sank onto the hay bales with a frustrated shake of his head. 'That there was still hope. Still hope for a different queen, a better Saddoriel.'

*Since when do you support me as queen?* Roh wanted to fire at him. But she bit down on the inside of her cheek, hard. Regardless of the clause, she didn't see how they could find a way back in …

'I'm guessing Izan is still alive?' Yrsa asked.

'Kezra said as much,' Finn said. 'Though I'd like to think he's a little worse for wear.'

'He didn't look great when I rushed past him on the bridge,' Odi offered.

'Good,' Finn muttered.

Roh rubbed the scales at her temples, the ember of hope already snuffed out. 'So that leaves the final option … I don't suppose you know what a *sacrifice of the highest order* entails, then?'

'No.' Finn met her stare with a challenging one of his own. 'Only that it means there's still a chance.'

Roh threw her hands up. *'But at what cost?'* Had she shouted? She wasn't sure. All she knew was that she couldn't lose him, or anyone else again. She wouldn't survive it a second time around. She could feel the others staring at her, the tension between them all was palpable, as though they were waiting for her to lose control. They didn't meet her eyes.

It was Finn who didn't look away.

Roh tore her eyes from his and left.

Roh wandered to the great ravine, something she'd avoided doing until now. The great height had been a brutal reminder of Finn's fall. Her heart was in her throat and her hands shook, even when she tucked them under her arms against the chill of the afternoon breeze. But somehow it felt like the right place to be now, when everything felt too big to contain. She needed to take in its vast depth, to spy the jagged mountains in the distance – where she knew Lochloria and Lamaka's Basin lay beyond. The brevity of such a landscape made her feel small and insignificant in comparison. She had thought coming here would make her problems seem like a speck of dust in the sky, a drop in the seas ... And yet as she stood before it now, nothing seemed insignificant or small. She couldn't let go, couldn't process.

Finn Haertel was alive. Valli had returned. There was a chance she could re-enter the tournament. Bigger still, there was a chance she could lose everything all over again. And what of her song? The very one that had supposedly wrenched Finn from the jaws of death? Had her magic truly travelled that far? Was it really *that powerful*? The last question left her reeling. Ever since the Strothos poison had left her body and her song had inhabited her fully, an inkling of wonder, of suspicion had nagged at the back of her mind. Her song was at odds with all she had ever learned of deathsongs. And she was untrained, her magic was raw and unyielding. Would she ever master it?

A gale of wind pummelled into Roh suddenly and she whipped around to see Valli landing awkwardly on the grass. He shook off the impact, almost bashful.

'There you are,' she said softly, taking in the sight of him. 'You are much changed, friend ...' It wasn't just his size, though that was enough to give her pause. Despite his clumsiness, the shine of his scales seemed brighter and the molten gold of his eyes was richer, older. He did not snap at her fingers nor flick his tail with impatience. He watched her, as though he knew she was still trying to understand that the beast before her was the same that had crowded the breast pocket of her shirt not all that long ago.

Roh ran her hand along the young drake's neck, his scales as smooth and soft as ever beneath her touch. He had glowed in the mountain pass. He had glowed when he found Finn … What did that mean? An instinct deep in Roh's gut told her it was important and that it was somehow connected to her, but how?

Valli lay down on his belly, wings outstretched to bask in the sun's last rays before it dipped behind the hills, ever a creature of leisure. He nudged her with his snout again, and she stroked his forehead, as he had always insisted upon when he was a drakeling.

'Thank you,' Roh whispered as she pressed her brow to his. 'Thank you for bringing him back to us. Thank *you* for coming back to us … I thought perhaps you'd gone to the seas, to find your kin …'

In the presence of the sea drake, Roh's deathsong hummed steadily within her. Those streams of magic that had shown themselves the night before glimmered at her talons and drifted outwards, towards the chasm of the ravine. Valli paid them no heed. Instead, he closed his eyes and Roh continued to stroke him.

As she watched the ribbons of magic play in midair, Roh knew that Deodan was right: she needed to master her magic, to understand it better, to control it. But who could teach her such things? Especially if she was to return to her quest? Deodan had implied it was no one they knew. Roh sighed, wishing she had brought the crown of bones and the topaz with her ... She could use all the guidance she could get. She sat back on her heels. She was torn between two paths: to run, and run forever, or to stand her ground and make *a sacrifice of the highest order*. She had seen firsthand the creativity of Saddorien cyrens' cruelty. Whatever sacrifice the council deemed acceptable would leave her altered forever, as much of this tournament had already.

'*Go where the fear is the deepest.*' The words came to her out of nowhere. Valli raised his head from the ground as though he too had heard it.

'What was that?' she asked him, recognising the words from the mountain pass.

Valli blew hot air from his nostrils, seemingly unfazed.

Roh's deathsong fell silent and the gold streams of magic around her vanished. Would there be no limit to what she didn't understand?

Valli's wings cast shadows across the ground as he sat back up and stretched. With a glance behind him, he readied himself, before launching skywards.

'Valli?' Roh whispered in his wake, staring after him as he became smaller and smaller in the distance, only to find a figure limping towards her.

Instantly tense, Roh stood.

'Someone said they saw a drake fly this way,' Finn said

when he reached her, leaning heavily on his staff. 'Figured you wouldn't be far off.'

Roh nodded, not taking her eyes off him. 'I needed to think …' She toyed with the key around her neck.

'I imagine you did,' he replied, glancing at the plummeting drop below without so much as a shudder. 'Find any answers?'

'To which of my many problems?'

'Are they all not one and the same?' Finn countered, regarding her with an amused look.

Roh's chest tightened. 'You think it's a simple choice? This clause?'

Finn shrugged. 'Nothing's simple.'

'But you have an opinion?'

'Don't I always?'

'Let's hear it, then,' Roh pressed.

'It's not my opinion that matters here.'

*Gods, he's infuriating!* Roh ground her teeth and clenched her fists. 'Since when?'

Finn adjusted the staff beneath his weight. 'I'm sorry,' he said quietly.

'You're sorry?' Roh's fingers fell away from the key around her neck and she gaped at him in disbelief. 'What in the realms do *you* have to be sorry for?' The words came tumbling out. 'That you risked your life for me? That I let you? That you nearly died? That you —'

'Only that I couldn't get here sooner.'

Roh stared at him, suddenly realising how close he now stood. She couldn't bear it, *him* of all people, apologising to *her*. She took a deep, trembling breath.

'You have no duty to me. You owe me nothing. It was I who put you in a —'

'Stop it,' Finn said sharply. 'We have been through this. It was *my* idea. It was *my* choice.'

The thick knot of guilt that had bound Roh so tightly squeezed her harder. 'You said it yourself, you had no choice.'

'I *never* said that —'

'I thought you were *dead*,' Roh's words were raw with anger. Anger at herself for letting Finn take her place, and anger at Finn for not accepting the magnitude of her mistake. '*I* sent you to die, not Izan Rasaat, not the council. *Me. I did.*'

Finn grabbed the front of her shirt and wrenched her to him, nothing but sheer rage shimmering in his lilac glare. 'It was my choice,' he ground out. 'You can't take that from me.'

Roh's whole body was taut with tension, her own fury rising up to meet his. Why couldn't he see what she had done? Why couldn't he accept that everything that had happened after his fall was because of her? That he was *her* responsibility and she'd failed him beyond measure?

'Whether you like it or not,' she spat, 'you're one of *my people*. And my actions nearly saw you killed. So, you owe me *nothing*. There is *nothing* that binds us together but for that stupid contract —'

Finn went rigid.

And all at once, Roh was even closer than before; she could almost feel his heart beating against hers. She looked up, moss-green eyes meeting lilac.

Finn's voice was low, his words hot on her face. 'Fuck the contract.'

Roh didn't know who moved first, and she didn't care. All she knew was that their bodies slammed together, her hands flying into his hair. He was warm beneath her touch as she pulled his face to hers and kissed Finn Haertel fiercely.

# CHAPTER TWENTY-SIX

Roh had been kissed before. But not like this. Finn's kiss stole the breath from her lungs and turned her magic molten. His stubble was rough against her skin, and his mouth hot and insistent on hers as she kissed him back, letting her tongue brush against his, sending a thrill straight down her spine. He tasted of rum and fresh bread, of somewhere like home. She caught herself savouring the scent of him, something she never thought she'd experience again. He smelled as he always had, perhaps with a little more dust and sweat. He smelled like *Finn*.

His hands were on her. One at the nape of her neck, the other at her waist. The imprints were like a brand and she heated beneath his touch. He had dropped the staff he'd been supporting himself on and was leaning against her, his body flush with hers.

Roh curled Finn's hair in her fist, drawing him even

tighter to her, pressing herself to him, deepening their kiss. There was so much want, she couldn't get him close enough.

'Gods,' he murmured against her lips.

Roh's gasp was ragged, overcome with her need for him. Magic and desire entwined and her knees buckled slightly.

'Do you want to stop?' he asked, pulling back.

'No,' she rasped. 'Do you?'

'Gods, no.' A low moan escaped him as he crushed his mouth to hers again and the sound nearly ended Roh. She let her hands drop from his neck across the broad sweep of his shoulders, to the muscular plane of his chest which rose and fell quickly beneath her palms. She could feel the warmth of him beneath the fabric of his shirt and her fingers found the buttons, fumbling with them.

'You want to undress me out here?' Finn smiled against her mouth as the breeze whistled through the ravine below.

Roh's fingertips brushed against Finn's bare olive skin, which was littered with scars and soft hair. 'Do you not want that?'

'I don't give a damn where you undress me, as long as you do.'

Roh pushed the open shirt from his shoulders, leaving it hanging at the crooks of his elbows as she drank in the sight of him, her heart pounding. She hadn't allowed herself to imagine this moment; of them, together. Not once. But what she felt … had been there for some time now, blooming between the stolen glances and the secrets shared. Roh had told herself it was nothing, that it was all in her head … She could no longer tell herself that. What was unfolding between them was real. The longing and depth of feeling for the cyren before her was deeper than anything she had experienced before.

Ever so lightly, she traced the toned globes of his arms, pausing with a start when she reached the thick *C* that had been viciously carved into his bicep. The blood promise between their families.

But he drew her to him, the scar forgotten as his fingers found the hem of her shirt, then grazed the skin beneath with his calloused palms. Roh's breathing hitched as he kissed her deeply and traced the shape of her ribs, toying with the band of her camisole so gently she couldn't stand it. She placed her hand on his and drew it up her torso —

A sudden blast of wind nearly sent them toppling over as Valli landed hard beside them, sending dirt and tufts of grass flying. His eyes were alert, full of warning, and Roh followed his line of sight back towards the township.

'Something's wrong,' she said, her skin prickling as she tried to scan the settlement in the distance.

Finn tugged his shirt back over his shoulders and hastily buttoned it, his face flushing.

Roh scooped up his staff and handed it to him. 'We need to go back.'

Finn studied Valli warily, evidently trying to determine the reason for his interruption. The beast huffed impatiently.

'I think you're right,' Finn said finally.

Touching her fingers to her bruised lips, Roh started towards the township, her cheeks burning at the thought of what might have happened between Finn and her.

'You can go ahead,' Finn told her. 'I'm slowing you down.'

But Roh shook her head. 'Whatever is going on back there, we're stronger together.' She glanced at Valli, who was prowling at their sides rather than taking to the skies again.

'What have you seen, friend?' she asked him quietly, but the creature just kept his steeled gaze ahead.

'Is that smoke?' Finn said, pointing to a column of grey cloud billowing into the sky. 'Is it normally like that?'

Roh inhaled sharply, her talons unsheathing. 'No … It's not from any building or kiln that I know of …' She unhooked her sling from her belt and loaded a hefty stone into its cradle, just as Yrsa had shown her.

Beside her, Finn cursed. 'I left my sword in the barn …'

'Here,' Roh said, offering him her father's quartz dagger.

Finn hesitated. 'You would have me wield that?'

'Why not?'

'It's a warlock weapon …'

'It's *my* weapon now. And any blade will do when it stands between you and death. Let's go.'

As they reached a crest in the land, Roh scoured the village below. A cart of hay was on fire and the sudden clang of steel on steel echoed up the hill. A skirmish had broken out in the centre of the township. Roh could see the glint of Deodan's cutlasses as they whirled through the air against a leather-clad opponent.

'The Jaktaren,' Roh said. 'They must have found our trail.'

'Or mine,' Finn said, his mouth a hard line. 'And it's not just the guild …' He pointed. 'A Saddorien Army unit is here, too.'

Roh swore, dread surging within as she watched the cyren warriors attack, their shouts fuelled by rage. 'Tell me you can't see Piri.'

Finn's eyes narrowed as he scanned the conflict. 'I can't, but that doesn't mean she's not here.'

Roh sought Yrsa, who was spinning her sling, slamming it into oncoming attackers with no hesitation, leaving them crumpled in her wake. Next, Roh spotted Odi … perched on the balcony of one of the private residences. He had Finn's crossbow, and was shooting bolts through the air, defending Deodan and Yrsa from the assailants they couldn't yet see. There was no sign of Harlyn, but Roh knew she would be nearby.

'We need to get down there.' Roh turned to Valli. 'Stay out of sight,' she told him, with a sweep of her hand across his brow. 'I don't want them to know of you, not yet.'

Valli growled in protest.

'Please,' Roh begged. 'Who knows what sort of weapons the Jaktaren and the army have at their disposal.' While Valli had grown, he wasn't yet big enough to cause a considerable threat against the numbers Roh could see pouring into the dirt streets. And he was clumsy, still not fully in control of his wings and his landings.

She steeled her voice. 'Go!'

With a final hiss, Valli spread his wings and shot into the sky, towards the ravine in the opposite direction.

'Was that wise?' Finn asked as they started down the slope, making straight for their friends.

'I guess we'll find out.' Roh didn't take her eyes off the township. She didn't allow herself to think of Finn and his staff and how he limped beside her. He could manage himself with or without that tonic, and right now, their friends – human, warlock and cyren alike – needed them.

As she surged forward, Roh prayed that Yrsa's partner wasn't among the attackers. A small unit of cyren soldiers advanced on a handful of Tess' villagers, but at last in range, Roh spun her loaded sling above her head. Heart pounding in her throat, she relished the momentum of her weapon, releasing the first projectile.

A yelp sounded as her stone found its target, striking the soft flesh of a man's neck.

'Damn,' she muttered. She'd been aiming for his head.

But the damage she'd done shifted the focus of the attackers from the villagers, and they brandished their swords at Roh and Finn, surging for them. Hands surprisingly steady, Roh reloaded her sling, ducking under the first incoming attack and sending a cyren soldier sprawling into the dirt with a single blow to the face. Muscle memory took over and her fingers were already plucking a new stone from her pouch and loading it to the cradle of her sling as she sidestepped the swing of a blade and the thrust of a spear. There was a rhythm to battle, she realised; it hummed around them and guided her movements, fuelling her magic just as music would.

She glanced to her side, where Finn wielded her father's dagger as though it was an extension of him. He moved with a violent dance of slices and lunges, driving the blade home with every strike. Enemy blood sprayed, all the while Finn balanced on his staff, sometimes using it as a second weapon to block a blow before slashing the sharp quartz across his opponent's throat. A life ended with the blur of a blade.

Nearby, Nicholas and Tess' brothers burst onto the street and charged at an incoming unit of Jaktaren. A fresh clash of swords rang through the township. Roh didn't pause, she was already running towards Nicholas and his sons as the opposing cyrens closed in fast. Her sling collided with the unprotected middle of one of the Jaktaren and he doubled over, gasping for air. She was in the heart of the fray, with no chance of reprieve as she loaded and reloaded her sling, strike after strike, bringing down her own kind in the defence of humans. Roh looked around wildly, narrowly avoiding a gash to the shoulder, and realised for the first time that not all of the villagers had the protective tokens – all it would take would be a few notes of a deathsong and they'd be nothing but piles of bone.

'Don't let them sing!' she shouted over the pandemonium, slamming her sling into a Jaktaren who had tilted her head to the sky, her mouth open, ready to deliver her deathsong. She crumpled to the ground, no noise escaping her.

They would have to win this fight without cyren magic, Roh understood, despite her power roiling beneath the surface, begging to be unleashed. She would not risk the innocents of the village, nor would she wield her song against her own kind, as her mother had done centuries ago.

A crossbow bolt whistled as it shot past her.

A sharp cry of agony sounded a few yards behind her. Roh whirled around to find a junior Jaktaren staggering forward, his hands wrapped around the bolt embedded in his abdomen, blood dribbling from his lips.

And Finn Haertel standing beside him, his face etched in shock as he slowly looked from his wounded attacker to the balcony where Odi grinned and reloaded his weapon.

'Roh, look out!' came a voice. Harlyn's.

Roh ducked just in time as a throwing knife came hurtling towards her. Horrified, she spun on her heel, but couldn't discern one opponent from the next. The streets of Serratega were a bloodbath.

Almost dazed, Roh watched as Harlyn darted across the open spaces, tugging crossbow bolts from dead bodies with her good hand and shoving them into a quiver. She caught Roh's eye.

'For Odi,' she called out. 'I have to help *somehow* —'

A cry of aggression drowned out her words as Yrsa leaped from a wagon, a sword in each hand, her body suspended in midair for a moment as she flew towards a soldier Roh hadn't seen creeping up on Harlyn.

Red blinded Roh and a soft thud sounded nearby.

Yrsa had cut the cyren's head clean off.

Her face spattered with blood that clearly wasn't her own, Yrsa called to Harlyn, 'I could use more projectiles for my sling.'

Harlyn yanked another bolt from a body and nodded determinedly. 'Got it.'

Only the chaos around them stopped Roh from staring at her friends with her mouth hanging open. Instead, she squared her shoulders and shouted after Harlyn, 'Me too!'

Harlyn darted across the street once more, towards the building where Odi was firing from. 'Coming right up,' she yelled back over her shoulder.

Roh and Yrsa surveyed the battle before them.

'No sign of Piri?' Roh asked her friend between ragged gasps.

'None,' Yrsa replied shortly and started forward at once, spotting a group of soldiers who had cornered Tess and some of the humans Roh recognised from the tavern.

At the sight of Yrsa and her swords, the soldiers blanched, clearly recognising the Jaktaren. But one of the older fighters sneered at her.

'She handed in her uniform,' he spat. 'She shouldered your disgrace, rather than take part in bringing you in to face Saddorien justice.'

Yrsa's advance faltered. 'Is she —'

'Stripped of her rank. Facing charges of treason.' The

cyren seemed to delight in sharing this news, watching the colour drain from Yrsa's cheeks and the horror set in.

'Surely she can be pardoned? No one can expect her to —'

'Do her duty? Yes, that's exactly what was expected and exactly what she failed at. She has no honour —'

The words died on his lips as Tess shoved a blade between his ribs. 'I think we've heard enough,' the human said.

Yrsa stood in shock while Roh and Tess took advantage of the distraction and sent the army unit scattering.

'What are you doing out here?' Roh hissed at Tess, knowing that Yrsa needed a moment to gather herself.

'You think I'd leave my family and my people to fight without me?' Tess snapped.

'Fair enough,' Roh panted. 'When did this all happen?' She reloaded her sling with one of her last stones and hurled it into the face of one of the army warriors, glancing across at Yrsa. She was still unsteady.

'Not long ago,' Tess managed as she deflected an incoming blow from a spear. 'But it doesn't feel like it. We can't hold them off forever …' She trailed off, something a few yards away catching her eye.

Roh saw it instantly. Deodan, his cutlasses gleaming as he cut down one cyren after another, every cleave of his blades charged with a fury she'd never seen. He fought three – no, four – Jaktaren at once, his face distorted in a wild rage.

'Perhaps we can,' Tess said, watching on in horror.

But another shout of pain sounded to Roh's left and she turned to find Nicholas backed up against the door of the tavern, holding a deep gash in his arm, blood pouring through the gaps between his fingers.

'No!' Roh yelled as a Jaktaren lunged at Tess' father to make the final blow. Her sling crashed into his face with a sickening crunch and the attacker crumpled. Bile burned the back of her throat, her gaze passing over the bloody pulp she'd created. She looked away, scanning the madness before them. The Jaktaren and the Saddorien Army were too many and too skilled against the candlemakers and honey harvesters of Serratega.

Yrsa was at her side again, her eyes alert and sweat gleaming on her brow as she offered a handful of rocks for Roh's sling. 'Here.'

With trembling hands, Roh took the projectiles, knowing she had to have faith that her friend could put her fears for Piri aside for the moment. 'We can't win this,' she said to Yrsa. 'We have to surrender.'

Harlyn flung herself beside them, panting hard. 'What?' Her eyes bulged. 'Surrender? Roh. We can't —'

'I will not have Tess and her family's deaths on my conscience. Nor the destruction of this entire town —' Roh lunged forward and struck another assailant with her sling, the impact reverberating up her arm. Her blood singing with power, she tried to catch the others' attention from across the way, but they were too entrenched in the fighting, too caught up in the swing of their blades and the spilling of blood.

'Deodan!' Finn's voice cut through the fray. 'Do it!' he

yelled. 'Do it *now*!'

Roh's hand faltered on her sling as her gaze snapped from the blood-soaked Jaktaren whose hands had just been tracing her skin, to the warrior warlock at the helm of the chaos. Deodan gutted the man he was sparring with before his hands shot to the vials at his belt. Finn covered him with the slash of the quartz dagger, slicing through any cyren who dared to lunge for the warlock. Deodan released the contents of the vials, whispering to the liquid floating just above his palms.

Panic squeezed Roh's chest, the shout for surrender tasting sour on her tongue.

Deodan's water magic burst to life as a swarm of nucrites, the moth-like creatures Roh and Odi had encountered in the first-ever trial of the Queen's Tournament. But these were no ordinary fluttering insects.

With bated breath, the skirmish seemed to pause, mesmerised by a stream of tiny winged creatures weaving their way through the conflict as one mass. For a moment, everyone looked around in confusion and then, the swarm split.

Water insects dived towards the attacking Jaktaren and cyren warriors, some having instinct enough to run. It didn't matter. The water magic caught up, and with the soft splash of a liquid wing against exposed flesh, weapons dropped to the ground in a rhythmic drumming.

And then the screaming began.

Every living Saddorien who had attacked the village

shrieked as they clawed off invisible demons, swiping at phantom forces, pleading and crying out. Some brought their blades to their wrists, some ran into stone walls, knocking themselves unconscious, others darted erratically across the street, fleeing from things Roh and her companions could not see.

A sickening pit of dread opened up deep inside Roh as she watched Deodan's magic take hold of every mind that had opposed them, in a way that was terrifyingly familiar to her. She found herself at the warlock's side, her mouth dry.

'Stop this,' she commanded. 'Stop this now.'

'I —'

Her knuckles nearly split; she was holding her sling so tight. '*Now*, Deodan.'

The warrior warlock muttered something, and instantly, the Saddoriens fell to the ground where they stood and a thrumming silence blanketed Serratega.

'How?' Roh bit out, scanning the dead and unconscious cyrens littering the street, dread sinking deep in her gut. She knew exactly what Deodan had used on the poor bastards, a substance she would never wish upon anyone, except perhaps Adriel. 'How did you get it?'

Finn's voice cut in. 'It was me. I gave the Strothos vine to him, back in Csilla. Figured we could weaponise it in some way.' He glanced around. 'Turns out I was right.'

The image of shirtless Finn by the river bank crouching over the star-shaped leaf came back to Roh instantly, as did the memory of the burning rash that had crept along her arm.

'We were going to lose, Roh,' Finn told her gently.

'These cyrens …' she said slowly. 'They were part of your guild, your family …'

'Our family is right here,' Yrsa said, coming to stand beside her.

Roh's magic sparked within her, desperate to unleash itself, but she locked it away. She couldn't do that here. All around her, Tess' people were lowering their weapons, their eyes wide with shock. Roh didn't know if it was due to the cruelty of the magic used, or the fact that she and her companions had defended them against their own kind. But whatever alliance had formed between them … it was now set in stone.

A gentle hand squeezed her shoulder. 'We won,' Deodan told her. 'We live to fight another day.'

*It doesn't matter*, the realisation hit Roh as hard as a blow.

'We emerged victorious this time,' she said quietly, more to herself than to the others. 'But there will always be another fight.'

A strange gurgling noise sounded. At the foot of the smouldering hay cart, a Jaktaren lay doubled over, spitting blood onto the dirt. A myriad of conflict whirred within Roh – pity for the state of the poor bastard and anger for his cause simmered to the surface.

'You going to surrender, bone cleaner?' he drawled. Even amidst his pain, his nose wrinkled into a sneer.

Roh went to him and crouched at his side. She hooked a finger under his chin and forced his gaze to hers. 'Don't think I need to at this point.'

Loathing filled his eyes. 'Rohesia of the Bone Cleaners,' he rasped, as though he was still performing an official duty. 'Former competitor of the Queen's Tournament. You broke the Law of the Lair. You fled Csilla rather than face your banishment from the cyren territories in light of your failure in the challenge against Izan Rasaat.'

'Are we not banished?' Roh replied, her tone steely. 'Are we not exiled from the cyren territories? No law was broken.'

The Jaktaren's laugh was dark. 'You took the crown —'

'A crown of bones,' Roh countered. 'It was no true crown of Saddoriel.'

'You stole the Mercy's Topaz, the key to the Willow's Sapphire and the property of the Jaktaren guild.'

'How many more units are there?' Roh asked, scanning his body for visible wounds and finding a laceration just below his collarbone. She pressed her thumb into it, hard. 'How many?' she demanded.

He screamed. 'As many as it takes to bring you to your knees.'

Roh ignored the eyes on her, boring holes into her back. 'They will not stop,' she muttered. She had known it all along, really, but the confirmation solidified as a lump of dread in her gut.

'Saddoriens do not give up, *isruhe*, even you should know that. The council will scour the realms for you and your sorry excuses for companions.' His eyes lingered on Finn, who stood close by. 'They will take you back to

Saddoriel and you will face a true sentencing for the crimes against the Law of the Lair. One that will make exile seem like child's play.'

'Have you not seen what we are capable of?' Finn ground out.

'You …' the Jaktaren spat. 'Have you no shame? You dare to speak to me, after tarnishing our guild? After aligning yourself with an *isruhe*?'

'I align myself with a true cyren,' Finn said, limping forward on his staff. 'You remember what they're supposed to stand for?'

'I remember nothing of the pathetic cripple before me —'

A wet shucking sound cut him off.

Roh looked from his widened eyes and mouth parted in shock, to the bone hilt of a dagger that stuck out from his heart. Not by Finn's hand, but by hers. She hadn't thought twice, she'd snatched the blade from Finn and driven it home.

Now, a cyren's blood was wet on her fingers. Until now, she hadn't considered those she had killed or maimed on the battlefield; there had been no time to descend into shock or question morality. But here and now, there was something incredibly intimate about holding a blade that still pierced a warm heart.

'I could have handled him,' Finn muttered beside her.

'So could I,' Roh said, pulling the dagger from the body and wiping it on the ground, willing her hands to remain steady. 'So I did.'

The entire town seemed to exhale as the tension of

violence and death dissipated. Roh was quiet, the cogs of her mind turning and Deodan's words echoing loudly: *We live to fight another day.*

Moments later, Odi emerged from one of the buildings and strode across the street, Finn's crossbow in his hands.

Finn dipped his head. 'Thank you,' he said. 'For what you did.'

'For saving your arse?' Odi grinned, offering the Jaktaren his favourite weapon.

Much to Roh's surprise, Finn answered with a grin of his own. 'Yeah, for that.' He pushed the crossbow back to Odi. 'Keep it.'

In the aftermath of the skirmish, while bodies were dragged away and Tess decided what to do with the prisoners, Roh's mind whirred. The dead cyren's words clung to her and refused to let go. There would be more skirmishes, more blood on her hands before the end. She sat on the steps of the inn, watching Tess' people organise the turmoil that had swept through their town as she toyed with the key around her neck. None of her companions were in sight. Roh guessed they might have gone off to find some peace and quiet, to process what they'd just inflicted upon their own kind.

The words came back to her again. *The council will scour the realms for you ...* Roh swallowed the thick lump in her throat. He was right. It was only a matter of time until the next unit found them, and the next, and the next. They would be running forever, until they could run no more.

Making up her mind, Roh got to her feet and started towards the barn.

She froze at the doorway. Waiting inside was Yrsa, Finn, Harlyn, Odi and Deodan, with their packed bags at their feet, their hands resting on the grips of their weapons.

'What are you doing?' Roh managed.

'Braiding each other's hair,' Harlyn retorted. 'What's it look like? We're coming with you.'

'But … you don't know where I'm going …' Roh stammered. 'I'm … I'm going back to Csilla, to face the council … I won't run for the rest of my life. I won't let you all be hunted like prey.'

'We know,' Yrsa said, stepping forward, holding out Roh's pack.

Roh baulked. This was not part of the plan, which was to take the attention *away* from her companions, to face the fate she had carved out for herself alone. She looked at each of their faces, imploring them, but every pair of eyes that met her gaze was brimming with determination. She knew that she could argue with them until she was blue in the face, but they were not going to budge.

Something sparked anew within Roh.

*Hope.* And the knowledge that she was not alone, not now, not ever.

She took her pack from Yrsa's grip. 'Alright,' she said. 'Let's finish what we started.'

# CHAPTER TWENTY-SEVEN

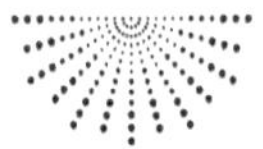

With emotionally charged embraces and well wishes, Tess gifted them fresh horses for their journey. They bypassed the redwood forest and followed the river south, *all of them*, leaving their human friend and the village of Serratega far behind.

It was during the initial hours of the ride that Roh forced herself to come to terms with the fact that she had made her decision, and her companions had made theirs. She could not control or influence their choices, nor would she keep trying to do so; she respected them all too much for that. They were in this together now, until the end. Perhaps they had always been. Crossing the threshold between Talon's Reach and the realms beyond felt like a lifetime ago to Roh, and in spite of everything that had happened, part of her was quietly glad, glad she had longed for more than the life of a bone cleaner, had yearned for adventure, something more than what she was born with.

*I know I won't always feel like this*, she mused to herself as they rode alongside the river. *But for now, I want to savour that feeling, the lack of regret, this revelling of sorts in the short life that I* have *lived.*

Even in the face of what surely awaited them in Csilla, Roh couldn't help but steal glances at Finn. She could still feel the whisper of his hands on her skin and the intensity of his lips bruising hers. The imprint of him was the only thing stopping her from believing that she'd imagined the whole thing.

The Jaktaren rode straight-backed in his saddle, the wooden limb Nicholas had fashioned for his stump hanging above the silver stirrup, but he looked at ease, somehow more himself than Roh could remember seeing him. He guided his horse with subtle movements and kept his gaze ahead, though Roh could have sworn her skin prickled in a way that told her he knew she was watching him. She trained her gaze on the sword strapped to his back where his crossbow would have been. That weapon graced Odi's shoulders now, and Roh felt a smile tug at her mouth at the thought of the unlikely friendship that had grown between musician hunter and master pianist.

Roh turned her gaze to Yrsa, who had been quiet since their departure. She knew the Jaktaren's thoughts were with Piri and whatever fate awaited the soldier who had been stripped of her rank and honour. Roh had seen Yrsa's face stricken with raw grief these past few weeks, but the pain etched on her face now was of a different nature: distraught, desperate for some semblance of control. Roh wanted to wrap her arms around her friend, to offer comfort and reassurance ... but where they were heading, there was none to be had.

'You alright, Roh?' Harlyn asked, nudging her horse up alongside Roh's.

'I don't know,' she said honestly.

'You thought about it? What you'll ... About what you'll offer?'

'I'm working on it,' Roh told her, not unkindly.

Harlyn seemed to understand not to press her. Instead, she sighed heavily. 'I still hear her, you know,' she said.

Roh's gaze snapped to her friend's. 'Orson, you mean?'

'Yes ... At least once a day, as though the wind carries her voice to me, from wherever she is. Do you think about it? Where she might have ended up?'

'I do,' Roh answered. 'But I don't like to think on it for long. Do you think she's still alive?'

'Yes,' Harlyn said, without hesitating. 'I feel like we'd know if she wasn't? I know that doesn't make sense, but ...'

'It makes sense, Har,' Roh told her.

'Good.' Harlyn sighed. 'Deodan mentioned that we need to find someone to train you in Csilla, to help you master your magic.'

Roh nodded, recalling the warrior warlock's words. 'Hopefully, Kezra will know someone, at the very least she'll let us use the Csillan library. We might be able to find something there.'

'Did you ever suspect it?' Harlyn asked.

'Suspect what?'

'That your song would be so powerful?'

'Har, you know that I feared I'd never find my song at all, so no. I didn't.'

'I knew,' Harlyn said confidently. 'I always knew you'd be different.'


Days of travel passed and whatever appreciation Roh had experienced for the adventures beyond Saddoriel was soon snuffed out as they reached the cold gorges of Csilla. Reality set in once more, icy wind whipping through her chopped hair and worn clothes, while above, the grey skies opened up, setting a downpour upon them. As they navigated the gorges, Roh's mind was *loud*. She knew that they couldn't have run forever, but it didn't make her decision any less terrifying, to face the council head-on, to fight for what she'd already fought so hard for. She desperately tried to piece together all she had learned from *The Law of the Lair*, from Deodan and Finn and Yrsa, from Odi and Harlyn and the Csillans, too. She recalled Ames' words from before the very first trial in the Queen's Tournament: *'What do you know how to wield? What do you know about the tournament? About your fellow competitors? There are lessons and tactics to be taken from all around you. If only you would open your eyes.'*

Her eyes were wide open, perhaps for the first time in

her life, and yet with each step closer to the Bridge of Csilla, slowly but surely, Roh felt she was one step closer to her execution. Knowing Saddoriens, it was a worse fate that awaited her and her companions. More than once, she delved deep into that dark recess of her mind, where her thoughts festered, each more poisonous than the last. But she refused to stop calculating and scheming; she would scour her mind until the last possible moment.

All at once, that moment arrived.

The Bridge of Csilla came into view, as glorious as she remembered it, even amidst the pouring rain and grey skies. It was as though it kept the jagged cliffs at bay, as though it commanded the gorge itself, a power of its own —

A flutter of movement snagged her attention and Roh's head whipped around to see Deodan's water bird fly into view at last, coming to hover by the warrior warlock's ear, relaying whatever it had learned.

Then, Deodan's gaze locked with Roh's. And she knew everything she needed to know. It was true. It was all true. Her foolish trust of Incana's advice and her brash actions that had followed with the fields of wild draketail and monke's thorn had led Akoris to ruin, to death and despair. The pity in Deodan's stare told it all.

'Gods.' The word came out a choked sob. But there was not a moment to process, to understand the full extent of what she had done, of what she had inflicted upon the innocent cyrens of Akoris —

Roh could suddenly hear music. The intoxicating notes of two fiddles, she realised. Her eyes went straight to Odi, who had paled considerably. There was no question; his stepbrothers had been brought to Csilla, which could only mean one thing: the council meant to thoroughly punish Roh, her companions and everyone who had ever laid eyes on them.

Roh's throat went dry as a Csillan guard appeared, meeting them at the pathway to the bridge, as though they were expected. The Csillan wore formal attire and a grim expression, greeting them with a respectful dip of his head. Without a word, he motioned for the entourage to dismount and follow him down the narrow path. As they left their horses behind, Roh knew that the likelihood of Kezra greeting them was low, but it worried her nonetheless that the Arch General wasn't there. Had she been incriminated in their escape? Had the council discovered that she'd assisted Finn? But this was not the time for questions, Roh knew that much at least, for she didn't know who might be listening or whom she could trust. She spiralled as she once more tried to sift through the scraps of her remaining options. So much hung in the balance; the lives and livelihoods of her friends, her own future, and the future of all those she had wronged in Akoris. Roh didn't notice where she stepped or where the passage curved or inclined, she existed only in her own mind, only to find a way …

When at last, Roh and the others stepped out onto the Bridge of Csilla clutching their travel packs, Roh sucked in a breath. It was dark but for a few candles and valo beetles glowing across the marble, in such stark contrast to the beacon of light it had been at the gala when she had seen it last. The atmosphere was strange and sombre but for a crowd of Saddoriens and former competitors, who seemed to vibrate with anticipation. The council awaited them on the dais, their intentions clear: they meant to make a ceremony, an example of her.

Roh missed a step with a start, instantly recognising Adriel's face at the forefront of the masses. He seemed thinner, older even … But when his gaze caught hers, he gave that same serpentine smile he had before and Roh couldn't help the shudder that racked her body. There was something darker in his gaze now – not just the desire to conquer and possess, but … the yearning for vengeance.

'What is he doing here?' she hissed to Harlyn, not taking her eyes off the Akorian Arch General.

For the first time since their capture, Roh's heart truly stuttered in her chest. Up until this point, she had convinced herself that she could handle whatever was thrown at her. She had dealt with worse, after all. But at the sight of Adriel, she shrank into herself. Remembering his possessive stare, and the way he'd forced his kiss upon her. She remembered that entitled sense of ownership that had dripped from his very being.

The lump in her throat was like a rough stone. *No, they can't give me to Adriel as punishment, surely …?*

At her side, Harlyn was equally horrified. There was no measure to the torment scorned cyrens could inflict, it seemed.

Roh ground her teeth as she spotted the Eery Brothers at the far end of the bridge, locked away in a cage of bones, their fiddles pressed to their chins, their clothes hanging limply from their wasted bodies.

*None of this is right.*

Without warning, she and her companions were forced out onto the bridge at sword point, like animals to be gawked at, and she found that her steps were not her own as she drew closer to the dais, where the Council of Seven Elders sat glaring down at her in disgust. The Haertels gave away nothing as always, no glimmer of surprise to find their only son alive after a fall that had meant certain death.

Roh glared back at them. They had no business being leaders of Saddoriel, of cyrenkind, not after all they had done to Finn.

She scanned desperately the other faces around the dais. Winslow Ward, Yrsa's aunt, stood at the very end of the group of elders, her hands clasped before her, her lips pursed. Roh guessed that to a stranger, her expression might seem like one of disappointment, but from what Roh had heard of her, she knew it was fear, fear for her kin.

*She's right to be afraid,* Roh thought, clenching her own hands so tightly her talons threatened to pierce her palms. Her shirt was damp with sweat. *Where is Delja? Where's Ames?* Surely, they would be able to give her some clue as to what was going on? But she found no source of comfort amidst the crowds. Roh couldn't see Kezra or Floralin. The few Csillans present kept their faces blank – the bands of bone that had graced their arms at the gala were gone – while the Saddoriens appeared outraged by her presence. She had heard it all before: she was an insult to their kind, to the lair they cherished above all else. A rogue bone cleaner who had dared to enter the tournament and disrespect their order, their way of life. An *isruhe* who had befriended humans and warlocks, who had stolen the Mercy's Topaz for her own gain and the key to the Willow's Sapphire.

*Perhaps I am as bad as they think —*

She staggered as someone shoved her to her knees before the council, her bones crunching against the marble, hard. Around her, the others were given the same treatment. Roh winced as she heard Finn's wooden leg being kicked from under him. He swore as his whole weight landed on one knee and he went sprawling.

She wished she could go to him, but a meaty hand held her in place. She could do nothing but watch as the most revered Jaktaren in all of the cyren realms was brought to his knee, the secret he'd kept for so long on full display to a gawking crowd. Although many had been there at the challenge, shock rippled through the masses at the sight of Finn's flapping trouser leg.

Odi swore at the guard and helped Finn get upright. Human and cyren gripped arms in solidarity and knelt side by side, ready to face their fates.

Roh steeled herself against the icy fear clawing at her insides. She would not let it end here.

'Rohesia of the Bone Cleaners.' Taro Haertel didn't raise his voice, and yet it rang out across the entire bridge, powerful and commanding. The melancholy notes of the fiddles fell silent, as did any hushed whispers of the common cyrens.

The elder's eyes were cold as they scrutinised her. 'You have returned to us to face your sentencing. You kneel here as a breaker of our most sacred laws, a disgrace to the lair. You are hereby *formally* eliminated from the extended Queen's Tournament, due to your failure at the trial by combat.' He let each word echo through the crowds, each pause between them like a beat of shame against an already tarnished name. 'By the order of the council, you will return the bone crown, the Mercy's Topaz and the key to the Willow's Sapphire to Queen Delja.'

Roh felt the ripple of power pulse across the bridge before she saw her. Delja the Triumphant flew through one of the open archways and landed in the centre of the bridge with a deft beat of her wings. She wore her crown of coral and a shimmering blue gown that flowed around her body like water. Roh stared at her, at the cyren who looked so different to the one who had held her at the end of her challenge in Akoris, so at odds with the cyren who had sent her racks of garments to choose from, who had spoken soft words of wisdom in the throes of the gala. There was no softness to the regal figure who walked towards them now, and she did not meet Roh's gaze.

'Furthermore,' Taro continued. 'As punishment for fleeing your formal banishment and for stealing the property of both the lair and the Jaktaren guild, your companions will be exiled to the work fields of outer

Talon's Reach, to serve as crop pickers. The Prince of Melodies will be returned to the Jaktaren. While you … you shall be transported to Akoris, where you will serve the Arch General personally. These sentences are lifelong. They cannot be challenged or undone. It is the Law of the Lair.'

Whatever spell the elder had over the crowd broke and murmurs of disbelief washed over the masses. There had never been anything like this in history. This would be recorded in the *Tome of Kyeos* for the rest of time.

Roh herself did not move, not a muscle. She ignored the tightening grip of the thick hand on her shoulder and she didn't break eye contact with Taro Haertel.

'Hand over the gem, bone cleaner.' His voice was laced with hostility. 'And the crown of bones. *Now.*'

But Roh made no move to reach for her pack and the objects within, nor the key resting warm against her sternum. Instead, she lifted her chin. 'I would, Elder Haertel,' she said, drawing up her strength and magic from deep inside. 'But I wish to invoke a different Law of the Lair.'

Taro Haertel faltered, for the briefest moment, risking a glance at his wife. Bloodwyn was the crueller looking of the two, a permanent sneer marring her harsh but otherwise beautiful face. She waved a long hand fleetingly, some private signal between the two.

Taro inhaled deeply, seeming to gather his patience. 'And to which law do you refer?' he asked, his tone grating.

Roh twisted out of the guard's grip then and stood,

shoulders back. 'Clause seven hundred and forty-one.' She addressed the entire council, bringing the words to the forefront of her mind. '*In respect to formal competitions and tournaments, should a competitor be eliminated at the hands of a fellow cyren, grounds for reinstatement are as follows: proof of an unjust trial, the consequential or immediate death of the competitor's opponent, or a sacrifice of the highest order ...*'

An unnatural stillness fell across the Council of Seven Elders as Roh's words washed over them. Rage, she realised, an ancient rage that came when one's own laws were used against them.

It was Winslow Ward who broke the pulsating silence. 'And on which grounds do you request to be reinstated?' she asked.

'There is only one that the bone cleaner qualifies for,' Bloodwyn Haertel said, her eyes narrowing. '*Sacrifice.* She must make a sacrifice of the highest order.'

Roh inhaled through her nose, clasping her hands behind her back so no one would see them tremble. 'Yes.'

Murmurs broke out across the bridge and no number of glares from the council could silence them.

'We will confer with the reigning queen,' Elder Haertel announced loudly, at last having to raise her voice to be heard.

Roh's gaze went straight to Delja, disturbed by the coral crown that had so swiftly found its way back atop her head. Since her first meeting with the former queen in Saddoriel's Prison, she had two sides to her: the gentle, caring cyren who might have been a maternal figure to her in another lifetime, her helping hands bound by the laws of the lair … and then there was the cold, regal ruler whom Roh didn't know at all. She had the distinct, sinking feeling that it was the latter who joined them today.

'Roh,' Harlyn hissed, her eyes wide with panic. 'What's the plan? What in the realms are you doing?'

Roh's heart ached at the sight of Harlyn and their friends on their knees, their very lives in the hands of those who would do wrong by them.

'Everything I can,' she replied, forcing herself to look away. She needed to stay strong for this, whatever awaited her.

The council and Delja conferred in hushed whispers upon the dais, not sparing Roh and her companions a second glance as they decided their fates. Roh's magic sparked at the fury coursing through her. She had vowed she would never feel helpless again and had done everything in her power to make it so, and yet …

The council broke apart and Bloodwyn Haertel came to stand at the front. She smoothed her robes down unnecessarily, her cruel gaze finding Roh's.

At last, the chatter of the crowd died down. Roh could feel their anticipation thick in the air, though she had no idea what outcome they might hope for.

'You have chosen to make a sacrifice of the highest order,' Elder Haertel said. 'The council have decided to honour this clause and we have determined what that sacrifice must be.'

Roh didn't so much as breathe.

'A life.'

Roh nearly choked.

'A life must be sacrificed to Saddoriel. The resulting death must be most meaningful to our lair of bones. You may choose one: the warlock, the Prince of Melodies, or …' Elder Haertel paused then, the enjoyment plain on her face. 'Your deathsong.'

At the words, Roh's magic caught alight, amplified by the hundreds of voices that now filled the bridge as the shock barrelled through every cyren there.

Roh's companions rushed to her side.

'Roh, Roh … we can figure this out —' Harlyn, always the optimist.

'We can still accept their sentencing,' Finn said. 'We'll plan our escape later —'

'I can play, Roh. I can play for them if I have to —' Odi, peeling away his fingerless gloves and already turning to the council.

Yrsa grabbed him. 'We're beyond that now —'

It was Deodan who turned Roh towards him, his expression set with determination. He took her hands in his. 'Give me your word that you will return Lochloria to the warlocks, Roh,' he said. 'Make that promise, and they can take me.'

Roh glanced back at the council, who watched on, taking pleasure from the panic unfolding before them. Bloodwyn Haertel met her stare, the hatred pouring from her almost tangible. At the subtle movement of her hand, several guards surged forward, snatching Roh, Deodan and Odi, and dragging them away from their group.

'No!' Harlyn shouted, but more guards held her, Finn and Yrsa back.

Thick hands bruised Roh as she was forced forward, shoved out into the open before all of Csilla.

'Step into the ring of sacrifice,' Bloodwyn said, a cruel smile playing upon her crimson lips. 'Tell us what you choose to give.'

A circle of flame shot up from the marble floor, surrounding cyren, warlock and human, threatening to engulf them. Roh jumped, pulling her friends towards her, gripping their hands at her sides, her heart hammering so hard it might have cracked her chest wide open. Cyrens hated fire, and this ... was a nightmare incarnate.

'Roh ...' Odi shifted as the flames licked closer, singeing their clothes.

Through the hungry blaze, Roh could still see Bloodwyn Haertel. The council elder's gaze was full of satisfaction, of retribution. 'What shall you give us, bone cleaner?' she asked.

Roh knew in that moment that whatever she gave would be devoured by the flames. At her side, Deodan gently pried her fingers open and traced something on her palm. What little magic he still harnessed left a thin shimmering line of blue there. Roh couldn't swallow the lump in her throat as she stared at it. It was half a pair of wings, the symbol of the alliance that had once been between warlock and cyrenkind.

Deodan spoke once more, his voice soft and full of

regret: 'Give me your word, Roh, and I will be your sacrifice.'

Roh's eyes burned with tears as she carefully completed the second half of the sketch, her lines glowing lilac on her skin.

She turned to Deodan, meeting his gaze with her own tear-lined eyes. 'You have my word.'

A voice echoed in her mind, one she'd heard before: *'Go where the fear is darkest.'*

And before Deodan could offer himself to the council, before one more drop of blood was spilt in her name, Roh turned back to the elders and the former queen.

'My song,' she told them. 'I give my deathsong.'

As the words left her mouth, the flames surged, rushing towards her, changing colour to a brilliant blue as they sucked at her magic, demanding that she fulfil the promise she had spoken in the ring of sacrifice. Roh's body was not her own, she wielded no control as she tilted her head back, her eyes shut against the glimmering ceiling, and sang.

Her deathsong was wrenched from her, more vibrant, more powerful than ever.

Ribbons of shimmering gold poured from Roh. They streamed from her chest, her mouth and her talons, toying with the blue flames dancing around her, illuminating the dimly lit Bridge of Csilla and reaching out towards arched windows.

A pulse of power shot out across the crowd, but Roh didn't hear the gasps of shock or see the cyrens scramble back, away from her. Deodan and Odi were nowhere to be seen, but with her head still tilted to the gods, all she knew was that her magic was being pulled from her into the realms, leaving her body in violent waves.

Blinding pain took root in Roh's heart as the essence of her very nature was torn from her by the blue flames, slashing at her magic. Time slowed and it seemed to take forever for her to stagger to her already-bruised knees. She couldn't scream and she couldn't stop. There was nothing but the white-hot agony of being ripped apart.

*I'm going to die.* The thought came to her amidst her internal sobbing, calmly and matter-of-factly. *There's no such thing as a songless cyren.* She should have known that a cyren wouldn't survive without a song, without the very thing that defined them.

Suddenly, Roh was untethered from her body. She was floating away, just like her deathsong, disconnected from all that was happening to her, the pain becoming more and more distant. Dazed, she watched as her magic crossed the threshold of the bridge arches and drifted in the gorge beyond. Something deep in her bones told her that it was waiting for her, she only needed to follow it —

She wasn't sure if she was still breathing, only that the magic flowing from her was waning. Little by little, it drained from her, and as it did she slowly came back to herself, ignoring the call of her deathsong dancing in the wind, letting the pain return to her husk of a body.

Around her, the blue flames sputtered out. A violent shudder took hold, as the last threads of power left her.

The ribbons of gold drifted out into the gorge and faded into nothing.

# CHAPTER TWENTY-EIGHT

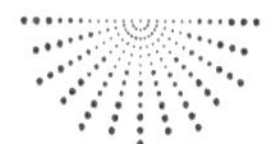

At first, there was only darkness. And a dullness of the senses. Roh knew she was on the Bridge of Csilla, but there was nothing to tell her so. It was as though she was suspended in the pitch black of the night's sky.

But all at once, she could feel the gentle grip of a hand around her arm, trying to help her up. She wasn't ready to stand, not yet. She wasn't familiar enough with the body she'd come back to. It didn't feel like her own. Instead, it felt like an empty shell.

Another pair of soft hands closed around her other arm, and regardless of her own intentions, Roh was pulled to her feet, which felt like useless lumps of flesh beneath her liquid legs.

And yet she remained upright. *How?*

'Roh …' A familiar voice said in her ear. *Harlyn.*

Another spoke on her other side. 'We've got you, Roh.'

*Yrsa.*

And they did. Roh did not fall.

Slowly, she peeled her eyes open, squinting against the sudden brightness. For the bridge that had been dimly lit only moments ago, was now flooded with light. Numb, Roh peered at the crowd of cyrens … Every single one of them had a kernel of gold flickering above their heads, as though witnessing the stripping of her magic had coaxed theirs to the surface.

Roh leaned into her friends' arms as she surveyed the rest. The Council of Seven Elders and Delja the Triumphant stared at her, awestruck, flecks of magic floating above them as well. Roh turned her gaze to where Deodan and Odi stood, mouths open. They were alright, untouched by flame, which was now nowhere in sight. And the others, Finn and Yrsa and Harlyn … They were all almost exactly as they had been before, and yet … She herself was much changed.

'Rohesia of the Bone Cleaners …' Bloodwyn Haertel began. Though her voice was steady and clear, Roh could hear the note of shock that rippled through it. 'You chose to sacrifice your deathsong …' It was as though the elder herself couldn't quite believe it.

Roh wasn't sure she believed it, either.

Elder Haertel seemed to gather herself, and she smiled coldly, as though she was now revelling in the absence of one of the most powerful forms of magic in cyren history. 'You sacrificed your deathsong in order to save a human and a water warlock … Two inferior races.'

Something was pressed into Roh's hand, something cool and smooth. She felt a familiar warm pulse of power, of sincerity.

Her voice came back to her suddenly and raw as her fingers tightened around the crown of bones now in her grip, the topaz still gleaming at its apex. 'They're not inferior to us,' she rasped. 'We are all of the same realms.' She straightened, with the help of Harlyn and Yrsa. 'I was birthed by a cyren, fathered by a warlock and named for a human. In the past, our kinds stood together … and so it will be once more, under my rule.'

Her words rang out across the bridge, stark and true. Though she could feel no hint of magic within, not a single note of song, her words claimed her identity enough on their own.

The Council of Seven Elders bristled, but before they could say anything, Roh took a step forward, towards the dais. Harlyn and Yrsa's hands fell away from her as she found her strength once more and ascended the stairs. She let her gaze rest upon each of the council elders.

'I trust that my sacrifice was of the highest order. And that I have been reinstated in the Queen's Tournament.' It was not a question. They would not deny her. Not the cyren who had gone where the fear was darkest. Roh placed her crown of bones atop her head.

The quiet of the council did not threaten her. Roh waited, her hands clasped before her, her gaze unflinching.

A muscle twitched in Erdites Colter's jaw. 'You have,'

he said. 'You may continue your quest for the birthstones of Saddoriel.'

Roh stood rigid on the dais. She did not look at her friends or scan the crowds for a familiar, comforting face. Instead, she trained her cold eyes on the council. 'I require a private audience with my guardian.'

*Require.* Not request. Her order hung between them as clear as the notes of the fiddles had been, what felt like a lifetime ago.

Elder Colter gave the slightest dip of his head and then the crowds were parting, with Ames emerging at the foot of the dais.

It was Kezra who led them swiftly across the bridge and into her private study, the heavy door clicking closed behind her as she left. The sound of it seemed to echo in the silence, and at last Roh loosed a heavy breath. She had intended to interrogate Ames about her father, about the girl she was named after but whom he'd failed to mention last time. But at last, in the privacy of Kezra's study, Roh came undone. With her back to the cool stone wall, she slid to the ground, the emptiness inside her threatening to swallow her whole. Tears burned her eyes and tracked hot down her face.

Ames took three strides towards her and joined her on the floor. Her vision blurred, Roh glanced across at him in surprise, finding his weathered face softened with awe. She'd never seen that expression on him before.

'I …' His voice cracked. 'I am moved by your sacrifice.' He placed a gentle hand on her shoulder.

Roh rested her head in her hands, opening her

mouth to speak, to say what, she didn't know. But she stopped, palming away her tears, her brows furrowing as she turned her attention to Ames' hand still on her shoulder.

It was trembling.

'You …' she said.

When Ames removed his hand, he did not hide it from her as he once had. It rested in his lap, its tremors plain for Roh to see.

But Roh didn't just stare at his hand. Her gaze trailed up, to the patch of discoloured skin peeking out from beneath his collar.

'Ask it, Rohesia,' Ames said, watching her. 'I cannot deny you answers. Not after all you have done.'

Roh's voice was small. 'You're him …'

'Him?'

'The patient from the journals … There was a water warlock, Killian … He documented his life before the Scouring of Lochloria and the days leading up to it. He was a healer of sorts, trying to cure a patient whose body seized and whose skin discoloured. I was *so sure* you were him. But … but you can't be. I asked …' Roh's hand went to her crown, taking it from her head and staring at the golden gem glinting in the candlelight.

'What did you ask the Mercy's Topaz, Rohesia?' Ames said.

'It didn't work. I … I exchanged the code name in the journals for yours, seeking its guidance towards sincerity.'

'I see.'

'And nothing happened. It wasn't true. It couldn't be.' Roh's whole body sagged as she held the crown limply.

Ames' warm arm fell around her shoulders, and for the first time, he offered Roh the comfort a caring guardian might. She drew her knees up to her chest and allowed herself to lean into her mentor, fresh tears spilling down her cheeks. For nearly eighteen years Ames had watched over her, but had never offered this sort of reassurance. She hadn't realised how much she needed it.

'You had the right idea,' Ames said, his voice rumbling above her head.

Roh blinked, slowly pulling back. 'What?'

'It might have worked,' Ames told her. 'Only I didn't go by that name back then.'

Roh peeled herself off the wall and faced her guardian. 'What are you saying?'

'I'm saying, that had you used my given name, the name I was gifted at birth, my true name, the topaz would have told you something different.'

'What would it have told me?'

Ames smiled sadly at her. 'That I am who you believe me to be, I am the patient in those journals. The patient whose body was racked with tremors, whose skin discoloured. Killian was my lessons master, my healer, and later, my friend.'

Roh's mouth hung open, her heart hammering. 'But that's not possible. That would mean you're well over six hundred years old. That you're the same age as —'

'Delja? And Cerys?' Ames finished. 'I'm younger by a

few years, actually. Though I'm aware I don't look it. Chronic illness and prolonged life will do that to a cyren.'

'Ames,' Roh warned. 'How ... what ...?' Words abandoned her as she stared at the cyren she had always thought she'd known. 'This can't be.'

'I assure you, it can.'

'How?' Roh asked.

'We're all connected. Delja, Cerys and I ... Your father, too. We grew up together, you see. For a time, we were incredibly close. Back then, water warlocks were not so reviled as they eventually became. Cerys, Delja and I, we learned alongside them for years, with Killian as our tutor. But as time went on, the realms began to change for the worse. Saddoriel and Lochloria became places of darkness, places not fit for the dreamers of this world. But Deelie and Cerys ... They were determined to make change, to better cyrenkind and our way of life. I was young and often ill, so I wasn't privy to a lot of their plans. They were always scheming together, and Eadric and I were always two steps behind them.' Ames drew a tired breath, as though recalling the events of the past drained the very life out of him.

But a name clanged through Roh: *Eadric*.

'Eadric, my father?'

'Yes.'

Roh's heart stuttered as the pieces fell into place. 'So the Eadric in the journals, the one that Killian speaks of ... That's him? That's my father?'

'I imagine so, yes. Your father was a student of Killian's as well. He was there with us.'

For a moment, Roh was back standing before the teerah-panther enclosure, running her talons across the name in the journal, convincing herself it was nought but coincidence.

'It was him … it was him all along,' she murmured, before she remembered herself. She turned back to Ames and waited.

Thankfully, he pressed on. 'Long before The Dawning, Deelie went off on her own for a while. It was very unlike her. She was always by Cerys' side, as though she was worried she might step away to find her gone. But not this time. It was Deelie who left. We didn't see her for weeks. And then, when she came back, she … Well, she told us she had found a way to extend our lives. All of us, Eadric too. She insisted we needed more time than normal cyrens and warlocks were given in order to make true change.'

'There was an Ashai – a human magic wielder from afar who could take and gift years of life as he pleased. It's my understanding that Delja made a deal with him.'

'And …?' Roh whispered.

Ames sighed heavily, his head dropping into his hand. 'And without our knowledge, linked our lives to hers.'

Roh hadn't realised she'd got to her feet and had started to pace Kezra's study. 'But why you? Why —' Roh cut herself off, freezing mid-step. When her gaze met Ames' again, understanding simmered there. 'What was your name?' she asked. 'What was your given name?'

Ames pinched the bridge of his nose. 'Marlow,' he said. 'It was Marlow.'

The topaz sent a pulse of warmth from the top of Roh's head to her toes, and two moments in time flashed before her as the name seemed to echo through the study …

*Cerys' eyes widened as her gaze settled on Odi, her mouth parting as though she was remembering something.*

*'Marlow?' she croaked, pressing her face against the bars.*

*Roh stared. 'Marlow?'*

*'Marlow, you've come,' Cerys rasped, a thin arm reaching out.*

*'Who in all the realms is Marlow?' Scowling, Roh looked from Cerys to the human, who'd frozen in terror.*

*'Your uncle,' said a quiet but melodic voice from behind her.*

*Roh whirled around, finding herself face to face with the queen – Delja the Triumphant.*

And then Roh was in the same place, at a different time …

*'He has already come.'*

*Roh threw herself against the bars, clutching the lengths of bone in her hands as Cerys had done so many times before. 'What? What do you know of the stones? Of the* Tome of Kyeos?' *she pleaded. 'Who has already come?'*

*'Marlow,' Cerys said simply.*

*Roh's heart sank instantly. Marlow. Her supposed long-dead uncle.*

. . .

Now, Roh gazed upon her uncle in dumbstruck wonder. 'You're … *alive.* And … and you've known me my whole life?'

'I am. And I have,' he replied, warily following her steps across the study. 'I'm so sorry I wasn't able to tell you. It was part of the conditions when you were passed over to me at the prison after your birth.'

Dizzy, Roh braced herself against Kezra's desk, trying to wrap her mind around everything Ames – *Marlow* – was saying.

'I don't understand why Delja would link her life to yours? To that of a sickly cyren?'

Ames smiled sadly. 'When Cerys and I met Deelie, she was a lonely nestling, all but abandoned by a cruel mother and mostly apathetic sisters. She had no one. During lessons, Cerys took her under her wing, as she often did with strays, and begged our mother to adopt her. It was rare that anyone said no to Cerys. Our mother was no exception, and she saw how Deelie's own mother treated her. So Deelie became part of our family. She travelled with us to Lochloria when I was ill, and she grew up with us. Even in my haze of sickness, I always knew she had a soft spot for me. We were the family she had always wanted but never had. *That's* why she linked me to her, along with Cerys. She couldn't let us go, even when she wanted to. Deelie cares for us … She cares for you, in her own twisted way. She tried to keep you for herself, you know.'

'What?'

'When you were born. She tried to change the Law of the Lair so that she could take you in as her own. But for once, the council stood by their own rules. As it happens, there are some lines they're not willing to cross, and having the offspring of Cerys the Elder Slayer as their princess was one of them.'

'So Cerys …' Roh's voice was a croak. 'Cerys isn't mad, is she?'

Her uncle shook his head. 'I've never thought so, no.'

'But … but you told me to stay away from her! That she was dangerous?' Roh blurted, outraged. For all these years she had lived as an orphan, when not one, but *two* family members had been within arm's reach.

'Well, that's not entirely untrue. And you had to believe those things, Roh. At least at first —'

'I had to think my own mother was insane?!' A hollow laugh escaped Roh at the absurdity of it all.

'*Yes*,' he said. 'It was part of the plan.'

'*What plan?*' In the heat of the moment, Roh nearly called him Ames and she realised with a shock that she had no idea how she was meant to address him now. Ames? Marlow? Uncle? They all felt wrong.

'The plan to keep you *safe*, the plan to pave the way for your future. The one your parents sacrificed so much for.' Ames frowned. 'Did the journals say nothing of Eadric and Cerys?'

The question momentarily quelled Roh's anger. She sifted through her memories. 'Killian mentioned Eadric obsessing over something to do with the Pool of

Weeping, but it sounded like … Well, like he thought he was insane?'

Ames huffed a dark laugh. 'We all did, at first. Eadric had some very far-fetched notions about that pool. Or so they seemed at the time.'

'Tell me,' Roh urged. 'Tell me about the pool.'

Ames studied her thoughtfully. 'You already suspect it. I imagine Deodan put you on the scent.'

'I suspect that I did not partake in the First Cry, as other nestlings do. That is all I suspect, and I have no idea how this could be part of some grand plan hatched by a bunch of dead warlocks.'

'You're right,' Ames told her quietly. 'You did not partake in the ritual. Eadric ensured it.'

'How? He was dead, wasn't he?'

'Yes. He was dead. But he had put measures in place. An enchantment.'

Roh's skin crawled. 'What kind of enchantment?'

'The very one that still echoes in your mind. The one I heard you quote countless times to Orson when she was upset. The one Harlyn has told me you chant in your sleep …'

Roh's hands went numb and her throat was dry. Her next words came out as a rasp.

*'Little nestling, little nestling,*
*We cry not in the ancient deep.*
*Little nestling, little nestling,*
*Follow my voice, to the land of sleep.*
*Hush, hush, little cyren, so strong yet so small …'*

Ames nodded. *'For down in deep Saddoriel, we let no tears*

*fall*,' he finished. 'A warlock enchantment,' he explained. 'Originally, it was to soothe unsettled infants, but … well, Eadric modified it for you, his daughter, so you would never shed a tear in your infancy, so you would never be able to sacrifice to the Pool of Weeping.'

It was as though a thick fist clenched around Roh's heart, squeezing so hard she could hardly bear it. 'Why?' she managed.

'Because you were meant to be different. Don't you know what the pools are?'

'Sacred sites. Ways for the ruler and the council elders to travel …?'

'More than that. They hold the essence of every cyren in history. Except yours.'

Roh loosed a breath.

'Your parents didn't want your magic linked to everyone else's, didn't want your power, your development at the hands of the queen,' Ames told her.

'What does that mean?'

'It means you will be the one to break the cycle. It means that your father, even in death, found a way for you to carry on his work, your mother's work. They sacrificed everything to ensure you will be the one to bring us all together, Rohesia. You will lead us from the darkness.'

Roh gave a hollow laugh as Ames' grand words echoed around her in the face of all she had just lost. 'We were supposed to find me a trainer, you know … Someone to help me master my magic …'

Ames – Marlow – studied her intensely. 'The only

person who can train you, is locked away in the bone cells of Saddoriel's Prison.'

'Cerys? Cerys could have trained me?'

'No one else has ever understood the power of an Irons' song.'

Roh swallowed, trying not to sound as broken as she felt. 'Well, there's no need for that now.'

'This is far from the end,' Ames said.

'You sound like Deodan,' Roh told him bitterly. 'All these lofty statements and no concept of reality. I am *not* *queen*, Ames. Not by a long way. And when I am? *If* I ever am? I'll have no song, *none* of the Irons' power that can supposedly unite warring races.' Pain pulsed behind her eyes. 'I refuse to be a pawn in a game played by a bunch of ancient warlocks and cyrens.'

'Roh, you are no pawn. You are our queen —'

A sharp knock sounded at the door and their visitor didn't wait for an invitation.

It was Delja who ducked inside, her expression tight. 'What's going on here?'

'Deelie, please,' Ames said.

Delja's eyes widened and she turned to Roh. 'I don't know what he told you, Rohesia —'

Roh flung her hand out as she cut her off. 'It doesn't matter what he told me,' she said. 'I am tired of half-truths, of being manipulated. The *Tome of Kyeos* will tell all before the end.'

Shock flashed in Delja's eyes, but Roh was done.

Turning on her heel, she left her uncle and the former Queen of Cyrens alone with their secrets.

Back on the Bridge of Csilla, the crowds had departed, with only a few stragglers remaining on the outskirts. There was no sign of the Eery Brothers and their fiddles, nor Roh's companions, but the Council of Seven Elders was stalking the dais impatiently.

'We will depart immediately,' Taro Haertel announced as soon as he spotted Roh. 'You and the Csillan Arch General will escort us to the mirror pool at once.'

At the foot of the dais, Kezra nodded dutifully.

'I won't be escorting you anywhere,' Roh said, her voice sounding as hollow as she felt. 'I will no doubt see you at the next challenge for my reign.' There was no question that there would be another. 'One final thing,' she added, steeling herself against the loathing in their stares. 'The disgraced soldier, Piri? She remains in Csilla.'

The council elder standing to Taro's left stepped forward, a breastplate of coral peeking out from beneath her luxurious robe. 'You cannot make those demands.'

Roh observed the twin rapiers hanging from her jewelled belt. 'You must be Isomene Sigra.'

'You dare address me after what you did in Serratega? To *my* army unit?'

'We were attacked without warning and we defended ourselves,' Roh argued, fighting to keep her voice even. 'If you expected us to lie down and die, then you know little of Saddorien cyrens for someone who's in charge of the lair's defence.'

'I know enough to know that you are no Saddorien.'

'Tell that to your army,' Roh snapped. 'Now, the soldier. She stays with us.' Roh made sure there was no weakness, no compromise in her voice, only the pure command of a cyren who'd just sacrificed her deathsong and lived to tell the tale.

Elder Sigra, her face flushed with fury, opened her mouth to argue, but was cut off by Winslow Ward.

'We have no need for dishonoured cyrens in our ranks,' she said, her voice deceptively cold. 'Keep her. She has no further value to us.'

Roh didn't let her gratitude show. Instead, she let her gaze trail across each of their faces. 'Safe travels, elders.' She made it sound every bit the dismissal it was. The cyrens before her had never supported her and she would never win their favour now … The time for that had passed. Roh watched them go, their luxurious robes billowing after them. Emerging from Kezra's study, Delja followed with a meaningful backward glance at Ames, who hurried behind, pulling Jesmond in tow.

Roh's former-mentor-now-uncle's eyes were filled with regret, but she watched him go the same as the rest, wondering how many more secrets stood between them.

Afterwards, Roh wandered the halls of the east wing, numb and alone. Her lack of deathsong left a hollowness within that seemed to grow with each passing moment.

*There's no such thing as a songless cyren …* The words echoed in her mind as she cradled that broken part of her, wondering if she was destined to feel emptier and emptier until she could no longer bear it. Cyrens weren't meant to exist without song. It wasn't natural, that much was clear to Roh. Some fundamental piece of her had been ripped away from her body, just as vital as a lung or a heart.

And then there was Ames … Her uncle … There were the secrets he had kept from her for her whole life. The reason she hadn't shed a single tear until she thought she'd killed Valli before he'd even hatched. A damn warlock enchantment, crafted by her father, the why of it *still* unknown. And there was Akoris, too … How could she undo what had happened there? She still didn't know the full extent of it. Her life was a series of unending questions, it seemed.

As she walked aimlessly, she knew she was postponing the inevitable: facing her friends. What would they make of her decision? Would it change things between them? Her stomach churned and she shook her head, trying to rid herself of the unhelpful thoughts. There was still the Willow's Sapphire to obtain, and now there was significantly less time to travel to Lochloria, after whittling away their weeks in Serratega. But what if they *could* achieve these things? What would that mean for her now? To be a cyren queen, without the most meaningful of cyren magic?

*Rohesia the Songless* … The name rushed through her in an icy wave. That's what they would call her …

'Roh?' a quiet voice said tentatively. The young nestling, Mora, peeked her head around the corner. 'What are you doing?' she asked inquisitively.

Roh looked around. 'Uh … walking.'

Mora blinked. 'Why?'

Roh wanted to tell her that it helped her think, but as the words formed on her tongue, she realised they weren't true this time. 'I don't know,' she admitted. Sometimes hidden truths were best shared with a nestling – they did not judge.

Mora skipped to her side. 'Everyone is waiting for you.'

'Are they?'

'Yep,' she announced, slipping her small hand in Roh's. 'Come on, I'll show you.'

Dazed, Roh let the small cyren lead her through the east wing back to the royal guest chambers. Mora used her entire body weight to push the door and hold it open for Roh.

Everyone was there. Harlyn, Odi, Yrsa, Finn, Deodan, Floralin, Kezra and Sol all stood as she entered the room, their eyes gleaming with an emotion Roh couldn't quite pinpoint. The cyren Roh recognised as Piri, now in plain Saddorien attire, stood a little further back from the group.

And Valli … Valli took up the entire sill of the large arched window, his barbed tail swinging, his molten-gold eyes intent on her. Relief rushed through her. He had found her once again.

But it was Deodan who came forward and took her hands in his. The warrior warlock knelt before her.

'My Queen.' He bowed his head, his hands warm and firm around hers.

'Deodan,' she said, unsure of what to do. He had seen her during her darkest days, he had witnessed the depths of her mistakes and the hollowness of her heart … and yet he claimed her still.

The others didn't kneel, didn't bow, but as Roh glanced from the warlock pledging his allegiance to her other friends, she realised what glimmered in their gazes.

*Pride.*

And so Roh pulled Deodan to his feet and met Finn's lilac stare from across the room.

'Last I heard, you had figured out a way to retrieve the Willow's Sapphire from the teerah panther … is that still the case?' she asked.

Finn's face split into a wide smile, his dimple showing. 'It is.'

Roh steadied herself. 'Then what are we waiting for?'

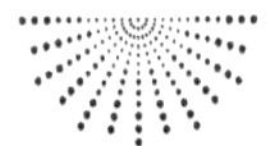

Roh stood before the teerah-panther enclosure, her palms growing clammy at her sides as Finn and the others explained the plan they'd hatched long ago: *Finn's plan*, the strategy she thought she'd never hear. They were all so confident, even Harlyn, who up until now, had avoided being anywhere near the enclosure. The emptiness inside Roh expanded as she gazed upon the foliage beyond the glass.

*I have to trust them*, she told herself, toying with the key around her neck.

'Does everyone know what they have to do?' Finn asked, folding his arms over his chest.

'Yes,' Roh replied through gritted teeth, palming her father's quartz dagger.

'And you know that if it comes down to one of us, or him …' Finn added, loading his crossbow meaningfully. Though he'd gifted it to Odi, the human had insisted that

Finn wield it for this particular venture, the scheme of his own making.

'I know,' Roh said, her heart heavy. Regardless of their past failings to retrieve the birthstone, she still didn't want the beast dead. She felt a strange sense of kinship with it. It was caged as she once had been, a gold collar clamped around his neck just as the gold circlet had been forced around her head. After all that she had endured, the death of this creature, whether by her hand or order, seemed like the one thing she couldn't allow. But as it had been from the moment she'd left Saddoriel, this quest was no longer just about her. If one of her friends was at risk, she wouldn't hesitate to signal Finn.

Finn made for the entrance to the enclosure with only a slight limp. One of the Csillans had made further alterations to the prosthetic limb Nicholas had made, and Finn seemed to be adjusting well enough. Roh was yet to ask him why he hadn't started taking the healer's tonic again.

'Ready?' Deodan asked, his water vials clutched in his hands.

Yrsa nodded, brandishing the net she held with Odi. 'Ready.'

Harlyn waved a silver whistle at the warlock. 'You hear this, you run.'

Roh consulted the timepiece Floralin had loaned her and drew the key from beneath her shirt. 'Kezra should be in position now.'

Finn nodded to the door. 'If you'll do the honours, then, Roh ...'

Roh gritted her teeth and fitted the key to the lock, which clicked loudly as she turned it. 'Now …' she said, the door swinging inwards.

As quietly as they could, Roh and her companions slipped inside the enclosure. Roh crept forward, one tentative step at a time, silently praying that all had gone to plan on Kezra's end. Leaf litter crunched beneath her boots and she scanned the surrounding foliage for any sign of that gleaming black coat and gnashing fangs.

Roh motioned for the others to follow. They inched deeper into the forest, Roh's heart hammering in her throat and her blood roaring in her ears. The cool air of the enclosure prickled against her skin and she felt a bead of cold sweat drip between her shoulderblades.

*This has to work*, she told herself, craning her neck to peer into the depths of the enclosure, flinching at the sound of the smallest twigs breaking. But Roh's companions moved as a single unit, in tune with each other's steps and positions, no hesitation among them. It was their conviction that spurred her on, and for a brief moment, she marvelled at how far they had all come together —

She held up a hand suddenly and the others froze behind her. It was somewhere here … she could feel it. Was it watching them? Was it readying to pounce? Roh blocked out the memory of Harlyn's piercing scream from the attack in the Gilded Plains, and the vision the Rite of Strothos had shown her, where Harlyn had lost her arm entirely.

'*Sing, sing, sing …*' the Council of Seven Elders had

chanted then. Now, Roh couldn't even if she wanted to, even if her life or Harlyn's depended on it. She took a deliberate step forward, as though if she kept moving, her thoughts would remain at bay —

A low growl vibrated through the entire enclosure.

The panther was here.

Roh nodded to the others, who readied themselves, falling into position as though they'd been working together all their lives.

An ear-splitting screech drowned out all else, followed by a powerful gust of wind that nearly flattened the surrounding trees.

'Go!' Roh shouted, surging forward into the dense undergrowth at the signal.

Valli had arrived, offering a distraction, as planned.

Roh and her companions darted through the forest, towards the sound of both legendary creatures squaring off. The enraged roar of the teerah panther echoed off the walls, but it was silenced by Valli's defiant shriek.

Roh burst into the clearing, where her glowing sea drake bared its fangs to the teerah panther on its haunches. The Willow's Sapphire glinted in the gold collar, as though sensing the presence of its sibling stone in the crown atop Roh's head.

'Gods,' she murmured, signalling the others into position while Valli kept the beast's attention elsewhere, his gold scales illuminating the dense jungle. Roh tore her gaze away from him and eyed the panther's body, taking in every scar, every old wound, and at last went to its back leg, to the spot Finn had told her about. Between the animal's heel and its calf, a large metal barb pierced the tendon, where thick yellow pus oozed. Roh could smell the sour odour from where she was at the edge of the clearing. A torture device, crafted by the cruel minds of the council to keep the beast in a permanent state of fury and aggression.

Valli shrieked again, eyeing the teerah panther in challenge. He was no longer a pestering drakeling now, he was as big, if not bigger, than the wild cat before him, and he clawed at the ground, his long body glimmering and his wings outstretched in threat.

'Now!' Roh cried, leaping towards the panther.

Around her, the others burst into action. Deodan spilt his vials of water and whispered his enchantments, creating miniature creatures in Valli's image, surrounding the panther. Finn trained his crossbow on the beast as Odi and Yrsa sprang from the bushes, throwing a huge net over the panther and pulling down hard, a similar manoeuvre to the one Yrsa and Finn had attempted against the sea serpent back in the third trial of the tournament.

Roh was already at the animal's wounded hind leg, doing her best to dodge its enraged kicks. She clamped her free hand around its ankle, using every ounce of her strength to draw the wound to her. She nearly gagged at the rotten stench of it. The poor creature's flesh was hot under her touch.

'Easy,' she soothed, more to herself than to the thrashing beast.

Harlyn came to her side, the silver whistle between

her teeth, her brow gleaming with sweat. Her good hand gripped the panther's back leg, stabilising the hold Roh had, enough so that she could examine the barb. It went straight through the animal's tendon.

When Finn had told her about the torture device he'd discovered, she thought she might be able to ease the thing out slowly and carefully. But that was not the case. The horrific thing would have to be pulled all the way through, and fast.

'Do it,' Harlyn grunted, struggling to maintain her grip on the creature.

Roh didn't hesitate this time. Her hand closed around one end of the barb and with all her strength she wrenched it through the flesh —

A near-deafening roar exploded from the beast and the net broke free, sending Yrsa and Odi sprawling into the bushes. Yrsa was on her feet in an instant, whirling her sling, ready to defend them. Roh grabbed Harlyn and dragged her away, avoiding being trampled by a hair's breadth.

Finn stood his ground, his eyes trained on the panther, who reared up in agony, swiping at the air before him, where Deodan's water drakelings flew around his head. Still clutching the barb, her hand drenched in blood and pus, Roh eyed Valli from across the clearing.

The drake seemed to study her in return, as though he somehow sensed she was very much changed. He blinked, his molten-gold eyes glinting, before he took a deliberate step towards the teerah panther, who was now growling and panting on all fours, white spittle foaming at its mouth. It looked up, taking in the measure of Valli and his glorious wings, as though it might mean to attack, to tear through his scales —

'Roh,' Finn warned, raising his crossbow slightly higher.

'No,' she told him. 'Wait.'

Carefully, Roh walked towards Valli, coming to stand in front of him, laying claim to him before the panther.

The panther snarled, its body shuddering as though in recollection of the pain.

Roh threw the blood-coated barb at its paws, an offering.

The panther huffed, its yellowed eyes moving from the source of all its agony, to Roh, its blood and pus still dripping from her hand.

Roh didn't breathe. She didn't think the others were breathing either, as the teerah panther took a single step towards her, a pained groan escaping it.

Roh felt the gust of wind Valli's wings sent in his direction, a warning. But she didn't look back at her drake; her eyes were fixed on the panther as it approached her.

A gasp escaped her as the beast lowered itself to the ground and gazed up expectantly at her.

Without thinking, Roh's legs were moving beneath her, the topaz in her crown guiding her. She went to the beast and knelt before it in the damp earth. Her whole body was tense as with trembling hands, she reached for the beast's gold collar. Blood smeared against the smooth, pristine surface as her unsteady fingers found the clasp.

Up close, she saw the exhaustion in the creature's eyes. For how long had it suffered? For how long had its fury kept it alive in the face of so much pain?

Something clicked beneath Roh's hands and time slowed as the heavy collar fell from the teerah panther's neck and into her lap.

The beast exhaled a hot breath, the sound akin to a long-held sigh of relief. With a half-hearted growl, the panther lurched to his feet.

Behind Roh, Valli moved, standing at the edge of the clearing, stretching his wings and staring keenly at the injured beast. Roh watched on in amazement, as the sea drake led the teerah panther from the enclosure, through the hidden exit, and into the wild gorge beyond.

'Roh.' Yrsa's hand was gentle on her shoulder, drawing her attention back to the prize in her lap.

With her friends surrounding her, Roh turned the heavy collar over in her hands, leaving bloody fingerprints on its surface. The Willow's Sapphire winked back at her from its inset.

*Is this real?* she wondered abstractly. *Could a songless cyren really retrieve a birthstone of Saddoriel?*

She ran her talons over the deep-blue stone, feeling its magic pulse beneath her touch. Slowly, she took her father's dagger in her hands and set the quartz blade against the gold inset. With a deep breath, she prised the Willow's Sapphire free.

As soon as the weight of the gem hit her palm, so too

did its power. She felt it course through her body, a warm strength filling her hollow shell as the Willow's Sapphire lent her its endurance.

'You've done it, My Queen.' Deodan crouched by her side, staring in wonder at the stone.

'*We've* done it,' Roh corrected him, removing her crown of bones and setting the sapphire in its place beside the Mercy's Topaz.

The gems gleamed back at her, their magic knitting together seamlessly, settling around her like a warm blanket. Roh knew the comfort and reprieve from her emptiness was only temporary, but she leaned into it as she placed the crown back atop her head and stood.

'What now, Your Majesty?' Harlyn asked with a wink.

Roh allowed herself to smile, linking her arm through Harlyn's good one and looking to the rest of her companions, her final gaze coming to rest on Deodan. 'We make for Lochloria, the scholar's city.'

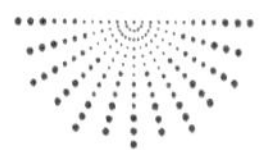

That night, Kezra and Floralin insisted on preparing a feast in Roh's honour. The kitchen smelled divine and the companions, along with the addition of Piri, each took up their stations, more than happy to help. The wine and mead flowed freely, and to Roh's great surprise, Harlyn offered to play the lute.

Her friend sat on a stool in the corner, with Mora and Sol planted at her feet as she brought the instrument to her lap and tentatively plucked the first few strings.

'You can do it, Har,' Odi called over his shoulder, a pile of peeled carrots on a chopping board in front of him.

Harlyn waved him off, her brow furrowed in determination. She seemed to gather herself, and then, she began.

A rough melody filled the kitchen, glancing off the pots and pans and coiling around Roh, lining that endless hollow inside her. It had been an age since she'd heard the peculiar resonance of the lute; its gentle yet rich sound. Harlyn gained confidence with each note, with each steady strum of her fingers across the strings and pluck of the chords.

It wasn't perfect, not by any stretch. But it was *beautiful*.

Harlyn didn't sing, she never had when she played the lute. The instrument she had carved with her own hands was perfect for solos, its tuning full of intricate shading and delicate nuances of colour, which Harlyn wove throughout the song. She stumbled across the fingerboard and her hand jarred at the lute's neck, but it didn't matter. Harlyn gritted her teeth and played on. It was a new composition, Roh realised. Something that Harlyn had been working on with Odi, by the sound of things. It had his imprint on it – melancholy laced with the sweetest notes of hope.

The melody blossomed around them, sweeping Roh up in its waves of feeling, pulling at her like a strong current, whipping around her, as though she was in the eye of a heart-wrenching yet exquisite terror tempest.

Roh found her cheeks damp with tears, and on the final note she shot to her feet, applauding loudly. She rushed to embrace her friend, all too aware that her actions would do little to reflect the depth of her pride, her joy for Harlyn.

'Amazing,' she gushed. 'That was, and you are, amazing.'

Harlyn's cheeks reddened, but a smile tugged at the corner of her mouth and Roh knew she was pleased.

'Told you that you could do it,' Odi said with satisfaction.

'Uh-huh,' Harlyn snorted. 'You're just an expert on everything, aren't you?'

'Pretty much,' Odi retorted.

The preparations went on, interspersed with laughter, warm conversation and numerous refreshments. In the distance, the Csillan choir sang.

Not for the first time, Roh found herself sneaking glances at Yrsa, who was constantly by Piri's side. There was a quiet joy in every touch between them, from Yrsa straightening Piri's apron to Piri wiping a smear of flour from Yrsa's cheek. Roh marvelled at the intimacy that pulled them together, even when they stood across the kitchen from one another. For the first time in a while, Roh was glad – *grateful* – to see such elated affection, rather than grief, lining Yrsa's face.

Everyone's cheeks were tipped pink, their eyes bright as they sank into each other's company. But it was the little nestling, Mora, whom Roh sought. Soon after Harlyn's performance, Roh pulled her aside, crouching before her.

'I have something for you,' Roh told her, digging through her pocket.

'A present?' the little cyren asked, her eyes wide and eager.

'I suppose so,' Roh replied, drawing her hand from the folds of her jacket. 'Here.'

She lay her palm flat, offering the two pieces of gold to the nestling. 'This was my circlet.'

A grin wider than the Csillan gorge split across Mora's face. 'You had one?' she exclaimed with glee as her small fingers reached for Roh's offering.

'I did. And I remember you saying that you wanted one like your brother.'

'I do, I do!' The girl was practically jumping up and down.

'Well, I checked with your ma, and she said you could have mine. I'm sorry it's broken.'

That fact seemed inconsequential to the nestling. She grabbed the two pieces of gold and shrieked with delight. 'Sol!' she shouted to her brother. 'Sol! Look what I have!'

The youngster darted over and peered into his sister's palms, intrigued.

'It's a circlet, just like yours! We can be the same now.'

'But Mora,' he said cautiously. 'It's broken.'

'That's okay. We can fix it, can't we, Roh?' Mora glanced up at Roh, no trace of doubt on her face.

Roh smiled. 'I believe you can,' she answered. 'Flo said she'll take you to the forge tomorrow. I've heard that sometimes when things are broken they can be welded back together, to be stronger than before.'


Despite the festivities, Roh waited for the opportunity to present itself and slipped away from the kitchens. The emptiness was yawning inside her to the point of madness and she had to take a moment or two for herself. Was this how she would be from now on, forever incomplete?

As soon as she was alone, Roh couldn't help her mind wandering to all that awaited her in the days to come. Deodan had told her that there was no such thing as a songless cyren, but there was now. *She* was that cyren, up against the most treacherous and cunning of her kind, not to mention time itself. There was only a matter of weeks until her seven moons were up. A handful of weeks to reach Lochloria, contend with an inevitable challenge and retrieve the final birthstone of Saddoriel: the Gauntlet Ruby.

The magic of Harlyn's lute playing had ebbed away, leaving Roh emptier than ever. Whatever power the topaz and the sapphire contained, it was no longer enough to fill the void her deathsong had left behind. For the first time since her sacrifice, Roh allowed a sliver of grief to slip through her mental armour, the pain of it so poignant it nearly brought her to her knees. She leaned against the wall in the hallway then, tipping her head to the ceiling as she choked back a sob.

'Roh?' Finn's voice echoed down the hall as he approached her.

She hastily tried to gather herself, but it was too late, he'd seen her gasping for air. His hand was instantly on her shoulder, and he peered into her face, his brows knitting together in concern.

'What is it?' he asked.

Roh wished he hadn't asked, wished he wasn't there, for all the question did was intensify the sorrow within her when she had been trying so hard to push it down.

Words refused to form, but he must have seen it in her eyes for he quickly began folding her into his arms.

His body was warm and firm against hers, reassuring and strong. She let herself sink into his embrace, into the comfort he was so freely offering. They hadn't so much as touched since that afternoon by the ravine in Serratega, and for a moment she wondered how she'd gone so long without him. She breathed him in, the pain slowly receding as he held her, making no move to step away.

'Is this where you tell me it'll all be alright?' she said into the hard plane of his chest.

'No,' his voice vibrated against her. 'It's where I tell you I'm here, that we all are, for you.'

Roh failed to swallow the thick lump in her throat, unable to tell him what that meant to her, the gratitude feeling all too much as it drifted alongside all her other raging emotions. Instead, she lifted her face to his and kissed him. The kiss was hard and hungry, a desperation taking hold of her. She needed him, every part of him. She needed to *feel*.

His hands tightened around her waist as he kissed her back, deeply, his tongue brushing against hers, making her stomach dip, a heat blooming within. Every inch of her sang out, begging to be beneath his touch. Gods, she wanted this. She'd wanted it for longer than she could remember. The feeling was utterly intoxicating, completely uncontainable. She had to have *more* of whatever it was. She had to have all of it.

His kiss devoured her and she ran her palms over him,

savouring the feel of his muscles before daring to drift her hands lower —

He caught her by the wrist.

'This isn't right,' he managed, his breathing ragged.

Roh froze.

'You're upset,' Finn said hurriedly. 'I shouldn't have —'

'It's alright,' Roh told him. 'You're not taking advantage of me. I *want* this.'

'No.' The word was like an icy bucket of water tipped over her. Finn met her stare, something hard glimmering there. 'I don't want this to be a balm for an open wound.'

'Then what do you want it to be?' Roh pulled away from him, straightening her clothes.

'I …'

Pain bloomed anew in Roh. 'Can I ask you something?' she said instead.

Finn took a step back, eyeing her warily. 'Yes.'

'Why did you get me that sketchbook?'

Pink stained his cheeks. 'You found it?'

Roh nodded stiffly. 'Yrsa told me it was for me. Why? And what was the inscription meant to say?'

'Back in Thornhill, I heard Harlyn telling Yrsa that it was your eighteenth name day soon. I'd seen you cramming your sketches into every corner of your old sketchbook, with no new pages to spare. I thought … I thought you could use a new one.'

Roh's heart hurt. 'And the inscription? What was it meant to say?'

'Odi interrupted me as I was writing it weeks ago. I … I can't remember what I meant to write.'

'Oh,' was all Roh managed, feeling incredibly foolish. Her face flushed. She'd thrown herself at him and he'd said no, and now … *Gods, now he regrets buying me a gift …?* Roh stepped away from him completely, putting a decent space between them. 'I've got to go,' she heard herself say.

'Roh, wait —'

But she was already moving. She couldn't be there a moment longer, she couldn't look at the pity in his eyes while her lips were still bruised from his kiss. It was too much. And so she ran. She ran through the corridors, down through the levels of the east wing, the stairs a blur beneath her boots, the cold air of the hallways crisp on her skin. It felt like one giant spiral, making her dizzy, but she didn't care. She just needed to put distance between Finn and the others and her. It was why she'd left the dinner in the first place. She needed solitude, she needed to process the gaping emptiness inside her. Down, down, down she went into the depths of Csilla, every loss, every sacrifice barrelling into her. In the distance, she could have sworn she could still hear the choir singing, but the music was somehow out of reach; it did not touch her as she continued to run, her lungs burning.

After an age, she skidded to a stop, finding herself somewhere she'd never been before, but a place she recognised immediately: the mirror pool.

Resting her hands on her knees, she gasped for breath, staring. It looked almost the same as the pool in Akoris and its mother in Saddoriel with its large expanse of ice-blue water surrounded by willow trees and a stony shore.

At last, a sob escaped her. The place taunted her – a

source of secrets, of her own isolation. It was the last place she wanted to be, another reminder of something she lacked, another thing she didn't share with her fellow cyrens. She had never made her First Cry as every other nestling had in history. Her first tears had never been sacrificed to the Pool of Weeping as they should have. And for what? *Why?*

Warmth from the birthstones pulsed downwards. She'd forgotten she was wearing her crown. Since giving up her deathsong, it felt more like a mockery than ever before. So when the gems tugged her towards the water's edge, for once, she fought against them, her hollowness momentarily filled with an irrational rage at the stones themselves. But what little magic remained in her was no match for the Mercy's Topaz and the Willow's Sapphire. Crying openly now, every hurt bleeding from her, Roh wrangled with the will of the birthstones right up to where the water met the shore. There she fell to her knees, gasping, tears streaming down her face.

*Is this what I've become?* Her mind was screaming for her deathsong. She needed it, she couldn't live without it, let alone ascend the Saddorien throne and become Queen of Cyrens. It didn't matter how many birthstones sat in her crown.

But the topaz and the sapphire sent another pulse of heat into her body, this time bordering on hot. It shocked her enough to take her head from her hands and look up, into the rippling water.

When she did, she cried out.

For an older version of herself looked back. Her hair

was waist-length once more, her face slightly thinner and her eyes were lilac, hard with determination.

Roh stared at herself, at her unflinching gaze.

'That can't be me,' she murmured at the shimmering reflection that was both her and not her. Her song was gone. Her eyes would never be lilac, would never radiate the fearlessness that this imposter displayed. But …

The Mercy's Topaz and the Willow's Sapphire hummed in Roh's crown and sent a pulse of reassurance, of *truth* down through her entire body. A silent request to endure, to have faith …

And when Roh palmed her tears away and gazed upon the mirror pool once more, her older self smiled knowingly, unfolding a great pair of wings at her back.

ACKNOWLEDGEMENTS

I wrote this book during the most challenging year of my career (so far). So, with that in mind, my dear readers, brace yourselves, for these acknowledgements are lengthy.

First, this book is dedicated to one of my beautiful readers, Anne, who came into my life via email in late 2018 and has been a very special part of my journey ever since. Over the years, Anne has sent me heartfelt encouragement and support, and all the virtual hugs an author could ask for. She also happens to be one of the strongest warriors I know; she fights grief and a debilitating chronic illness daily, constantly pushing through despite the pain and always seeking to uplift those around her, no matter what. *The Fabric of Chaos* explores a lot of those themes, so it felt only fitting that it be her book. Anne, this one's for you. Thank you for your unending faith in me and my stories.

This book, and in fact, this entire series, would not have been possible without the input and support of my partner, Gary Ditcher. On a creative level, I'm so grateful that you're so involved in this process, from start to finish, and I've never had such fun, wine-fuelled feedback sessions. On a 'life' level … For a bit of context, during the writing of this book, my income took a massive hit. I won't go into specifics, but as a (relatively) young person trying to make a living writing books (while also trying to buy my first home in a country with an actual housing crisis), it was dire, to the point where I was seriously considering hitting pause on writing and finding a salary-based job. This notion plagued me constantly, but each time, it was Gary who talked me out of it, who told me that there was no way I should give up, that he would support the pair of us if need be and that every financial loss was simply an investment in our future. Never have I known such a gem of a human being. Thank you for your incredible encouragement and for ensuring that I always live up to my potential.

Thank you also to Alexandra Nahlous, my editor of five years. Her generosity, kindness and belief in this series helped bring this book to you all.

Of course, my immense gratitude is also owed to my beta readers, Aleesha and Claire, who have gone above and beyond, as they always do, to help me grow as a storyteller. I'm so lucky to have you both along for this wild ride. Thank you for all that you do.

Also, a special thank you to Aleesha, who was the

mastermind behind the book's title. For the longest time, this book went by another name, but as with all things in an author's life, unexpected complications arose with the cover and the title. So, I went to Aleesha for help and she came up with the beautiful name, *The Fabric of Chaos*, which suits this story more than I could have imagined.

Over the years, both in previous acknowledgements and online, I've mentioned how lonely this job can get. However, despite writing the words, I don't think I *fully* comprehended just how lonely I was during the early years of this strange and wonderful career. However, over the course of writing this book, that changed drastically as the author, Sacha Black, came into my life. To me, Sacha is one of those people who I felt instantly comfortable with, she was someone who 'got me' and everything I was trying to achieve, and who was equally driven herself. Sacha, your friendship gave me a new lease on life when I needed it most. Thank you for playing such a huge role in my development as an author and as a businesswoman over the past year, and for the epic friendship that spans numerous voice memos each morning.

I'm also incredibly grateful to Sacha for introducing me to her ragtag crew of author friends. So, on that note, a huge thank you to: Jenna Moreci, Katlyn Duncan and Daniel Willcocks for also welcoming me into the fold and offering your support and friendship.

To my amazing patrons: I didn't know what to expect from launching a Patreon page, but I've been blown away by the incredible community that has emerged both there and in the HS Universe on Discord. Thank you to each and every one of you.

To Eva and Lisy, as of writing this, it's been two years since I saw you last, but when I'm feeling down, I look over to my favourite part of my office … It's the shelf that houses a bit of all of us: a plant from Eva, a painting and dried flowers from Lisy, and *War of Mist*, the book dedicated to you both. It brings me a quiet sense of joy, knowing that you're with me every day as I stumble along on this journey.

To Mum, Dad and Yas … It's also been over two years since we've seen each other last. Thank you for your ongoing support from afar and holding down the Sydney branch of Author HQ.

Thank you to Natalia Hunter, Fay Wood, Hannah Jermyn, Benjamin Stevenson, Margot Butler, the O'shea family, the Mulhollands, the Zapperts and Delzoppos, Erin Mealey, Brad Davis, Emily-May Norman, Jordan Meek (and Jordan's mum, hello again!), Danielle Noah, Phoebe Woodward, Maria Carroll and fellow author Nattie Kate Mason.

More special thankyous to these incredible bookstagram friends: itsmejayse, thebooktweeter, bookbookowl, apapergarden, bookscandlescats, bookishbron, leezland, elle.cheshire, emilyandherbooks, just_perfiction, queenof_midnight, labsandliterature, missdysfunktion, readingmadly, catsandpaperbacks, zanybibliophile, books.and.hangovers, clareapediabooks, coffeebooksandmagic, devoured_pages and readthewriteact.

And last, but never least … Thank YOU, dear reader, for choosing to stick with me on this magic-fuelled adventure.

Helen Scheuerer is the YA fantasy author of the bestselling trilogy, *The Oremere Chronicles,* and the *Curse of the Cyren Queen* quartet. Often likened to the popular series *Throne of Glass* and *Game of Thrones,* her work has been highly praised for its strong, flawed female characters and its action-packed plots.

Helen's love of writing and books led her to pursue a Bachelor of Creative Writing at the University of Wollongong and a Masters of Publishing at the University of Sydney. Now a full-time author, Helen lives amidst the mountains in Central Otago, New Zealand and is constantly dreaming up new stories. You can find out more via her website: www.helenscheuerer.com